FLOWERS NEAR ME

LOVE BLOOMS IN THE SHADOWS OF OLYMPUS

ALEXIS REX

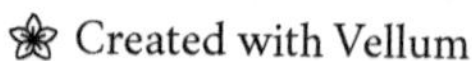 Created with Vellum

For Matt and Lindsay - You two deserve compensation for your support.

"WHAT WONDER THAT I LOVED HER…
THE IMMORTALS KNOW EACH OTHER AT FIRST SIGHT,
AND LOVE IS OF THEM…
I KNEW IN A MOMENT WHAT OUR LIVES MUST BE…"
—OWEN MEREDITH, *THE WANDERER IN ITALY*

INTRODUCTION

Flowers Near Me is a *very* loose re-imagining of the Hades and Persephone myth with **mature content that's intended for readers ages 18+.**

Although this book has been edited and proofread, unwanted mistakes still slip in. If you find an error, please email authoralexisrex@gmail.com (I have two cats that love to dance over the keyboard as I edit. I blame them.)

Has it been a while since you read about the Greek gods and goddesses? Here's a quick recap of their mythological titles. Don't worry, you will not be quizzed.

Happy reading!

In alphabetical order:

- APHRODITE - GODDESS OF LOVE
- ARTEMIS - GODDESS OF WILD ANIMALS, THE HUNT, VEGETATION, CARE OF CHILDREN, AND CHASTITY
- ASCLEPIUS - GOD OF MEDICINE AND HEALING
- CHARON - PSYCHOPOMP-BEING WHO GUIDES SOULS-WHO TRANSPORTS MORTALS VIA THE RIVER STYX INTO THE UNDERWORLD AFTER DEATH

- CHLORIS - Goddess of flowers
- DEMETER - Goddess of the harvest, mother to Persephone
- HADES - God of the Underworld
- HECATE - Goddess of magic, witchcraft, and sorcery
- HEPHAESTUS - God of metallurgy, metalworking, craftsman, fire, and volcanoes
- HERA - Queen of the gods, marriage, women, and childbirth
- HERMES - Messenger of the gods
- PERSEPHONE - Goddess of spring
- POSEIDON - God of the sea
- TYCHE - Goddess of fortune, luck, and prosperity
- ZEUS - King of the gods, thunder, and lightning

CONTENTS

CHAPTER ONE

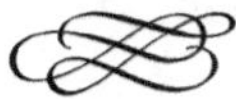

THE SHADOW OF DEMETER

PERSEPHONE

Tonight, Persephone would close the deal of her career. Better yet, she'd do it before Hades could get his slimy hands on it. The contract just needed one more signature, and then all of Olympus would know she was more than her mom's shadow.

The clack of Persephone's heels echoed in the glass atrium of Demeter's Bounty HQ, keeping in time with her racing heart.

"Good night, Ms. Ioulo!" a spry intern called from the front desk, balancing a laptop in one arm and a compostable coffee cup in the other.

"Enjoy your weekend. Don't stay too late." Persephone gave a quick nod and smile.

The intern beamed, her eyes wide as she waved.

Pulling her phone from her skirt pocket, Persephone opened the reports her assistant had forwarded minutes before. With her eyes glued to her phone, she used her shoulder to push the main revolving door open and took a deep breath of the evening's humid air.

Grocery delivery sales outperformed competitors AGAIN, read the email. Her heart soared and a smile bloomed on her face. She stowed her phone into her bag and nearly collided with a man carrying two overflowing cloth grocery bags bearing the wheat emblem of her mom's company.

She quickly sidestepped to avoid knocking over his things and muttered a brief apology, but didn't miss the way the man's face lit in recognition. He replied, "Oh, it's my fault entirely, Ms. Ioulo. Sorry about that."

Persephone continued down the city sidewalk, weaving through a sea of fellow mortals. It would've been nice if she could magically teleport to her meeting like her mother, Demeter. Blessed with only fledgling magic, Persephone had to arrive on foot.

One shrill ring sounded from her vegan leather bag—a daughter of Demeter could *never* own animal skin—and she answered without missing a step.

"Hi, Mom. I've got five minutes."

"Sephy, I tried to catch you before you left the office. Where are you?"

Persephone's chest tightened, but she straightened her spine. "I'm headed to a dinner meeting."

"With?" her mom prompted with a tinge of interest in her melodic inflection.

It'd been a challenge to keep the app acquisition a secret from Demeter, but she wasn't about to slip up now. "It's a surprise. You'll find out soon enough."

Although Persephone had negotiated deals for Demeter's Bounty before, this was the first one she'd worked alone and without her mom's knowledge. Market research, risk analyses, and even fighting off interested investors—she'd handled it all and was closing in on the final step of acquiring a flower marketplace app named *Flowers Near Me.*

"Fine," her mom said, but the flat reply belied Demeter's annoyance. "Did you read this quarter's report?"

A smile burst onto Persephone's face as she stopped at the crosswalk, waiting for the light to change. "I did."

"Another record quarter. All thanks to the grocery deliveries." The sound of a cork popping echoed through the receiver.

Persephone pictured her mom standing in the office—her silk ensemble free of wrinkles—with a champagne flute in one hand and phone in the other. Her mom's golden, waist-length hair would be twisted into an effortless bun by this time of the day, framing her symmetrical face. Delicate strands accentuating verdant green eyes. It was a cruel act of the Fates to give Persephone the dimmed versions of her mom's best features.

"The grocery delivery app is really paying off then?" Persephone joined the crowd crossing the street.

"Better than expected. This is huge." Pride coated her mom's words.

It *was* huge.

Hades may have owned the largest online marketplace—Underworld Unlimited—but now only Demeter's Bounty grocery chain grew, sold, *and* delivered food. *A necessity even for the gods,* her mom would say.

Persephone enjoyed helping her mom build the Demeter's Bounty empire, but she was eager to make moves of her own. The secret app acquisition she was moments away from making gave her a real chance to earn the respect of the gods and goddesses of Olympus.

Soon she'd become president of Demeter's Bounty. Her mom would always be CEO, but overseeing daily business decisions under Demeter was Persephone's ultimate goal. After that, she could pursue a partner and start a family.

Persephone's grin grew larger until her mom continued.

"Don't let this win cloud your judgment. We can't let our guard down even when things are going well."

Gritting her teeth, Persephone kept her tone cool. "I know."

Her mom made a low, disapproving hum over the line. "Hades' team would've shared the same results with him by now and you know how vindictive he can be. Remember when he patented those product scanners before our contractors could?"

How could she forget? He stole a product out from under the noses of its inventors. Patent law was his weapon of choice and he wielded it without mercy. Thankfully, Persephone had instructed the *Flowers Near Me*'s developer to submit the necessary patent paperwork ages ago.

"He could shut down our delivery app with a claim that it violates some law he wrote," her mom warned.

Chin lifted, Persephone replied, "I'd like to see him try considering his app is pretty similar to ours."

Not for long, though. With the addition of the *Flowers Near Me* app, she'd gain new tools that would give Demeter's Bounty the upper hand in their profits race with Underworld Unlimited.

Demeter laughed but with a stern voice added, "I mean it. He plays by his own rules."

Her throat went tight. Now the sweat forming on her brow wasn't from the evening heat. "Don't worry. Bye, Mom."

"I love you, my clever girl."

SOFT YELLOWS and oranges reflected off the white marble facade of the restaurant. Shoulders back, Persephone held her head high and entered through the bronze revolving doors. Chilled air greeted her, and she pulled her hair out of the bun, letting it fall past her shoulders. Walking toward the hostess stand, she glanced at the large, ornate clock on the wall.

With her mom's warning to *be careful* fresh in her mind, she scanned the lobby. Could Hades have spies here? Hades wanted this app almost as much as she did, but he wasn't the one with an in-person dinner meeting, even if his dark, towering building was right across the street. Was he bold enough to disrupt her meeting with the developer, Eurydice? *If he had nothing better to do, he would.* She silently prayed to the Fates he wouldn't dare. She needed this more than he did.

A raven-haired hostess greeted her with a tender smile. Backlit by warm candlelight glowing from the tables and minimalist chandeliers hanging from the high ceiling, the server looked like a siren in front of a glittering oasis in a sea of black.

"Good evening. Thank you for dining with us, Miss Ioulo."

Persephone stared for a moment before answering. "Hi... yes, thanks. Reservation for two."

It had only been a month ago when her mom revealed to all of Olympus that her dedicated operational executive was, in fact, her youngest daughter. Nepotism be damned, Persephone had earned her leadership role when coworkers all thought she was a nobody, and she was glad she didn't have to hide who she was anymore. But she mourned her former anonymity when out in public.

"Please follow me. Your guest is already here." A different but still beautiful server guided her past black-clothed tables set with dark gold cutlery and vases filled with gardenias.

On her left, a curved bar ran the length of the dining room. At the opposite wall, floor-to-ceiling windows boasted an enormous view of the picturesque metropolis. The server gestured towards a secluded corner booth where a young woman sat.

"Thank you," said Persephone as she gave a slight dip of her chin.

With an outstretched hand, Persephone approached the woman she recognized from their video calls. "Hi, so nice to meet you in person, Eurydice."

"Yes, it is. Thank you, Persephone. This means a lot." A wide-eyed Eurydice stood and shook Persephone's hand with the firmness of a seasoned professional and not of a recent grad. A smile spread across Persephone's face at Eurydice's cheery grin, easing the anxiety in her gut. They settled in their seats and a server set sparkling water on the table before taking their drink orders.

A giddiness fluttered inside Persephone. *Eurydice is going to sign with me.* She was certain of it by the way Eurydice's cheeks pinched in barely restrained joy.

Persephone sat tall. "Let's talk business first, then we can enjoy our meals." She set her phone in her bag, intent on giving Eurydice her undivided attention. "I sent you an updated contract. Have you read it?"

Nodding, Eurydice pulled out a tablet from her purse. "I did. Thank you for making those changes."

Thank me? This app promised to be huge and the fact it came with enviable intellectual property any distributor would want made it irresistible.

The waiter returned with their drinks and took their food orders, and they quickly got back to their discussion of the timeline for launch. Persephone was ready to release it as soon as possible, where Eurydice wanted a longer testing period so that there were no bugs.

It was important to Persephone that Eurydice understood and was content with the terms of the acquisition. They'd be working together for the next year and as much as the gods claimed that *business wasn't personal*, Persephone found that it most definitely was.

By the time Eurydice's blackened grouper and Persephone's braised butternut squash arrived, they had all but signed the deal.

"Are you certain you want me to be the spokesperson?" asked Persephone. It was a last-minute addition Eurydice had requested, and Persephone worried the young developer was concerned with stroking Persephone's ego. The gods may have liked that type of worship, but Persephone didn't. "Because Aphrodite would be a much better fit—"

"No. It has to be you." Clipped and firm. Eurydice's immediate reply caught Persephone off guard. She hadn't expected her to be so adamant. It should've made her pause—why her, when Aphrodite would be a natural fit? But she shook off the thought. The deal was nearly sealed. That's what mattered.

Flowers Near Me opened up the flower market to the masses. All you had to do was snap a photo of the flowers you were selling, share your location, and name your price. Any user could go on and search for available flowers in their area. The seller set a meeting location to meet the buyer and it was done.

Such a simple app for the users but monumental for Demeter's Bounty because of one glorious piece of tech: *dynamic tracking of users' location data.* It was an absolute gold mine and her pickaxe was diamond sharp.

Persephone put a hand over her heart. "Well, I'm honored to promote the app. I know it's precious to you and its success is a top priority for me."

Eurydice nodded as she pulled up the contract on her tablet's screen, Persephone's signature already inked and dated at the bottom. Holding her breath, Persephone watched Eurydice drag her finger to sign.

"You turned around the changes quickly," remarked Eurydice. She smiled, but kept her eyes averted from Persephone's.

If either party backed out now, Eurydice would have to wait a year before she could shop for buyers and Persephone would be back to square one. And for as big as Olympus was, news traveled fast, and rumors of bad business traveled even faster.

As they ate their meals, they discussed their shared love of gardening. Working with someone with a common interest had Persephone imagining how fun it'd be to show each other their latest planting triumphs. What a sweet idea for Eurydice to turn her hobby into a business.

"I'm so glad I got to you first before someone else tried to snatch you up." Persephone gave a light laugh, but Eurydice shifted in her seat as she looked at her phone.

Persephone cocked her head. "Are you alright?"

"I'm so sorry, but could you excuse me for a minute? My dad keeps calling and sent a cryptic text."

"Of course."

Eurydice sighed audibly. "Thank you." Standing up, she pressed her phone's screen, then brought it to her ear. "Hey, is everything..." Eurydice's voice faded into the buzz of the crowded restaurant as she walked off.

Suddenly, the temperature in the room plummeted, the scent of leather and cedar curling through the air. Beside her, a deep voice murmured, rich with wicked amusement, "Persephone. Caught at last."

As she turned to the god standing next to her, Persephone's gaze jumped from a tapered waist, up past broad shoulders covered by a tailored suit jacket, and landed on a stubbled jawline and gray eyes. Her eyes narrowed on the enemy she'd avoided meeting in person for years.

Hades.

CHAPTER TWO

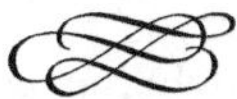

A SEAT AT THE TABLE

PERSEPHONE

She'd been warned countless times, "Don't meddle with the gods." Immortal. Powerful. Vengeful. Capricious. Even her mom could throw a fit that would scare the bravest mortal. And no good ever came from a god's flirtation.

Persephone followed the length of Hades' arm, where his hand rested against the back of her booth. A bold move as if they were *familiar* and not business adversaries. If a god wasn't being terrifying, then they acted insufferably. Restraining the quip on her tongue calling out his insolence, she wracked her brain for something less antagonistic to say.

She forced a grin. "You must be Hades."

He lifted his head with a laugh, then offered his hand. The suit jacket moved with him as if the material was his own personal armor, accentuating a muscled upper torso and lethal grace.

"Persephone, it's thrilling to finally meet you."

Her racing thoughts shackled her to the seat. Never once did she imagine she'd be meeting him by happenstance. Certainly not like this without her mom around. For as much as their businesses competed in the same market, they'd never been at the same place at the same time.

She struggled not to spiral into the depths of her mom's countless warnings of him. Never-ending acquisitions that turned into monopolies. Cutthroat lawyers with unlimited time and money. Iron-clad contracts that ruined business partners. Fates, even his own brothers had told her mom they avoided working with him, and Zeus and Poseidon were considered his equals.

He kept his hold on the booth's frame behind her. The whole display felt like an intimidation trick, but she conjured the weak magic within her and masked her feelings with an unbothered expression. Her own defense.

She extended her hand, keeping her back rigid. "Yes, nice to meet you." *Not at all.*

With a firm yet surprisingly polite handshake, Hades released her hand then slipped into Eurydice's vacated booth.

It was disappointing to see up close how picturesque his features were. A slim, strong nose that fit perfectly with his wide-set jaw and sharp features. As a child, her mom often reminded her that the most dangerous gods were always the most tempting.

"I was beginning to think we'd never meet." The silky quality of his voice and the way he kept his eyes locked with hers prickled her skin. She couldn't deny she was intrigued. *Is he using his power to draw me in?* Better that than genuine interest.

She cleared her throat. "To what do I owe the pleasure of your company?"

Please don't stay and chat.

Hades unbuttoned his suit jacket with a flick of his fingers and settled with his forearm leaning on the table. He looked pretty-damn comfortable.

Dread slowly rose in her gut. A part of her felt the urge to tell him about the deal with Eurydice, to gain the upper hand in a situation that was increasingly putting her on edge. But she had to keep her cool. She needed to know why in the Fates-damned world Hades was here, sitting across from her in the booth. Might as well be a cage given his larger than life energy.

He gave her a lazy smirk. "I've been hoping to run into you."

Run into me with your car is more like it.

Determined to appear indifferent, Persephone steeled her nerves. Using her napkin to wipe the sweat from her palms, she asked, "Do you come here often? I've never seen you here before." She counted in her head and inhaled slowly, careful not to break eye contact and show even a hint of her rising unease.

Her gaze kept bouncing from his full lips to his smoke-colored head of hair. What a curious thing it was for an ageless face to have silvery white hair crowning it. Every immortal Persephone had met in person was an enigma like this—even her own mom—and it never lost its alluring effect. Once you thought you'd seen the most exquisite deity, you'd meet another who was even more stunning. Even though she'd grown up around the gods, their brilliance never dulled.

"I started coming more often after I heard a certain someone was frequently spotted here." He gave her a smile that made her heart rate spike.

"Who? My mom?" Maybe it was foolhardy to pretend she misunderstood the *someone* he referenced but she'd hoped the reminder of who she was related to would make him lose interest.

Hades released a mirthless laugh and leaned closer across the table. "Speaking of Demeter, how is your mom?"

Persephone cleared her throat. "She's well. Business grows

with the city. How's Underworld Unlimited?" She had no intention of divulging more to her mom's enemy.

Hades waited a breath before answering, keeping rapt attention on Persephone's face. "I'd hate to make our first meeting about business, and I doubt my company's endeavors could impress the heiress of the world's biggest producer of food. But thank you for asking anyway."

Why did the Fates hate her so? How much longer would she be stuck with Hades, *alone*, caught under his heavy gaze?

"How are you liking Olympus?" Hades drew Persephone's attention back to him sitting across from her in the shrinking booth.

She tightened the fist on her lap. "I see its appeal. There's a lot to enjoy."

"Hm, there is," he murmured. "If you ever want to see the shadows where your mom's domain doesn't touch, let me know. I'd love to be your guide." The slight tilt of his head exposed the bobbing of his Adam's apple. Imposing shoulders drifted forward and eclipsed some of the light behind him.

A quick breath flooded her nose with the intoxicating scent that had to be his power. Leather and cedar. She opened her mouth to pull in fresh air and avoid falling under his spell. Turning towards her dinner and picking up the filigreed fork, she pushed some roasted fiddlehead ferns around her plate.

"Is this something you offer to all Olympus newcomers?" She met his eyes again.

He narrowed his gaze. "Only you."

Fear tangled with something else, something she refused to name. A hum of laughter escaped her throat. "I bet that line has worked on plenty of women." Fates, it shouldn't be working on her.

Hades' mouth dropped open. A hand pressed to his chest and fake shock coated his features. "How low is your opinion of me?"

Persephone chuckled. "I don't know enough about you to have formed much of an opinion."

She wasn't sure why she said it. It held a partial truth—she didn't know him—but his every move was covered in business news or celebrity gossip, and she was not a fan. Not to mention the stories her mom had told her over the years she'd been battling him for power in the city. How could she ever look at the god who mocked Demeter's Bounty in the press with anything but disdain?

The light in his gray eyes dimmed. "Oh, how I wish that were true. But perhaps we could spend time together and get to know each other, Sephy."

A shiver shot through her at his breathy purr of her nickname. Only her closest family called her that, in their own loving or cajoling way. And no one ever repeated it in a meeting or gathering, even if they'd heard her mom or sister speak it aloud.

Wiping a napkin across her lap, anything to not have to keep eye contact, Persephone said, "I doubt we have much in common. You own the largest e-commerce enterprise and I'm a lowly operations employee for a grocery chain." The last bit wasn't accurate, but she guessed he wouldn't know that.

"Now we both know that's not true," he said with lids lowered and a boyish smirk. "You've outranked me in product distribution for the past two years. I'd say we have much more in common than you're willing to admit." He gave a quick wave of his hand towards her as he added, "You may be much better looking than I am, but otherwise we're equals."

Was that right? Persephone wracked her memory of the past two years' earnings. Why was he trying to butter her up? This had to be a trap.

She replied, "It's a big market with plenty to go around, but you've kept Underworld Unlimited at the top. No one's come close to matching your total revenue." No harm in being honest.

Hades' company was the largest online retailer for practically everything—clothing, home goods, electronics, books, you name it.

His head tilted and the corners of his lips turned up. "That's nice to hear from a respected colleague. I don't know if this day can get any better."

Intending to refute his assertion of them being *colleagues*, she stopped as he slipped from the booth.

He buttoned his jacket and turned his head towards the stairs. "It looks like your original dinner companion has returned."

She went to ask him how he knew who she'd been dining with but seeing the weight of his full attention back on her, she held her breath. A pleased smirk grew on his face.

"Next time you come here, it should be with me. But if it's not, *please* don't let it be with a date. I'd hate to have to remove one of your admirers from the premises." His satisfied grin proved he *relished* the idea of ruining any of her future dates.

Returning to the table, Eurydice's eyes widened as she took in Hades. Poor woman was probably just as shocked to see him here as Persephone was.

"Hi, Eurydice. It's good to see you again." He patted her shoulder, and she bobbed her head with a tight smile.

"Hi, Hades. Hope you're doing well."

Eurydice's gaze flicked to Persephone's before it fell to the table as she took her seat. Persephone offered her a smile, but inside her heart pounded.

"You two know each other." More statement than question, Persephone bristled at the realization.

"Our paths have crossed a few times," Hades replied, keeping his gaze fixed firmly on Persephone.

Everyone in Olympus knew him. He was a staple in the tech community, so it was possible Eurydice had met him while she was still in school.

Persephone wasn't about to question Eurydice in front of Hades but at some point, she needed to know what connection —no matter how insignificant—Eurydice had to this god.

Hades dipped his chin, winked, and strode off, leaving Persephone with her pulse speeding, her thoughts tangled. She'd expected his arrogance. She hadn't expected... whatever this was. And she definitely hadn't expected him to know Eurydice.

CHAPTER THREE

OLYMPUS' SWEETHEART

PERSEPHONE

Persephone knocked twice on the painted door of her sister's red brick townhouse. Twisting the handle, she stepped over the threshold with an eager, "Hello!" and hung her overnight bag on a burnished bronze wall hook.

"Aunt Sephy!" Helena squealed, racing from the kitchen to the foyer. Her small arms hugged Persephone's waist. Persephone hugged her back, then reached past her niece's shoulder to place a handful of pale pink peonies and a to-go box onto the lacquered credenza. Helena released Persephone with a giggle. A sparkle from the chandelier above reflected in the little girl's brown eyes.

Stroking the silken strands of her niece's straight black hair, Persephone said, "I brought your favorite flowers today. Look." She gestured her head towards the bouquet.

Helena's eyes widened as she hopped to retrieve her gift. "Thank you!" With her arms full, she sprinted down the hall.

Laura, Persephone's half-sister, called, "We're in the kitchen."

"So glad it's the weekend," Persephone shouted back and lined her pumps next to her sister's tennis shoes.

She wrapped her hair into a low bun, then grabbed her bag to drop it in the nearby guest bedroom before joining Laura and Helena in the kitchen. While both Persephone and Laura had their mother's long, light brown hair, Persephone looked more like their mother with her green eyes, olive skin, and tall frame. Meanwhile Laura had her father's dark brown eyes, ivory complexion, and the gentle curves of motherhood.

Tall windows overlooking the tree-lined street cast a golden glow on the white countertops and warm wood cabinets. Laura plucked a glass vase from a live edge shelf as Helena bounced on her heels, the pastel peonies bursting from her grasp. After filling the vase with water, Laura trimmed the ends of the flowers and handed them back to Helena. The little girl got to work arranging them on the table in the breakfast nook.

Turkish cloth in hand, Laura swiped fast circles over the countertop and blew a lock of hair from her forehead. "What's in the box?"

"Chocolate cake. I had a dinner meeting."

"A dinner meeting? Or a date?" Laura raised her brows.

The edges of Persephone's mouth lifted. "Not a date. I bought an app from a developer named Eurydice." It was nice to finally be able to talk about it with her sister after keeping it hush for so long.

"Another app?" Laura's brows raised. "What's this one do?"

Persephone pulled out her phone from her pocket, opened the app, and turned the screen towards Laura. "It's a mobile flower market. Anyone can upload a photo of flowers they want to sell, and buyers can search for flowers in their area."

Laura held Persephone's phone in her hand, swiping through the products. "Won't florists hate it?"

"No, because they can list on there as well. It's meant to help them offload surplus stock. In fact, I got Helena those peonies from a local florist who had leftovers from a custom order."

Laura handed Persephone her phone and asked, "Are you an early investor then?"

"More like a partner and brand ambassador."

Laura's brow pinched. "Does Mom know?"

Pulling a glass from the cupboard, Persephone filled her cup with water from the fridge. "I'm going to surprise her with the signed contract." She almost couldn't believe her luck. To acquire technology like the *Flowers Near Me* app was a feat for the gods, let alone a simple mortal like her. Demeter would be proud.

Laura set plates and forks on the counter and opened the satin ribbon tied over the black to-go box.

"You won't believe which god showed up at the restaurant, though," Persephone said.

"Who? Poseidon?" Laura cut a slice of cake, setting it onto a plate.

Persephone was quick to shake her head. "One of the brothers but not that one."

"Zeus?"

Persephone took the offered cake slice from Laura. "No."

Laura's knuckles turned white as she gripped the cake knife. "Hades?"

"Yes."

Mouth agape, Laura asked, "Did he talk to you?"

"Get this, he sat at the table when Eurydice left to take a phone call."

Laura's hazel eyes stared back. "What did he say?"

"Not much. It seemed like he just wanted to introduce himself. He asked what I thought about Olympus and how Mom's doing. He knew who I was. I'd thought for sure he didn't know me or would pretend he didn't."

"What makes you say that? Aren't you famous now as Demeter's business-savvy daughter?"

"Demeter's shadow is more like it."

Laura laughed. "Have you read the articles about you?"

Persephone shook her head. "I've tried not to."

"Awe, maybe you should. They're calling you Olympus' newest sweetheart."

"Oh Fates. That makes me sound annoying." Persephone rubbed the bridge of her nose.

"I don't think so. Everyone assumed you'd be cold like Mom but you're not and they're surprised."

Persephone's shoulders slumped. "They just don't know me yet."

"True, but Mom can be a real bitch." Laura's expression turned sly. "Anyway, is Hades handsome in person? Or just photogenic?"

"No, he's handsome and knows it."

Laura scrunched her face then with a loud exhale said, "Well, if you said anything he didn't like, I'm sure you'll hear about it from his team."

Laura was right. They'd run an article claiming Demeter's daughter had said something offensive or unsavory to the mogul. Baldfaced lie or not, whatever served their purposes, they'd publish it.

She started running over every syllable that had passed her lips. She'd been careful. She knew she had. But with Hades, careful was never enough. Her stomach twisted, the rich chocolate cake turning bitter on her tongue.

CHAPTER FOUR

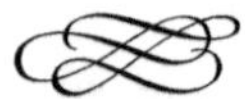

THE BETRAYAL

PERSEPHONE

Several slices of dark chocolate cake later, Persephone sank into the deep-seated couch beside Helena, the hum of the television lulling her into a rare sense of peace. Laura clattered in the kitchen, packing up leftovers, and for the first time all evening, Persephone let herself believe that tonight would end quietly.

A commercial for Demeter's Bounty's grocery delivery app played loudly on the screen. Lifting the remote, Persephone muted the TV then turned to look at her niece fiddling with a beaded bracelet.

"Where did you get that?" Persephone pointed at the accessory in Helena's hands.

"I made it in school today." Helena held out the bracelet like a precious relic.

"You made this?" Persephone ran a gentle finger over the beads, admiring her niece's handiwork. "It looks like something from a boutique."

"I did!"

"It's very well crafted. And I love the blues and purples you picked."

Helena beamed.

"What's been your favorite part of first grade so far?"

Concentration etched Helena's angelic face. "Um… I like my teacher. She's nice. And she has two cats."

Persephone chuckled. "Really? Did she show you a picture of them?"

"Yes! One's named Pancake, and the other is Butter!" Helena's big almond eyes and thick lashes stared expectantly at her aunt.

"I love those names. Do you know how old they are?"

"Uh… I think she said they're six."

"Just like you?"

"Yeah!"

Helena's toothy grin stirred warmth in Persephone's chest. If she had a child that was even a fraction as sweet as her niece, she'd be in heaven. A family of her own—someone to come home to, someone who loved her not for her last name, but for who she was—felt like an impossible dream. And if she let herself want it too much, it would only hurt more when it stayed out of reach.

Although envious, she wasn't jealous of Laura's life because she knew how hard her sister had worked for it. Both Laura and Persephone wanted to have thriving careers before building families of their own. For Laura, it meant becoming a trauma surgeon before having kids. For Persephone, it meant becoming president of Demeter's Bounty before having a serious relationship.

Lowering her voice to a whisper, Persephone asked, "Do you want a cat?"

Helena nodded.

"What did Aunt Sephy say?" Laura's voice startled Persephone as she and her husband, Peter, entered the room.

Giggling, Helena scooted forward on the couch.

"I asked Helena if she wants a cat." Lips pressed in a devilish smile, Persephone kept a challenge in her eyes.

"Oh." Laura sat and glared at Persephone. "Will Aunt Sephy be coming over to care for this cat?"

Peter's muffled laugh sounded from behind his wife.

Persephone replied, "I can't. You know the estate is too far from here."

Helena said, "You could live here." Persephone laughed, about to tease her niece—until Laura nodded seriously.

"Moving to the city makes sense. Everyone knows you're Demeter's daughter now. And Mom wants you to take on more responsibility at the company anyway. Stay with us while you're apartment hunting."

Persephone swallowed. "If it were to be closer to you three, I'd do it. But we all know there are other obligations that would take over."

"Your mom?" Peter asked.

Persephone pointed her finger at her brother-in-law. "Her and all her allies and enemies. I've avoided her politics, and I'd like to keep it that way."

"Well, you might've rocked the boat tonight," said Laura.

Peter leaned forward in his chair and looked at Persephone. "What happened?"

Persephone cocked her head and pinched her brow at her sister. "You think the flower app is a mistake?"

"Gods no. I just think your little run-in with sworn enemy number one could come back to bite you."

Peter's incredulous face went from his wife to Persephone. "Hades? How?"

Concern pricked at the back of Persephone's mind as she considered Laura's comment. "He dropped in on my meeting at Narcisi. I didn't think the demon himself would show up."

"What did he do?" asked Peter.

Persephone and Laura exchanged a brief look before both glancing at Helena. The little girl had unmuted the TV and stared at the screen.

In a hushed tone, Persephone said, "He tried flirting."

Confusion coated Peter's expression. "What do you mean, he *tried?*"

"He said a few discreet pickup lines, winked at me... kept a confident air, then left abruptly."

"He sounds like Poseidon," said Laura.

"I'm certain he'd hate that comparison," Peter remarked.

"Hopefully it's my only run-in with him. If someone snapped a photo—just one—Mom wouldn't care about context. She'd see betrayal and would never let me forget it."

Laura cut in, "I think you should flirt back next time and use it as leverage against Mom. You can threaten to date her nemesis."

Laughing, Persephone said, "You and I both know she'd flip. She might force me to live with her in the penthouse. And I can't promise I wouldn't try to push her out a window."

"Yikes," Peter whispered, but Laura laughed along with Persephone.

"Who are you talking about?" Helena's sweet voice asked.

"Yaya," Laura replied without hesitation.

Helena leaned on Persephone's back, craning her head past her aunt's shoulders. "Noooo. Who's the *other* person you're talking about?"

"What do you mean?" Peter asked.

"Who flirted with Aunt Sephy?"

Persephone, Peter, and Laura exchanged a quick glance. Busted.

"Oh, ha... just some god who thinks he's special. And how do you know what flirting is?" Persephone leaned back on the couch, and Helena hopped over her to sit on her mom's lap.

"I don't know. Why does he think he's special?"

"Because he's rich," Laura answered, and Persephone shrugged with a nod.

"Aunt Sephy, aren't you rich?"

"We all are, but it's not polite to talk about it," Persephone said.

Helena, seemingly satisfied with her aunt's answer, crawled off her mom's lap and went back to watching the TV.

"Sorry," Persephone mouthed to her sister and brother-in-law.

"She understands more than we know," whispered Laura.

Persephone glanced at her niece behind her and smiled. "She gets that from you."

WHEN PETER TOOK Helena up to get ready for bed a couple of hours later, Persephone followed her sister back into the kitchen to tidy up.

"Do you think it's weird I happened to run into Hades the same night I bought the app?"

"Oh no, not at all," Laura said as she slid onto the suede bar chair by the marble island. "It was only a matter of time before you two were in the same place."

Persephone pushed the dishwasher closed and the buzz of the machine sounded. "There's more. It seemed like Eurydice and Hades knew each other. I didn't push the issue with her, but now I'm wishing I had."

"Do you think they're *together*?"

"If they are, then he's worse than Mom says. She looked uncomfortable around him so maybe she knows him from the technology sector? They didn't seem like former lovers. And I think she's too smart for him, anyway."

They each huffed a laugh.

Persephone continued, "But I don't like that he showed up right after I signed the agreement. I trust our lawyers and they know anything that remotely touches Underworld Unlimited is a nonstarter, but how does Hades know Eurydice? I'm concerned it may have something to do with the app."

"Ask her Monday. If you just signed with her, then I'm sure she won't mind telling you how she knows him."

Persephone nodded then pulled off her hair tie and started fussing with the strands.

Laura asked, "Why would he be interested in the app?"

Persephone hummed a low note. "There's IP he wants."

"IP?"

"Oh, intellectual property. Like a copyright for the tech, but don't you quote me on that because I'm certain there's a more accurate way to phrase it. There are predictive location tracking capabilities that a company like Hades' would love to have. It could help their e-commerce platform."

Anyone would want that IP.

Laura's phone lit up, snagging her attention. "Sephy, what's the name of that app again?"

"*Flowers Near Me.*" Persephone watched the concentration on her sister's face, waiting for her to look up. When she didn't, Persephone prompted, "Why?"

Laura frowned as she held out her phone. "Look."

The phone screen showed an article titled *Underworld Unlimited Smells the Roses and You Can Too.*

The date of publication was today's date.

The timestamp on the article mere minutes ago.

Persephone scanned the text, skipping from paragraph to paragraph hoping for a clue that would discredit her budding fear.

Rising tech star, Eurydice... hit the jackpot with her debut app, Flowers Near Me...

Users can search, order, and sell flowers from anywhere...

Thanks to Underworld Unlimited's recent acquisition, all users of their online market can add fresh flowers to their shopping lists...

Persephone looked at her sister's concerned face, then reached for her own phone. With furious fingers, she punched in the words, "Flowers Near Me" and "Underworld Unlimited."

The results made her body go cold. Recent posts all confirmed that Hades did indeed own the *Flowers Near Me* app.

How? Was the contract she'd signed with Eurydice now void? What was going on?

"Is this a joke? Who did this? Did Peter design this? Because bravo... you've scared me shi—"

Shaking her head, Laura cut her off. "Oh no, Sephy, it's not a joke. I get search alerts anytime your name shows up online."

Persephone couldn't believe it. If he had already bought the app, then how did Eurydice sell it to *her* mere hours ago? And why was her name attached to his announcement?

She scrolled down the page and saw a photo of Hades and Eurydice shaking hands and smiling at the camera. Both were wearing the same clothing they'd worn at dinner. Based on the lighting in the background, it'd been taken outside of the restaurant *after* she'd met with Eurydice.

Persephone stopped breathing when she spotted another photo. One of Hades and her looking extra cozy on the bench together. *She* knew her polite smile was wary, but a reader wouldn't. They could've been a couple enjoying a romantic dinner.

"Oh, Fates, kill me now." What kind of ploy was this?

Persephone's face flamed hot as she read:

"When asked about the app, Hades said, 'It's a joy to bring Flowers Near Me to our customers looking for an easier way to buy and sell flowers. Eurydice promises to be a force within emerging tech and e-commerce. If that wasn't exciting enough, I'm also pleased to welcome the brilliant and incomparable Persephone Ioulo as our newest partner in bringing Flowers Near Me to the world. We're elated to have her represent this new brand and I can't wait to begin our partnership.'"

She finished reading the last sentence of his quote when an insistent notification covered her screen with one name.
Mom.

CHAPTER FIVE

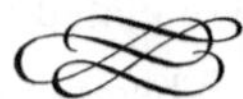

MOM'S NOT HAPPY

PERSEPHONE

The device in Persephone's hand burned with unleashed fury. She looked at her sister, hoping for some inspiration for what to do, some sign that this was all a dream, but for once her sister looked as gobsmacked as she felt. Persephone's throat went dry.

Please don't be real.

Her phone buzzed impatiently, and she sucked in a breath before answering the call. "Hi, Mom. Are you in on Laura and Peter's joke, too?" *Fates, let this be a nightmare that I wake up from.*

"What?" Demeter screamed. "I swear on Zeus' chariot… Is this a joke? Is this your surprise?"

Her mom sounded crazed. Now Persephone was hot despite her short sleeves and silk shorts. Could her mom's power reach her over the phone? She didn't think so, but the terror flooding her veins made her consider the possibility.

"What's going on, Persephone? I have every god and goddess

sending me messages with their condolences and surprise. What did you sign with Underworld Unlimited?"

Sweat beaded on Persephone's brow and palms as she stood up from her chair and muted the call.

With as threatening a voice as she could muster, Persephone said, "Tell me the truth, Laura. Is this an elaborate joke?"

"Definitely not a joke." Laura held Persephone's gaze. A stone sat on her chest.

Persephone unmuted the call. "Mom, let me talk. I didn't sign anything related to Underworld Unlimited. I signed a partner and rep agreement for a new app. Our lawyers checked into their funding, and I met with the developer tonight. There's no way—"

"You signed before consulting me? Why would you do that? What were you thinking? Do you have any idea what you've done?" Her mom's seething tone made her dizzy.

Persephone closed her eyes and slowed her breath, waiting for her thumping pulse to quiet. "I just told you that the lawyers researched it. They gave me the go ahead. I don't know how Hades finagled this. Underworld Unlimited was never a part of my agreement with Eurydice." The last part sat like cotton in her mouth. How could she have made a mistake like this one?

There was a brief quiet on her mom's end until her sigh broke the spell. "The damage is done whether you like it or not. People are saying you've jumped ship to Underworld. How can I justify your position to the board now? They were already wary after you went public as my daughter."

Persephone felt the anger rising in her veins. "That wasn't *my* choice to announce our relationship and I'm not jumping ship," Persephone hissed as she braced her damp back against the kitchen wall.

Her mom asked, "How selfish can you be?"

Persephone took a deep breath and rubbed her forehead. "I

won't go through with any of this. I'm calling it off with the developer once we hang up."

"At this point, I don't care what you do."

The dismissal in her mom's tone triggered a rush of adrenaline. She fought it off with another slow inhale.

"You and I both know that's not true. I'll fix this. Yes, the press is alarming, but nothing we can't navigate. I'm sure Hermes is scrambling as we speak to draft my public statement refuting Hades' claims."

"Don't put out a statement until I've talked with our lawyers and PR team. And send me that Fates-damned contract immediately." Demeter yelled the last bit.

"I'll do that right now, but I'm putting you on speaker so I can open my email."

"Just send it," Demeter snapped.

Standing nearby, Laura rolled her eyes, muttering *typical* under her breath.

Persephone opened her email. To her horror, her inbox had exploded with a slew of unread emails from Underworld Unlimited. Each one with attachments and subjects starting with "Please sign and return ASAP."

Poor Hermes. If her assistant had already caught wind of this disaster, then he was probably pacing around his loft, yanking his curly hair. For his sake, she hoped he hadn't checked her email after work.

"Alright… I just emailed you and your PA."

"Got it. Don't talk to anyone until I call you back. You know how Hades is with contracts. If you make any more mistakes, it could cost us every cent we've earned this year in profits."

The racing of her heart threatened to cut off her voice, but she managed a reply. "Of course. Keep me posted on what the team says."

Persephone ended the call, silenced her phone, and wiped the sweat from her brow. Laura squeezed her shoulder. "Don't worry. If anyone can fix this, it's you. Plus, Mom won't stay mad at you for long."

She doubted her mom's rage would subside soon, but she appreciated Laura's confidence. There had to be a way to get out of this mess, she just needed to figure it out.

CHAPTER SIX

THE FINE PRINT

PERSEPHONE

*P*ersephone counted twenty texts she'd sent to her mom. Each with the same question of, *What can I do?* All receiving versions of the same reply. *Stay put,* and, *Don't know yet.* Disappointment filled her when she saw the last text in their thread was the one she'd sent right before she tried to fall asleep. Persephone had only managed four hours of sleep and woke at six a.m.

No word from her assistant, Hermes, either. Perhaps he hadn't caught wind of the announcement and was sleeping in after a packed night out. Who would blame him for his fun? He was much younger than Persephone and she appreciated his zest for life.

After a quick shower, Persephone dressed and stretched. The tightness in her jaw and neck loosened, and her thoughts soon turned to coffee. After putting on some tinted moisturizer and a decent application of mascara, Persephone looked as put together as she could, given the circumstances. Now, wearing loose jean shorts and an oversized sweatshirt, she could pretend for a bit that it was a normal Saturday morning.

The buttery smell of pancakes and the sound of Helena singing greeted her as she entered the kitchen. Helena was coloring at the kitchen island while her dad tended the stove.

"What a pleasant pair you two are," Persephone said as she kissed the top of Helena's head.

"Good morning. Are you hungry?" Peter asked.

"I'm good. Thank you."

Persephone touched the coffee pot and relished its warm exterior. She grabbed the large mug she'd used last night and rinsed it in the sink.

"Sorry I kept Laura up late. How did you sleep?"

Peter turned to Persephone with a smile. "Oh, I assumed you two would stay up. Of course, our little night owl over here still woke up at five thirty, even after staying up past ten."

Helena giggled.

"Are you tired?" Persephone asked as she sat next to Helena.

"Nope!"

So much like Laura. Her niece's quirks and resilience mirrored her mother's natural confidence, something Persephone had always tried to emulate, even if she'd never admit it.

Helena picked up a blue crayon and began shading the shirt of a figure on her paper, her little hands moving with focused intent. Calming swirls of blue and purple filled the page. Persephone found herself entranced by the simple rhythm of the strokes, the soothing colors, and the melodic hum of Helena's song. The pressure in her chest slowly unraveled, tension bleeding away with each sip of coffee.

But two cups later, her mind began to spiral again. *Why hasn't Mom called me back? How did Hades manage to buy an app I already owned? Was Eurydice a traitor, or was she forced into it?*

When Helena had to touch her aunt's cheek to get her attention, Persephone snapped out of her thoughts, offering a quick apology. Excusing herself, she retreated to the guest room to grab her running shoes, sunglasses, and a baseball hat. Within minutes, she was outside, the townhouse door clicking shut behind her.

Sprawling oaks lined the sidewalk and the air smelled like laundry and baked goods. She walked past a woman wearing leggings and a fitted tank top with a yoga mat slung over one shoulder. Minutes later, an older man nodded a hello as he held the leashes of four tiny but vocal dachshunds. Eventually the sidewalk widened, and rows of bricked buildings turned into taller oaks and maples. A few fiery leaves peeked through the green branches. An iron fence spanned the perimeter of a grassy field with footpaths and flowering shrubs. Persephone rolled her shoulders back and picked up her walking pace. Parents pushing strollers lifted one hand in greeting, squirrels darted left and right on the sidewalk, and the crisp air grew heavy.

Reaching into her shorts' pocket, Persephone pulled out her phone. There was one unread message from her mom, which she opened immediately.

MOM

Ran into issues. Will keep you posted.

Persephone's heart sank. She typed back:

PERSEPHONE

Alright. Let me know what I can do.

She dabbed the sheen of sweat on her face, then pushed up her sleeves and continued on the park's path. She drew deep breaths in and out, trying—and failing—to shed the worry at her mom's reply. After fifteen minutes, she left the park and headed back to her sister's townhouse when her phone pinged.

LAURA

Get back here. Hell has broken loose.

PERSEPHONE
What happened?? I'm coming!

She broke into a run, halving the length of the return trip. *Fates,* what had Laura meant by that? Now her heart was racing so fast, she felt a pounding in her ears.

Parked outside the townhouse was a gunmetal-gray SUV with impossibly dark windows. Two suited men she didn't recognize stood near it with arms crossed and tight frowns on their faces. Once she approached the front steps, they each gave her a smile and nod. Too confused as to what they were doing outside her sister's, she returned the gesture and hurried to the townhouse's entrance.

Skipping steps two at a time, Persephone launched herself towards the door and swung it open.

"Persephone!" Her assistant Hermes stood in the middle of the foyer, dark bags under his eyes and the tight curls of his hair tousled. Persephone rushed towards him as she yanked off her hat and sunglasses.

"Hermes!" They exchanged a brief hug. "Why are you here?"

Had he been crying? No tears lined his brown eyes, but the whites were red.

"Your mom asked me to stop here this morning."

"Oh? Why didn't you text me?"

"She said not to contact you. I'm so sorry. I really wanted to reach out, especially last night. I can't believe this is happening."

Her coffee churned in her stomach. A mix of low voices sounded from the kitchen. "What's going on? Did Hades steal the flower app?"

"Don't you know? I thought you signed the new agreement?"

Lightheaded, Persephone gripped Hermes' arm. "What new agreement? Is my mom here?"

"No." Hermes gulped. "Has anyone from the office talked to

you?" He looked as sick as she felt, his tawny complexion grayer than its normal, warm hue.

Shaking her head, Persephone begged, "Please tell me what's going on."

"You might want to sit down," he began. But the unmistakable sound of a determined god approaching from down the hallway made Persephone and him stop in their tracks.

A shadow loomed beside them. Then, a deep voice said, "Go on, Hermes. I'm eager to hear your explanation."

Hermes' throat bobbed before he shot her a sympathetic look then fled into the kitchen. *Some help he was.* She could hardly blame him.

With the fiercest scowl she could muster, she straightened her back and leveled her eyes at Hades' self-satisfied face. She was Demeter's daughter and wouldn't tremble before anyone. Especially not him.

"*Hades.*"

His smug expression turned sinister as he smiled at her, displaying brilliant white teeth. "Good morning, Persephone. It's nice to see you again so soon."

The last thing she needed was to exchange pleasantries with him. "Where's my mom?"

"She's not here, but I have her on the phone." Hades reached into his pocket and pulled out his device. One tap on the screen then he said in a cold voice, "Demeter, I've got Persephone."

Her voice sure and strong, she asked, "Mom?"

"Persephone, listen carefully. You're bound to a six-month contract with Underworld Unlimited as the spokesperson for *Flowers Near Me.* Hades will fill you in on the rest of the details."

"No, I've signed *nothing* with them. I signed with Eurydice, an independent developer." She glanced at Hades, and he raised his brows in return.

In a flat tone, her mom replied, "Hades owns the patent for

the technology used in the app. Any contract signed thereafter becomes his."

Persephone blinked. No. That wasn't possible. It wasn't how this worked. She knew contracts—she'd studied them, obsessed over them, ensured every clause protected her.

She glowered at Hades. He grinned back at her. He thought he'd won, but there was no way he could've pulled off something like this.

Persephone's voice was strained as she said, "No, Eurydice owns the patent, not him. I made sure of it."

"Not anymore. She sold the patent to him."

This was the first bit of good news she'd had all day. "Then the contract she signed with me is void if she didn't own the tech at the time of signing."

She heard her mom clear her throat. "Normally it would be void, but you forgot to include a key clause in your contract. Had you consulted with me first, we wouldn't have made this mistake. But alas, you didn't and the contract you drew up didn't include any dissolution clause in case of an existing patent. Eurydice is still part-owner and any contract she enters must be reviewed by the patent's co-owner, Hades. It's his to decide now."

"That can't be right. The legal team reviewed it and accounted for existing IP."

Demeter's audible huff sounded. "No. IP law isn't some magical catchall that protects you from patents, Sephy. You should've talked to me first. I'd never make this mistake. And unfortunately, Hades caught your misstep."

Persephone's heartbeat pounded in her head. If it was up to him, then maybe she could convince him to dissolve it? Why would he ever work with her? There was no way he *actually* wanted her to be the spokesperson now that he owned all rights to the app.

The bite of shame sunk its teeth into her and she stared at

the floor. How could she look at the rival who'd bested her? It didn't matter that he was a god. She should've known better. *Mom would've known better.* She'd never be president of Demeter's Bounty now.

Interrupting her thoughts, her mom added, "Hades is offering you a six-month employment term to avoid binding you to a lengthy non-compete. I suggest you take it. Don't make a fuss and don't involve my team."

The strong tone of her mom's final statements left no question. There was nothing her mom could do right now to reverse it. That didn't mean Persephone gave up hope that she'd get out of it. Demeter just needed more time, and Persephone needed to play nice long enough for things to get sorted.

Hades held up one finger to Persephone. "Demeter, is there anything else you want to say to Persephone before you hang up?"

Persephone's mouth dropped open and her brows pinched as she stared back at Hades and held her breath. Hades' word may be law in Olympus, but he had no right to keep her from speaking to her mom.

"You're bound to the six-month agreement, Sephy. Don't fight it when there's too much to lose."

Was there regret hiding in her mom's words? Sadness? No one trusted Hades, least of all Demeter. How could she abandon Persephone to him now? Why wasn't she berating him? Her mom was the most cunning god she knew; there had to be a reason she wasn't fighting this. Now Persephone needed to keep calm despite fear filling every cell of her being.

Hades bent towards the phone. "Take care, Demeter."

He ended the call and smirked at Persephone.

CHAPTER SEVEN

WELCOME HOME, SEPHY

PERSEPHONE

"Come with me and I'll explain everything." Hades held out one arm and gestured towards the front door behind Persephone.

"Hold on," she said with a raised hand. Craning her neck, she stretched her head past Hades' shoulder to peer down the empty hallway. In the kitchen doorway were the backs of two figures wearing suit jackets. The unknown voices speaking earlier were now silent. Probably too busy listening in on her conversation with Olympus' most feared god.

"Laura," she called, wanting a witness to whatever was about to transpire.

A relieved breath escaped seeing her sister appear between the suit-wearing pair. Laura entered the foyer with a giddy Helena skipping along. "I told him you don't know any of the details of the acquisition." She expected Laura to look incensed that Hades and his crew had bombarded her home. Instead, her sister's face was pinched in confusion.

Bouncing and smiling, Helena hugged Persephone's legs. "Have fun, Aunt Sephy! Mom says you're going to start a new job and that you're moving to Olympus forever."

What? The foyer grew smaller, the air thickening in her lungs.

Throwing a frenzied look at her sister, Persephone bent down and distractedly hugged her niece, murmuring, "If anything, I'm going to prison, Helena."

"Sephy!" Laura scolded before pulling Helena back to her and saying softly, "Honey, Aunt Sephy is joking. She's in shock and saying weird things." Laura's eyes bugged out as she scowled at Persephone. Too upset to care, she gave Laura a blank look.

Hades offered his palm. "It sounds like you were kept in the dark and I'd like to fix that. Let's talk in the car as we go to your new apartment. I can explain the contract's terms."

"I'm not going anywhere with you." Tears pricked her eyes, but she refused to let them fall. Laura would save her. She had to. Looking at her sister, she pleaded, "Tell him there's no enforceable contract."

Laura stepped close and whispered, "Sephy, you know the way of the gods better than I do. There's no way out of this without you fulfilling your end of the bargain."

In a hushed tone, she argued, "But I never made a bargain with him."

"I know," said Laura. "But he's decided to uphold part of the deal you signed with Eurydice. I don't think you can stop this." With a flick of her eyes, Laura gestured towards Hades standing nearby. "It's too dangerous for you to fight it. Please just go with him and text me later. Okay?"

Through gritted teeth, Persephone said, "Let me get my bag."

Laura touched her arm, a gentler look in her eye now. "Your stuff is already in his car. Don't worry if you left anything here. Hades invited us over to your apartment for dinner tomorrow."

Squinting at her sister, Persephone tried to make sense of the words. She lived at her mom's estate. Not in an apartment. And why in the Fates' names would *he* be inviting people over to *her* place?

No one was listening to reason. She needed to regain her composure and clear her mind without Hades hovering nearby. "See you later, then?"

Laura's tender gaze held Persephone's. "We'll see you later."

"Bye, Aunt Sephy!" Helena held onto the side of her mom's leg and gave her aunt a big grin.

Persephone managed a stiff smile. She pulled her phone from her pocket and gripped it like a lifeline. Turning to leave, she walked out as Hades held the door.

Was her family really going to let her leave with *him*? When he offered his arm, she took it, but stared at the hand holding him as if it were not her own. What option did she have? Her mom's terse recommendation had left her head spinning and Laura's resignation cut like an axe.

If her mom hadn't stopped it and Laura accepted it, did that mean she was truly stuck working for Underworld Unlimited for the next six months?

A strange numbness filled her veins as she walked with Hades towards his dark SUV.

The car's interior exuded the now-familiar, bewitching scent of leather and cedar. Warm lights glowed along the floor, but Persephone was too tense to appreciate the luxury.

Once the door closed, the intoxicating smell of his cologne begged her to come closer. She closed her eyes, wishing her body wouldn't react like this. He wasn't just one of the Olympus elite, he was *Hades*, her vicious rival who'd stop—had *already* stopped it seemed—at nothing to do what he pleased. And she'd do well to remember she was a bug under his leather loafer.

"Tell me what you know, and I'll fill in the rest," Hades said, his voice a smooth command.

Persephone clenched her fists. "I signed an acquisition agreement with Eurydice to buy her app and *somehow*, you now own the patent of that app." Frustration sharpened her words.

He leaned his forearms on his thighs and studied her face. "You did sign an agreement, yes, but here's the thing: you've signed on as a spokesperson to promote an app that was already owned by me. So, for the next six months you're my employee who's agreed to be the face of *Flowers Near Me*."

She stared back, unable to process what he meant. Was she in shock?

Noticing her confusion, Hades added, "You should know that if you don't fulfill the terms of the contract, you're stuck in a twenty year non-compete which prohibits you from working with *any* company in Olympus."

Her heart stopped. "Even *you* can't do that."

"Oh, I can." He straightened in his seat. "You signed an agreement with tech *I own*. Now Underworld Unlimited's contract terms are in play, and I have a strict and comprehensive noncompete."

Fates. She'd walked right into one of his traps. *Don't break. Not in front of him.*

The deep timbre of his voice pulled her attention back to his face. *How could someone so ruthless have a voice that divine? Only a god, of course.* It wasn't fair.

"Your mom's team missed a clause," Hades continued, eyes gleaming. "My retroactive terms kick in immediately, binding you to my company and its spokesperson requirements, which include an honor code to protect brand integrity and a handler to be assigned to you."

Persephone couldn't believe it. *Wouldn't* believe it. *Mom just needs more time for the legal team to reverse this.* She'd never let her fall into Underworld Unlimited, alone. That level of cruelty might come from others, but never her mom.

And if there was one lesson Demeter had drilled into her, it was how to outsmart a vicious god. *Don't provoke them but guide them gently to your desired conclusion.* She simply needed to have him see how terrible of a plan this was and that he was better off releasing her from the agreement.

Persephone pressed her fingertips to her mouth before asking, "How do you see things playing out if I'm the app's spokesperson?"

He glanced out the window before looking back at her. "Perfectly. There's no one better than *Olympus' newest sweetheart* to promote a flower marketplace app."

Cocking her head to the side, she asked, "But why not a respected figure? Sort of undermines the app if it's me, doesn't it?"

His brows furrowed. "How do you mean?"

This is good. He's listening. "Think about it. If I left Demeter's Bounty after working there for well over a decade, forsaking *my own mom* to do business with our main competitor, how do you think that looks?"

"It looks like the app is too good to pass up." He smirked.

She leaned back and pursed her lips. "So you're saying that if a child of Zeus went off to promote a competitor's product, you'd assume the product was *that* good."

Hades shrugged. "Probably. I'd be curious enough to download the app and see what all the fuss was about."

"Okay, but what if the product had nothing to do with his kid's expertise? What if everyone saw it like a distractible child going from one shiny object to another?"

"Then I'd want to see the shiny object. It's like I said. I'd want to see what the fuss was about."

This wasn't going how she wanted. How could she convince him? What did he value?

"How could having me as the spokesperson benefit your

bottom line?" Was it about the money or was it about getting back at Demeter's Bounty?

"The people of Olympus adore you. If you're selling it, then they're buying."

Gods, she wanted to wipe that pleased look off his face. Maybe with the back of her hand flying at a high rate of speed.

"I've never been the face of a brand. And I'd never trust my enemy's daughter with a new product."

He simply crossed his arms and smiled like she'd said something cute.

She sighed. "What about Chloris, the Goddess of Flowers? Or Aphrodite? *Titans*, even Artemis is a better choice."

He shook his head. "You're not going to change my mind, Sephy. Now let's get back to what's included in your agreement."

Oh, she would change his mind. It just might take more than one conversation.

She shrugged. "Fine. You were saying I'll have a handler?"

"Yes, and good news for you." Hand on his chest. "I've assigned myself."

She stared at him and with a clipped tone replied, "Wonderful." This penchant for dramatic revelations was not something she'd encourage with a shocked reply.

Outside, clusters of pedestrians filled the sidewalks. The car rolled along slowly, embedded in the start of Saturday lunch traffic.

If Hades was her *chaperone* for the next six months, she might have a lot of freedom given his many commitments as CEO. Her mom worked sleepless nights and marathon days. Surely, he did the same. One can't run hell without toiling all day and night.

The air grew cold and she shuddered at the sudden change. Hades cleared his throat. "It's in your professional best interest to comply with these new contract terms, Persephone. Your ability to sell this app reflects on your reputation, and it'd be a pity to see Demeter's top executive fail when she's no longer under the protection of her mother."

There it was. Revenge after Demeter's Bounty's recent success. Why would he do the work of embarrassing her when she could make a fool of herself?

The worst part? He wasn't wrong. Painful as it was to admit, her reputation was on the line, as was the public's perception of Demeter's Bounty. That didn't mean she had to put him at ease, assured that she'd do a good job. She half-grinned, forcing the epitome of innocence through a rounded-eye look.

"Of course."

Hades pointed his pinched fingers at her. "This resignation…" He hummed low in his throat, then shook his head. "I don't buy it."

Persephone leaned back in her seat and clasped her hands, trying to hold back a smile. Maybe he wasn't getting the frantic reaction he'd hoped for? Thank the Fates he couldn't read her mind or he'd know just how rattled she was.

Shifting forward, Hades held her gaze. What felt like a century passed, but she didn't crack under his scrutiny. He settled back into his seat.

"Once we get you set up in the apartment, you'll have time to review the documents that have been signed on your behalf," said Hades.

She tightened her jaw. *Signed on your behalf?*

He crossed an ankle over his knee, looking every bit the arrogant mogul he was. "While the brand team plans the marketing campaign, you and I will attend a few events together."

Persephone took in a slow breath. *Enough time to figure out an exit.*

Hades had yet to look away from her. Like he knew she'd snap if he just stared long enough. His full lips tipped up on one side as he said, "To kick things off, we're going to start to do things together that a couple would as they enter a courtship."

Persephone almost snorted. "Courtship? If this is all about dating, why the business partnership? There are plenty of sites where you can find an escort."

"I'm glad you're asking. You see, this teasing comes so naturally because we're a great pair." He gestured his hand between the two of them.

She pinched the bridge of her nose. "What are you talking about?"

"Romance sells flowers," Hades said, leaning in. "We pretend to date, and the app becomes irresistible. People crave a love story."

She squinted as her upper lip curled. "Sounds manipulative." *And phony, and borderline idiotic.* But she'd keep those descriptions to herself.

"All good marketing is." Hades' mouth curved up in a devilish grin.

Rubbing her brow, Persephone asked, "We'll pretend to date so that when I promote the app, people will be more excited?"

"Yes, that's basically it." Was that contentment painting his face? Would he still look pleased if she shoved him out of his moving car?

"And what does this false romance look like?" He intended to embarrass her, but she'd get ahead of his scheme. He had no clue of the emotional control she'd honed working for her mom.

Hades leaned forward within arm's reach. "Whatever you want it to look like."

Persephone straightened in her seat, but kept her gaze trained on him. "I'm not touching you to sell an app."

He laughed. "I'd hope not. I'd rather you touch me because you wanted to."

She spat out a laugh. "Charming."

His eyes narrowed. "This can be as real or fake as you'd like. Personally, I'm keeping an open mind."

"This could never be real," she said, forcing herself to meet his gaze.

A wicked smile played on his lips. "We'll see."

Once the car stopped, she closed her eyes and took a deep breath. Her eyes shot open when Hades unbuckled her belt, his thumb brushing the side of her thigh. That tiny point of contact lit a fire in her veins. The scent of a winter forest and his eyes locking with hers ensnared her for a brief moment. When his gaze dipped to her lips, the spell broke, and he ducked out of the car.

The fiend used his power on me. Such a dirty trick of the gods. It could be amusing to watch it happen, but it was *infuriating* to be subjected to it. She'd seen her mom move negotiations in her favor with her power of compulsion but hated it when she'd done the same to Persephone to get her to eat all her vegetables, clean her room, or—after she'd become an adult—work countless hours on a project.

Persephone looked up at the obsidian skyscraper as she accepted Hades' offered hand and exited the car. Across the street, Narcisi, the restaurant where she and Eurydice had met last night, sat quietly, unaware of how well it had lured her into Hades' realm. He didn't let go as she stepped onto the sidewalk, so she sent him a curious scowl.

Seemingly unconcerned by her reaction, he faced forward and coaxed her along with a gentle tug towards Underworld Unlimited's headquarters. Panic twisted in her gut. Right now, she could be seen holding his hand, walking into the lair of her mother's greatest rival.

Her mother's words echoed: *the damage is done.* Would Persephone truly have to keep up the charade of this so-called relationship?

As they entered the imposing lobby, the gray-streaked

marble floors reflected the crisp morning sunlight. The attendants behind the front desk nodded at Hades as he led Persephone towards a doorway behind them. Standing in a straight line facing the counter, the reception team looked like a row of toy soldiers. Sleek, dark pants cinched at their waists. Their black crew neck sweaters must've kept the cool air at bay.

They approached a steel elevator. "Here's how you access the apartment," he said, pointing to a half-sphere camera. "Facial recognition will unlock it."

She nodded absently, the dread in her chest deepening. The door opened with a low gong, and they stepped into the mirrored elevator. Hades' hand hovered near her shoulder blade, his presence suffocating.

"B13 takes you to the apartment. We'll get your fingerprints into our system today."

He pressed a button. *B13*. Basement Level Thirteen. Her pulse thudded in her ears. Could a mortal safely go that far underground?

"Hold on!" Persephone punched the red STOP button. "I'm not immortal, Hades."

He cocked one eyebrow. "Are you sure?"

"Positive." She took labored breaths in and out, all former composure forfeited now the threat of being stuck that far below the earth's surface weighed on her.

He threw her a confused look. Of course he wouldn't understand. He was an immortal god. "Fear not. I've brought mortals down here before and they were fine." With a wink, he pressed B13 again. "Better than fine in some cases."

Persephone would've rolled her eyes but needed to put her hand on the metal railing before she tipped over. *Is the air thinner here? Fates, is that what happens below sea level? Or is it the pressure that'll kill you?* She leaned one shoulder on the mirrored glass for support.

Looking annoyingly unbothered, Hades smiled. "Are you

jealous that I've brought others down here, Sephy?" He placed his hands in his pockets. "I didn't think we'd progress this far the first day."

She gripped the railing harder but held her other palm up at him. "Save it."

The elevator plummeted, and her stomach flipped. Pressure built in her chest as B3, B4, B5 quickly ended in B13. The doors rolled back, and her ears popped. Every sound grew louder around her until she swallowed.

A warm hand gave a tender squeeze on her shoulder. "Are you alright?"

She hadn't fainted. Through clenched teeth, she said, "I'm fine."

Hades looped his arm around her back and held her side against him. The reminder that she wasn't alone in the deep trenches of the earth was an odd comfort. Hades wouldn't have been her first choice as a companion, but his steady grip had her leaning into his side. He ushered her out of the elevator, but she put distance between them as soon as she felt stable on her feet.

She followed him over the lush runners lining the textured stone entryway, hammered golden sconces on the wall. The space opened into a vaulted ceiling with a room the size of a temple. In the center of the main living space, suede sofas circled a fire pit carved into black marble. Off to one side, a rectangular marble island protected a large kitchen. Near the kitchen, a modern staircase of bronzed metal holding pinewood planks led to a balconied room.

The sound of nails scratching the floor announced the arrival of a shepherd-type dog with fluffy blue merle fur.

Hades held up his hand, and the dog halted, then lay down. He bent with one knee to scratch behind the dog's ears. When he stopped, the dog tilted his head and looked, unblinking, at Persephone.

"Wait—why is there a dog here?" she asked.

Hades turned to her, a wicked grin spreading across his face. "Because you're living with me."

Her brief calm shattered. "What?"

He spread his arms wide, satisfaction gleaming in his eyes. "Welcome home, Sephy."

CHAPTER EIGHT

THE HOUSE OF HADES

HADES

There she was at last. Persephone Ioulo, in his penthouse, elegant fingers stroking Cerberus' ear like she belonged here.

Tempering his joy, he reminded himself that not only was she not there *willingly*, but she looked ready to flee the moment the opportunity presented itself. "Would you like something to drink? I have coffee, tea, and a bunch of mineral waters," he asked as he reached into the pantry to grab coffee beans.

Too bad for her, he'd put this plan into place months ago and he wasn't about to let her slip through his fingers now. She was too valuable an asset in the e-commerce space to lose. It didn't seem like she knew her worth either given how she'd undersold herself during their first meeting at Narcisi. Demeter had kept Persephone a secret for decades and must've known just how much anyone would want Persephone on their team. Yet, there was so much more he wanted, and he had no intention of pursuing her with dear old Demeter breathing down his neck.

On unsure feet, she entered the kitchen with Cerberus in tow, trotting at her side. She went to reach towards the streaked marble island but pulled her hand back before she touched the smooth surface, as if touching it would hurt her. Instead, she crossed her toned arms and swept her light green eyes around the place. She was exquisite and she was finally *here*.

"This is a beautiful home, but I'm not living here."

"An interesting deflection. Coffee or water?"

"Coffee's fine. But I need to go."

Hades filled up a hammered bronze kettle and set it on the stove. After a wave of his hand, flames burst and burned under the pot. There was no way he'd give her the stale, leftover coffee from that morning.

"You'll have to tell me your drink preferences at some point. It looks bad if I don't know what your drink order is. Staff pick up on these things, you know, and they like to talk."

"Drinks are one thing, but living together is another. Most couples wait a while before making that leap."

Hades nodded. "We're not like most couples." How could they be? Two titans in Olympus, each seated on a throne of their own creation.

"We're not a couple at all."

Hades took his time answering, watching the way she braced herself. "Legally, we are."

"H-how so?" Persephone sounded like she choked on nothing.

Hands in his pockets, Hades turned towards her. "My assistant, Charon, will review the contract with you later today so I'll leave it to her to explain the specifics, but if you haven't guessed, you and I are *together* for at least the next six months. It'll be much easier to be spotted with each other if we live in the same place. Makes it more believable." This way he'd get as much time as possible with her to try and win her over. Of course she despised him right now, but he was determined to show her they'd make great partners—in work and life.

"How is any of this in *any* type of contract? I'm wondering what happens if I just leave, because none of this seems enforceable or legal."

Cerberus nudged her leg, and she rubbed one of his ears while still managing to glare back at Hades.

He wouldn't stop her if she walked out. Not really. But she wouldn't get far. Every deal, every opportunity—he had control over them now. She just didn't see it yet. He wasn't here to ruin her. He was here to show her she didn't have to fight anymore. He'd already won.

"It's meant to protect both the rep and the brand. Think of it like a pre-nup."

"Make Eurydice the brand's rep. *She's* the one who created it."

Ah, yes. Eurydice would have some explaining to do to Persephone, wouldn't she? When there's a choice between one contract and another that's paying three times the price, everyone chooses the one that lines their pockets.

"Neither Eurydice nor I want that. No one else is better. Olympus adores you, and mortals trust you." He leaned against the counter, his expression almost casual. "I'd prefer for you to stay. And in time, you'll see—I'm a reasonable partner."

Her jaw tensed as she stared at him.

"You could walk out, Persephone. But you won't." He drew a slow breath in. "Because if you do, I'll take what's owed. And not just from you." He stepped away from the counter, rolling his shoulders, standing tall. He didn't want her fear, but he needed her compliance. "I never quit. And I can always go lower."

Persephone grimaced. "And as part of this agreement, I'm *forced* to live in your apartment?"

Hades gestured towards the middle of the large room. "You just said it's a beautiful home."

She scoffed. "We're thirteen floors underground."

"You're not stuck here all hours of the day. You're only expected to spend your nights here. That's it." He lowered his voice, as he pressed his fingers to his chest. "And you'll have me for company."

Her pretty face scrunched in a scowl. "That's another part that concerns me. We don't know each other and a roommate *situationship* is a bad thing to mix with a business deal."

He relaxed, leaning his hip on the counter. "You're too focused on what could go wrong."

"You're not focused enough on the risks. Fates... I bet your COO is on anti-psychotics."

"Hecate's my COO and she makes her own potions." He smirked and chuckled to himself when she rolled her eyes. "Anyway, Eurydice is exceptional and deserves to have the best team in her corner to launch this. You'd have to know this given the app's capabilities. There's a lot to love about it."

Her face paled in defeat.

He asked, "Are you upset that I've commandeered her IP for my company?"

She moved towards him. "Wouldn't you be?" He loved that she wasn't backing down.

"It's why I had to have it." *So I could get you.*

"When did you first learn about Eurydice's app?" Persephone asked.

He met her eyes. "Through Aphrodite and Hermes about five weeks ago."

"Hermes? My assistant, Hermes?"

"One and the same. To be fair, he didn't know he'd given me the information. I asked Aphrodite to seduce him and find out your social calendar. You'd been awfully quiet after Demeter introduced you to Olympus, and I was curious about you. So when he told Aphrodite about your current projects and how excited he was for his friend, Eurydice, to meet with you, I started looking into the developer as well. Then I loaned a large sum of money to her parents with the contingency that I'd own the app once she secured you as the spokesperson. Oh... and they signed an NDA so you wouldn't hear about it."

"Seems like a lot of effort to secure a pawn if you ask me."

Did she think she was a pawn and not the prize? "No one would ever mistake you for a pawn."

The kettle on the stove whistled and Hades made quick work of two pour-over coffees.

He shot her a slanted smile. "Cream? Sugar? Some alternative dairy-free milk substitute?"

"Black is fine." Her eyes wandered around the main living area and landed on the backlit slag glass wall near the hallway to the guest rooms.

"That's how I take it too." Hades ushered Persephone towards the sofas in the middle of the penthouse's largest living space, two mugs balanced on his palm.

As she sat down, Hades noticed her studying a small bundle of books stacked next to his favorite oversized leather chair. "This is as much your home as it is mine. Make a list of things you need that aren't here. I'm not too picky with the interior, but tell me first if you want to get rid of something."

He sat at the other end of the couch and set her coffee on the low, smooth stone table in front of her.

"Thank you." Her voice sounded lost as if still in shock.

"So tell me what questions you still have. I'd imagine this is overwhelming."

She scoffed. "Well, let's see if I'm understanding. We're going to pretend to be a couple to drum up buzz around the app. Once your team finishes the campaign's plan, I'll fill in wherever a brand rep is needed. And I'll be living here, *with you,* for the next six months, so it looks like we're seeing each other."

Sipping his coffee, he hummed. "You've got it."

"Okay, then what about my actual job? I'll need to go into the office or at least participate in meetings with my team. I'm not keen on using your internet to do work, no offense, and I have responsibilities I can't shirk. This rep agreement was never a full-time thing, but given that you've taken me straight here while the ink dries, I'm worried about my availability."

"Starting today, you work for me. Demeter's Bounty has let you go." He swallowed his sip of coffee. "Congratulations, Persephone. You're now a treasured member of Underworld Unlimited."

Persephone's face reddened. Quietly, as if only whispering to herself, she remarked, "I didn't think I'd lose my job at DB."

The poor goddess was reeling from the day's events. He felt a little bad but it was better to rip the bandaid off.

"If you impress me, Persephone, there's a future for you here. You could do very well under me." He regarded her for a moment. "And I think you'd like it."

She ignored his innuendo and scooted further away. Pulling her phone from her shorts, she typed away on her phone.

"Not sure if I've mentioned this yet," Hades said, "but all of your cellular communications will be monitored. It's our safety protocol."

Her lip raised a fraction before she threw him an incredulous look. "You bugged my phone?"

"I don't have to. You're within my domain and my team monitors all communications in and out—especially a new employee from a rival company." Surely she knew this. He'd bet his whole business that her mother did the same.

"A new employee who *you* stole via some in-no-way-legal twisting of the law. Can you access everything on my phone?"

"If I wanted to, yes." He took another sip.

"Will you?" She leveled him with a raised brow.

Frankly, he was too curious not to. Everything about her interested him but he chose to be coy. "I'm not sure yet. I don't know enough about you to form an opinion of whether or not I can trust you." His lopsided smile provoked a scowl from Persephone.

"I've got limited options here and no allies. I've been cut at the knees. What harm could I do?"

"Well," he said smoothly, "between the two of us, I'm a known entity. Olympus has spent centuries scrutinizing my every move. But you were a ghost until a month ago. Now, you're an asset. And if anything, I'm the one taking on more of a risk inviting—"

"Forcing," she interjected.

"*Welcoming* a new companion into my home. Besides, what if you try to destroy the brand?" he mused. "Inspire a coup? Or if you're feeling particularly bold, release your magic and end me?"

Persephone shook her head.

"I'm your greatest ally. You can fight it, but I think you'll come to see that this is the best move for you." He leaned in slightly. "Work with me, and it won't feel like a chore. It'll feel like power."

She could resist all she wanted, but resistance only worked if it led somewhere. He'd already written the ending.

The chime of a doorbell called their attention. His assistant, Charon, and a few uniformed staff carted Persephone's luggage into the apartment. His smile grew wide.

CHAPTER NINE

HADES' NEW PRIZE

"Good morning, Miss Ioulo. Please excuse us while we place your things," said a petite woman with long, jet-black hair.

Persephone looked up from her seat, drawn to the woman's polished navy dress and sharp heels. It was an outfit she'd wear to the office.

She rose from her seat. "Thank you."

The woman nodded, a small, polite grin gracing her lips before she turned to direct several staff members carrying Persephone's bags down a hallway off the main living space.

Dark brown eyes met Persephone's, and for a fleeting moment, she saw Helena in them. The resemblance softened her, drawing a rare smile to her lips. Would her carefree niece grow up to be this poised? This composed?

"My pleasure." The woman extended her hand and a delicate gold charm on a thin chain caught the light with the movement. "My name is Charon. I'm your new assistant."

A sharp twist of unease tightened in Persephone's stomach. This was too real.

Although Charon introduced herself as Persephone's new assistant, she looked more like her superior with her graceful movements and impeccable style. Perhaps she could help Persephone get out of the contract? And someone with eyes as sweet as her niece's had to be kind as well, right? This could be a good ally if Persephone ended up having to serve the full six-month term.

She dipped her head. "Nice to meet you. You can call me Persephone."

CHARON SCOOTED her chair next to Persephone at a long table in the center of a formal dining room in Hades' home. Connected by a simple stone hallway with golden sconces lining it, the dining room ceiling boasted a vaulted stonework that was the smaller sibling of the one in the main living space. Papers fanned across the obsidian table as Charon reviewed each agreement.

"Wow, Charon, you already look happier now that you're Sephy's assistant," Hades teased as he entered the room.

"Nice to have someone new on the team." Her focused gaze never left the documents as she replied. This woman hadn't slouched one bit since she'd entered the apartment.

"I'll let you two get on." Hades threw a wink at Persephone as he left.

She took a deep breath. It was a relief not to have him lurking nearby as they went through the contract's finer details. Unlike the gods, goddesses didn't perceive her as a thing to be conquered or a threat to be eliminated.

"Charon," Persephone said slowly. "Please excuse my ignorance, but what are you the goddess of?"

Utterly still, Charon's eyes flew from the page to Persephone's face. "Oh no, I'm not a goddess. I'm a psychopomp. A spiritual guide for souls but mostly Hades' personal assistant these days now that Underworld Unlimited basically runs itself."

So, a glorified grim reaper turned corporate executive? Psychopomps didn't have the same power as a god, but they were no mere mortal either. Persephone often wondered if her own assistant, Hermes, was one as well. He was faster than some of the gods.

Former assistant, she reminded herself. According to everyone else, she worked for Underworld Unlimited now.

"Will you need to attend to Hades as well during my time here?" Persephone asked. Was she loyal to Hades? Or could Persephone win her over?

Charon leaned back in her chair with a grin. "Not at all. He was very clear that I see to all your needs and I'm more than happy to oblige."

Persephone waited several breaths before asking. "Is this agreement legally enforceable given that I didn't have prior knowledge of who the patent owner was when I signed the contract with Eurydice?"

Charon clicked her tongue. "I'm not the law. Hades is. You'd be hard pressed to get out of this agreement without losing your ability to work in Olympus again."

"There's no way out?" It came out like a sigh.

"Best thing for you is to complete the required six-month term. I can appreciate your frustration, but I genuinely believe you'll do well here and might come to enjoy it."

I doubt it. Charon might be all-in, but she wasn't the one who'd been tricked into working for Underworld Unlimited. Yet, there was wisdom in what Charon had said and as much as it pained Persephone to admit it, her only option was to play along. If she tried to continue to fight this, it'd be her career that suffered.

"What other reps have worked for Hades under a contract like this?"

Charon's fingers rubbed the charm dangling on her long necklace. "Zero before you. We've only ever had one face of the company."

"Hades," muttered Persephone.

"Right. Yes. And now we've partnered with you—a former competitor—we want to do this right."

Hades had used that same word, *partner,* when referring to Persephone's contract. Didn't seem like much of a partnership if one person's life changed completely while the other simply gained a new employee/girlfriend. Again, what was she to do but go with the current than rage against it.

Gathering the papers together on the table, Charon grabbed a folder and tucked the signed copies inside.

Persephone nodded, then accepted the newest stack of papers from Charon's hand. She read from the paper in front of her. "*Required to dine together for at least one meal a day.*' Why?" Throwing a hand in the air, Persephone continued, "Surely he doesn't intend to enforce this. I understand the need for a rep to maintain a certain public image, but now I'm concerned you're about to tell me which toothpaste brand I can use and how many circles I need to make as I brush my teeth."

Charon gave a light chuckle. "Oh no, your toothpaste choices are yours alone. Same with all food and drink. There are no stipulations regarding those things. Think of this more about *where* you'll be seen and with *whom.*"

It continued like this for the next hour as they went through the contract. Charon politely reframed each one of Persephone's complaints. There was no getting past any of it. Truth be told, if the living arrangements were removed from the contract, it wasn't that different from the brand rep agreements Demeter's Bounty used.

Skimming through another clause, Persephone joked, "You'd think I was marrying the god. This is absurd."

Next to her, Charon stiffened. Persephone snuck a side-eyed glance at the straight-backed assistant. "Charon." Persephone's fingers curled around the edges of the contract. "This isn't a *marriage contract,* is it?"

With her hands folded on the table, Charon turned to look directly at Persephone. "Would you like it to be?"

"That's not an answer." Persephone's tone was firm.

"No, it's not a marriage contract but it shares similarities to a pre-nup."

Pinching the bridge of her nose, Persephone drew in a slow breath.

"Why?"

"Why what? Why is it similar to a pre-nup?"

Persephone nodded.

Charon tilted her head. "Shared assets mostly. This is the way of the gods. They protect what is theirs."

Persephone leaned one arm on the table to turn to face Charon. "I'm failing to see how I'm the threat here. What would I take? I could do as much damage as an inmate could to a high security prison. Beyond trying to escape, there's no real harm I could cause."

Charon tapped her fingertips on the paper. "You're the asset. If you walk away, you'd be taking the one entity he wants."

Persephone buried her face in her hands, trying to massage her temples and banish the ache blooming there. Lack of sleep was now catching up to her. She almost asked, *Why didn't Hades approach me outright?* But she knew the reason. She'd never agree to work with him willingly. But why did he want *her* and not someone else?

"No offense, but he has no idea whether or not I'm an asset.

I've never worked with anyone from Underworld Unlimited before."

Charon's gaze went to the ceiling. She counted with her fingers as she listed, "We know you oversaw the successful rollout of the area's first grocery delivery service. Within the first six months as operational director you increased DB's logistical efficiency by 300 percent. Every new system you've implemented enterprise-wide was fully functional at least ninety days ahead of schedule with minimal operational impact. You've brokered contracts with Olympus' most difficult gods and goddesses when they've refused to work with anyone else, and you've exceeded profit projections every quarter regardless of which department you oversaw." Charon shrugged at her. "You might as well spin gold, Persephone."

Somehow this psychopomp assistant knew more about Persephone's resume than her sister did. "How do you know any of this?"

Charon gave her a confused look. "There aren't many secrets among the gods."

Shifting forward in her chair, Persephone pondered Charon's comments. "So why am I the spokesperson and not Chief Product Officer?"

Charon smiled widely. "Would you accept the position of Chief Product Officer for *Flowers Near Me?*"

Not so fast. This was Underworld Unlimited. She had no idea how they handled a position like that one, and she wasn't about to take on more responsibility here to help Hades. "Spokesperson sounds fine for now."

Time passed with relative ease given the circumstances. Charon patiently explained the terms whenever Persephone had a question. Perplexed by Charon's calm demeanor, Persephone studied the psychopomp's mannerisms and decided Charon was too skilled to show a hint of concern. In fact, the only sign that Charon may have found any of this odd was the way her fingers kept brushing the small torch charm hanging on her necklace.

After placing the entire contract into a thick folder, Charon said, "I think this will be *too* easy for you."

Persephone stilled. "You sound awfully sure."

Charon's fingers lightly traced the small charm at her throat. "Let's just say... you wouldn't be here if Hades thought you *couldn't* do it."

A casual statement, one that made Persephone's stomach turn.

Then why do I feel like I've already lost?

CHAPTER TEN

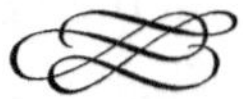

SMOKE AND MIRRORS

PERSEPHONE

After the detail-intensive meeting with Charon, Persephone lay on the canopy bed in the guest bedroom that would be hers for the next six months. A backlit bubble glass wall stretched from the floor to the high ceiling behind her, casting a pale blue glow across the soft comforter.

Cut honey-hued Teddy Bear sunflowers stood in a white flute vase on the bedside table. Persephone stroked the fine petals with her fingertips and drew in a slow, deep breath. Her mom used the bittersweet flower to decorate culinary dishes back home.

Laura had laughed off her request to file a police report, but replied to every question and concern she'd texted in her several-paragraph-long messages. How Laura wasn't unnerved, she didn't know, but her sister's acceptance helped her own. Albeit in a tiny way.

Rubbing her eyes, Persephone swore aloud when she looked at the black smudges on her fingers. She hopped off the bed and washed her face in the en-suite bathroom. Floral filigree lined the edges of the porcelain sink, tub, and shower. Plush cotton towels were folded neatly and placed around the space, and Persephone lingered on each one as she moved about. Duplicates of every bath and beauty product she owned were packed into a linen closet.

Slumped in a desk chair on the opposite wall to the bed, she searched her name online. When she saw that the only articles that mentioned her were the same ones she'd read, then reread last night, her shoulders relaxed. She went through texts from her former team with requests to meet for coffee or lunch soon. Each kindhearted message carved more from her chest. When would she work with them again?

Charon had packed her calendar with activities with Hades. Everything from formal events to picking up takeout together. There weren't many free blocks over the next ninety days because Hades wanted people to believe that not only were they excited for their new business partnership, but they were also a real couple who spent every moment together. Not to mention the fact that they were launching a new product, but that seemed to be a secondary concern to Hades. Her throat tightened as she reviewed her calendar for the tenth time.

Hades had told her they'd have dinner together at a new steakhouse tonight. He'd showed her the dark slacks and black cashmere sweater Charon had laid out for him. The high-waisted loose slacks and silk blouse Charon had picked for her would match nicely. She may lose her mind during these next six months, but at least she'd look posh.

After a short nap, Persephone fixed her hair and makeup. The dark circles under her eyes this morning looked less purple. Dressed with shoes in hand, she padded out towards the kitchen.

She had twenty minutes until their reservation, and with Hades nowhere in sight, she set down her shoes near the elevator then headed towards a desk and some barrister book-shelves off in a corner of the main living room. Neat stacks of paper sat atop the shiny surface and a high-backed upholstered chair stood askew. Never once had Persephone wondered what the *God of the Underworld's* apartment looked like. She'd been inside other gods' homes—her mom's, of course, and Hera's, Athena's, and Artemis'. But those were bright, opulent, and blessedly above ground.

Shelves packed with thick business and technology law books lined the outer edge of the open-floor plan in what looked to be Hades' office space.

With a light touch, Persephone pressed her fingertips to the lock on the enclosed glass door of the bookshelf. A warmth emanated from the metal, but as she made contact, the heat subsided and the door opened. As a child, her mom discovered she could open enchanted doors and compartments. Shortly after, her mom's protective spells became more elaborate... and painful.

Picking up a title boasting itself as *a must read for every tech executive,* Persephone flipped to a middle page and skimmed.

Picturing dinner tonight, knowing she and Hades would be photographed together, she imagined what her sister and mom would think when they saw the photos. Laura would get a notif-ication on her phone and Persephone was certain someone on her mom's team would alert her with a screenshot and a link to the post.

Did they know about the fake relationship part of the deal? Was that why Mom had been so cold?

She focused on what she thought her sister's reaction would be and not her mom's. Laura would see the photos and laugh. Probably send a teasing but good-natured congratulatory text to her. She'd torture herself later with her mom's certain disap-pointment. If Persephone had a daughter who'd got stuck working with her rival, she'd be gutted too.

"Find a good book?" Hades' husky voice trailed over her shoulders.

Slamming the pages shut, Persephone turned to see him a couple of paces away.

"*Blade of the titans...* You're silent as death."

He gave her a wolfish grin. "You look lovely."

"Charon has great taste."

He looked past her to the bookshelf. "I'm glad I left this unlocked. I should've invited you to peruse the books sooner."

She held her tongue, not wanting to correct him.

With a wave of his hand, several clicks followed by the creak of the bookshelves' doors rang out. "Now you can peruse at will."

"Ah, thank you." She held up the book in her hands. "I'm putting this one back."

Smiling, Hades held out his hand, and Persephone set the book in his palm. He set it on top of his desk and offered his arm.

"Are you hungry?"

She looped her hand through the crook of his elbow. "Always."

The hooded-lid look he gave her as he said, "Me too," ran a tickle down her spine.

Persephone cleared her throat and asked, "Does my mom or my sister know about the fake relationship part of the deal?"

"They do not. Only you, me, Charon, and Hecate."

"Oh," replied Persephone. Regardless of his rules, she'd tell Laura the truth.

THE CAR RIDE to the restaurant passed too quickly for Persephone. "Tonight, we don't need to act in love—yet," Hades told her. "We just need to be seen together, enjoying ourselves, so people start to wonder."

She bobbed her head. If Hades wasn't a god, she'd be elated to be seen with a handsome, successful date like him. But this was the god of Underworld Unlimited. The company known for its ruthless takeover of Olympus' e-commerce space. If you wanted to buy something online, you *had* to use his site.

Hades frowned at the gathered crowd packed onto the sidewalk, where their car stopped.

Persephone's heart kicked up a notch. *It's just dinner. Smile.* The words played on repeat in her mind as Hades opened up her door and offered his hand. She gave him a polite nod and released his hand the second she stood on the concrete. She loved tiny gestures like an offered hand, but why did it have to be *him*?

Hades used one arm to part the small crowd of phone-wielding journalists and the other kept a featherlight pressure on her upper back. She donned a relaxed expression, and her head pointed down at the ground as she walked past the cameras.

They entered through imposing oak doors into a steakhouse lounge filled with dark wood floors, matte black tables and chairs, and sleek industrial lighting.

A suit-wearing host greeted, "Miss Ioulo and Hades, welcome."

"Thank you," answered Hades, who kept walking and applied gentle pressure on Persephone's back, leading her down the line of identical tables.

Hades gestured to an open booth set with a bottle of ambrosia on ice. Before sliding into the booth, Persephone snuck a glance at the couples and groups nearby. A few eyes peered her way and smiled politely when they met her gaze. She nodded a silent greeting, then settled in her seat. By the time Hades sat across from her, she'd folded her cloth napkin into a neat triangle and laid it on her lap. Persephone's back was to most of the room, but she could see the reflection of the busy dining area and bar in the framed mirror on the back wall.

It was only yesterday evening that she was sitting across from Eurydice, making—what she thought was—the biggest play in her career. Oh how quickly things had flipped on her. Instead of a quiet weekend, enjoying the company of Laura and her family, she was dining with the one god she never wanted to meet in real life.

She reached for her ambrosia-filled cup. "Do you get tired of crowds following you?" she asked.

"What makes you think I always have a crowd following me?"

Persephone focused on the landscape painting on the wall nearest them. "Well... the herd we walked through tipped me off."

"Ah, yes. If you're concerned that's a constant thing, don't be. Most days, I move freely without anyone noticing."

"I doubt that."

One of Hades' brows quirked up. "Why?"

Glass in hand, Persephone swirled the golden liquid, watching it spin. "It feels like every week there's another news story circulating about you." She took a sip and watched him over the rim.

He laid an arm on the back of the bench. "Have you been following the stories about me?"

Persephone released an airy laugh. "You're not one to be ignored. I think every time I've opened social media, your image is plastered like graffiti on my page. I'd say you enjoy the attention."

"Hm..." Hades' eyes narrowed, but his shoulders were still loose and leaning back. "I only want *your* attention, Sephy."

These little flatteries kept pouring out of his mouth and she feared that he'd never stop. He was immortal, and she'd die long before she'd ever fall for him.

"Why, Hades? What's the point?"

Hades straightened in his seat before leaning his elbows on the table and tilting his head to one side. The shadow of smugness on his handsome face made Persephone's breath still. "Do you really think it's a coincidence your feed is flooded with images of me?"

Yes, she thought, chewing on his implication, trying to make sense of the taste.

She scooted forward. "What are you implying?"

His smirk deepened, his voice was thick with amusement. "That maybe we were always going to meet."

She bristled. *Like fate?* The thought unsettled her more than she cared to admit.

She resisted the urge to press her fingers to her temples, catching sight of her own exhausted reflection in the mirrored window beside them. Instead, she ran her fingers through her hair, smoothing it down. It wouldn't do to look furious on their first public outing—but the god sitting across from her was making it a challenge.

Lowering her voice to a whisper, she said, "This is going to be *excruciating* if you keep laying it on this thick."

Hades leaned in just enough to make his presence feel like a shadow pressing against her. "You don't have to believe me for it to be true."

She straightened, placing more distance between them.

A server arrived to take their orders. Hades' suggestions sounded delicious and Persephone wasn't one to fuss over a free meal. He made a few recommendations and whenever her face lit up with interest, he added it to the order.

"You're happy to go toe-to-toe with me when I flirt, but you're as docile as a lamb when I'm ordering food," said Hades, though his tone carried the lilt of a question.

Persephone gave a carefree shrug. "I love food. *You?* I'm not so sure about."

Chuckling, Hades quipped, "Give it time. You may even end up desiring me more than you desire food."

"Oh, Fates. There's no way."

Hades raised one brow in a challenge, and Persephone took another sip of her drink. She asked, "So tell me. How do you plan on using the tech in *Flowers Near Me?*"

His throat strained as he swallowed his drink and answered, "Same as you would have. Apply it to all e-commerce delivery, then use the location data for custom ads."

She nodded, unsurprised by his answer but intrigued that he'd admit it so freely. "Must be nice to know you'll regain your revenue lead in delivery sales."

"Oh, love, this will definitely level the field between your mom's company and mine. No... I take that back. Now that I have the app and *you*, I've gained an immeasurable advantage." His eyes bore into hers like a predator cornering its prey. "If only you'd stop living in Demeter's shadow and cast your own."

"I enjoy working for her." Persephone's reply was quick, instinctual. But was it actually true? Was Hades onto something when he said she lived in her mom's shadow?

"Maybe, after some time with me, you'll change your mind." Hades sank back in his seat.

"Not sure about that," said Persephone. "You are the villain who snatched me away from my thriving career."

"Or maybe I'm the hero who rescued you from perpetual mediocrity?"

She chuckled. "I know a few salespeople who would love the way you think."

Their first course arrived and despite the flitting in her stomach, Persephone had no issue savoring the roasted vegetable tart and its accompanying arugula salad.

Hades pulled her back to their conversation. "Your niece, Helena. Where does she attend school?"

Persephone's spine went rigid. Why would he ask about Helena? He could find that information on his own if he really wanted to, so there was no point in lying or avoiding the question. But that didn't mean she needed to say more than the school's name.

"Mount Olympus Academy."

"Great school." Hades relaxed in his seat, his expression nostalgic. "I remember when it opened."

Built several centuries ago, most gods still considered it a newer establishment. Odd that someone who looked to be barely a decade older than her had lived many of her lifetimes already.

As a server cleared their plates, Persephone scanned the bar through the mirror's reflection. There were a few gods and goddesses she recognized from events her mom had hosted over the years. Of course, most of them hadn't known who she was until recently.

She went to ask him a question but stopped when his face hardened at a sight behind her.

"Brother!" a deep rumble of a voice called before a tall, well-dressed god Persephone knew as Poseidon slid into the booth next to Hades.

"Poseidon," Hades said in a flat tone. Any exuberance he had a second ago drained from his chiseled face.

Poseidon showed off his pearl white teeth that contrasted with his tanned complexion. "You must be Demeter's daughter, Persephone." He extended his hand across the table. Persephone went to return the handshake, but he tugged her hand to his mouth and kissed the back of it.

"That's enough." Hades swatted at Poseidon.

"So Persephone," Poseidon continued, "how'd you end up

stuck working with him?" He thumbed towards Hades while keeping his attention on her.

There was a moment where Persephone wondered if Poseidon suspected she'd been unknowingly tricked into the contract. Even if he did, she doubted he'd be any help. So she gave a lighthearted smile and answered, "Olympus is only so big. It was only a matter of time before I ended up working for someone other than my mom."

With a sly tilt of his head, Poseidon said, "If I had known you were on the market for a business partner, I would've snatched you up."

Hades tugged on his sleeves. "Well, you didn't and now you're interrupting our pleasant evening. It looks like your date has returned and is looking for you." He flicked his nose towards the bar.

Poseidon wrapped one arm around a frowning Hades. "I only just got here." Poseidon beckoned the woman sitting at the bar. "Why don't we join you two?"

Hades' jaw flexed. Clearly outrageous flirting was a family trait of theirs, and she had no interest in chatting up two of Olympus' major gods. The handsome one she now lived with was bad enough.

Persephone chimed in, "That's sweet, Poseidon, but we'll have to take a rain check. With the impending launch, all social outings for the next few months have to serve the dual function of a business meeting as well. I'm afraid we'll make for poor company tonight."

Poseidon's eyebrows lifted. "Is that right?"

Nodding, Persephone added, "Afraid so. But we'll schedule something with your team. In fact, we'll host dinner in his apartment." Hades had invited her sister and family to join them tomorrow night. Why not extend an invitation of her own? At least it would buy some time for her to ask Hades in private why he looked like he wanted to jump out of his own skin at the prospect of speaking to his brother for a minute longer.

Poseidon grinned. "I look forward to it. Lovely to meet you, Persephone." He dipped his head at Hades and said, "Have a good evening," but snuck a wink at Persephone as he left their table to sit at the bar. *Typical god behavior.* Persephone smirked and shook her head.

Exhaling, Hades leaned back and dropped his shoulders. "I'd tease you for inviting someone over to our place, but I won't look a gift horse in the mouth. Thank you, love."

"You looked ill sitting next to him."

His nostrils flared. "Poseidon is an acquired taste I have yet to acquire."

She wondered if she should've made Hades sweat it out with Poseidon and his date. But had she let the conversation continue, there was a possibility she'd slip up and say something that would complicate their arrangement. *Don't make a fuss and don't involve my team.* Her mom's words played in her mind and confirmed she'd made the right call to placate Hades and not entertain her own curiosity.

"Speaking of siblings, tell me more about Laura."

Persephone pressed her lips tight then answered, "She's one of the smartest people I know. Which is why I'm going to tell her the truth about us."

He inclined his head. "You're certain that she won't tell others?"

No one except Peter, but he'd never tell another soul. "I'm sure."

A beat of silence stretched between them. Then, with an easy nod, Hades leaned back. "Then it's fine by me." His next words, however, carried a quiet sincerity. "If it helps you settle in, then I have no objections."

No smirk, no game, just an unexpected willingness to meet her halfway.

For the rest of the meal, Hades asked her about how she got into distribution as a career, what it was like growing up on her mom's estate, and the reasons she had remained there instead of moving into the city. He seemed genuinely interested in her answers. It was either that or he really was the best actor in Olympus. Most likely it was the latter, but for a moment, she allowed herself to enjoy his company. By the time dinner ended and they entered his car, she'd almost forgotten he'd tricked her into living with him.

CHAPTER ELEVEN

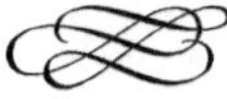

THE PRICE OF A GOD'S INTEREST

PERSEPHONE

To fake a relationship in front of your friends and family wasn't easy. Fooling your sister? *Impossible.*

Which was why Persephone had no intention of doing so.

Laura, Peter, and Helena would arrive a little later that Sunday afternoon and their visit couldn't come soon enough. Hades agreed to let Laura and Peter in on their fake dating arrangement, and Persephone was grateful for that concession. She would've told Laura regardless of what Hades wanted—contract be damned—but to know he obliged helped her feel slightly less angry with him.

Persephone paced the massive living space after scrolling through social media for an hour. Photos of the previous evening's dinner with Hades circulated through every Olympus gossip column and even made it into a few live stories. They looked good together which made her equal parts intrigued and terrified. Now was *not* the time to start warming to him, even if he'd left croissants from her favorite bakery on the counter for when she woke up. It had barely been a day since he'd stolen the *Flowers Near Me* app from her and forced her to work for and *live* with him.

She dug back through photos and news articles of Hades online. Finding images she had seen before: beautiful women on his arm at lavish events celebrating his successes—always someone different. Now she was the latest on his list. Hopefully she'd be forgotten in the mix, and her next business venture would eclipse the failure of this one.

Persephone rubbed the back of her neck as she meandered around the couches, chairs, and Cerberus. The dog sprang up whenever she moved. The two of them were sure to wear treads in the woven rugs on the hardwood floor. Cerberus bumped her hand with his head as he trailed after her, leaving a dusting of grey, white, and brown fur wherever he went. The cutie was impossibly fluffy—like a large ball of blue merle fuzz. He made her want to get an American Shepherd or two for the estate.

She dropped to one knee and massaged the dog's head. Those pointy ears molded to her grip, and she kept squeezing and pulling as Cerberus closed his eyes and panted. Worried she might've been too rough, she paused for a moment. His eyes shot open, and he butted her hands with a whimper.

"Alright." She resumed petting. Hairs from her own head tickled her face, and she pushed them behind her ear. If she didn't know better, she would have sworn her hair had grown an inch or two longer overnight. It fell to her waist now. Even her power, which was usually a small tingling feeling, now felt like a thrumming pulse in her veins. Perhaps the shock of this weekend's events had her magical defenses blooming?

Soft footfall announced Hades' presence beside her.

"I never understood my brother's desire to shape shift until now."

Persephone rolled her eyes and stood up. "If you want me to scratch you, then ask nicely."

"*Please* scratch me," he said in a deep voice.

She looked at her nails. "I don't know. I just painted these."

By the mercy of the Fates, she'd survived her first night in Hades' lair, completely unscathed. In fact, the guest room she slept in was cozy enough for her to get a real night's sleep and the shower was much larger than the one she used back on her mom's estate. Being underground felt claustrophobic enough to make her even more appreciative of the spaciousness of Hades' penthouse. And Hades' taste in coffee matched hers, which was the greatest relief. Who knew what kind of disgusting, pre-ground trash most bachelor gods drank? Thankfully, Hades wasn't one of them.

Chimes echoed from the entryway and Hades boomed, "Come in," before a line of uniformed staff filed in, pushing food carts with covered metal platters. Some set trays on the countertop as others carried plates and silverware and disappeared into the hallway leading to the dining room.

"All this for hosting my sister and her family?"

"The alternative would be me making scrambled eggs." He cocked an eyebrow. "I'll save my breakfast cooking for you."

Persephone let out a light chuckle. "Now that we're roommates, I'm sure we'll try each other's breakfast cooking at some point over the next six months. I hope you like burned bacon."

"Not just roommates. A *couple*," Hades added with a smirk.

She stepped towards him, invading his space. His eyes lit up as she came closer. "Yes, a couple of roommates."

"Sure." Hades winked at her. "What drink should I get for my roommate?"

She narrowed her eyes but there was no bite in her words. "Water's great. Thank you."

The chimes sounded again, and Cerberus whimpered and ran to snatch a chew toy from between pillow cushions. He hurtled towards Hades before sitting at his feet.

Charon's voice called, "They're here."

Laura and Charon entered first, with Peter and Helena behind them. Laura held a potted snake plant. Probably the only thing that could survive with no sunlight in Hades' underground apartment.

"Welcome." Hades shook Laura and Peter's hands, then offered a palm to Helena. She high-fived him, still clutching her father's leg.

Together, Peter and Hades gazed at the ceiling as Hades pointed towards different features.

Laura placed the plant on the coffee table then embraced Persephone and whispered in her ear, "What's really going on?"

"I'll fill you in later." Persephone squeezed Laura's arm as Helena sprinted towards them shouting, "Aunt Sephy!"

She lifted Helena in a hug, instantly feeling lighter seeing the little girl. "Are you hungry? I heard there's gourmet mac and cheese."

"And cookies. That's what Miss Charon said."

Charon smiled at Helena. "That's right. Dessert will be brought down later, along with a coffee tray."

Laura glanced at Persephone, raising her eyebrows.

"Charon, will you be joining us for dinner?" Persephone asked.

"Thank you but I need to help shuttle guests to an art exhibit tonight. I'll check back with you later." With a slow nod, Charon said, "Enjoy your dinner," and walked out behind the departing staff.

"She seems nice," Laura said. Her gaze shot to Hades and Peter before whispering, "Why are your texts so cryptic?"

Casting a furtive glance towards Hades, Persephone ushered Laura and Helena towards the kitchen. "I didn't know how much I could tell you before, but this contract includes a fake dating arrangement in addition to spokesperson duties." She ducked her head down and asked, "Helena, do you want to pet the dog?"

"Yes."

"Yes, please," Laura added.

"Yes, please," Helena parroted and scurried towards a curious Cerberus whose tail began to whip back and forth happily.

"So, why are your texts so weird?" Laura stepped near Persephone.

Persephone leaned in towards her sister. "Hades can read anything I send from my phone."

Laura's face scrunched. "Why would he read the messages on your phone?"

"To ensure I don't compromise the brand."

"Can he do that?" Laura eyed Hades.

Persephone nodded. "To be fair, Mom does it too."

"Course she does. Most paranoid goddess in Olympus."

With a shrug, Persephone replied, "She's careful."

Laura lowered her voice. "What else is included in this contract? Hand holding? Kissing? Sex?"

Persephone swallowed hard, trying to keep a serious face. "You wouldn't believe the vile things I have to do. He's depraved."

Mouth agape, Laura put her hands on her sister's arm. "Damn the Fates. Like what? Shit. I should've filed a police report."

Persephone giggled, which prompted Laura to swat Persephone's arm.

"Seriously?"

"I had you there for a second." She laughed. "No, nothing physical beyond living in the apartment. It's mostly public appearances and acting like we're a couple. He thinks it'll help sell the app." Persephone worried her lip. "Laura, why did you let Hades in your house yesterday? Did he threaten you?" In the chaos, Persephone didn't think to question it, but now with her sister here, she wondered what had happened before she'd got back to the townhouse.

Laura shook her head. "No, he was polite." She hesitated, as if replaying the moment in her mind. "It was a shock to see him, but right after he introduced himself, he said he was there to rescue you from Demeter's Bounty. And honestly? That was the best thing he could've said."

Persephone's brows shot up. "What? How is that a good thing?"

Laura sighed. "Because maybe this is the push you needed to get out from under Mom's rule." Her voice softened. "You know she controls everything. Despite how much money you've made for her company, she barely acknowledges your work."

How could anyone understand her working relationship with her mom? "I do get credit. I make—"

Laura cut her off with a firm shake of her head. "Mom has never given you your due, Sephy. She loves you, I know that. But she treats you like an asset, not a daughter."

"And you don't think…" She motioned her head toward Hades, eyeing him from across the room. "That he sees me the same way?"

Laura shrugged. "Maybe he does. But at least he's putting you out there instead of keeping you hidden while taking credit for your work. He wants you to be a spokesperson. At DB, you built an entire grocery delivery system from the ground up, and whose name is on it? Mom's. Not yours."

"It's her company."

"Exactly. And it always will be." Laura crossed her arms. "This flower app? It's going to be yours."

"It's Underworld Unlimited's." Her sister didn't understand how these things worked. But even if Laura's faith in Hades was misplaced, it felt good to have her in her corner.

Laura leaned in. "Before you got back to the house yesterday, I overheard some of Hades' conversation with Mom."

A wary knot twisted in Persephone's stomach. "And?"

"He told her he couldn't believe a goddess would be so jealous of her own daughter that she'd hold her back from greatness."

Persephone's lips parted. "He probably wanted you to hear that."

"Maybe. But that doesn't make him wrong." Laura's expression was resolute in a way Persephone seldom saw. "You know what else? He talked about how sharp you are. How everyone in the city respects you. How humble you must be, considering you never seek the spotlight."

Something conflicted came over Laura's face. "I've never heard Mom say half as many good things about you in all my life."

Persephone swallowed. "He's a flatterer."

Her sister's voice softened. "Call it flattery if you want. But I think he actually sees your greatness and wants to unlock it. Not exploit it like Mom does."

Persephone's chest tightened. "I hope you're right." Her sister usually was, but Laura loved her too much to be objective.

"We'll have to wait and see."

The moment was eclipsed when Hades and Peter approached, Helena holding onto her father's back.

Hades' piercing bluish gray gaze locked onto hers, his smirk just shy of smug.

Laura whispered, "I don't think he wants you here just for the app."

DURING THE MEAL, their conversation hopped from Helena's swim lessons to Peter's latest cooking mishaps and Laura's recent interest in mystery audiobooks. No one seemed to want to address the elephant in the room, not even Laura.

Persephone speared fusilli noodles with a fork as she studied her sister's face. When Laura caught Persephone's stare, she mouthed *what*, right as Peter pulled out his phone to show Hades his best batch of croissants. Persephone shook her head and stuck to furtive glances for the rest of the dinner. What did Laura really think of all of this?

When they'd finished, Hades invited them to lounge in the living room. Nearby in the kitchen, Helena sat in the seat closest to the dessert tray on the countertop and chewed on a cookie. Crumbs cascaded from her lap, falling towards a rapt Cerberus, catching the morsels like snow.

"Laura, did you ever want to work with your sister?" Hades asked.

"And work for our mom? Absolutely not. My dad begged her to let him train me when I showed an interest in medicine." Laura stroked Peter's shoulder absentmindedly.

Persephone cut in, "She was making splints for injured livestock before she was ten."

Hades smiled, then turned his gaze to Persephone, something unreadable flickering in his expression. "And you? You were restructuring distribution channels and negotiating logistics before you were twenty. I've read every proposal you've ever written—your strategic efficiency is unparalleled."

Laura blinked, studying him. "You've reviewed all of Sephy's proposals?"

Hades nodded, unbothered. "Of course. She's brilliant. I was waiting for the right time to recruit her."

Persephone stiffened. "You mean steal me."

Unapologetic, Hades replied, "Semantics."

"You shouldn't have been able to access those proposals," added Persephone.

How had he procured DB files? In response, the fiend simply shrugged.

Laura's expression turned questioning as she regarded him. "That's a lot of effort to put into understanding someone's work. What is it about Persephone that makes her so valuable to you?"

Hades held Laura's gaze. "Because she's extraordinary."

Laura tilted her head. "Sounds more like a personal reason than a professional one."

Turning towards to Persephone, Hades answered, "It is."

Laura released a small laugh, eyeing her sister. "Well, I suppose it makes sense. Persephone's always been exceptional. Even among the elite in Olympus, her origin story is one of a kind."

Hades' attention sharpened. "How so?"

"She was made," Laura clarified.

Hades shifted forward in his seat with a pinched brow. He leaned closer to Persephone. "You were *made*?"

Funny *that* was the point he decided to focus on and not the fact he'd all but forced her to work with him. "Not like how you or my mom or any of the gods were. I didn't start as an adult. I was born an infant and have aged just like my fellow mortals."

Hades sat back, a pensive look on his face. "That's why Demeter declined to name your father."

"Well, you can't name someone who doesn't exist," said Persephone.

Hades asked, "How? Who did she bargain with?"

"The Fates."

Hades' brows shot up. "*Really?*"

He seemed surprised by that answer which didn't make sense to Persephone. Who else would a goddess bargain with?

"Our mom pleaded with them for another daughter," Laura said. "They told her to eat a field of poppies and then she'd become pregnant. That's what she did, and here's Sephy."

Lips pressed tight, Hades nodded, clearly deep in thought. Persephone wondered why the revelation held his mind captive.

Peter sighed. "What do you think? Should we get Helena to bed soon?"

"No! I'm not tired," shouted Helena from her chair. Mouth full of cookie.

"Oh, yes." Laura held out her hand to Hades. "Thank you for having us. This was very nice. We'll host next time."

Hades shook her hand then Peter's as he said, "Thank you for coming."

"Thank you," replied Peter. He walked over to his daughter and scooped her up from her seat. The definitely-not-tired girl rested her head on her father's shoulder.

"We had a great time," added Laura. "Helena's already calling this the 'cookie cave.'"

"It *is* a cookie cave," Helena giggled.

Laura pulled Persephone into a hug. "I'll see you soon."

As Hades, Peter, and Helena headed for the elevator, Laura whispered, "He's obsessed with you, Sephy."

Mumbling low, Persephone said, "He's good at playing the part."

"Maybe. But I don't think it's an act."

"He's a god. They're the best liars."

Laura looked over her shoulder at the others, out of earshot. "Just be careful. He's not bound by the same rules as the rest of us."

"No shit, Laura. You think this is how I wanted to spend the next six months?"

Laura's eyes shot up to the high ceiling, then she shrugged. "Could be worse."

CHAPTER TWELVE

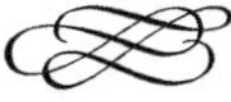

A DANGEROUS GAME OF PRETEND

PERSEPHONE

Monday morning, Persephone woke at 6 a.m. to a quiet apartment. Hades and Cerberus were both gone, leaving her alone with the soft hum of the city above. Sitting on the kitchen counter was a tray of coffee and croissants, along with a handwritten note.

> *My dearest Sephy,*
> *I'll be back by 11 a.m. to take you to lunch.*
> *Floor B10 has a gym filled with equipment and a*
> *400m track. Text Charon if you need anything.*
> *Your favorite roommate,*
> *Hades*

She smiled faintly, sipping the coffee as her phone buzzed with messages. No word from her mom, despite her attempts to reach out. The silence gnawed at her. Demeter had always been there, hovering at the edges of her life, controlling and distant. But this? It was… unusual.

As Persephone scrolled through her inbox, a new String of Pearls succulent caught her eye, its delicate vines spilling over the edge of the table. She frowned. Not only was it toxic to Cerberus, but it also needed far more sunlight than this dim, subterranean apartment could provide. She'd have to move it soon, or it would wither. Hades really needed to stop buying her plants because for all his business know-how, he was clueless when it came to caring for plants.

Her eyes went back to her phone screen. Still no reply from her mom.

She tried distracting herself with reading but nothing was sinking in. Sighing, she reached for her phone and began scrolling through social media, pausing at images of Hades, always with someone new, someone gorgeous. Her heart sank before she quickly locked her phone and shoved it back into her bag. Soon, she'd be another one in the mix. The thought startled her because she had no reason to care. So what if Hades moved on after her? It's not like they had real feelings for one another. This was a business arrangement.

Today was the first weekday of her imprisonment with Underworld Unlimited and she was already antsy. Next week, she'd go into the office to meet the team, but she wasn't sure what she'd do between now and then. She ought to embrace the quiet, knowing that as long as she was idle it meant she *wasn't* helping Hades. But habits formed over her entire professional life had her fingers itching to do *something*. Even if meant helping the arrogant god.

Besides, she needed to speak with Eurydice. How had she read that situation with the developer so incredibly *wrong*? Hadn't Eurydice been excited to work with Persephone? Technically, they still would be working together, but the circumstances were unfortunate, and they needed to talk.

Shaking off those thoughts, she threw on some athletic wear and headed to B10, ready to clear her mind and fill her time.

Lights flickered on all around the gymnasium once the elevator doors opened. Pine wood slats framed the large gym and mirrored sections ran along the sides. The air was crisp with a slight chill and the scent of wood stain. Even by the gods' standards, it was an impressive underground facility.

Persephone set her bag down on a bench near the track. Headphones in, she walked two laps before turning up the volume, then jogged. Translucent, backlit privacy screens surrounded the clay track. She sprinted the straightaways between the bends covered with a scant layer of sand.

Whenever her chest hurt and her mouth tasted copper, she'd slow her pace. Once her breathing evened out, she sprinted the straightaways again.

Why hadn't she heard from her mom? It wasn't like Demeter to blow her off. And what did this mean for Persephone's career? As hard as it was to admit, her mom was the keystone holding her professional future together.

When she slowed to a jog, she checked her phone.

CHARON

Good morning! You have a lunch reservation with Hades at 11:30 a.m. at a new restaurant uptown. Need anything?

Persephone stopped as she typed her reply, feeling more like a sidelined housewife than a new app's spokesperson. She wasn't used to a morning free of meetings, reports, and calls.

PERSEPHONE

All good. Thank you!

She stretched, gathered her things, and headed back to the apartment to shower. On her way she texted Hermes. There was nothing to do here so why not check in on her former assistant?

PERSEPHONE

How's the team doing? Tell them I miss them.

She rushed through her routine, then put on the black midi dress Charon had laid out for her.

Her phone buzzed.

HERMES

We miss you. Your mom is MIA.

She rubbed her temples and tapped quickly. Demeter wasn't an 'MIA' type of boss. Something was wrong.

PERSEPHONE

No one has seen her? Her PA?

Three dots appeared, then a reply.

HERMES

She's canceled all meetings for this and next week.

Persephone pressed her fingers to her bottom lip. This didn't sound right. Her mom rarely canceled meetings so why had she canceled two weeks' worth? She wanted to call her mom but the conversation they needed to have was not one she wanted anyone to overhear—especially not Hades' team. And he made a point to remind her that her phone activity would be monitored while she was on his network.

PERSEPHONE

She hasn't messaged me back. Keep me posted.

HERMES

Will do.

There was one person she trusted to dig deeper to see what was going on if she couldn't do it herself. She fired off a text to Laura.

PERSEPHONE

Mom's lost it. Canceled mtgs for next 2 wks. Haven't heard back.

Placing her phone on vibrate, she slid it into her purse and took several deep breaths. It wasn't just her that Demeter was avoiding. It was both a relief and concern because maybe her mom wasn't simply angry with her. Maybe Demeter was furious with everyone?

HADES CAME BACK to the apartment before 11 a.m. with a small square box wrapped in matte purple paper and topped with a black satin ribbon bow. "Open it," Hades said, his voice more command than request. "It'll match that tempting little black dress you're wearing."

Tempting? The dress' neckline exposed her collarbone, but nothing more. Even the skirt fell past her knees in loose pleats. The tasteful, form fitted bodice hugged her middle, but Persephone wouldn't consider it *tempting.* She scrunched her nose but thanked him as she took the gift.

The satin bow slid off, pulling the wrapping paper off a cushioned box with the symbol of a hammer and anvil embossed on the cover. Inside was a simple black leather watch with golden hands. The matte clock face highlighted the metal numerals. Stitched dark thread spelled her name across the band.

Persephone hesitated. "I can't accept this. It's leather." And it's from *him*.

Hades smiled, slow and confident. "It's synthetic, Sephy. Not leather."

Her mouth parted in confusion, but he continued. "You never wear animal products. It's not much of a mystery."

Right. Fashion bloggers had been buzzing about her wardrobe choices—ethical, organic, always cruelty-free.

"It's exquisite." The words fell out before she'd given them much thought. "Do all your employees wear these?"

Hades tilted his head. "Why would you think that?"

She laughed. "It has your name, like a pet would have their owner's information on their collar. I'll match with Cerberus." Come to think of it, she wasn't sure what the dog's collar looked like or if he even wore one. Still, her meaning was plain.

She held his gaze even as the most mischievous smirk a god had ever given her spread across his face. "It's a gift." His smile grew. "To commemorate our partnership. Nothing more."

He reached out, gesturing for her to offer her wrist. "May I?"

His vulpine features curled into a sly grin, his eyes sparkling with mischief. *He wants to put it on.* Was that so bad?

She offered her wrist, watching him fasten the band, skimming his fingertips over the sensitive skin. Nerves danced in her throat. This small act was the exact thing she'd picture a lover doing. If it was any other person, it'd feel romantic.

Staring at the watch felt safer than looking at Hades after that delicate touch.

Hades picked up her purse and extended his arm. "Shall we?"

He was a natural flirt. Even that small, effortless gesture made her knees weak. Why did it have to be him and not someone else—*anyone* else?

As THEY SAT in a restaurant surrounded by bustling patrons, Persephone found herself unsettled by the way her heart raced and cheeks warmed whenever he'd look at her with his intense gaze.

Hades poured sparkling water into Persephone's cup before topping off his. "How was your morning, Sephy?"

He regarded her as if he actually cared about her answer. "Your gym is impressive. Do your staff use it?"

"Not while I have a guest." He cleared his throat. "Wasn't it nice that no one else was there?"

"I mean…" Persephone started but pressed her lips tight.

"Yes?" Hades leaned closer to her.

"I don't like to exercise in public, but I hate treadmills more."

Hades inclined his head. "Don't enjoy dealing with admirers?"

"I'm not a fan of sweating and heaving in front of others."

After sipping his drink, he cleared his throat. "I disagree. Those two things are better with others."

Her traitorous cheeks blushed. "You know what I mean."

A server carried a tray filled with blanched vegetables, hummus, and cheeses towards their booth. Happy to see the lunch spread delivered to their table, her focus shifted back to Hades. With quick movements, he placed several items from the tray onto her plate. Little samplings of each thing, as if he wanted her to try it all and find what she liked. She already knew she liked everything on the board.

"You're certain Laura and Peter won't say anything about our arrangement?"

Surprised by his question, Persephone waited a breath to respond. He'd asked before, so why was he still worried? And from the way he'd carried himself yesterday with Laura and Peter, she swore he'd considered them new friends. "Never. Laura can keep a secret like no one else."

"Even from your mom?"

Right. He's worried about my mom finding out.

"Especially from her." She laughed to herself. The things Demeter knew about Laura were only the things Laura wanted her to know.

Hades hummed in understanding before tilting his head. "Are you trying to hide the fact that you're a goddess?" His brow pinched in genuine confusion.

"What?" She stared back at him, awaiting clarification. His question lacked the playful tone she was coming to expect from him.

Smirking, he replied, "You were made."

The query was serious. "Yes, then born. Not created like you." Even if Persephone was truly one of them—an immortal— she'd be at the bottom of the pack. Fates, even Demeter in all her power and glory didn't have the same clout or godly lineage as the top three brothers did. Hades, Zeus, and Poseidon were set apart. Set *above.*

Hades shook his head. "Doesn't matter. If you're made, you're immortal."

A rise of heat hit Persephone's cheeks. There was no way she was immortal. Surely, she'd know if she was because her mom would've told her. She had a goddess mother but no father. At most she was a demigod—still a far cry from having power like Demeter or Hades.

"Why don't I have powerful magic, then?"

Hades sat taller and crossed his arms. "Oh, you definitely do."

She shot him an incredulous look, studying his face for any hint of jest.

"Friday night in Narcisi. You used it on me. You still have me in your thrall." He held her with a heavy-lidded look.

The intensity of his gaze was too much so she looked out at the other diners. No one seemed to be watching them. "Stop. No one is paying attention, so you can dial it back. It's beneath you."

"Not much is beneath me. I live several stories underground, remember?" said Hades. "Besides, I felt it with all my senses. Why do you think I approached you in Narcisi?"

This line of questioning felt too personal for something between two business partners—even two who were faking a relationship.

One eyebrow shot up. "To intimidate me."

He scooped a few items onto his plate. "No, I was *drawn* to you."

"That's the reason?"

He shrugged. "I could tell you weren't charmed by me."

What an insufferable god. He was so used to people falling at his feet that he assumed anyone who didn't was magic. This was typical god behavior to expect anyone and everyone to gush over their power, looks, and wealth. "Did you use this spokesperson clause to prove that I could *like* you?"

Hades leaned forward, his elbows on the table. "I did it because I wanted to get to know you before others could."

Persephone crossed her arms and gripped her biceps until her fingertips bit into her skin. So this *was* a game to him. She was the pawn, too distracted by a business opportunity to spot the danger lurking nearby. Her skin heated in anger. Even a few deep breaths did nothing to dampen the simmering rage. If he was a viable partner, maybe she could understand his desire to lay claim to her. But this was *Hades* and there was no future to be had between the two of them after this contract ended.

Trying to keep her tone even, she sat taller in her seat. "Should I piss a circle around you, then? Make it impossible for others to approach you without fear of repercussions? If what you say about my power is true, then it should be no problem for me to enact my will on any admirers *you* have."

His features tightened into a deep frown. "Would you have preferred Poseidon wooing you?"

Persephone leaned in, her chair scraping the floor as she closed the space between them. Her whisper came out strained. "Don't you think you've put me on his radar in the worst possible way? He might try to break your new toy, *Hades*. I didn't want to be a fixture in society, and I was equally determined to not become one of its victims. You're looking to stir up drama, and who better to do that with than your rival's daughter?"

His full lips parted, and eyes lifted. "You think I want to harm you?"

"You took my chance to meet the rest of the gods and goddesses on my own terms. I think you want to embarrass me and my mom so everyone will talk about your app while they're laughing at Demeter's mindless daughter." She knew better than to bait him like this, but after the weight of her new reality began to settle, it was too much to keep inside. He admitted that he wanted to keep others from her so that he could get to know her. But it seemed to her it was more about him getting to call dibs before she got to choose who she wanted to get to know.

Hades' eyes widened. "Why would I embarrass you? You're representing one of my products. That wouldn't bode well for business."

Scoffing, she replied, "All press is good press, right? You've got your image as the top villain, so wouldn't the perfect plan be to destroy the new kid in town?"

He stilled. "How would I go about destroying you? Tarnishing your reputation?"

The confession spilled out. "Making me look like a lovesick idiot, then getting 'caught' with someone else." She'd seen it before with the other gods and now it looked like he was going to do the same to her.

He sucked in a long breath. "Persephone, I would never do that to you."

"Oh? Change of heart?" she sneered, arms still crossed, her face a mask of disgust. Yet, beneath it all, her chest felt achy and raw.

He straightened in his chair, leaning back with hands on the edge of the table. "You speak as if this is how I do business. I've never pulled a stunt like that."

Throwing an exasperated look his way, she stared off, lost in frustration. Regardless of the truth of his true intentions with their arrangement, what control did she have in the situation? Her goal for the next six months was to protect herself, so why did he have to play with her like this? Make it seem like he was genuinely interested just so their inevitable break-up would be even more dramatic. And why did this bother her? She shouldn't care.

"Tell me specifically what you're worried about." His pleading tone gave her pause.

She knew he was no different than the other gods. Growing up around these deities gave her a front row seat to their ever-changing romantic whims. Even Demeter had suitors one day who would disappear the next and her mom was one of the more reasonable, grounded gods. Persephone wanted someone to share her life with, not some fake boyfriend who'd forget her name as soon as their contract ended.

The best move was to keep quiet, but she couldn't. Her future dangled in his grasp, and maybe a touch of honesty would soften him enough to end the charade. Her confession spilled out like seeds onto a garden bed.

"I don't want to be seen as 'Hades' ex' after this is over. I've just completed one of my best launches and it's already clouded by this nonsense. Nothing will change for you. And unlike you and the gods, I intend to be loyal to my beloved and not hop around warming beds or having a rotation warm mine. That thought makes me sad." Oh, how she wished she was immune to these feelings. It had only been a few days, and she was already bracing herself for disappointment and hurt after their arrangement ended. How *ridiculous*.

Hades shook his head. "I won't embarrass you. Ever. And maybe Charon skipped this detail when reviewing the contracts, but there's an infidelity clause."

It offered some protection, sure, but could she trust him to honor it? "Charon said it was like a pre-nup."

"Almost identical," he replied. "Protects both of us in case you break my heart."

"Please stop." She rubbed her temples, eyes closed, until a horrible thought struck her. Her fingers froze, and her eyes flew open. "We're not married, right? You didn't sneak something like that into our contract, did you?"

He chuckled, slipping his phone back in his pocket. "Not yet."

Her mouth tightened as his slid into a slanted smile.

CHAPTER THIRTEEN

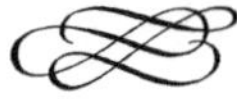

A GODDESS IN THE MAKING

PERSEPHONE

The Underworld Unlimited business floors were strikingly similar to Demeter's Bounty's. Both buildings boasted sprawling square footage with private offices lining the walls, conference rooms in a range of sizes, and open workspaces next to water and coffee stations. Most importantly, both were *aboveground,* high in the mid to upper floors of their respective skyscrapers.

"Here's your executive suite." Charon pushed a set of frosted glass double doors open, revealing a spacious workspace that was twice the size of Persephone's office back at DB.

Charon pointed towards the kitchenette. "Stocked mini pantry and espresso station over there." Tapping a screen on the wall, she instructed, "You can control everything from the room's temperature, to the lighting, and even the shade level of your windows on this panel here." Charon swiped an on-screen lever and the floor-to-ceiling windows dimmed.

Persephone stepped behind the corner desk, admiring the

large screens and brand-new laptop sitting on the marble desk-top. She ran a finger across the floral notebooks stacked on a nearby shelf.

"Bit excessive for a spokesperson, don't you think?"

Charon laughed as if Persephone had made a joke.

Hades knocked once on the door, drawing their attention before stepping in to join Persephone and Charon. "How do you like your office?"

Deadpanned, she replied, "It's sufficient." She snuck a wink at Charon who returned the gesture with a lopsided grin and exited her office.

Hades threw Persephone an amused look, clearly not buying her feigned nonchalance. "You know, if you like it here, you can stay as long as you'd like."

"What do you mean?"

Hades walked to the windows and looked out over the city. "After your current contract expires. If you wanted to stay on with Underworld Unlimited, you could."

What was he trying to do? There was no way he actually wanted her to stay with Underworld Unlimited. Maybe this was his way of getting her to drop her guard. "I didn't apply to work here, remember? You bought the patent rights of an app that I was supposed to acquire."

He sat in a chair on the other side of her desk. "You didn't need to apply. Your work speaks for itself, and I don't let talent go to waste. So why wouldn't I want the best?"

Nothing stroked Persephone's ego like a compliment to her professional prowess. If Hades were a mortal executive paying her tribute, she'd be melting. Especially with how good he looked in that suit. And if she had to guess, this office was meant for a C-suite partner and not just any Underworld exec-utive. The gesture was incredibly flattering, and *Fates*, it was making her soften towards him.

"I think whoever this office belongs to will want it back after

I'm gone." She distracted herself with her phone in an attempt to shake off these unwanted feelings of appreciation.

Hades stood with a smile. "Come on. Allow me to introduce you to the team." Holding the door open, he waited for Persephone to walk through.

It felt incredible to be back in an office building, meeting a new team of marketers and developers. Hades personally introduced her to each employee, remarking how *lucky* they were to have *someone of her caliber* join the app's launch. She held back her smile, not wanting to seem too eager—or let Hades see she was happy and think he had something to do with it.

"Think about all that she's done in the e-commerce sector and imagine what she'll do here," said Hades to the fresh-faced communications team gathered around long conference table.

Expecting to see eye-rolls and hear muffled scoffs, she almost stumbled in place next to Hades when the group smiled back at her.

Later, when she was walking back to her new office alone, a woman around the same age as her stopped her, whispering, "I shouldn't admit this, but I use your new grocery delivery service all the time. I love it." Her eyes darted past Persephone.

"Glad to hear it," said Persephone who smiled as the woman rushed off.

She settled into her cushioned desk chair, powered on her new laptop and started the initial setup. After a few minutes logging into her email, calendar, and shared drive, Hades entered.

"You look right at home here, Sephy." There he was, using her nickname again. Had it been some other handsome man saying it, she'd think it cute for someone to give it a try and not be afraid to flirt with her.

"When we're in the office, you should call me Persephone."

He let the doors close behind him, stalked towards her and leaned to sit on the side of her desk. "Why? Do you not like it?"

Was that any of his business? Even if they would be faking a relationship soon, he didn't need to be so over the top with the endearments. "Only a small group of people call me it and not a single one of them has ever tricked me into working for them."

He smirked. There was playfulness in his tone as he asked, "Really? Not even your mother?"

Persephone stared back at him, sitting up straight in her chair. The god was imposing with his dark suit and tall frame, but his relaxed shoulders and gentle expression put her at ease.

He lifted his hands in surrender. "Fine. I'll stop using it in the office. It can be our special thing when it's just the two of us."

No. He was *insufferable*. Unfortunately, he was pleasant to look at. It'd be easier to stand firm in her distaste if he was ugly. Right now, her stomach did flips as his gray eyes bore into hers. To have someone look at her as if she were a work of art was thrilling. Too bad it was him.

"Did you need something from me?" She meant to busy herself with emails, but her treacherous laptop was still loading an update.

Adjusting his cuffs, he said, "I'll make this quick. I have to go across town this afternoon for a meeting, but I'll see you for dinner tonight at the apartment. Try not to miss me too much." He stood, tapping two fingers on the edge of her desk.

"I'll see you later then."

ALTHOUGH PERSEPHONE APPRECIATED the office tour Hades and Charon had given her, she wanted to walk around on her own and get a real sense of the space. DB had been her stomping grounds from early childhood and she could navigate its halls with her eyes closed. She needed to learn the ins and outs of her new jail. But if she was being honest, she hadn't seen Eurydice yet and wanted to have a word with the developer.

When she considered Eurydice's situation, she'd be a liar to say she wouldn't have done the same thing. To have two executives dedicated to the successful rollout of your app was a once-in-lifetime opportunity. You had to take every advantage you could to get a leg up in the tech industry. Olympus had mega stars—gods for Fate's sake. But that didn't diminish the lingering frustration Persephone felt at Eurydice's two-timing antics.

A little lost in her thoughts, Persephone grinned when she caught Eurydice filling her mug with coffee at the beverage station.

She inched closer, careful not to make a sound until she was within arm's length. "Well, look who it is. Good morning, Eurydice."

Eurydice whipped around, sputtering a polite, "Good morning, Miss Ioulo."

Persephone hummed a laugh. "Given that you've bested me *and* I already gave you permission to call me Persephone, I'd say we're past formalities. How are you?"

"I'm well. And you?" The lost look on Eurydice's face made Persephone feel a little bad about ambushing her.

"I've been better, but I shouldn't complain." Persephone paused, gathering her thoughts. She needed to clear the air and not toy with the young woman like her mom would. Fates, her mom would have this poor girl sweating bullets if she'd tried to trick Demeter.

"Eurydice, I don't like that you hid the patent ownership from me, but..." She softened the look on her face, hoping to convey sincerity. "Had I been in your situation, I would've done the same thing and held out for the best deal."

Eurydice sucked in a breath. "Really?"

Persephone nodded. "It was opportunistic, but that's what it takes to be successful in Olympus." Shrugging, she continued, saying, "And it would've been foolhardy for you to try to convince me to work with Hades, so I can't blame you for not saying anything to me. But I hope that moving forward, you'll trust me enough to share all of your hopes for the app. I meant it when I said that your tech is impressive and that you've got a bright future ahead. I think *Flowers Near Me* is clever and I'm proud to be associated with it."

"Thank you. This means a lot." Eurydice gave a restrained smile.

"I mean it. I'm here to do a good job and promote this app with everything I've got." *And somehow get it away from Hades' hands.* She kept that last part to herself. "Let's get this out of its beta version and ready for the masses. No hard feelings, okay?"

Eurydice nodded. "Thanks, Persephone."

Persephone smiled. "I'll see you around." With a parting wink, she turned and headed back to her new office.

HECATE'S long black hair glinted purple where the light hit it as she walked into Persephone's office. Her sleeveless wrap dress cascaded into a flowing skirt that ended mid-calf and displayed her heeled gladiator sandals. Persephone stood to greet her.

"Nice to see you again, Persephone." Hecate pulled Persephone towards her and placed a light kiss on each cheek.

"Likewise. It's always good to see you." Persephone had fond childhood memories of Hecate coming to visit Demeter's estate. The goddess always made a point to exchange pleasantries with her.

"Did you know that Hades claims you're his COO."

Hecate laughed. "His COO? For fuck's sake. He needs to stop using that joke."

"So, you're not?" She needed to know.

"Fates no. I only do freelance consulting for his team. I work with your mom too, but I doubt she told you I'm on her staff."

Persephone huffed a laugh. "Good point."

"Well, he asked me to take you to lunch because he wants me help you feel more at home at Underworld Unlimited," said Hecate. "I say we can use it as an excuse to get you out of the office for several hours every day."

This was good. Hecate was stuck between Demeter and Hades too, so she could understand Persephone's situation, but unlike Persephone, Hecate was *powerful* and could offer protection that Persephone couldn't give herself.

Hecate used her powers to portal them both to a bistro sandwiched between a packing and shipping store and a plain office building. The outdoor sitting area was in an alleyway behind the tiny restaurant with olive and oak trees and small tables placed under the canopy of leaves. A tiny forest within the city. Such a welcome sight.

Hecate swiped lip gloss over her pursed lips. "Have you been here before?"

"No. I haven't been to many parts of the city."

"Right. You've lived on the estate. I'm sure you miss it." Hecate poured two cups of tea, then waved her hand over the hot drinks.

"It's beautiful there, as you know. Lush. Orderly. Quiet. Everything that Demeter wants it to be. Olympus has its charms, too. My sister's lived here since her residency."

"Yes, I've met Laura a few times. She's brilliant. Great sense of humor." Hecate brought the teacup to her mouth.

Mirroring Hecate, Persephone took a sip. A burst of lemony rosemary and honey swept over her tongue, sending a soothing warmth through Persephone's chest as she swallowed.

"What kind of tea is this?"

"Green tea that I doctored just a little." Hecate winked and took a long sip.

Magic, of course.

"It's perfect. I like to think I can make a good cup, but this is special."

"I'll show you. It's not hard."

Persephone gestured her cup at Hecate. "For you, I'm sure it's second nature, but I don't have powers like you or my mom."

Hecate shook her head. "Yours haven't fully emerged yet. This will be easy once it does."

"Why haven't they already?" It wasn't as if she hadn't tried many times before. If she could portal instantaneously from one place to another, she'd have no reason to take transportation or walk everywhere.

"It might be waiting for a certain event."

What Hecate said sounded reasonable. If anyone would understand the quirks of magic, it was her. "Like what? I'm well past puberty and young adulthood. I've tried to conjure things but stopped because it never works."

Hecate shrugged. "Magic is fickle. Have you been reaching for it recently?"

"Not really. I tried it a few nights ago, but it was weak."

With a delicate movement, Hecate set her tea on the table, then interlaced her fingers on her lap. "You know... I've known of your origin since the beginning."

Persephone stared at Hecate. Of course she had known she was Demeter's daughter when most of Olympus only knew of Laura, but the ominous way she said *your origin* raised the hairs on the back of her neck.

"I didn't just help your mom find the field of poppies you were made from, you know. I enchanted them myself." Hecate wiggled her fingers.

With a hand pressed to her lips, Persephone regarded her

with a new interest. "Why didn't my mom tell me you helped create me?"

Hecate's lined eyes softened. "I don't think Demeter likes the idea of sharing you with anyone."

How true.

Hecate ran her fingers through her hair. "You were never *mine* and your mother needed you. Laura was so much like her father even as a small child. Demeter was desperate for a daughter that was all her own."

She wasn't sure what to make of that. Her mom's love was fierce and more isolating than she'd realized. Perhaps her mom's recent avoidance was simply an attempt to give Persephone space to grow. Learning Hecate's involvement was a welcome revelation, but she really wished her mom was here with her and Hecate. "So, if you enchanted the poppies..."

"Then you absolutely have power. *My* magic."

Butterflies in her stomach, Persephone sat straighter in her seat. Maybe she didn't need to be a goddess to be powerful.

CHAPTER FOURTEEN

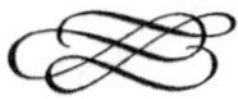

THE KING'S GAMBIT

HADES

Over two weeks had passed since Persephone had moved into his apartment. Seeing her in the office every day confirmed just how right everything was now that she was here. Even when she wasn't trying to be helpful, she had a way of naturally improving his employees' moods by lending a hand wherever it was needed. A few days before, he'd caught her negotiating with a marketing vendor who'd given one of his event planners a hard time. Persephone had the vendor eating out of the palm of her hand by the end of the meeting.

His chest still fluttered every night, knowing she was just in the next room. He'd started adding more plants to his space after seeing how they thrived under her care. Even cut flowers seemed to bloom in her presence, as if rooted in a sunlit field.

Lying in bed with a book in his lap and thoughts of her consuming his mind, Hades watched the flames dance along the wick of a jasmine candle. He'd moved enough belongings into the guest room closest to hers to make it look like his own—

clothes, shoes, books, and toiletries. If the captivating goddess ever wandered in, there'd be no reason for her to suspect the room was anything but a proper bedroom, furnished with heated stone floors, rich woven rugs, and the dark velvet furniture Charon had chosen.

They had settled into a routine of morning coffee and shared dinners, but it wasn't enough. Soon, once the marketing proposal was approved, she'd spend all day on the video set, and he'd lose those precious, fleeting moments with her. He'd even asked Charon to align as many of his commitments with Persephone's studio sessions as possible, but it barely freed up any extra time.

Every morning, he rushed back to the apartment after checking in with Charon, lingering in the hallway by Persephone's open door while she was at the gym. The guest room smelled of vanilla and jasmine—like her.

Earlier that day in his home office, Hecate asked, "You've already burned through the candle?" She quirked her brow with a sly smirk.

"It was barely a tea light."

"And enchanted. I gave it a seventy-two-hour burn time. Did you burn it for three days straight?"

"No."

Hecate crossed her arms and leaned against the door frame, her brow quirking even higher than Hades thought possible.

Hades said, "I had to extinguish the flame when I moved it back and forth from here to the cookie cave."

"*Cookie cave?*"

"Helena's name for my apartment. We had cookies the first time she visited and every time since. You've met Persephone's niece, yes?"

Hecate cocked her head to the side. "Does Demeter know her granddaughter visits you?"

Hades' chair creaked as he rested his back on it. Demeter

would have future grandchildren *living* at his apartment if he got what he wanted.

"Of course. I told her as we gabbed over cocktails."

Hecate rolled her eyes, then sunk onto the settee by the glass wall displaying an underground waterfall trickling over layers of rock. "Have you heard from her since the acquisition?"

Thank the Fates, he hadn't, but it wasn't cause for celebration. Demeter might not have the same power he did in Olympus, but that didn't mean she was any less formidable. Up until recently, she employed the one person he'd ever wanted by his side.

"Not yet. She fought hard in our negotiations and now she's licking her wounds." He traced two fingers along the mouse pad of his computer and scrolled through his email.

Hecate clucked her tongue. "Don't be careless. Demeter loves Persephone more than you and I could ever imagine."

Hades frowned. The admonishment sat like rotten food in his gut. He didn't have a mother's love for Persephone but the unrelenting need to be with her felt primal.

Turning to look at Hecate, he quipped, "You're friends with her. Put in a good word for me."

Shaking her head, making her long hair swish, she said, "No, I have my own worries. You stole her daughter, Hades. There's no coming back from that. Even if you two were amicable before, it'd be a serious problem."

Hades released a long sigh. Of course, Hecate disliked his method of getting Persephone to spend time with him. Buying *Flowers Near Me* right out from under Persephone in order to get her into a contract with him wasn't a traditional way of dating, but he had to be creative. Besides, Demeter and he had been adversaries in the distribution space for decades, and it wasn't like he could approach Persephone in the open with her guard dog looming.

Strangely, he suspected Demeter's anger stemmed from

disappointment in Persephone. When he'd met with Demeter and her team, he learned she knew little about Persephone's true interest in *Flowers Near Me*. Demeter grew quieter as negotiations carried on and that was unlike the formidable goddess of the harvest he knew.

"Have *you* heard from her recently?" Hades asked.

"No, and I think that ought to give you pause." Hecate's dark brow quirked again.

Hades' eyes narrowed. The worst scenario bubbled to the surface in a rolling boil. "You think she's working with my brothers?"

One shoulder shrugged. "Or something worse."

He grimaced but remained silent.

Hecate left shortly after their conversation, but the shadow she cast lingered.

He fired off a message to Charon.

HADES

Find out who Demeter's been talking to.

Returning to his computer screen, he opened a document on his desktop labeled "Marriage License." The words washed over him, but his chest tightened at the blank line next to his signature. Underneath in black text read: "Persephone Ioulo" and he tried to imagine the swirls of her signature decorating that line.

Charon's reply lit his phone.

CHARON

Will do.

HADES

Good. Hecate thinks Demeter's on the move.

Marrying Persephone would devastate Demeter, but that wasn't why he wanted to. This six-month contract was a temporary fix until he could convince her to love him. If she left him at the end of it, he'd be the one gutted. Desperate for whatever foothold he could gain with her, he was using the contract to give himself time to show his interest. And his interest had become longing quicker than Cerberus could devour Helena's cookie crumbs from the floor.

It only took one chance sighting of Persephone, accompanying Demeter to lunch, for his obsession to bloom. Fates, he'd bought the restaurant Narcisi outright because it was the first place he saw her. The goddess sat tall at the table, with the most beautiful smirk and smart green eyes. Where Demeter exuded arrogance throwing annoyed looks at who he assumed were Demeter's Bounty middle management, Persephone emanated power. Her understated confidence entranced him and after this short time together, there was no way he'd let her go.

Deep in his being, he knew they'd be together—the Fates had promised him as much. But given the duplicity of the Fates and the fact that Persephone's continued professionalism proved her immunity to his charms, he had no clue how to make it happen. Women typically adored him. So why wouldn't this siren start flirting back? It was maddening.

INSIDE HIS UNDERWORLD UNLIMITED OFFICE, Hades listened to Charon rattle off team reports as they each ate their salad and talked between bites.

"Legal took issue with marketing's phrasing and now they're reworking the ads. There are concerns regarding the app's use of users' locations when setting up meeting spots," explained Charon.

"How much more time?"

"Four weeks," Charon replied in a strained tone. "They know

it'll push the release date as well. They can't record anything with Persephone until they finish the scripts."

Hades glanced at Charon, then nodded. "Push the gala back one month."

"Will do. But it'll fall after the end of Persephone's current contract. Do you think she'd agree to a new one?" Charon put a small bite of salmon in her mouth.

"I'll check with her. Keep the invite list the same."

Charon finished a few more bites of salad, then asked, "Have you told her you want to marry her?"

How could he? "It's still too soon."

Charon nodded. What he'd give to be as unbothered as her about the situation.

Hades grabbed his phone. "What's my day like tomorrow?"

"Well, it *was* packed with meetings for *Flowers Near Me*, but seeing that things are delayed..." Charon scooted her chair towards the laptop she'd set on the other side of Hades' desk. "Your day is mostly free."

Hades was no longer hungry. This meant he'd have more time to spend with his little goddess.

"Book a tee time at Artemis' manor tomorrow afternoon for Persephone and me."

"Of course." Charon typed on her keyboard. Was that a smile lighting her face? "Weather should be perfect. Do you want me to reach out to any reporters?"

Hades stood up and paced by the windows near his desk. "No, keep this a secret. Don't tell Persephone either. I want to surprise her."

"Alright..." Charon's voice trailed off. She was focused on her laptop, but the cheery glint coloring her cheek was unmistakable. Charon must've enjoyed booking these dates. "You're set for tomorrow."

"Excellent. And setup an annual contribution to Mount Olympus Academy." He sat back down at his desk.

"The school Persephone's niece attends?" Charon cocked her brow with a slanted smile.

Hades nodded.

More clicks sounded from Charon's keyboard. "How much?"

Sucking in a slow breath, Hades considered for a moment. "See if their development office has a capital campaign that needs funding."

"Will do," Charon hummed as her fingers flew.

"Charon," he said as he waited for her to look up from the computer. "Do you think Persephone could be happy here?"

She played with the charm hanging on the long necklace she wore every day. "I do, sir. I doubt she thinks that possible at the moment, but once she realizes she's got the whole Underworld empire at her disposal, she may relax enough to build a life with you. Can't blame her for not trusting any of us. I know I wouldn't if I were her."

He put his pointer finger on his lips then asked, "If you were me, how would you convince her to let her guard down?"

Charon's eyes lifted thoughtfully towards the ceiling before landing back on Hades. "She's an executive like you. She trusts power and opportunity. Show her that you want to give her both but be vulnerable about it. You staked her reputation on this project, so show her what's at stake for you."

He considered Charon's words. Persephone had no idea, but he'd staked his whole empire on her success. But it was too soon to admit that. "Should I tell her about the bargain I made with the Fates?"

Charon pinched the torch charm dangling on her necklace again. "I don't know."

CHAPTER FIFTEEN

THE FIRST STROKE

PERSEPHONE

The two of them had settled into a daily routine in the apartment. A small breakfast together before they'd take the elevator up to the offices. During the workday, Hades was sometimes playful but mostly professional towards her. It seemed that most of his employees gave him a wide berth.

The forward, flirtatious Hades she'd met that first night in Narcisi started to feel more like a friendly roommate. Sure, he still complimented her at every turn, but his praises felt tailored to her desires. Somehow, he knew exactly what she wanted to hear. Before living with him, she never would've described herself as attention-starved. But the way he'd gift her new notebooks and pens, surprise her with lunch, or leave her notes thanking her for her work, made her think that maybe she was lonelier than she realized.

It pained her to consider the possibility that *maybe* she actually liked being around him. Was it his godly allure and power that drew her in? It had to be that and not something real. Now as they sat close together in his car, she couldn't help the flip of her stomach when his thigh brushed hers.

"Why am I dressed like a figure skater?" Persephone asked Hades, who was sitting next to her in the back of his car.

"You'll see. And you look lovely, by the way." His eyes drifted over the black athletic dress covering her arms, torso, and upper thighs. What looked like scrutiny at first turned to appreciation.

She brushed her fingers across her pleated skirt. "Thank you. So do you."

The tailoring of his outfit put his lithe yet muscular figure on display, and the deep black made his hair and eyes more brilliant. A mock collar, half-zip top, and simple, fitted pants tapered slightly at the ankle. Persephone held out her forearm, comparing the color of her outfit to his. Both the same shade of midnight.

"Are we playing tennis?"

"Good guess, but no."

She stroked the soft fabric of her skirt between a finger and thumb. Persephone guessed again. "Ice skating? It's too warm for that unless we're headed to a rink."

Hades chuckled. "Not ice skating. You're getting colder in more ways than one."

"Ha." Out the car window, the city disappeared as they wove through lush suburban gardens filled with vibrant cornflowers and azalea bushes the size of one-story homes. Ancient oaks and pines began to fill either side of the road with fewer homes peeking through the woods. A calm silence blanketed the back seat, and Persephone heard a sigh so soft escape from Hades that she was certain he didn't know she noticed.

"Golfing?"

Hades beamed at Persephone. "How did you guess?"

"A bit *on the nose,* don't you think?"

"What do you mean?"

Persephone gestured to him. "You're an executive who likes to golf. It's a cliché and not even an interesting one."

He shrugged. "Lots of people like to golf."

"Okay, but how does a golf date sell a flower app? Because I've never played so you'll have a lot on your hands trying to teach me."

"You know, I'm delighted to hear you're thinking about yourself and my hands."

Persephone's cheeks heated and with a subtle eye roll, she turned her head away towards the window.

Hades said, "It's a chance for us to get to know one another better. It'll just be the two of us on a practice course."

Being comfortable with one another would help their fake dates look more believable. And it wasn't as if she had anything else to do but wait until the marketing team finalized the ads' scripts. She tried to keep herself busy, but she also wasn't trying to help out Hades too much either.

"Have you swung a club before?" Hades asked.

"Never." She held her breath, nervous about trying a new sport. Artemis' Estate crested through their view. She'd attended events there before, but she'd no clue it had a golf course.

Once they arrived, an attentive pro-shop employee helped fit Persephone with proper shoes and clubs. She then joined Hades, who patted the seat next to him as he sat halfway in the golf cart, one long leg stretched outside, touching the gravel path.

Cozied next to him in the cart—made smaller by Hades' large form—they whirred down the bending road, weaving through a scattering of towering cypress trees. Metal clapped together as their golf bags jostled. Apple green lawns lay before them like pressed bed linens across the expanse of the course.

Unbelted, Persephone bumped in her seat, hitting the side of Hades' leg with hers.

"Sorry," she said as she braced herself.

"Don't be. Hold onto me."

One side of his mouth quirked up as he lifted his elbow. She placed her hand in the crook of his arm, mesmerized by its steadiness as the golf cart dipped, jostled, and turned.

Past more cypress trees a lazy, rolling field of sage green grass. They pulled up to a driving range. Hades parked their cart and gathered the golf bags. Meanwhile, Persephone took in the rolling field before them.

Hades grinned as he set down their clubs. It was no surprise that the weight of two hulking golf bags proved to be no problem for him. Gods had unimaginable strength, but this display of raw power and slight twist of broad shoulders made her head spin. Fates, she needed to get serious about dating after all this was over. Just watching him had her almost drooling and that was simply not okay. This was the *last* being she should be lusting after, no matter how incredible he looked.

Persephone pushed hard into her shoe's sole, adjusting to their hug on her feet, trying to distract herself from her traitorous thoughts.

"Here you go." He handed her a glove.

She slid her hand into the glove with a strong tug to stretch out her fingers. "I hope you're a patient god."

This was not gardening which allowed for imprecision. Nature could always course correct when it needed to. Golf demanded control and focus—and adept hand-eye coordination. Things Persephone grappled with in the best of circumstances.

Hades chuckled, putting on his glove, then grabbed a club from each of their bags. He handed her the driver and gestured with his towards the driving range.

"We'll take it slow. Just focus on making contact with the ball."

She muttered, "That's what I'm most worried about."

"You'll do great." Hades positioned his feet slightly wider than shoulder-width apart, facing Persephone. "For a driver, you'll use a wider stance than the other clubs. You're trying to give the head as much range of motion as you can while powering your hit with the strength of your hips and core. But remember, no matter your size or athletic ability, anyone with training can still drive a ball far. Focus on proper form and strike quality and don't try to swing the club as hard as possible."

Half of those terms made sense. The other half sounded naughty. "So... don't swing it like a baseball bat."

He smirked. "Right. You could get lucky but more likely, you'll miss the ball or smack your club off the ground. The club is designed to propel the ball forward with the range of the head's path. Focus first on getting your form right and making contact."

"Alright."

"See how my feet are positioned with my lead foot turned just a bit. Grip the club with your dominant hand's pinky inter-locking with your other hand's pointer finger. We can mark your gloves so you can line your grip correctly with the shaft." Persephone's eyes jumped from his hands to his face, expecting a smirk or wink, but he continued with a straight face and calm tone.

"I'll bring back the club with my lead arm straight and my back one at an angle, like this." Hades demonstrated the motion with his eyes fixed on the ball on a tee. Persephone couldn't help noticing the way his shirt strained across his muscled torso, emphasizing his broad shoulders and the sleek taper of his waist. He truly looked like a god.

With impossible speed, Hades brought the club into a full swing and ended with his back foot twisted yet stable under him and his arms and club nearly wrapped around his back. There was a distinct *thwap* sound, then the ball sailed, disappearing against the bright sky then descending onto a trimmed green patch far down the course.

"I thought you said don't swing it as hard as possible."

Hades let out a small laugh. The rise of his cheeks softened his sharp features. *He looks so much younger when he smiles.* But he had never been young. Not in the same way that Persephone or her sister had been. What would he have looked like if he'd been a child? She'd never know. *Unless you had his child.* The unexpected thought scared her so much that she missed whatever he had said to her.

"Everything okay?"

She shook off those amorous notions, chiding herself for her lapse in judgement. What was she doing? "Yes, sorry. Go on."

He smiled. "Let's have you give it a go without a ball. This way you can get a feel for the club."

Persephone mirrored Hades' stance.

"Grip it like this." Hades interlocked his pinky with his other hand's pointer finger and wrapped his hands around the rubber grip.

"This feels weird." She tried not to squirm from the strange pressure in between her interlocked fingers. "Really? This is how to grip it?"

"It's one of several ways but it's the best one. Now, slowly bring your arms back." He twisted to demonstrate.

She did her best to turn her shoulders and twist her back while still keeping an eye on his form.

"Hit your peak, keep your grip, and bring your swing all the way through. Keep your eyes down where the ball would be. Don't fight your feet. Let your back foot twist as it needs to."

With a half-hearted effort, she swung the club and promptly smacked the head into the ground. A chunk of grass covered dirt flew a few feet away.

"Oh shit," Persephone's voice dropped with concern before she chuckled. "I didn't mean to do that."

Hades put his hands on the sides of her arms, his voice hurried and strained. "Are you hurt?"

"I'm fine. Why'd I miss?"

"It's not your fault. I should've had you check your distance from the tee to your club. I'm sorry about that." His pain-etched face made her pause. If she didn't get control of her racing feelings soon, she'd start believing that he truly cared for her.

"That's alright. I'm sure you've trained others who were more capable."

Had he trained others? The question tightened around her throat, and she tapped the divot with her shoe. It shouldn't bother her because it wasn't her business.

"I can assure you, I haven't. Let's try again but with the right positioning this time."

Hades stood next to Persephone and held out his club angled to the ground. She did the same, and he asked, "May I?" before guiding her hands to a different spot.

This time when Persephone swung, the club whooshed through the swing and ended with her wide grin. After several practice swings, she tried hitting a ball off the tee with moderate success. A few times the tee flew and the ball rolled, but Hades lined up the next ball each time, occasionally sneaking a wink at her.

Golfing was proving to be much more enjoyable than she'd thought. "I might put in a driving range on the estate when I go home. I'd have to figure out a way to gather the balls from the field, though." Persephone followed the ball as it landed near a few others from earlier shots. When she looked at Hades, he was staring off down the range with a fisted hand pressed his mouth.

"What if you didn't have to gather them?" Hades asked. He turned his eyes to hers, the weight of his attention causing her legs to waver.

"What do you mean?" Persephone asked.

A hint of slyness peeked through his features. "What if the balls disintegrated in the rain? If they were made of dirt or fertilizer, then you'd never have to gather them."

Envisioning little brown nuggets scattered across one of her mom's gardens or fields. "What if you put seeds in them?"

Hades' brows quirked. "Brilliant."

"I'm certain they already exist. How could they not?"

Hades shrugged. "Doesn't mean we couldn't make our own."

They emptied a bucket of balls but for every one Hades hit, Persephone hit at least five. There were a few moments where she caught him watching her. Once, when she flicked her head to knock flyaway strands of hair away. After she hit her longest shot, he'd complimented her effort. The shadow of a grin across his mouth made her blush. She needed to rein in her emotions. It didn't matter how kind he was being or how much fun she was having, this was *Hades*. It was all a game to him. Her feelings meant nothing to a god who had everything.

When they left the range and opted to try a few holes, Hades pulled out whichever club was best for each shot.

"How do you keep track of which one to use?" Persephone asked.

"Lots of practice." He swung as if the act was the plainest thing he'd done all day.

After a few missed swings, Persephone groaned. "What's happening to me?"

His light laugh was still deeper than a voice should be, she reasoned. "You're twisting from the wrong place. You'll have better power and control if you focus on your hips and legs and not your back and arms." He stashed his club in his bag, pulled off his glove, then stood within arm's reach of her.

"I'll show you, but I'll need to move your center." Gesturing with both hands on the sides of his hips, he twisted to one side then the other.

Persephone stared for a moment, unsure she heard him correctly.

"Go ahead," she said, hoping it didn't sound breathy.

Whenever they were alone in the apartment, he rarely touched her outside of offering his arm. Whenever he put a hand on her upper back, it was always with others around. She could admit to herself that the idea of his hands on her in this moment sounded exciting. Maybe she could allow herself to enjoy the moment just this once? Her mind knew it wasn't real. Her body held still, anticipating his touch.

"Perfect. Get into your stance."

She did, feet shoulder-width apart and her six-iron firm in her grasp. His fingertips pressed into her hips, his voice in her ear. "Bring your club back." The effort it took for her not to shudder held her breath hostage.

She raised the club as Hades pulled and pushed her hips, giving her a longer reach. He brushed his fingers down the side of her skirt-covered thigh. A soothing warmth followed the trail of his touch. "Put your weight on this leg. As you swing through, shift your weight onto your other. Ready?"

"Mm-hmm," was the only response she was willing to give through her pressed lips. Too enraptured by the heat on her back from his proximity, she figured there was no way she'd hit this ball. It wasn't her fault. She'd have an easier time weeding acres upon acres of wildflowers than ignoring how her body reacted to him.

Hades released his hold on her, and she swung. Eyes on the ball, she watched it wait for its ride, then sail down the fairway. It was her longest shot of the day. Persephone coughed out an incredulous laugh, dropping her club. She spun around, closing the space between them, and squeezed a surprised, stiff Hades in her arms. When the god didn't move, didn't breathe, she immediately released him. Why did she do that?

"I can't believe how different that feels. Er—the uh—stance."

Understatement. If he had any idea how much he'd captivated her with his touch, she'd have no chance of protecting her heart. To her dismay, it appeared this effect was one-sided. *Good.* She needed the reminder that his efforts to win her had nothing to do with genuine interest.

"Beautiful shot," Hades said with high brows. One hand remained tucked into his pocket as he reached down to pick up her club.

She cleared her throat and wiped her palms down her skirt. "The weight shifting. It's a good trick."

"You move like you were made for this." Hades held out his ungloved hand and helped her in the cart. The controlled gesture proved this was simply a business deal between them.

Still, the headiness of their golf excursion clouded her thoughts all through the rest of the day into the evening.

While lying in bed, the moment with Hades' hands on her hips replayed on a loop until she fell asleep.

CHAPTER SIXTEEN

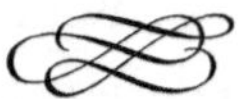

A DANGEROUS GOD

PERSEPHONE

As soon as the marketing team received approval for the ad campaign, Persephone's calendar filled with endless studio sessions, leaving only a handful of minutes with Hades each day over the past few weeks. It'd been almost two whole months since she'd been forced to work for him. Yet, every second with him felt borrowed when it should've been a relief that they were too busy to spend much time together.

Hades asked to join her when she ran on the track to which she replied, "Isn't it *your* track?" It was nice to have company when exercising. Hades made a great workout companion too. He'd share how other parts of Underworld Unlimited were faring and would invite her opinion on the matter. Afterwards they'd shower and dress separately before returning to the kitchen to sip coffee and read the news on their phones. Their shared morning rituals were silent echoes of each other, a stubborn tether Persephone clung to, even as their schedules pulled them apart.

After Persephone watered the ever-growing, nature-defying garden in the apartment's large sitting area, she'd play fetch with Cerberus. It wasn't the dog's fault his owner was evil. Between Hades' and her continual acquisition of plants, the room was starting to resemble a greenhouse. How these sun-loving flowers were surviving with the artificial lighting, she had no clue. But Hades was convinced it was her magic. More likely, he or Hecate enchanted them before delivering the plants to the penthouse.

Charon, as usual, met her in the lobby with a fresh cup of coffee. For the past three weeks, she'd spent hours in front of the camera, reciting lines she'd rehearsed, but today, it was simple B-roll footage. Even straight-backed Charon had looser shoulders and a lively gait when they entered the studio.

"If they get enough footage this session, you'll have more than one day off." Charon set her tablet onto the table.

"That sounds great." Persephone took a sip then asked, "When's your next day off? Do you sleep?"

Laughing, Charon crossed her legs and rested her inter-locked hands on one knee. "I like being busy." No surprise there. It seemed like Charon never stopped working. She was always available whenever Persephone texted, called, or emailed her.

"But what about hobbies?" It felt like something Persephone ought to know by now. They'd spent so much time in the office together but hadn't discussed anything personal. "What do you do for yourself?"

Charon tilted her head. "I work. That's what I like to do." There was more, but it didn't look like the psychopomp was ready to reveal it yet. Whatever Charon did in her free time was not something she let spill into her work life. Could Charon secretly be a gambler or partier? It was silly but Charon's tight-lipped manner intrigued Persephone.

"Have you always worked for Underworld Unlimited?"

"Yes, since the beginning. You know how it is with a career.

Once you've worked somewhere long enough, you know all its secrets. It's satisfying to have the power you need to complete the tasks ahead of you. I like the feeling a lot."

Persephone hummed her agreement, holding her phone tighter. It was a Thursday and had she still been working at Demeter's Bounty, Hermes and she would be in the middle of their ops team's weekly debrief. Wondering how they were doing, she typed a short message to Hermes. She hadn't heard much about DB in weeks.

The stylist began combing Persephone's hair.

PERSEPHONE

How's everything going? How's my mom?

Three little dots appeared immediately, and Persephone watched the screen.

HERMES

Has she called you?

PERSEPHONE

No. Is she in the office?

Her heart sped. Why did Hermes asked if she had called? He ought to know more since he was still at DB. Why hadn't her mom called? Even checked in? It wouldn't take more than a minute for her to say she was thinking of her.

It would do her no good, fretting over her mom's behavior. Demeter was a capable goddess. And if Persephone kept worrying, she'd look angry or sick in the recordings. She stashed the phone into her bag.

"Is everything okay?" Charon asked, leaning closer to Persephone.

Persephone swallowed. "I'm fine. It's fine."

"Oh. Okay." Charon's expression softened in understanding.

They sat in a companionable silence as the stylist worked on

Persephone's makeup. The nagging worry of her mom still lingered. If Demeter could just say something, *anything*, then she could let it be. She stopped texting after the first couple of weeks of trying to get a hold of her. Eventually, she gave up. She'd have to wait until her mom was ready.

Charon asked, "So tell me, what are *your* hobbies?"

Chasing after my mom, was her first thought. "I love to garden. Back home there are fields of wildflowers and herbs I've tended for years. That's why I was so excited about *Flowers Near Me* in the first place."

"It sounds beautiful. The potted garden you've grown in the apartment is so lush. I bet your wildflower one is unlike anything else I've seen." Charon's calm voice stirred something in Persephone's chest.

"I would love to show you. It's funny because when Eurydice first told me about the app, I pictured gathering bundles and bringing them to the city to sell. Of course, each time I was called into the office, I was in such a rush that I never did it."

Charon chuckled. "Why not grow more flowers in the apartment?"

Did Charon really not know how to garden? She seemed more than capable of keeping a plant alive but maybe not if all her life she'd lived underground. "Flowers need a lot of sunlight."

"Not when *you're* tending to them," Charon quipped. "Anyway, your mom's estate sounds lovely. We should've shot footage there."

Persephone shook her head. "I doubt my mom is keen on helping with any of this."

"Have you spoken with her recently?"

Persephone swallowed against the thickness that grew in her throat at the mention of her mom. She wasn't normally one to let her emotions get the better of her, but the weeks of no contact from Demeter were starting to take their toll and she was perilously close to tears as she said, "I haven't."

Charon fiddled with her necklace. "Want me to bring her to you?"

Persephone's eyes widened, her lips parting in surprise. "You could really do that?"

With a quick bob of her shoulders, Charon replied, "I'm fairly good at retrieving people. We have several mutual friends so I'd imagine it wouldn't take long."

"Good to know." Persephone's comment trailed off and she put her fingertips to her pursed lips. Charon was better than she let on.

"So… would you like me to setup a meeting with your mom?"

Should she? Would her mom appreciate the effort or be disappointed that Persephone needed others to advocate for her? "No, that's alright. Hermes could make her meet with me if it were an emergency. I'll wait for when she's ready."

Charon gave Persephone a contemplative look. "She's angry with *you*?"

"I think so. She hasn't responded to any of my messages. And since I'm no longer her employee, I can't use a work meeting to lure her out either."

"I'm sorry. I'd assumed she'd be upset with Hades. Not you."

Shrugging, Persephone said, "She means well. I know she cares, and I can't imagine it's been easy on her."

A producer shouted for Persephone from the hallway leading to the set. She handed her purse to Charon and held her head high. She hadn't checked to see what else Hermes had to say and now she'd determined to put her mom out of her mind for the rest of the day.

THE DIRECTOR HAD Persephone arranging flowers and pretending to use a phone to snap photos. The task that felt more tedious with each passing minute. She scanned for Charon but only caught quick glimpses of the woman flitting around the set. Hecate appeared instead, lounging in a director's chair with effortless grace, her sandaled feet draped over the armrest, the silky train of her skirt pooling like liquid moonlight. Strands of her dark hair floated as if lifted by an unseen breeze, a testament to her ethereal magic.

"When are you done today?" Hecate called out.

"Not until later," Persephone replied, adjusting a stubborn rose. "But if we wrap quickly, I might have a few days off. Why do you ask?"

"I wanted us to grab lunch." She inspected her nails, and wisps of plum-colored smoke curled from her fingertips, carrying a sweet, soothing fragrance like lavender and butter cookies.

Persephone's nose crinkled in delight. "Is that smell from you? Or is someone baking lavender shortbread?"

Hecate tilted her head. "You can smell my magic?"

"Of course. It's amazing," Persephone said, fussing with the flowers again. "Can't everyone smell it?"

"No, not everyone," said Hecate as she gave a feline smile. Before Persephone could respond, the director called out, "Clip the flower stems a bit, Persephone."

She picked up the shears, but her gaze met Hecate's, who seemed ready to ask a question, her crimson lips parting before she pressed them shut. "What's wrong?" Persephone asked.

Hecate cleared her throat. "Nothing. You have keen sense for magic."

Keeping her shoulders loose, Persephone replied, "I've been around it my whole life."

"It's in you," Hecate replied. Based on what Hecate had shared with Persephone—that she had helped Demeter to consume a field of poppies which led to Persephone's conception—the goddess and her were magically linked. Just like she could sense the intricacies of her mom's power, she would recognize Hecate's as familiar too.

Hecate asked, "Enough about my magic. How does it feel to be done with filming all the speaking parts?"

"It's a relief. I never want to see myself on video again."

Hecate laughed. "I heard you've done a great job. The only one that's complained about any of it is Hades and that's only because it's kept you busy and away from him. You know... he's watched then rewatched all the footage of you. I've caught him drooling at his computer screen too many times to count."

She couldn't imagine Hades drooling, ever, but the thought of him transfixed, watching her made her face grin and stomach flip. Despite her healthy fear of the god, she enjoyed his attention. What Hecate said couldn't be true. When she'd hugged him on the golf course, he'd frozen in horror. He just knew how to appear doting when the moment called for it.

Persephone replied, "He's probably regretting choosing a brand ambassador who lacks on-screen experience." *They should've picked Aphrodite.*

"Not a chance. He's so besotted he thinks you can do no wrong. It's quite entertaining to see the mighty Hades act like a lovesick fool."

Persephone tried to laugh off Hecate's insinuation but the memory of their golf date lingered. She thought back to the gentle way he'd taught her to swing, and how his touch had set fire to her veins. A burst of leather and evergreen in the air pulled her back. The camera was still recording so she schooled her features to try not to look like a swooning idiot. Maybe it wasn't as one-sided as she thought.

Hades' deep voice called out from behind the monitor the director had told her was called a video tap. "Go back ten seconds. Yes, right there. That's *the* shot."

From her peripheral, she caught the outline of Hades' broad shoulders as he stood next to a seated Hecate. Immediately, her treacherous heart started to thud.

"What were you just thinking about a moment ago? You looked euphoric."

Not willing to admit she was thinking about him, she stammered, "I-um…"

Hecate groaned. "Yes, yes. She's lovely to look at but keep it to yourself so she can work."

Thank the Fates for Hecate. She met Hecate's eyes, and the goddess gave her a sly wink.

Hades chuckled. "Hecate, did you know that attractive people are less likely to receive compliments? Everyone assumes they're used to admiration, but it's often the words left unsaid that matter most."

"Speaking from experience? That's why no one compliments you?" Hecate cocked one brow, and Persephone held in her giggle as the corners of her mouth lifted.

"Such wit." Hades adjusted his watch. "Sephy,"—his gaze lingered on her—"is Hecate bothering you? Say the word, and I'll remove her. I'd much rather have you all to myself."

Hecate rolled her eyes and a light purple mist surrounded her. "I came here to invite her to lunch, not flirt with her."

"She's been keeping me company on set," added Persephone.

"Persephone, I'll text you later when your guard dog isn't around." The hissing of falling sand sounded, and Hecate disappeared from her chair.

"Sir, want us to take a break?" the director asked Hades.

"Please. I need your star for a moment." Hades strode onto

the set and offered his hand with an unmistakably possessive intensity in his eyes.

They walked together to her dressing room and Persephone closed the door.

"What does Hecate's magic smell like to you?" she asked.

Hades furrowed his brow then inclined his head. "Hm, something akin to herbaceous pastries. Why do you ask?"

"Just curious. It smelled like lavender cookies to me."

"Do you know how your power smells?"

What did it smell like? Did it have a noticeable presence? If there was a scent, would it have notes reminiscent of her mom's?

"Faintly floral? I'm not sure I have enough power for it to smell at all."

Shaking his head, Hades said, "If you picked up Hecate's, then you'd have enough to emit a scent. If you had no power, you'd only *feel* her magic and your other senses wouldn't pick it up."

Persephone considered his statement. Interrupting her pondering, Hades said, "Yours is jasmine and vanilla. It's the best thing I've ever smelled."

Persephone held him with a glare. "The best thing you've *ever* smelled?" She shook her head. "Anyway, why are you here? I thought you'd be stuck in meetings." It came out harsher than intended but perhaps that was for the best. She disliked how much she was softening towards him.

"I was," he admitted, his voice a low rumble, "but I needed to see you." He reached out, his fingers trailing gently along her ear before tucking a stray lock of hair behind it. The touch lingered, sending shivers down her spine. "What were you thinking about on set? You looked... radiant. Almost blissful."

"Don't remember. Probably thinking about food." No way would she tell him the truth. Instead, she gave him a slanted smile. "How are things with the app?"

He leaned back against the vanity, backlit by the bulbed

lights, his eyes narrowing at her change of subject. "The dev team is having issues with a bug, but they're making progress."

She could still feel the trail of his touch around her ear. "Is Eurydice worried?"

He raised his shoulders and crossed his arms. "Can't tell. She's always skittish so I don't know if I'd recognize worry in her."

"If I were her, I'd be skittish too. She's trusting you with her own creation."

Amusement glinted in his eyes. "Charon said you've earned a few days off." He put his hands on the edge of the table at his sides.

"Yes, as long as they get what they need recorded today. Why don't I use the time to help with this tech issue? I'm familiar with QA testing and app launches."

He fussed with his cuffs. "You don't want a break?"

"Not really. I'm much better behind the scenes than in front of the camera. I'd rather be ensuring the app's successful launch than the face promoting it."

His silver eyes lit up. "Why not do both? Charon said you rejected the offer to be the Chief Product Officer. Would you reconsider?"

She crossed her arms. "I'm happy to help, not take someone's job."

Hades laid a hand on his chest. "My job, Sephy. I've been managing the role until you'd step in."

"You didn't hire or re-assign someone for the position?" Surely someone else had stepped in.

"I was waiting for the right talent to become available. When can you start?"

This type of experience better suited her long-term goal of becoming DB's president. "Immediately. When's the next dev team check-in?" Sure, Charon had offered her the role back on her first day in Hades' penthouse, but Persephone wasn't an

Underworld Unlimited insider at the time. Now she'd seen more of its operations and knew this could be a good opportunity to do more than be the face of a product.

"Hold on there. You've just wrapped a month's worth of filming, and as eager as I am to have you as CPO, there are a few loose ends we need to tie up."

What loose ends were there? "Do I need to sign extra paperwork?"

Hades made a noncommittal hum in the back of his throat. "Only a new employment agreement for your pay increase." He paused. "I'm more concerned about us taking this next step in making ourselves a more convincing couple. I suspect some think our relationship isn't real."

Waving one hand, she replied, "It isn't. So, why are you concerned? Did someone say something?"

"No, and that's part of the problem. There were a few murmurings and some well-placed articles back when you started with us but not much since. It's time to tell people that we're living together." Hades stood up from the table and circled Persephone at a polite distance.

Persephone remained still. If they went public, how much ridicule would her mom receive for her daughter not only working for but flirting with the enemy? Would she become angrier? *Would she finally reach out?*

Of course her mom knew of the business arrangement, but not that their *relationship* was faked for the media. Maybe this would inspire her to respond?

The thought held the sourness of immaturity but Persephone's lack of options sweetened the bitter taste. Four more months and she'd be free of the contract and able to explain everything to her trusted circle. Until then, most of her day-to-day was out of her control.

An idea bubbled to the surface. If her mom thought she actually was dating Hades, maybe Demeter would *finally* contact her?

"Hades, aren't we supposed to be going on public dates? You know... if we were seen out together again doing something a couple does. Even with your busy schedule, we could fit in a lunch or dinner and make it look convincing."

As soon as the words spilled out, Hades grinned like the cat who'd got the cream.

"Sephy, that's a wonderful idea and I'm elated to hear you suggest it." He stepped close behind her, his mouth inches from her ear and his cedar cologne causing her to swallow hard. "How do you suggest we make it look convincing?"

Persephone turned her head towards his. She gritted her teeth but kept a cocky smile. "I'll have to think about it. This is my first fake relationship, so I'm not sure."

Hades' eyes dropped to her mouth for a few seconds before he straightened his back and stepped around to face her.

"It's never been fake for me," he confessed, his eyes searching hers. He took a breath. "What if, just once, you didn't have to pretend? Let me take you somewhere we can be seen but still have a quiet moment, just the two of us. Drop your guard, even if only a little, and let me try to earn your heart."

Persephone sighed and closed her eyes. She wished that was true, but how could she believe him? Her whole life she was surrounded by gods and learned very quickly that they couldn't be trusted.

Releasing a long exhale, she said, "Look. I'm not like you. I don't have a long line of past lovers I've moved on from. I... um..." Persephone looked off to the side then met his gaze again. "We're business partners, yes?" She gestured between them.

"Yes, of course. Equals too."

"Right. Well, as my business partner, it's my responsibility to be honest about my capabilities and limitations."

"Okay…" Hades' face tensed in concentration.

"It has to be completely fake for me." Even one date where she allowed herself to consider it real was foolhardy. That golf date had messed with her brain.

His eyes and mouth softened and his voice lowered to a strong whisper. "But why can't *one* date be real? It could be similar to our golf outing, but with the general populace around."

How could she make a god understand? The golf outing was a prime example of why she couldn't do this. He could turn on and off his feelings as easily as snapping his fingers to make Cerberus sit or fetch. Apparently, she no longer had that kind of command over her heart.

"Human hearts don't work that way." Her hand shot up before he could interrupt, telling her she wasn't a mortal. "There's only real or fake. I can't give you a real chance because it could become real to me and then in four months, I look like an idiot and feel even worse. I won't do that. My heart is soft and pliable so I take great care with it. What you're suggesting is careless."

"How are you so certain you'll look like an *idiot* in four months?"

"I mean, come on. I could end up mourning real feelings from a publicity stunt. It's pathetic." She stood behind the lone dressing room chair, pinching the black fabric stretched across its back. This is how it was with the gods. They'd say or do anything to get what they wanted. Mortals were *nothing* to them.

"I told you from the beginning, this could be as real or as pretend as you wanted. But my desire for you, Persephone, is very real. I'm not playing a part when I say I want you—beyond the contract, beyond all of this." His voice grew husky. "I'm already yours. Tell me how I can prove it."

With a light laugh, she replied, "Fates, you are so convincing."

Mortals were toys with expiration dates. She did well to remember that.

Hand on his heart, a stern-faced Hades said, "It's the truth. Why do you think I orchestrated the *Flowers Near Me* acquisition?"

"Because of the IP. We discussed this."

He shook his head. "That was an afterthought I shared with my team. We already have IP similar to it. I knew you had interest in the app and saw an opportunity for us to spend time together."

"Forcibly," she warned.

"Would you have ever agreed to a date otherwise?"

His assumption was correct. She wouldn't have and they both knew it.

"Probably not. But what happens when your next project or deal is to be made and a more advantageous match is found?" Persephone crossed her arms with fingers splayed on her biceps. "When this no longer suits your or Underworld Unlimited's interest, then you'll move on without hesitation. I think sometimes you forget who my mom is and that even if I haven't lived as long as you, I still know how gods operate."

Hades' gaze dropped to the floor. "I can understand your hesitation, but I have not made promises or assurances to others as I have with you." Hades gave her a devious smile. "I intend to prove you wrong. You'll see that I love you."

Love? This was too much. She wanted to sneak into a closet and scream into a pillow. Or throw herself into a wheat field and let the stalks consume her. Whether from tension, frustration, or anticipation, she wasn't sure, but she needed to bolster her defenses before she was sucked into his orbit. The gods could warp one's mind with their alluring words from their perfect mouths.

The most tempting is the most dangerous.
And Hades the most dangerous of them all.

CHAPTER SEVENTEEN

GAME WITH THE GODS

PERSEPHONE

A mountain of clothes covered the end of the bed. Persephone pushed the mound with her feet to free more of the comforter, but ended up knocking part of the pile onto the floor. Muttering a curse, she reached for her phone to check the time. A jolt of adrenaline shot through her at the 9:30 a.m. on her lock screen.

"Oh shit," she said to herself, jumping out of bed with her phone. Scuffling to the bathroom, she checked her calendar and released a sigh of relief.

There were no meetings except for one twelve-hour block labeled, "Quality time with my future husband."

Rolling her eyes with a breathy laugh, she brushed her hair then put on loose joggers and a sweatshirt. She massaged her face with moisturizer before applying lip balm and quick swipes of mascara. She couldn't help herself. Laura would have turned the tables on him by now and here she was hoping he'd say she looked nice.

Damn the Fates. Damn my heart. And damn that god.

She gathered the clothes from the floor, placing them in hampers or back in the closet. The unacceptable mess was a clear indication of being overworked. Yanking and tucking the sheets into the bed, she stuffed a few hair bands into her jogger's pocket, then shook out the comforter.

Her thoughts circled around this nagging desire to be wanted by him. Who didn't enjoy a well-timed compliment, especially from a single and handsome god?

There were worse things.

The last time she'd spoken with him was in her dressing room on set the day before. When she returned to the apartment late last evening, she was too tired to check if he was home. Cerberus had greeted her and curled up on her bed, but had whined to be let out of the room before she fell asleep.

The dog scratched at her door now and she greeted him before heading towards the kitchen. Satisfied with a few pets behind his ear, Cerberus lay down on a rug by the couches.

"There she is. Good morning, Sephy. Ready for a well-deserved day off?" Hades beamed at her. The sleeves of his black dress shirt bunched at his elbows and strained against muscles as he wiped his hands on a rag. Was he flexing?

Tailored charcoal gray pants and a matte black belt finished his ensemble, and Persephone hid her perusal with a feigned cough.

"Good morning. According to my calendar, I'm spending the day with my future husband." She pretended to scan the apartment, trying to hold in her grin. "When will I meet him?"

Hades smirked and poured her a cup of coffee. "I'll introduce you to him at lunch. He's quite the catch. You ought to embrace him with a passionate kiss when you meet."

She took the mug gratefully. "Thank you and I will not be doing that," she said before blowing steam and taking a tentative sip. "I hope he's someone normal like a teacher… or a professor. And that he's soft spoken."

Hades' brows shot up. "A common man? Sephy, in what world would that be an appropriate match for you?"

She shrugged and sat in one of the chairs at the kitchen counter. "Why wouldn't it be an appropriate match? I'm quiet and reserved." The richness of the coffee tasted like heaven on her tongue. Taking a long sip, she held Hades' wide eyes.

He placed both palms on the countertop across from her and dropped his shoulders with a playful sigh. "You're no wall-flower. Whether you like it or not, you're part of the elite now. There's nothing plain about you."

Her stomach grew wings. The dryness in her mouth alerted her to her parted lips which she closed immediately. It sounded so good coming from him and although she thought to argue, she was learning it was better to accept his compliments and move on. "That's kind. Thank you."

"Besides. You're meant to be with me and I'm not a teacher or a professor and have no lack of words. And right now, I want to tell you all about our fake-for-you-but-real-for-me date."

Persephone went to speak, drawing in an incredulous breath of air, but Hades continued on. "I'm stating facts. I still under-stand your reasoning for considering it fake but wanted to remind you of my interest." One corner of his mouth quirked up in a half smile. "We're going to a Teppanyaki restaurant."

She was always down for a hibachi restaurant. "That sounds good. What time are we going?"

"We have reservations at two. There'll be a few columnists there but otherwise we'll still have some semblance of privacy." He winked.

Before Persephone could reply, the elevator doors to the apartment chimed and Hermes stumbled in. The brim of his baseball cap stood up from his head, but he righted it as he approached. She stared at him, unsure if she was seeing a ghost or was seeing her former assistant for the first time since their fateful parting in Laura's townhouse.

Lacking all warmth, Hades greeted, "How did you get in, Hermes?"

Hermes threw an apologetic look at Hades then said, "Zeus sent me."

"Ah," Hades replied and went to sit at the kitchen counter.

"Persephone," Hermes drew close, "your mom's taken down the grocery app and halted all food deliveries to stores."

Persephone's eye twitched. It'd felt so long ago since she'd spoken with Hermes. And now, after months of silence, her mom shut down the grocery app. It didn't make any sense. "What? How do you mean? I—uh. Why? So there are no deliveries arriving? Distribution is completely stalled?"

Hermes glanced at Hades before returning to look at Persephone. "Your team was told to cease operations."

Things must be very bad. Whipping her phone from her pocket, she opened the Demeter's Bounty app and clicked on grocery delivery.

"For how long?" she asked.

"Indefinitely. Most of the DB staff are worried they're going to be laid off and now customers are buying up everything they can in the stores before the supply is gone."

The app displayed an error message even after restarting her phone. Pressing her fingers to her mouth, Persephone debated whether to call Laura so she could settle her nerves or her mom so she could try to get the app back online. Would her mom even pick up the phone? This needed to be fixed immediately. Thousands of employees depended on that app's existence.

Demeter was calculating and purposeful, so why shut down the app now? She tried to put herself in her mom's shoes but struggled to make sense of the timing. She suspected the reason had something to do with the extremely annoyed god currently leaning on the counter.

"Did she say why?" She hoped his answer would remove the sting of her mom's silence during the past two months. Maybe her mom hadn't been ignoring her out of spite, but instead had been plotting how to get her out of the contract with Hades.

Hermes bobbed his head. "No, but she's demanded a meeting with Zeus and Hades."

With a tight-lipped sneer, Hades said, "Ah, yes. Let's not keep them waiting."

Persephone cleared her throat. "I'm coming too."

Hades turned towards her, placing his hand on the side of her arm. "Are you sure? Zeus isn't one to treat uninvited guests well."

"My mom will be there. It'll be fine." She'd visited the capitol decades before as a student. The domed center, stretching pillars, and marble sculptures were a staple of class field trips. One time, her class got to go inside Zeus' office.

The pity on Hades' face caused her heart to drop. He didn't trust Demeter to defend her.

"Ready?" Hades asked.

Persephone nodded. Hades touched her arm and an electrical shock bolted through her system. Body tensing and jerking, Persephone flailed as her feet scrambled for solid ground. After a painful moment, a warm touch blossomed on her back, and she opened her eyes to a blinding light. As she found her footing, a dark figure moved into her vision. Whoever it was smelled like Hades.

Persephone blinked until Hades' face sharpened before her.

"Are you okay?" he asked.

"Um, yes. I'm fine," she whispered and brushed her hands down the front of her sweatshirt and joggers. In the hurry to appease Zeus' summons, she'd forgotten to change her clothes. "It's been a while since I've portaled like that. Normally I vomit, so I'd say it was one of the better trips."

"Sorry, love. Next time, I'll go slower," said Hades.

"Persephone?" Demeter's voice cut through Persephone like a knife, and she whipped round to see her mom standing next to a white marble desk, gaping at her. Zeus was beside her. His white hair was brighter than the white of his jacket and shirt. He was statuesque like Hades but with rounder features and a weathered face.

Up close, they didn't look like brothers. Hades appeared much younger with strong vulpine features—cunning and lethal.

Her mom's heliotrope colored silk blouse and cream linen pants looked pressed, as if she were headed into a board meeting. A meeting with Zeus warranted fine clothes, even from a goddess. Yet Persephone stood frozen on the spot, caught in her mom's stare and Zeus' frown, wearing athleisure wear.

Zeus shook the floors, saying, "Brother, why have you stolen Persephone?"

Persephone turned to look at Hades and realized that his hand was still on her upper back. He shot her a wink and playful smile then whispered, "Don't worry, Sephy. Your future husband's got this."

Hades strode towards Zeus and Demeter. "I believe you meant to ask why did I *abduct* Persephone. You don't steal a goddess. You abduct them." Hades snapped his fingers and a stack of paper fell with a loud thud onto Zeus' desk. "Even so, this accusation is off base. Persephone is my contracted employee."

Hermes surprised Persephone at her side as he sidled up to her and bumped her shoulder. He spoke softly out of the side of his mouth, "Has he hurt you?"

"No. He's just a shameless flirt, but that's how they all are." Persephone pointed her chin at the trio of her mom, Hades, and Zeus, who all stood cross-armed and brooding around Zeus' massive desk.

Hermes gave a quiet laugh. "That they are."

Now that her eyes adjusted to the room's light, she took in the wall of windows behind Zeus' desk that looked out onto fluffy cloud tops. Gilded columns and golden streaks in the marble tile floor reflected a warm light. The large, circular room dimmed slightly as her eyes adjusted. More white marble covered walls and floors.

Zeus spoke with his thunderous voice again, filling the office with a building storm. High above them, stone gray wisps fattened into bulbous clouds ready to burst. "Demeter," Zeus said as he flipped through the contract. "Your daughter's signature is all over this. Only Hades has the power to dissolve a contract like this one anyway."

Heels clacked on the shiny marble floor as Demeter stepped closer to Hades. She stabbed a finger in Hades' direction but kept her focus on Zeus. "You don't understand. Persephone purchased the app first and then Hades took it. He's claiming his contracts are retroactive because he bought the patent."

Still and smirking, Hades shrugged at Demeter. "It's true."

"Persephone." Zeus' voice had her spine ramrod straight.

She cleared her throat and squared her shoulders. "Yes?"

"Have you been mistreated in any way by my brother?"

Her gaze darted from Hades to her mother. The two of them glared at each other, their expressions locked in a battle of wills, both poised to strike. Someone was about to be very unhappy.

Directing her reply to Zeus, she said, "He's gone to great efforts to ensure my comfort. While I don't like how things started, working for him has been... surprisingly positive. I do miss my DB colleagues, though."

Hades hid the flex of his brow before Zeus looked at him. Her mom, on the other hand, stared blankly back at her. Fates, how she wished her mom would've communicated with her before this meeting. If she wasn't angry with Persephone before, then she sure as Tartarus was now.

Zeus dropped into his chair, rubbing his temples. "Demeter,

Hades is in the clear. His contracts are ironclad and retroactive. As God of the Underworld, he governs all legalities tied to our laws. My hands are bound." He turned to Hades. "What are the terms?"

Hades smiled but there was no warmth in it. "Six months, of which Persephone has completed two already. Then she's free to return to Demeter's Bounty if she wishes." His voice softened as he looked at Persephone. There was a tenderness in his eyes that made her stomach flip. "I hope I can convince her to stay indefinitely, but she hasn't warmed to the idea… yet."

Persephone's face flushed. Every smooth word he uttered chipped at her defenses. How much longer could she resist feeling wanted, even by someone as dangerous as Hades?

"Don't look at her like that," Demeter snapped, and the scent of jasmine hit Persephone like a wave.

Soon, cedar and leather overpowered the floral fog.

"Why Demeter?" Hades' friendly tone belied the jab underneath like a blade hidden in silk. "How do I look at her?"

Demeter stepped within arm's reach of Hades, not quite as tall but just as imposing. "Like she belongs to you. Like you'd rather shatter her into pieces than let her slip away." Hands fisted, Demeter squared her shoulders and wisps of sage smoke rose from her like steam.

Is that how he looks at me?

The churning pulse of blood grew louder in her head. Could anyone survive a game with the gods?

Hades' eyes narrowed, his voice a low, lethal whisper. "And yet," he said, leaning in ever so slightly, "we both know she's never been safer than she is with me. Or would you prefer I take a different approach—one that doesn't involve her willing cooperation?"

Demeter went rigid, her jaw clenching so tightly that Persephone expected to hear bones cracking. "My answer is still no," Demeter warned, her voice taut with fury.

A muscle in Hades' jaw twitched, but his expression remained coldly amused. "Very well." His tone was deceptively calm, like a predator conceding a small loss before a greater hunt. "Shall we proceed with the arrangement everyone here has begrudgingly agreed to, or do you wish to waste more of our time?"

Zeus grunted. "Not yet. Demeter, you have to reopen distribution. If you refuse, I'll be forced to remove you from power."

Demeter threw a conflicted glance at Persephone then faced Zeus. "Fine." A nauseating wave of rancid, rotting foliage filled the air as Demeter disappeared in an emerald cloud, unwilling to spare even one parting glance at Persephone. Yes, Mom was furious.

"Hermes," Zeus bellowed.

The lithe man approached the desk faster than any mortal could. "Yes, Zeus?" Meanwhile, Hades beckoned Persephone to his side. She held her breath for the few steps it took to reach him.

"I understand you've served as an assistant to Demeter and Persephone," said Zeus.

Hermes looked at Persephone with a toothy smile, and Persephone kept a brave face. Why Zeus was interested in Hermes' employment history at that moment, she had no clue. "That's right. Persephone and I have worked together for almost ten years."

Zeus turned to Persephone. "How did he perform as your assistant?"

Persephone threw a smile at Hermes before meeting Zeus' eyes. "Exceptionally well. He's the fastest at every task."

Zeus hummed an approval and held his chin. "Hermes, would you like to serve as messenger of the gods?"

"I-uh... yes. But what about Demeter?" Hermes readjusted the baseball cap on his head.

With a sheepish grin, Zeus pinned his eyes on Hades.

Groaning, Hades replied, "Fine. I'll get a contract drafted."

One load clap of his hands and Zeus boomed, "Excellent. I'll summon you later."

Hermes bowed and his hat slid off. Quick as a whip, he snatched it before it hit the floor. "Thank you." Turning on his heel, he gave Persephone a hug and whispered, "Talk soon?"

As they released each other, she nodded and he sped out the open archway at their backs.

Hades offered his hand to her. "I think we're done here."

"Persephone," Zeus called, rattling the columns circling the room. She turned.

"Welcome to the family."

The family of the gods or his family?

Quick as a wink, Hades scooped up Persephone in his arms, dislodging the question from her mind. Too stunned to yelp, she clutched his muscled shoulders as he portaled her to their apartment. Heat from Hades had her body relaxing. The trip back took longer this time but at least the room didn't spin when they landed.

CHAPTER EIGHTEEN

THE OFFER SHE CAN'T ACCEPT

PERSEPHONE

After the impromptu meeting with Zeus and her mom, Persephone and Hades returned to their shared apartment. When they landed in the main space, instead of setting her on her feet, he carried her to a plush chair.

"How are you feeling?" he asked, kneeling next to her.

Giddy. She was reeling from him sweeping her up and portal-ing her in a way that kept her from becoming ill. Why did he care if she got sick from the portal? Although her mom was never harsh, even she didn't slow her portal speed, no matter how much Persephone and Laura wobbled after the trip.

"Fine," she replied, unable to look him in the eye.

He must've noticed her hesitation as with a gentle touch, he turned her chin. It was impossible not to be captivated by the striking god with silvery eyes and a face so dangerously magnificent that only the Fates could've made it.

Smiling, Hades stood up and made his way to the kitchen. "Would you like a fresh cup of coffee?"

"Yes, thank you." Once her nerves settled, she got up from the chair and pulled out her phone.

Her thoughts turned back to the meeting and her mom. Was her mom's silence from the past few weeks because she thought she'd get her released from the contract soon? Or was her mom still angry with her? Zeus upheld the agreement so there wasn't much else anyone could do. Would her mom now accept the situation and communicate with her daughter again? Persephone hoped so.

What about Hermes? Did the messenger of the gods have a better life than an executive assistant? How would her mom react to that news? Again, if Zeus commanded it, you'd better obey or be prepared for a torturous fate meted out by her roommate.

She didn't remember sitting on the stool at the kitchen counter, but she knew Hades had been standing still with one arm holding his middle and a hand on his mouth for a few silent minutes.

"So… uh. Teppanyaki at two, right?" Persephone asked.

Hades made an affirmative sound from the back of his throat and kept his eyes fixed on the ground where a pacing Cerberus meandered near his feet.

"Everything alright?"

Hades looked up at Persephone. "Yes. Just thinking."

She cocked her head. "About what?"

With a tempered smile, Hades replied, "I don't know."

Now her mouth quirked. "Don't know? Or don't want to say?"

"A bit of both."

Sprawled on the floor, Cerberus released a low whine then plopped his chin on Hades' shoe.

She knew better than to push a god to open up, even if she was curious about his silence. He wasn't usually one to hold back. "Well, I'll leave you to your thoughts. How soon do I need to be ready? I might go to the track if there's enough time before we leave."

Seeing her mom after weeks of silence had given her enough mental fodder to last a full workout. The strange mix of incensed care and unnerving frustration from Demeter during the meeting in Zeus' office scrambled her mind. Still, buried deep inside her was the fact that she knew her mom loved her. Just because her actions or inaction didn't make sense, it didn't mean that she'd abandoned Persephone.

"Care if I join you?" Hades asked. A mischievous smirk lit his face, eliciting a smile from her.

"It's your gym." She wanted time to process the interaction with her mom, but having a bit of a distraction wasn't a bad thing. The meeting in Zeus' office was a lot to take in and perhaps Hades could offer some insight.

Curious, she opened the Demeter's Bounty app on her phone and breathed a sigh of relief. The grocery delivery option had been restored.

TYPICALLY, when Persephone visited the gym, she'd spend most of her time running the clay track with Hades. Occasionally, she'd lift free weights or stretch in the sauna—alone. But after the way Hades unapologetically hoarded her in front of Zeus and her mom, she couldn't help feeling shy. No one had ever expressed a desire for her the way he did.

She lingered by the bench taking far more time than ever before to stretch and tighten her shoes' laces to the optimal tension. He was clearly tied up in his own head. After she'd changed into her tank top and shorts to head down to the gym with him, he'd barely looked her way.

After a long, silent stretching session, they jogged the track together, Hades in the outer lane next to her. Did she always pant like this when she ran? Her breath sounded louder than the blood rushing in her head and she felt strangely self-conscious about it.

She assumed Hades would grow bored with her slower pace and would speed off on his own. When he didn't do that for ten minutes, she felt bad. In a strained voice, she said, "Don't hold back on my account. My legs are shorter than yours."

Hades turned towards her, his breathing steady and slow. "Nonsense. I asked to join you. This is perfect."

She huffed in between breaths. "I doubt it but alright."

Picking up her pace, her muscles eased into the movement and steps became lighter despite the effort.

"What'll happen to Hermes now that he's working for your brother?"

Hades kept his face forward. "He'll be paid more, I'm sure. And he'll be much busier than he was as your assistant."

"I figured as much." Would Hermes prefer Zeus to her as a boss? A small pinch of worry hit her gut.

He gave her an inquisitive look. "He'll be well taken care of if that's what you're worried about."

Trying to stifle her heavy breathing, she nodded. "Glad to hear that. He's a good person."

Hades slowed to a walk and Persephone stopped a few steps ahead and turned back to face him. "Everything alright?"

He approached her and gestured for her to continue walking with him. "Was it hard to see your mom?"

They'd spoken little of her mom since she'd lived with him even though the goddess remained on Persephone's mind. Would confessing her frustrations add to the betrayal her mom may have felt? Did it matter given that there were still four more months of contractual obligations, and the next events were public ones where Demeter would see her daughter flirting with her enemy? Perhaps one god could give insight on another's way of thinking.

She kept her eyes forward and rolled her shoulders. "It's the first time I've seen her since... well..." She waved her hands between them. "All of this."

His voice lowered. "I know."

Of course he did. Persephone was in his domain. The god probably knew whenever she sneezed and how much of his air she took with each breath.

"Do you wish to change the contract?" he asked.

Her steps faltered but she righted herself without stumbling. *Why would he ask that?*

"If you were me, what would you change?" she asked.

He turned to look at her, still keeping in step as they walked. "I'm too biased to give a fair answer."

She huffed. "Humor me. What would you change?" She kept her tone light despite the dryness in her throat.

"I'd remove the end date and have you join the executive team." A smile snaked its way up his stubbled face, making his eyes sharper. "Would you like to bargain for different terms?"

How could one construct a counter bargain so clever that even the God of the Underworld couldn't entrap you further? It wasn't possible for her to get out of her contract without breaking it.

"What kind of bargain?" She sounded so confident, but his self-satisfied expression made her heart stop.

One brow quirked, Hades replied, "One that would guarantee an elevated position within the elite in Olympus."

She shivered as the air grew colder and her sweat clung to her skin like ice. "Why? I liked my job at DB. I'm worried I won't be able to get it back after working for you." Could she ever become Demeter Bounty's president now?

He sneered but remained handsomely sharp. "Why would you want to go back to your old job?"

Because it was mine.

Sure, her mom had gotten her the first interview but every advancement after was hers and hers alone. Most of her coworkers had all but forgotten Demeter had recommended her all those years ago, until her mom announced Persephone as her daughter. Still, it was Persephone who oversaw the most recent grocery delivery launch with the logistical, technical, and promotional departments she hired and directed. For the most part, her mom was hands off with day-to-day operations.

Persephone swept her gaze around the pine rafters high above them in the gym. "Hades." His face flushed at the mention of his name from her lips. "Imagine losing all of this in one day."

As his eyes softened, he tilted his head and stared back, still in step with her. "Sephy, what did you truly *own* back in Demeter's Bounty? Because from what I've seen, you worked and your mom enjoyed the spoils of your labor."

Her skin prickled with unease. He had no right to criticize her mom that way, so why did it feel true? Why did it sound so empowering?

She tried to shake off her conflicted emotions. "I had a whole branch of the company at my disposal and a department I built myself. It's not a massive empire like yours but it was something I created. It was my responsibility even if it was under the ownership of my mom. She protected my interests and invested in my people. I know you each have your reasons for hating the other, but that doesn't change that she's successful in her own right."

Hades stopped to turn towards her. His warm fingers wrapped around the tops of her shoulders, halting Persephone. A chill swept through the air and the scent of cedar overpowered the salty sweat on her face.

He leaned closer without towering over her. "She protected her assets, of which you are the greatest one. But you've been under her thumb this whole time. What if you owned your own company without any other oversight? How would that compare to your division under your mom's dominion?"

Sighing, she replied, "Of course that sounds promising, but I don't know if I want my own enterprise. I was excited to run my mom's business." To be fair, Persephone hadn't imagined any other option. Why would she branch out on her own when she had access to her mom's vast agricultural resources?

Hades released a slow breath and ran his fingertips down the length of her arms. Scooping her hands into his, he raised them to his mouth and put a gentle kiss on the back of each one. "You should be partners with me. Consider it, love. You could have whatever you wanted with Underworld Unlimited."

Persephone's head started to spin. What was he offering? What trap had he laid that he now lured her into? The scent of his power warmed her from the inside even as the air around her grew colder. This was the exact type of career decision that she'd normally go and consult with her mom about. She'd never gone this long without her mom's input before. Now there was an ache in her chest at the realization she'd been without her greatest ally.

He continued, "What if you were Underworld Unlimited's CEO?"

A bucket of freezing water would've been more subtle. Her mouth dropped open. "*What?*"

Releasing one of her hands, he brushed his knuckles over the apple of her cheek. "I could step down and become president or join the board. You'd gain everything I have and could launch whatever venture you wanted. You'd never need your old job."

She stepped back and gave an awkward chuckle. "Why are you joking about this?" Crossing her arms, she conjured whatever power she might have inside her chest and was pleasantly surprised by the potency of jasmine and vanilla that filled the space.

He shook his head. "No tricks here. I'm asking you to run

Underworld Unlimited and hoping you'll agree. Sephy, I think we'd make excellent partners and it'd benefit us both. Now that everyone in Olympus already knows who you are, and that you're a part of my team, what's the harm? I doubt your mom would step down and let you take over even if it's in the best interest of Demeter's Bounty."

Persephone laughed and stared off towards the other end of the track. His proposal was ridiculous. Clearly, he wasn't thinking straight. Plus, why would her mom give away her company when the food empire dominated the market? Why build something so grand and toss it away? Not that Persephone couldn't be trusted with it, but her mom was a powerful goddess. Relinquishing her thriving empire to her inexperienced daughter would spell disaster. Persephone had decades to go before she could come close to her mom's abilities. Even then, it wouldn't be enough.

Returning his gaze, she said, "You're the one I should trust the least. And you have ulterior motives—you've already entrapped me with your questionable legal maneuverings. On what planet would joining your team permanently make sense for my self-interests? And CEO? Hades, this doesn't make sense." It was absurd.

He sighed and smirked. "I'll take this as a 'no' for now." Closing the distance between them, he twirled a section of her hair that had slipped from her headband. "But I won't stop asking. Not until I die and since I'm immortal, well…"

Her hand flew up and gripped his as it hovered by her face. "I'll keep saying no, so I'd suggest you let it go." With a step back, she continued, "Now come on, we haven't really exercised, and you've added to my stress."

She sprinted off at a speed she couldn't keep up for long.

CHAPTER NINETEEN

THAT'S NOT A KISS

HADES

*H*ours after their workout in the gym, Hades and
Persephone sat in the back of Hades' SUV as
Charon drove them through the loud streets of Olympus
towards the restaurant. The black fitted cashmere sweater and
umber woolen pencil skirt Persephone wore melded to her
frame like a work of art. A piece he'd worship for as long as
she'd let him.

Hades had known that when he first asked Persephone to
become his CEO, that she'd reject the offer or play it off. In
fact, he assumed she'd keep him at arm's length even if she
signed on as a permanent Underworld executive. This did
nothing to change his resolve. His once empty apartment was
filled with live greenery and Cerberus had regained all the
energy of a puppy since she had moved in. He looked
forward to returning home, knowing she'd be joining him for
dinner.

She didn't know it yet, but he'd bargained away his empire

158

with the Fates, granting her control over it all. She'd learn soon enough that she already owned it.

Of course her emerald eyes, sun kissed cheeks, and luscious body made her desirable. Yet there was a yearning more intense than any other attraction he'd felt for beautiful women—immortal or mortal alike. Everything about her felt *right*. There was no doubt she was his whether she recognized it or not.

The night of their first dinner together when his brother Poseidon had dropped in on their conversation, uninvited, and she'd respectfully dismissed him, she'd won his admiration. She could've driven him mad bantering with his playboy brother—other flames had had no qualms about doing that in the past—but she didn't.

When she'd stood up for him during the meeting with his other brother, Zeus, she'd won his whole heart. No one in her position would've vouched for him—in front of her own mother no less. Here, Persephone faced an unknown empire and had had every reason to slight him in that moment, but she'd still chosen to honor him.

The feats they could accomplish together would write history. Existence wasn't worth it without her at his side.

"Persephone, has Hades briefed you on the reporters who will interview you today?" Charon called from the driver's seat. His assistant's voice sounded warm and pleasant unlike the clipped, expeditious tone she often used with him.

"Yes. They're going to ask about the app's progress and if we're officially dating. Correct?"

Sitting one seat away from her, he studied the slope of her nose, the length of her dark lashes, and the way her hair trailed over her shoulder past her chest. He'd noticed that since she'd moved in, her face had more color, she stood taller, and her hair grew with impossible speed. It had to mean that she was exactly where she was meant to be. Now, figuring out how to convince her of that was quite the challenge.

And he was still kicking himself for going rigid in her arms at the golf course. She'd pressed that gorgeous body against him, and he lost all rational thought. At least he hadn't taken advantage of her temporary vulnerability and run his hands along her hips and waist like he'd practically done when helping her line up her shot.

Lost in his own musings and the sight of the beautiful goddess sitting next to him, he missed whatever question Persephone had asked him. She scowled. "Did I miss anything, Hades?"

Probably not, he thought but answered, "You'll be perfect."

His phone vibrated in his jacket's front pocket, and he swiped to open a message from Eurydice.

EURYDICE

Issue with testers. Call me.

"Eurydice wants us to call her," said Hades.

Persephone nodded.

The line rung once before Eurydice answered, "Hi, Hades."

"What is it?" he asked and flicked his eyes to Charon's reflection in the rearview mirror as he hit the speaker button.

On the other line, Hades heard tense voices arguing in the background. "All of the beta testers had their phones hacked. After they download the new version of the app, it sent push alerts of their location to everyone in their contact list. I have fifty angry testers demanding answers."

"Have you removed the latest version from their phones?"

"Yes. It hasn't stopped the issue, though. Whatever is causing this, used the app as a vehicle."

"*Wonderful.*" Hades groaned. "Other than the testers and their contacts, who else knows?"

"I don't know."

"Charon will meet you in the office soon. She'll alert PR to field all questions, and I'll talk to Hecate to see if she has any solutions." Charon met his eyes in the mirror again and gave him a nod.

"Thank you, sir."

Hades ended the call, fired off a quick text to Hecate, then slid his phone back into his breast pocket.

Persephone narrowed her eyes at him. He unbuttoned the top button of his shirt and caught her glancing at the action. The hint of interest in her cursory look and the slight blush on her cheeks made him rise a little in his seat. "Do you have the app on your phone?"

Persephone opened her home screen. "Not anymore. Eurydice had me remove it weeks ago when she started working on the newest version. Shouldn't we head to the office?"

From the driver's seat, Charon said, "Don't skip lunch. I'll come get you if they need you."

Persephone fidgeted in her seat. Hopefully he could put her at ease so she'd enjoy their date.

"There's nothing we can do now," he said as he lifted one brow at her and winked. There was no point hovering over the dev team as they pinpointed the issue. Plus, she'd promised to act like a more convincing girlfriend on this date. No way he'd pass up that opportunity, even if his empire was burning to the ground. Wanting Sephy's attention back on him, he asked, "How about we use that first kiss today?"

She rolled her eyes and straightened in her seat. "Stop."

Leaning towards her, he put his hand on the seat between them. "It's a good plan and you know it." The thrill in his chest clawed at him.

She wiped her hands across the tops of her skirt-covered thighs. "It's going to be awkward if we do that," she said. Her mouth tightened at its edges, a tell Hades was beginning to recognize as her way of hiding an incoming joke.

He made a noise low in his throat. "And why is that?"

Straight faced, she replied, "Because I've never kissed anyone."

He chuckled. It wasn't true because his team had already uncovered every previous romantic detail from her past. A few boyfriends but nothing that lasted long. Demeter kept her daughter under close watch—something he appreciated even if Demeter was *difficult*. It was protocol, he'd assured Charon, that any high-ranking member of Underworld Unlimited required a thorough background check. Charon had responded to the request with a most sarcastic, "*Sure it is.*"

A huge grin on his face, Hades said, "Is that so?"

Brushing her sleeves, she hummed in the affirmative.

"Well then, we ought to practice before we head into the restaurant. Work out all the kinks before the big performance."

Her face snapped to his. There was a glint in her eye he couldn't quite decipher. "No."

He feigned disinterest and adjusted his watch. "Sephy, it's lucky for you that you're sitting next to the world's most able lover. It'd be a shame not to practice with the best."

She huffed a laugh. "You're a confident one, that's for sure. And if you wanted to kiss me so badly, you should've put that into the contract."

"Funny you should mention the contract—"

Persephone cut in, "No. There's no way you could've finagled something like that into the agreement."

Crossing his ankle over his knee, he sunk back in his chair. "Not explicitly, no, but I like to think it's implied. Still, I won't force you to do anything you don't want to. Instead, let's make a deal. One kiss and I'll make a donation of any amount to Helena's school."

Her eyes widened but the rest of her stayed frozen until she pulled part of her bottom lip with her teeth. If she said no, he decided he would keep his contribution to the school a secret.

But if by some glorious turn of fate she agreed, he'd tell her on their drive home.

"Any amount?" she asked.

Hades nodded.

While she stared back, he imagined what it'd be like to kiss her now. In this fantasy, he'd unbuckle his seat belt and close the distance with one step. The moment she returned the kiss, he'd free her from her seat and pull her onto his lap. Her skirt's modest front slit could be easily pushed up her smooth legs. He hadn't stopped thinking about them since their time together in the gym. It had been hard not to stare at her in her shorts and tank top while they'd worked out together. His self-control had gone through a gauntlet these past couple of months.

Yanked from his thoughts as she replied, he had to ask her to repeat her answer.

"Setup an endowment fund. One that would support the school indefinitely and maybe I will kiss you," Persephone said in a crisp voice.

"Done." He beamed at her, delighted she'd agreed to a kiss. The crackle of power sealing the bargain filled the car's interior with a pungent cedar scent. "I'm starting to think you like this idea given that your suggestion barely covers what a kiss from you is worth. You might never admit it, but you cut me a deal and for that, I am grateful."

She pushed her hair over one shoulder. "You're impossible sometimes." The words coated with jest hung between them for a silent moment.

"While we're on the subject of our impending date, let's discuss what it is you're willing to do," Hades said as he leaned back in his seat and turned his head towards her. "May I hold your hand?"

She dipped her chin. "Yes, simple things like that. Don't fondle me and it'll be fine. What you've done in public so far has been acceptable so I assumed this would be no different."

One side of his mouth lifted. "Would you sit in my lap during the meal?"

She shot him a tired look and chided, "No."

He lifted his hands. "That's fine. Save that for in private... I understand."

"*Hades.*" She groaned.

Laughing, he said, "Don't blame me for trying."

Persephone's cheeks flared as she struggled to contain a smile, and the sight sent a pleasant shiver down his spine. He watched her as she turned to look out the window and the car came to a stop.

Charon said from the driver's seat, "I'll text you with updates after I get back to the office."

Unbuckling his belt then Persephone's, Hades replied with, "Thank you," and hurried out of the car to open Persephone's door. Her soft fingers slid into his offered hand, and he tamped down the desire to pull her all the way to his chest. The sweet hint of jasmine wafted past him as she stepped out.

"It's showtime," Persephone whispered near Hades' ear, sending his heart racing. They'd had a few meals together in public, but his excitement had only increased. Sure, she still rolled her eyes and batted away his advances, but her bristling had morphed into feigned annoyance and hidden smiles.

Walking hand in hand, they smiled at the journalists who parted and peppered them with questions. Hades slowed his steps and put a hand on Persephone's waist to turn them both towards the group.

"We'll answer a few questions," he said, his back to the restaurant.

A few reporters spoke over one another but ultimately yielded to a woman with a tight ponytail and tailored blazer.

"We've heard there are concerns about the *Flowers Near Me's* security. Can you comment?" she asked, holding out her phone.

Hades cleared his throat and kept his hand on Persephone's

slim waist. He knew this question was coming. *"Flowers Near Me* is undergoing the same rigorous testing all of our applications go through. Security is our top priority and once the newest version of the app is available for download, users can be assured of its safety."

"Persephone! Is it true your mom fired you?" another reporter shouted from the crowd.

Persephone smiled, poised as always. The picture of professionalism—graceful and unbothered. "There's a temporary conflict of interest but no ill will between us. Demeter's Bounty will always be my first home."

"Do you know why Demeter has refused all interviews?"

"Sounds like a question for her staff," Persephone called back.

One of the reporters in the front asked, "Are you two dating?"

Hades and Persephone exchanged a glance as he pulled her closer to his side. Still holding her with one arm, he tucked some of her soft hair behind one ear and dragged his fingers down the length of the strands. Judging by the way her body froze he had reached the edge of her comfort level. It was hard not to run his fingers back over her soft hair, but he gritted his teeth and kept a polite hand on her side.

"I'd say so. And we're ready to start enjoying our date. Good day." He gave the group a dismissive nod, released Persephone's waist, and turned towards the restaurant's doors with an offered arm.

Persephone threw him a conspiratorial look with her half smirk and hooded eyes. She held his arm with both hands, interlocking her fingers, and took a step that pressed her hip to the side of his leg. If this didn't grow into the relationship he was desperate for, he wasn't sure what he'd do. There were no delusions that she was giving him *earned* affection, but things between them felt natural. Like he was finally whole.

They settled into upholstered lounge chairs surrounding the long flat top grill. Emerald glass chandeliers hung from the high coffered ceiling, bathing the geometric, Art Deco wallpaper in a golden glow. He liked the cozy spot, tucked into a corner of the restaurant. A waiter grabbed one of the bottles of ambrosia at their table and filled their glasses to the brim before taking their orders and hurrying off.

"You were perfect with those reporters, Sephy." He took a slow sip of his drink, curious if she'd take the compliment or bat it away.

"Nothing a little Underworld media training didn't prepare me for." She huffed a laugh.

"I mean it. You're a natural. And still so pretty too. The Fates outdid themselves with you. Even the gods are jealous."

The blush on her cheeks had his heart soaring.

"Wow, flattery can get you anywhere, Hades."

"Where would I go, love?" He skimmed his fingers down her arm and scooped up her hand to bring her knuckles to his lips. "I quite like where I am."

"I can't believe you just wasted the kiss on my hand," she teased.

He grabbed her other hand and tugged her so she scooted closer to him. Soaking in the glory of her attention, he leaned in close and held her green eyes. The thin circle of green thinned as her pupils grew.

With his face inches away from hers, he said in a husky voice, "That's not a kiss."

CHAPTER TWENTY

THAT'S A KISS

PERSEPHONE

He's going to kiss me.

Persephone searched Hades' face. The dim light of the restaurant cast a cool glow over his silver eyes. As he tugged her hands, it forced her to the edge of the seat. Perhaps Hades recognized someone in the restaurant who would be sure to share the news of this public kiss? But when she looked past his shoulder, out at the rest of the dining room, no one paid them any attention.

Instead of leaning forward with eyes closed, like she thought he would, he came close and brushed the stubble of his cheek on hers. His breath tickled her neck, and a delightful shiver coursed through her.

Hushed yet strong like a brook, he whispered in her ear, "They'll be no question when it's a real kiss." Slowly, he backed away, his eyes fixed on her lips, and released her hands.

Persephone righted herself in the chair. The cool glass of

water provided a momentary distraction from the force of Hades' pull. Sucking in a deep breath, there was only a hint of Hades' cologne. Had Hades masked the scent of his power somehow? Or was she genuinely drawn to him?

All it takes is attention and I'm enthralled?

She hoped not, but the lines between fake and true affection were blurring and her initial fear of becoming attached to him started to feel like a self-fulfilling prophecy. Determined to complete the contract while protecting her heart, she reminded herself that this was a god *most capable* of lying. Despite how agreeable he was or how much fun she had, as soon as she got back into the car once the date ended, she needed to come back down to earth and not float away in this fantasy. Nothing was real. This was the only way to keep her resolve.

Soon, a chef pushed her cart up to their table and began prepping. The precise flips of the chef's knives held her attention captive. Bowls of rice, seasoned meat, chopped vegetables, and cooking oils paraded through her presentation.

The almost-kiss had her out of sorts. As they enjoyed their meals, Persephone's shoulders relaxed.

"So Sephy," said Hades. "What was it really like working for Demeter's Bounty?"

Her eyes lifted in thought. "Fulfilling. I know the company's priorities and that made it easier to have agency no matter which level of the company I worked in. I've been remote for almost my entire career and that's allowed me to pursue things I love without wasting away in an office."

"You've done well for yourself." Hades took a small bite of food and stared at his plate.

"I've learned a lot from my mistakes."

Hades huffed. "Same."

"Success is a terrible teacher," she said. "What is it that you like about Underworld Unlimited?"

"Other than it made it possible to work with you?" Smirking, he motioned his fork towards her.

"No, really. Why work at all? It's not like you have to." She was very curious.

As a teenager, Persephone couldn't understand her mom's desire to work. Their estate was self-sustaining and with her mom's powers, they wanted for nothing. But after a few years of working for Demeter's Bounty, she understood the appeal of power and the satisfaction of a job well done. It was exhilarating to see a project through, especially one that earned a sizable bonus at the end.

He inclined his head. "Well, I indulged in leisure for a while, but then mortals and their never-ending demands filled my time. But as I rose to power, people grew more and more reluctant to ask me for things. I studied law and figured out how to use the system to my benefit and found I rather enjoyed it."

Persephone said, "You like bargaining with people?"

"I relish being a god, love. You should embrace your own godhood and see how sweet it tastes." He tapped her arm with the back of his hand.

"It's hard when you don't have the ability to conjure things. Unlike you, I have to work for my meals," Persephone said with a challenge in her voice.

He cocked a brow. "That so?"

"Yes."

"Let me do the work for you, Sephy. I don't mind getting my hands dirty." Hades resumed eating. His words hung in the air as Persephone toyed with their meaning.

The nervous sips of water she consumed pooled in her bladder. "Excuse me. I'll be right back." She tapped Hades on the shoulder then headed towards the restroom.

Inside the quiet restroom, she checked her phone for messages and emails then tucked it away before entering a stall. Hades' persistent compliments continued to mess with her determination to never trust him. Everyone in her professional and social circles either feared or resented him. Fates, he'd managed to get her on his payroll with his underhanded law bending. Yet there was a warmth blooming as she spent more time with him. Her skin prickled when he touched her, no matter how insignificant the touch was. And his compliments were addictive like sweets. He kept her coming back for her next fix.

She finished washing her hands and checked her makeup. It dawned on her that she was not in one of Hades' buildings and thus not on his network. If she texted Laura then deleted the thread, there was a good chance he'd never be able to read her message. She hadn't worried too much about him monitoring her communications since there wasn't much she was sending these days beyond brief check ins with her sister, appeals to her mom to talk, and business related matters to be sorted with Charon.

PERSEPHONE

Any advice for how to protect your heart from a god trying to claim it?

She hit send before rereading it, knowing how embarrassed she'd be and how pathetic she'd feel if she acknowledged her predicament further.

Hopefully Laura would respond quickly as she typically did when she wasn't in the hospital or on call. Persephone had lost touch with Laura's ever-changing schedule so there was a chance her sister was elbow deep in a medical emergency and unable to answer her younger sister's text about god problems. It was trivial compared to the work that Laura did. How silly had she become?

Her phone buzzed and Laura's name appeared along with her message, bringing a wave of relief.

LAURA

Maybe you can't and that's okay? Try not be so
hard on yourself.

She wanted to cry and squeeze her sister. Using her shoulder, she pushed open the door smiling to herself as she made her way down the small hallway.

Perhaps if she allowed these feelings to flow freely, they'd pass and she'd been fine regardless of what came next. She deleted her own message but left her sister's there as a future consolation. That must've been her problem. Instead of letting her feelings be what they may, she had been tamping them down, creating a pressure that only increased their intensity.

Fresh confidence died a quick death when Hades' chiseled frame covered in an immaculate suit stopped her in the hallway. "Ah, there are you. I was worried someone whisked you away."

"No, I'm still here."

Hades grinned as he traced her arms. With a gentle touch, he took her hands and placed them on his waist. He felt like warm stone under her palms. She became lightheaded as his hands caressed her jaw and her skin went hot. Leaning his face to hers, there was no question whether or not he intended to kiss her. His full lips pressed onto hers and the scent of a winter forest flooded her senses. The press of his lips lingered for a halted breath, then he pulled away to straighten to his full height.

"*That's* a kiss."

Oh Fates. Was there anything to compare it to? She'd been kissed before but not like that. *Never like that.* The world narrowed until it was only him with his handsome face and smooth words.

"Why now? No one saw us," she asked, hoping she knew the answer.

Hades offered his hand and she took it. "Our first kiss should be for just the two of us."

Floating along, they returned to their seats. She was plummeting headfirst into his whirlpool and wasn't sure where she'd land. There were worse things than a broken heart—a destroyed career came to mind—but lovesickness was unfamiliar to her, and she never liked seeing the effects of it in others.

If his feelings for her eventually passed, maybe the same thing would happen to her? *But if they didn't...* she pushed some rice around her plate. *I can't think about it now.*

CHAPTER TWENTY ONE

THE GODDESS WHO COULD BREAK HIM

HADES

Sephy had asked that Hades portal them back to the apartment after their hibachi date. After some convincing from her—that she wouldn't feel sick from the travel—he relented. He relished holding her and took his time making the jump from the restaurant to the penthouse. If she was agreeable, he'd start to teleport her everywhere. It'd scared him to see how pale she'd become the first time he portaled her to Zeus' office.

Back home, she insisted that she'd be the one to call Eurydice. "I've dealt with misbehaving tech before. Let me handle it." She was the app's new Chief Product Officer, but he wished her first significant involvement wasn't overseeing a bug fix and handling any potential PR fallout.

Cerberus trailed behind her as she paced over a handwoven rug. The gray and brown fur ball watched the little goddess' every move around the apartment. The beast was almost as enchanted by their companion as Hades was.

Their kiss in the secluded hallway of the restaurant was better than he'd imagined it would be. And he'd imagined that scenario often. The soft feel of her lips mixed with her bewitching scent had the ichor speeding in his veins. He would forever remember the flush of her cheeks and sultry gaze after that kiss. She desired him. And even if it was only a flicker, he'd try to fan it into flame.

Eurydice's shaky voice came over the speaker of Sephy's phone, "I'm still trying to find out what happened to the app's code. It makes no sense. We'd tested it in-house before the testers were brought in."

"Do you still have their phones?" Sephy asked. She stopped pacing and fixed her eyes on Hades.

Eurydice answered, "We gave them back after we deleted the app."

"Are they still in the building?"

"Yes."

Sephy's eyes lit up. "Good. Make sure they're logged onto Underworld's network then pull all of their phones' data from the past six months. Tell them you're checking for lingering issues. Get everything you can." She counted on one hand, each delicate finger marking her list of: "Search and location history, messages, contacts, apps, anything and everything. Then have your team cull the data and look for patterns."

Hades choked on his coffee. Had he heard her correctly? Was she really telling Eurydice to investigate the beta testers for possible sabotage by sifting through all of the activity of their phones?

Why didn't I think of that? He'd expect seasoned gods like himself or Demeter to distrust contracted employees, but Sephy seemed less jaded than him. Maybe she was as calculating as he was? To rise through the ranks of Demeter's Bounty, she'd need a steely resolve and sharp mind. Demeter was notoriously distrustful of those outside of her confidantes and naturally she'd want her daughter to be the same. He'd want his children to be as cunning too. In fact, Sephy's balance of kindness and shrewdness was the perfect combination. She'd be an incredible mom if they had children.

"I-uh… are we allowed to do that?" Eurydice asked. The developer's voice lowered into a whisper over the phone.

Sephy tapped her screen to mute the call. "Beta testers signed a data use agreement, right?"

In no world should *that* sentence sound as seductive as it did coming from her lips. He cleared his throat. "Of course."

She unmuted the call. "Yes, we're allowed. It's important you get your team moving on this straight away. There's a good chance the virus came from one of them."

"Oh, okay. I-I'll get right on it."

"Thanks. Keep us posted." Sephy ended the call then quirked her brow at Hades. "What's wrong?"

He prowled towards her until his hands rested on the sides of her arms. "Nothing at all. You made the right call. We shouldn't rule out the testers until we've dug into their activities." All he wanted was to kiss her again, but he didn't want to force things between them, no matter what his body screamed at him to do.

She released a sigh. "I have a hard time believing it's bad code. I had the beta version on my phone months ago, and it worked perfectly." Something unreadable cast over her face. "Weird how things change."

Dropping his hands from her arms, he took a step back. Why hadn't she had issues? During the car ride to the restaurant, she told him she'd deleted the app. Was it possible she knew what caused this and offloaded the app before disaster struck? This paranoia had kept him steps ahead of his adversaries. As distasteful as it was to consider Sephy his enemy, he couldn't shrug off this worry. She was Demeter's daughter, taught to despise him. And he'd yanked her from a familiar, cozy place to come work with him.

To his horror, he remembered their conversation the first time she'd stepped into his place. She'd acted as if she didn't know that using a god's network connection meant they could access everything on her phone. Was she still playing him?

Perhaps it'd been a mistake to make her the Chief Product Officer. His infatuation with the little goddess had clouded his judgment and now his empire could die at her hands. Even he wasn't immune to the capricious nature of the Olympus consumer. If *Flowers Near Me* had bad tech running rampant on users' phones, what would that mean for the other apps and websites where Underworld Unlimited made its fortune? He'd already wagered his empire with the Fates in order to understand this charming goddess. What if she was taking it over only to crush it underneath her feet?

Sephy's sweet voice shook him from his thoughts. "Do you disagree?" Her head tilted to one side as her brows wrinkled.

She looks so sincere. This being before him was not the same cold, scheming goddess as Demeter. This wasn't him ruling out distrust, but he needed more information. He'd barely gotten to know Sephy even if his heart felt like they were an allied pair.

Mustering a smile, he answered, "No. I think your suggestion is right." He rolled his shoulders. "There's nothing we can do at the moment other than worry so let's do something else." *Anything else.*

Feeling at odds with her made his body sick with unease. Being sharp didn't mean she was devious as well. He needed to understand her better, that was all.

CHAPTER TWENTY TWO

WINNER TAKES ALL

PERSEPHONE

The teapot whistled, and Persephone removed it from the stove. Fragrant jasmine and green tea filled the air, curling into delicate wisps. The large common space was quiet, save for Cerberus padding softly in the background.

Laura's advice to lean into her feelings only highlighted her sister's misplaced trust in Persephone's ability to stay rational. Laura had married Peter—reliable, tender-hearted, and nothing like Hades. Of course Laura could trust her own heart. But Persephone? She had allowed her guard to slip, and now she couldn't stop replaying that kiss.

Tea in hand, Persephone sank into the opposite end of the couch where Hades lounged, his long arm stretched casually across the backrest, almost within reach. She tucked her legs beneath her and blew on her tea, doing her best to feign indifference. His mere presence made her pulse race, and the corner of his mouth curved, as if he knew it.

Hades leaned closer, the faint scent of pine teasing her senses. "Care for a game of dice?"

Persephone hesitated but gave a coy smile. "Why not?"

He placed an ornate obsidian tray between them. It was a beautiful piece inlaid with opal stones shaped into a bident and helm. "You know the stakes are high when you play with a god."

A thrill danced up her spine at the reminder, but she kept her composure, leaning forward as if studying the pieces. "I'm not afraid of a little risk," she murmured, her tone a playful dare. She knew she should be more cautious around him, but she was enjoying some of his games.

Hades' grin widened, and he inched closer. "Good," he replied, his voice warm enough to melt the air between them. "I like a partner who's not afraid to gamble."

Opening a velvet satchel, Hades placed black dice in the tray. As he set the small bag to the side, he asked, "Care to make a wager?"

Alarm bells flooded Persephone's head. *Titans no.* "Let's do a few rounds first. It's been a while since I've played. Which game?"

"How about Sevens?" He picked up a die and extended it to her, his fingers brushing hers as he offered it. "Let's see who goes first."

"Alright." Sevens was easy enough. Each round you removed any number pairs that equaled seven and totaled the remaining numbers for your score. You could take up to three tries, but the final one would be the roll you were stuck with.

With a small toss, Persephone rolled a five which beat Hades three.

"Are you good with thirteen rounds?" He gathered the dice in a cup to hand to her.

She nodded and rattled the cup then dumped it onto the tray. Unfortunately, she made two sets equaling seven—a one and a six and a three and four—thus loosing those dice from her score. Fortunately, there were a six and a three leftover.

"I'll stick with this roll," she said, knowing that she'd only have two more dice to use on a second turn, and they could end up being a combination that totaled seven and granted her no points. Nine points was decent for an opening round.

She watched his face as he slid a point counter on the edge of the tray, marking her score. He met her eyes and a smile immediately bloomed.

"Nicely done. Let's see if I can do better." He winked at her then placed the dice in the cup and rolled.

"Hm…" He tapped one finger on his mouth and narrowed his eyes. He rolled three ones, one two, one three, and one four. With feline speed, he removed the three and four combination. Something about the smooth movements of his hands and the smile that peeked through every time she caught him watching her warmed her chest.

"A five to your nine… I'm going to take my chances." Rolling the four remaining dice, another seven combination with a six and a one, and then two threes. With a sigh, Hades lamented, "Six it is. Your turn, love." He plopped the dice into the cup and handed it to her. Feeling bold, she brushed her fingers against his as she reached for the cup.

They continued until they reached the thirteenth and final round. Persephone's hearty lead of thirty points cast away her previous worries.

"It's been a while since I've been beaten that handedly. Rematch?" Hades asked.

"Why not? How 'bout the loser goes first this time," she answered with a wink. She'd felt bold after her win and knew she shouldn't be careless. She could hear her mom's words cautioning her to *never let a win cloud your judgement,* but she was feeling high.

Lines bracketed his mouth in a look between a sneer and smile. "How kind."

Hades reset the point counters and took his turn.

After eight rounds it was clear Persephone would win again.

"Using your magic, little goddess?" Hades teased in a deep timbre.

Her cheeks went hot at the accusation. Even if she could cheat by magic, she wouldn't. "No," she fired back with a laugh.

Hades smirked and hummed his suspicion. "Alright... let's see if I can climb out of this hole."

With two more pitiful rounds, Hades chuckled in defeat. "Well done, Sephy. Luck seems to favor you tonight. How about we set a wager now that you know I'm not a threat?"

Her brow dropped. "Why?"

"Why not?"

She glared at him.

"Come on, love. Think about how much more fun we'll have with stakes." He reset the counters, filled the cup with dice, then lifted his eyebrows at her.

She pursed her lips. "What kind of wager do you have in mind?"

By the way his eyes sharpened, she knew *exactly* what it'd be.

"Another kiss," he answered.

She shifted in her spot. The smooth long-sleeved shirt and joggers she wore felt cool on her hot skin. "Two kisses in one day?" She scoffed but inwardly her heart paced.

"Well... only if I win."

"You've had eons to play this game. You think you can lull me into a bet after losing two rounds?"

He cocked his head. "No, love. I figured I needed to lose at least three rounds before I'd fool you," he quipped. "One more chaste kiss. And only our lips can touch if that makes it easier. Plus, I'd have to win, and you have yet to offer your terms."

With a subtle grit in her tone, she said, "Fine. If I win, then you have to…" She considered a few options.

Agree to no more tricks?

Stop trying to make me fall for you?

Or kiss me until I couldn't care if you broke my heart? Shit.

She kept drifting into his undertow. "Hm… you have to promise to never speak ill of my mom again."

He straightened his neck and his eyes went wide. "What if she crosses me?"

"Really, Hades? You think she's the one trying to mess with *you*? Isn't her daughter living with you?" Her voice was surprisingly lighthearted.

"In public. I won't utter a disparaging word about her in public ever again. Would that satisfy you?" His gaze flicked to her mouth.

She tipped her head, trying to be nonchalant. It was surprising he'd agree to that so easily. "I think so." Curiosity took over. Would he change his approach with the game to win now that there were stakes? Or was he truly that unlucky?

"You sure you don't want to add something for yourself?" There was a regretful look in his eyes.

"I'm sure."

He released an audible sigh. "May luck favor me this time." He handed her the cup full of dice and the scent of his power filled the room. The same tickle of magic she'd felt in the car when they'd bargained for the first kiss brushed the back of her neck.

As Persephone considered her choices after rolling, Hades' phone pinged. He glanced at the screen then set it down face up.

She removed the one seven combination and asked, "Everything alright?"

"Hecate's making progress. Says she needs more time but should be able to figure out what caused the app's issue." He looked down at her roll. "Ah, looks like you've got a head start." Four fives stared up at them.

"Yes, I'll take it. And that's great—Hecate's close to figuring it out."

Persephone won again but with a smaller lead than the previous two games.

He shrugged one shoulder and gave a dismissive wave with his hand. "You got me again. I won't slander your mom."

Victory didn't feel as sweet as she'd expected, but in a tiny way, she had done something that could work in her mom's favor.

"One more game?" he asked as he took Persephone's empty mug.

"Sure, one more. Grab me a water please?"

"My pleasure." He reached into the fridge and unscrewed a bottle of mineral water. "Think about your wager this time. I'm going all out."

The hairs on the back of her neck rose. "Oh?"

Carrying her drink, he handed her the bottle then settled back in his seat. "Oh yes. Something big."

One side of her mouth lifted. "I'm not making any major life changes because of a game's wager."

He leaned forward, coming closer but still out of arm's reach. "No? What about a *real* date then? Where you don't put on an act or force a smile because you think someone is watching."

She cleared her throat. "I'm doing those things because we have a contract. Don't make it sound like I'm fake when I'm doing the job that *you* assigned me."

He licked his lips and the fact that she tracked the movement made her bite the inside of her mouth. He said, "The contract was the only way you'd give me a chance."

"And to get back at my mom."

His face fell but he took a slow breath. "There are more

sinister ways to do that if I'd wanted to. That's not why I want you here."

She leveled him with a stare and felt a surge of magic within her. The pungent smell of jasmine and vanilla made her eyes water and her skin tingle. "I can't help but wonder at the timing of things given that we'd just overtaken your reported profits last quarter. It's the kind of game you gods love to play."

Now the smell of cedar and leather overwhelmed the space. "Little goddess, if that's what you need to tell yourself so you keep me at arm's length, so be it, but I will close the distance. Last quarter wasn't the first, hundredth, or even thousandth time Demeter's Bounty outperformed Underworld Unlimited."

Was that true? To be fair, she hadn't kept score until she'd worked in the distribution department. That was only a few years ago so perhaps he was telling the truth. Her mom wanted her employees to be hungry for success, Persephone had heard her say as much in their board meetings. Maybe Demeter's organization fared much better than she thought?

"Okay, here's my wager. If you lose, then once *Flowers Near Me* becomes profitable, you have to sell it to Demeter's Bounty. All of it, including rights to all IP, no exceptions. And at a fair market price too."

Hades perked up. "Deal." He held out his hand to shake hers. She met his palm, and he promptly tugged her forward and laid a slow kiss on her knuckles. His eyes watched her the whole time. "In fact..." He lowered their joined hands to rest on his knee. "I'd give Demeter's Bounty the app right now, for free, if you agreed to become Underworld's CEO. You could start whenever you wanted."

It was equal parts tempting and ludicrous. She gaped, trying to gather her thoughts, unsure how to respond. Any hope she'd held for reclaiming the app after he'd acquired it had faded as soon as she was in his SUV, riding away from her former life. Would she want to be Underworld's CEO without the app? This should've been an easy no, but now she wasn't so sure what her future held. Maybe a CEO position at Underworld Unlimited even without the *Flowers Near Me* app could be a good thing for her?

She pinched the bridge of her nose and clamped her eyes shut for a few breaths. "What would happen if I tanked the company?" *Fates, am I actually considering this? Surely not. I'm simply curious how far he'll take his bluff.*

He stroked the back of her hand while still holding it. "Sephy, you've fulfilled every piece of the contract you could have so far. You've had every reason to fight it. But here you are, working hard and enchanting everyone."

His willingness to promote her to CEO made absolutely no sense. Why was he trying to give her control of his company? "I don't have the right experience."

"I disagree."

"Then why?"

"Because..." He paused and looked off, absentmindedly licking his lips. His gaze returned to hers. "You're someone worth investing in. I think you like bringing others' visions to life, but you deserve the chance to carry out your own desires. I've lived a long time, Sephy, and I haven't met anyone like you. You think like a god but act like a mortal."

She shook her head. As much as she wanted that to be true, he didn't understand her one bit. She was scrappy and stubborn. Those traits often presented like better ones—confidence and competence—but at her core, she was *afraid.* Afraid of rejection, failure, and loneliness. "I can't become your CEO, Hades." She sighed. "I'm keeping my original wager. I'll go on a real date with you if you win, but if I do then you'll nurture the app and sell it to Demeter's Bounty." This way, she could try to restore things with her mom and get back on track to becoming DB's president. That's what she really wanted, right?

"You've got it, love. It's a deal." He handed her the cup. "Thirteen rounds. Want to go first?"

Persephone shook her head. "I went first last time. You go."

"I'll accept your pity." He smiled and winked at her then rolled his highest scoring roll. "Look at that. We might end up having a real date after all."

"Ah, there are still many rounds to be played. And I haven't gone yet."

He marked his points with the counter as she tossed the dice. Somehow, she rolled three combinations of sevens and scored no points. "That's not encouraging." She chuckled to herself as she picked up the dice and handed him the cup.

"It's only the first round, we have twelve to go."

Seven rounds later, and Hades had pulled ahead so far that she wasn't sure it was possible to win or tie with him unless he scored zero points for the remainder of the game. She worried the inside of her bottom lip with her teeth as she counted in her head.

"Sephy, you've gone pale. Is going on a real date with me that horrifying? Because now I'm wondering if I should be offended." He shot her a playful smile as he handed her the cup.

She rolled her shoulders. "I'm not ready to admit defeat just yet. Text your lawyers that they need to draft a seller's agreement, friend."

Hades clutched at his chest. "Friend? Oh Fates, Sephy. Just drive a knife through my heart while you're at it."

She pressed her lips into a thin line before she replied. "Oh, save it. Besides, would a knife to your heart even kill you? I'm not well versed in how to kill a god."

His mouth dropped open. "Well, when you say it like that... I'm not sure I want to tell you." His face quickly morphed into a sly smile. "Keep turning me down and you'll render me into something worse than dead."

"You'll survive," she said in a flat tone, restraining the roll of her eyes.

"Think of Cerberus, Sephy... He's only just learned the love of a consistent female figure in his life, the closest thing to knowing a mom that he'll ever have. You wouldn't leave *him*, would you?" The traitorous pup whimpered at their feet.

Persephone laughed. "You both have Charon and Hecate, you nit."

"Not living here."

"Stop distracting me from my roll," she said as she dumped the cup. Another abysmal result fell on the tray. Her head popped up and she narrowed her eyes at him. "Are you cheating?"

"I'm not Tyche. Luck doesn't answer to me."

She mumbled, "That's not a direct answer," and rolled again with her remaining two die. A two and a five. No points.

The remaining rounds ended in Hades' favor and by the time she completed her final roll, she relented.

The beaming smile on Hades' face made her grin. So they'd go on a real date. It wasn't going to do any more damage than what he'd already done with that Fates-forsaken kiss at the restaurant.

"Rest up, Sephy. I'm taking you on that date once we wrap our press tour," Hades said to her, taking their drinks to the kitchen.

"Why not sooner? Where are we going?"

"It's a surprise. Unless you want to barter with a kiss now to find out." His eyes fell to her lips.

She laughed softly. "I'll wait to see."

CHAPTER TWENTY THREE

THE PROBLEM WITH PRETENDING

PERSEPHONE

Lounging on one of the leather chairs in the main living room, Persephone thumbed through photos of Hades and her from their late lunch the day before. Cerberus curled up on the floor nearby. A few news outlets had published articles with the photos, linking them to other social accounts with even more photos. She and Hades looked convincing as a couple—almost endearingly so. There were a few pictures where she was watching the chef, but Hades was smiling and watching her.

She didn't trust her intuition with him. Whether he was immersed in this role of her fake boyfriend or what he claimed he felt about her was true, he looked smitten. Even worse, she wanted him to adore her because she was enjoying their time together.

Soon, an ugly, unwelcome question formed in her mind. *How did he look when he was with other women?* Unable to distract herself with meditation and unwilling to set her phone down, she stared at photos of Hades at different events with immaculate dates on his arm.

She couldn't discern the type he seemed to prefer. His companions spanned the spectrum of beauty—slender, sumptuous, athletic, willowy, tall, short, dark or fair skinned and everything in between. Cascading hair to buzzed pixie cuts. Did he look happy? Smitten? Proud? In love?

Who knows?

The chime of the doorbell caused her to drop the phone on the woven rug, barely missing a now awake Cerberus. The dog popped up and trotted towards the hallway.

"Good morning," Charon greeted as she placed canvas tote bags filled with groceries onto the marble counter. She tossed Cerberus a treat and he carried it off into another room.

"Hi! I didn't realize you were stopping by." Persephone grabbed her phone off the floor and made her way towards the coffee pot. "What can I get you to drink?"

Plucking items from the bags and setting them into the fridge drawers, Charon replied, "Coffee if there's some left."

"There is. Hades left early and only had one cup." She poured the steaming liquid and grabbed a creamer she had seen Charon use in the office. "But I'm sure you already knew he'd be out this morning."

Charon laughed and began folding the empty totes. "You give me too much credit. Between the two of you, I tend to memorize your schedule and not his."

Persephone handed her the mug. "Do you have somewhere you need to be soon, or can you stay for a bit?"

"Actually, I'd like to stay because I have a few things I wanted to run by you if that's okay. I know it's your day off, but I'd like to get your dress fitting scheduled now that the gala's date has been set."

Did Charon help all those other women pick out their outfits too?

Charon probably did and did so with the same professionalism and respect she showed everyone. *Don't be an idiot.*

With a hand raised in surrender, Charon said, "I'm sorry. We don't have to do this right now. I thought—"

Shaking her head, embarrassed that her emotions were so clearly written on her face and that Charon had mistaken her insecurity for disliking her suggestion, Persephone cut in, "No, it's fine. Of course we can pick the dress."

They each sat in a chair and reclined with their coffees.

"I have a few I want you to take a look at," said Charon.

"Let's see them."

Charon nodded as she scrolled on her phone then Persephone's pinged with a message. There were five different dresses. All floor length but vastly different from one another in color, fabric, and style.

"These are all very pretty, but the black silk one is my favorite. I was thinking something black but didn't know if that would be strange for the launch of a flower market app," Persephone remarked.

Charon hummed in agreement. "The bodice is covered in petals, and I think the black is a nice nod to Underworld Unlimited. Plus, you look great in black."

Persephone blushed. Why the affirmation from Charon affected her, she had no clue.

"I'll ask the shop to pull more black silk gowns, and we can set your fitting as soon as they have an opening." Charon typed on her phone.

"Sounds good to me." It wasn't a workday but Persephone couldn't help talking about the app. "Did you hear the latest news?" Persephone asked.

Setting her phone down on her lap and picking up her coffee, Charon replied, "Yes. I was surprised to hear it was one of the beta testers who introduced a virus."

"I told Eurydice it could've come from one of them."

"It's a shame. I thought our vetting process was airtight, but whoever paid the tester did a good job covering their tracks."

"Who do you think sent them?" As soon as she said it, the obvious answer, *her mom,* popped into her head. "Sorry. I have a guess."

Charon gave a light laugh. "Honestly, Demeter is only one among a long list of people who might want to discredit an app Hades is backing."

That was probably true. Besides, why would Demeter want to hurt something Persephone was promoting as well.

"Anyway… tell me about your lunch," said Charon.

"Food was incredible. I think the pictures turned out well so overall, it was a success. I'll post the picture I took with Hades on my account later today."

With a nod, Charon said, "The photos looked so good that I'm wondering if you two might actually be in love."

Persephone's chest tightened, and her face heated. "I think you're underestimating Hades' acting ability."

"Oh no. When you've worked with someone as long as we have, you learn all their tells."

Persephone laughed as she pictured the way Hermes would bite his bottom lip when he was excited. Usually, it happened right before her mom was about to rip into a contractor who failed to meet a deadline or whenever the legal team got a little snippy. Goddess of the Harvest and queen of clap-backs, Demeter's retorts never disappointed.

If Charon knew Hades half as well as she knew Hermes, could she discern what Hades' true aim was when it came to Persephone? Would Charon's loyalty to him as an employee trump any loyalty she felt towards her? Or was Charon just as complicit in his act and Persephone was the latest toy Hades planned on discarding as soon as he felt it expired?

"Penny for your thoughts?" Charon asked.

With a weak sigh, Persephone said, "I'm worried I'll be one of many that Hades has chewed up and spit out."

Charon cocked her head and her eyes softened. "Why do you think you'll be chewed up and spit out?"

With an exasperated look, Persephone replied, "All you have to do is a simple image search of Hades and you can find the carousel of women he's dated. Anyone with internet access would know this."

"Ohhhh…" Charon's brows lifted. "You're here thinking he's dated all the women he's taken to different events." Right then, Cerberus' nails clattered across the floor as he rejoined them.

"I mean, come on. You've seen those pictures. Did you compliment those women each time and tell them how cute they looked together?"

Charon's eyes widened and her lips parted. "Oh Fates, no. Not like this." She scooted forward in her seat. "He's never had a lasting interest or legal contract like he does with you."

Persephone wasn't sure at what point she'd started trusting Charon, but she did. There was some comfort in knowing that her situation with Hades was unique.

"I'm sorry, Charon. I'm out of my depth here. I worked in distribution and operations. Those don't involve fake relationships and glamorous parties. It's efficiencies… facts, figures. You know. Normal executive responsibilities, not dining out with my pretend boyfriend. It's degrading and now my thoughts have turned childish." Persephone's gaze dropped to her lap.

A small, warm hand caressed her shoulder as a fluffy head nudged her leg. Charon said, "I'm sorry you feel degraded. That's terrible. Maybe I could shed a little light on the situation?"

"Sure." Persephone dragged her hand over Cerberus' side as Charon sat back down into her chair and took a slow breath.

"Where to start…" She met eyes with Persephone. "Let's look at some of the photos."

Persephone opened her browser's most recent page. "Here."

Charon took the offered phone then pointed at the screen. "That's Merope and this picture was taken the week before her art collection debuted in one of our event spaces."

Persephone went to sit on the arm rest of Charon's chair, and Cerberus scurried off towards the kitchen. "That makes sense. Just like I'm the spokesperson for one of your apps; he wants to be seen with me to help get my name out there."

Shaking her head, Charon said, "No. Here's what you're missing. Look at their body language. They're both standing straight as an arrow."

"High praise coming from someone with the world's straightest posture."

Charon's porcelain cheeks reddened. "Oh. Thank you." She zoomed into the photo, focusing on where their sides almost touched. "See here. They're not cozy. It looks like they are because they've got their hands around the other, but you can't see their hands because they're on each other's back."

Persephone's mouth pressed in a flat line. *That seems like a reach.*

Behind them, Cerberus panted loudly, but Charon drew Persephone's attention back before she turned to look.

"No. You can actually see me in the background here." She pinched and zoomed in on a woman looking down at her phone. As her eyes adjusted, Persephone could make out the outline of someone who looked a lot like Charon. "I was behind them. They kept a fist on the other's back."

"Hm." How had Charon remembered that detail? The woman was thorough, but that kind of memory was other-worldly.

Minimizing the photo, Charon typed in Persephone's name in the search bar and pulled up an image from yesterday's lunch. "I know it's not the same because you two aren't posing for a camera, but there are a few things I noticed." She pointed at Hades' face. "See how he's smiling here? Remember it because I want you to picture it when we look at some of these other ones."

"Okay…"

In the photo Hades had his hand on the back of her chair. She didn't know he'd done that until she'd seen the pictures later. It was taken shortly after their kiss, and it was hard to ignore how happy he looked or how seeing his delight now made her flush.

Charon was back to the original search and scrolled deliberately down the page. "Not smiling here… barely a smile… looks almost angry… looks…"—she squinted her eyes then laughed—"drunk, to be honest. Then… yes, this one. He's smiling and they're dancing." She pointed to a lithe woman mid-spin. "That's my cousin, Marin. Her boyfriend hated that she worked for Underworld Unlimited. He even said some nasty things about me. But this was taken shortly after she broke up with him. I asked Hades to stage this as a goodbye message." Charon turned, smirking with a glint in her eye.

"Oh my… you nymph," teased Persephone. "I'll have to tell Laura about that one. She'll get a kick out of it."

"Think that's good? Wait 'til you see this other one I coordinated." Charon skipped down the page, and Persephone inched closer until their arms touched. "Here." Persephone leaned in to get a better look.

Suddenly, Hades' deep voice provoked a clipped scream from each of them, sending Persephone hopping away from Charon, and causing Charon to drop Persephone's phone onto the floor.

He purred, "You two look cozy."

"Fuck the Fates, Hades. Where did you come from?" Persephone picked up then clutched her phone to her chest.

He stepped close to her and answered, "I portaled here."

"How long ago?" Charon asked as she took her coffee cup towards the kitchen.

"Well, good morning to you too. Did I interrupt an important meeting?" He cupped Persephone's shoulder.

"I came over with groceries," Charon called from the kitchen. "We're figuring out Persephone's dress for the gala."

Hades smirked at Persephone. "Find one you like?"

"We're working on it." Fates, she hoped he hadn't caught any of her conversation with Charon.

"Great. I'd like to see it once you have one picked. My suit should be coordinated around what you wear."

With a quirked brow, Persephone followed Hades into the kitchen. "Won't you wear a tuxedo?"

"Yes, but there are details that should complement what you're wearing."

"Other than the color and fabric of the dress, do you need to know anything else?"

"I guess not. But I'd still like to see you in it when they do the fitting."

Persephone sat down at the counter next to Charon and said, "Hades, you're not going to the fitting."

"What if the dress is too restrictive?"

"It'll be a gown, of course it's restrictive. I won't be exercising at the gala." The parties of the gods could be elegant, bordering on stuffy or downright debaucherous. Would it be the latter? Her head went dizzy at the thought of having to pretend to be a doting girlfriend at a party like that.

"Fine, but don't fault me for trying to help." He winked.

"Yes. Trying to help yourself to a free show," she quipped and heard Charon's stifled giggle beside her.

Moving around the counter, Hades stepped up behind her chair and laid his hands on her shoulders. "Is there a paid one? Because you know I'm very wealthy." He put his head right next to hers and her back stiffened. "Name any price, love. I'd spend everything I have on you." The sound of his inhale faded as he removed his hands. "But I bet you want it to be a surprise."

The conversation with Charon about the photos and the way he spoke of her like she was worth more than his existence, made her heart skip. She could admit she liked having his attention—even if she shouldn't.

CHAPTER TWENTY FOUR

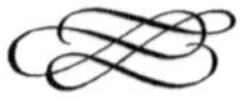

WHEN A GOD FALLS

HADES

Finally.

Sephy had agreed to go on a genuine date. Not a scheduled one to promote the app or a contracted event. Sure, Hades used a game that he *slightly* tipped in his favor to get her to agree, but she knew the terms.

What will she wear? Is she excited? The joy almost burst from his skin.

He'd unintentionally overheard Charon and Sephy's conversation in the apartment earlier. Most mornings, Sephy went to the gym, so he hadn't expected to find her there, sitting close to Charon. When he'd portaled into his apartment, he remained silent, watching the little goddess' attention dart between Charon and her phone screen filled with photos of him from the past few years.

Charon's calm voice spoke a carefully cultivated truth about each picture. Sephy's stiff body slowly unwound with each explanation.

Did she have any idea how perfect the living room smelled when she was in it or how warmth spread from his chest when she was near?

After Charon left, Sephy cleaned her mug over the sink. He took a few deep breaths as he admired her concentrated face, squinting at the dish in her hand.

"I've been thinking about our date." With a snap of his fingers, the mugs sparkled cleanly, taking Sephy by surprise.

Wide eyed, Sephy, backed away from the sink. "Thank you."

"Leave the dishes to me." Grinning, he offered his hand, curious to see what she'd do. "Come here."

He'd tried so hard to not touch her when they were alone for fear that he'd scare her off. Yesterday at the restaurant, as he'd sat in his seat waiting for her to return from the bathroom, the thought of their first kiss being shared with others made his insides twist. He'd hoped she'd grown fond of him enough that he might kiss her in private. His urge to hold her was growing with each passing moment.

He stood close to her in the kitchen, and Sephy answered by reaching for his hand. He pulled her into a hug, wrapping one arm around her shoulders and placing his palm on her soft hair. She melted into his embrace, and his mouth bloomed into a smile. She seemed to be warming to him. How had he become so fortunate that the Fates would allow this? A faint earthy smell filled his nose mixed with the vanilla and jasmine notes he'd come to enjoy.

He released her and motioned with his head towards the couches.

Hades sat next to Sephy once she slid onto the couch. "For our date, I was thinking we could spend a few days outside of the city. Do a short trip to get away from Olympus. What do you think?"

Sephy's brow furrowed, but her cheeks darkened to a rosy hue. "I thought we agreed to a *date*. Not a weekend getaway."

Hades shrugged, unrepentant. "We never agreed to a certain length of time. Besides, we're about to start the next phase of promotion and will need a break after a month of press tour interviews."

"Where will we go?" she asked.

"I want to surprise you, but I will say it's in the countryside but still near some great food places."

He'd hoped she liked his choice of destination. The moment he'd asked his team to draft Sephy's contract, he'd instructed them to prepare his retreat property for an eventual trip with her.

Sephy studied him before asking. "Is it off the grid?"

"There's internet, temperature control, staff available as well. We're not camping, if that's what you're wondering." He laughed at the image of him sitting on a picnic chair, eating a s'more. Although picturing Sephy doing the same stirred desire low in his gut.

"How will I know what to pack?"

"Charon will prepare your bags."

"Quite an elaborate date," she said with a grin.

Hades loosened his tie. "When your soulmate finally agrees to a date, you take her on a proper one."

Her nostrils flared as she glared back at him, restraining the smile tugging at her lips. "Oh, we're soulmates now?"

"Yes, of course we are," he replied. Soon enough, she'd recognize it too.

"Alright, *soulmate,* what are we up to today?" She mocked him, but he didn't care. Even teasing, it sounded lovely from her lips.

"Absolutely nothing. In two days we have to begin preparations for interviews and after that it's non-stop for almost a solid month. Let's order in and try to do as little as possible." The hope of a relaxing evening made him want to shed his suit.

Sephy tucked her legs under her. "That sounds perfect to me.

Do you want to go to the gym together before we do all this relaxing?"

He blinked, surprised. Had she just suggested they do something together? "I'd love that. Give me a minute to change."

Excitement rushed through him, and he took the stairs two at a time to his suite. He swapped his suit for an athletic top and shorts, then grabbed his shoes. As he tied the laces, realization struck him like a lightning bolt.

Fates.

In his rush, he'd forgotten to go to the guest room he'd been pretending was his. He'd headed straight to his real bedroom.

She won't notice... or she'll think it's just a spare closet... He clenched his jaw, trying to steady his nerves.

She's going to know.

Taking a deep breath, he walked back downstairs, determined to act unaffected. No one intimidated him. Not even her.

But there she was, leaning against the railing, arms crossed, a smirk playing on her lips. "I thought that room was your home office," she called out, eyes glinting with amusement.

She knew.

CHAPTER TWENTY FIVE

IT'S JUST THE START

PERSEPHONE

Heart racing, Persephone straightened her back as she pushed off the railing and waited for Hades at the bottom of the steps. With just the two of them in the apartment, she'd had little else—other than Cerberus—to watch. She knew which room he slept in and it wasn't the one he'd emerged from just now.

The smarmy tilt of his head was the only indication that she might be right. Otherwise, he stepped evenly down the staircase, a calm smile on his face, like a cat sauntering past another, poised to attack yet masking interest with nonchalance.

"Can't a god have multiple closets?" he quipped and swept a stray lock of hair behind her ear.

A low hum sounded in her throat. "Do you have some magical horn of plenty in there filled with workout clothes?"

Heading towards the door to leave the apartment, Hades said over his shoulder, "Are we headed to the gym or the loft?"

She didn't follow. Feet planted, she waited for him to turn

around. When he did, his brow lowered as a half smirk lifted on his face.

"Show me your office, Hades."

He stalked towards her, his smile growing with every step. "Sure thing, love, but it'll cost you a kiss."

"Oh, for Fate's sake." She stopped her eyes mid-roll. "Not every question is an opportunity for a bargain, you know." Though her shoulders were tall, butterflies danced in her stomach.

Invading her space, he dipped his head low to hers. "So what do you say? Will you sneak up there on your own later to take a peek? Or kiss me now and see whether or not you're right?"

He was baiting her, but she wanted to bite. Reaching one hand out, she grasped the back of his neck with a slight dig of her nails in his skin and closed the gap to kiss him. She pulled his bottom lip between hers with a gentle tug before releasing him and backing away. The intensity in his eyes made her wonder if he was upset. With an abrupt turn, she spun on her heel and started up the steps. If she remained facing him, then he'd see the flare of need she felt building within her. It was better to turn away, distracting herself with the reveal of the room in the loft.

Over her shoulder, she called, "Come on. No secrets between *soulmates,* right?"

He appeared at the top of the staircase before she made it to the last step.

Her cheeks flushed when he leaned in to whisper, "I'd be honored to show you our suite." The word *our* conjured a vision of her permanently living with him, and she wasn't as put off at the idea as she should be.

Like a grander version of the bedroom he was staying in downstairs, this room had a high ceiling, lush furniture in rich gem tones, and dark oak touches. Not a speck of dust to be seen. A few well-placed art pieces decorated the walls, and there were books stacked next to a bedside table lamp. Giddiness fluttered in her chest as she imagined herself waking up in the soft sheets, stepping over the woven rugs, and running a hot bath in the large porcelain tub.

She ran her fingers along the back of a velvet settee. "Did you move downstairs to keep an eye on your captive? Worried I'd sneak off in the night?"

Facing her, he said, "I wanted to be close to you. And sorry to disappoint, but my hidden vaults aren't connected to this room."

Laughing, she headed towards the door. "I've seen enough. Let's get to that workout."

"I'll portal us." He held out his hand, then transported them to a bench near the indoor track. Surprised by the ease of the portal, she'd expected her stomach to revolt as it typically did. Instead, she smiled at the looseness in her shoulders.

"I'll get us water and towels. Start without me." Hades gave her a nod then jogged towards the locker room.

Skipping a warm-up stretch, Persephone jogged along the clay track. The cool, piney air hit her lungs as she found her pace. A prickly sensation needled her skin, but she fought those first uncomfortable moments that running ignited. She pushed through, her feet pounding on the path and the woody scent of the rafters fading into a powdery, floral smell. She carried on, but her vision faltered, and she stumbled early into her jog. This type of strain wasn't normal.

Confused, she shook out her limbs. Once her vision returned to normal and her head wasn't spinning, she walked.

In the distance, the flare of something red trailed around the track. Scattered along the path she'd run were thousands of bright red poppies.

"*Titans*," she breathed out.

Hades' approaching footsteps sounded. "Sephy, are you alright?"

While she gaped at the flowers crowning the track, Hades held her shoulders and checked her face. "Persephone, are you okay?"

Her attention snapped to him. "Yes, I..." she replied. Her skin tingled but her breathing resumed its normal rhythm. Her arms relaxed at the point of his contact. "I'm fine. I got lightheaded, then I noticed this." She gestured at the poppies.

He kept his eyes on hers and then searched her face before he turned to see the flowers. "Wow," he said. "Everywhere you ran, they've sprung up."

She nodded. "Why?"

"I think it's your power, love. It appears you can grow flowers... well, poppies to be more specific. They're quite beautiful."

"Not sure how poppies help anything..." If she was going to have a power, couldn't it have been something better than creating flowers from her footsteps? A stab of disappointment hit her gut. Her mom could grow fields upon fields of produce. Why couldn't she do something incredible like Demeter? Or Hecate, with her mastery of magic?

"I think it's only the start of what you can do."

CHAPTER TWENTY SIX

FORMER ALLEGIANCE

PERSEPHONE

Clicking her pen, Persephone half-listened to the Marketing Director.

"Upbeat, happy, convenient," he droned. "Producers may test your confidence with rumors about tech issues, so speak decisively…"

Persephone tuned out, already knowing the script: assert the importance of testing. Across the table, Hades caught her eye and winked. She smirked.

Charon appeared at the frosted glass door. "Lunch is here."

Persephone's stomach growled as she shut her notebook, following the group out. Hades held the door, leaning in as she passed. "Bored already, little goddess?" he whispered, his voice dangerously low.

She arched a brow. "You're not?"

He chuckled, but his eyes held a hint of something darker as he turned to Charon, who handed him a folder.

"Here's the report you requested. Hecate is ready to meet in five minutes," Charon said. "Persephone, Hermes is here to see you in the lobby."

Hades and Persephone parted ways and she headed off to meet her former assistant in the ground-floor lobby. Rumblings from her empty stomach demanded that she grab her meal first, but she hadn't seen Hermes since the meeting in Zeus' office. Hermes was always speedy. It'd be quick, she was sure.

The elevator doors opened to the busy lobby, and Hermes, dressed in an off-white sweater and gray slacks, waved with a grin. "Persephone! I've missed you."

She hugged him, catching the familiar scent of his rosemary hair oil. "I've missed you too. How's life working for Zeus?"

Hermes pretended to adjust an invisible tie. "Living the dream." He led her to a quieter hallway.

Persephone laughed. "Any backlash from DB?" The acronym felt foreign on her tongue.

Hermes shrugged. "Your mom was fine with it. Zeus' orders."

Strange. Demeter didn't let go of people easily, but Persephone pushed the thought aside.

Hermes' smile faltered, eyes darting over her shoulder. "Your mom misses you, but… that's not why I'm here."

Persephone's curiosity spiked. "Then why?" His anxious fidgeting set her on edge.

"I need a favor," he said, lowering his voice. "It has to stay between us. Not even Eurydice or Hades can know."

Her eyes widened. "Is it illegal?"

He hesitated. "Maybe… sort of. It depends."

"Spill," she demanded, heart pounding with equal parts worry and intrigue.

"There's someone on Eurydice's dev team that I've been seeing." Not what she expected him to say. His darting gaze caused a tremble in her gut.

"Oh? What's their name?" she asked.

"Sophia. You may have already met her."

She had. As the new Chief Product Officer, she'd introduced herself to all of Eurydice's team.

Hermes continued, "We've seen each other a few times. It's been great, but she's been different since I saw something on her phone."

Persephone leaned closer to Hermes. "What did you see?" Knowing him, he'd snooped.

"I couldn't read all of it, but I saw my name. Remember that guy, Thaddeus, I was seeing two years ago?"

How could she forget? That ex of Hermes had broken things off with him—very loudly—at a product launch party. Hermes wasn't entirely innocent, but things were said that now haunted Hermes.

"Is she seeing *him*?" Persephone asked.

"I hope not, but I don't know. It was his name I saw on her phone and when she saw me looking, she was quick to hide it."

"I mean… can you blame her? Maybe she was seeing him and now she wants a clean break and doesn't want to bring you into their parting drama? It might not be as nefarious as you think." At least Persephone hoped that was true.

Hermes shook his head. "When I asked her about it, she said don't worry. I tried to pry, but she kept dodging my questions."

"Sounds like she doesn't want to tell you. You have to let it go until she changes her mind."

Sighing, Hermes tilted his head back. "It's so stupid, but I really care for her and need to know what it said."

Her brow furrowed. If Persephone was in his spot, she'd feel the same way. Tortured over what an ex said about her to a new lover. It sounded maddening. Thankfully she'd never been with anyone long enough for their parting to be anything but amicable. Usually, she'd lost interest, and they'd hated how busy she was with work.

"You want me to try to read her texts?"

Hermes nodded.

"Fates. That's asking a lot. I'm not sure I could even pull that off if I wanted to." Deep within her, she felt the stirring of her magic. Could she try to use her powers to help him? It was too risky and her ability was questionable at best. What if she caused a scene making errant poppies sprout around the cubicles. She embraced the humming in her veins but only enough to calm herself.

His mouth fell into a flat line as his eyes settled on hers. "Of course you could. You're the spokesperson for the app she's working on. Ask her to take a photo with you to post on social media then say you left your phone behind. Snap the photo and tell her you'll put your contact info in, then check the message."

What a rascal! He'd clearly thought through this scheme already. "*Hermes,* that's too many lies and some sleight of hand."

"*Please,* Persephone." Was Hermes making puppy eyes at her?

She stared at the floor, wracking her brain for something better—or at least less daft—of a plan to suggest to him.

"I'll bring you in," Persephone said. "I'll distract her; you check the phone."

Hermes nodded, tension easing slightly. "But make sure she can't see me. I only need a minute."

With closed eyes, Persephone tried to calm her heart as it rattled around her chest like a squirrel who'd been plucked off a branch and shoved into a purse. "Okay, I'll do it. When are we doing this?"

"Right now," Hermes said, nervously running his fingers through his curly hair.

"Charon just brought lunch; she's probably eating with her team..." Persephone thought for a moment. "I'll see if the dev team will follow me into the conference room for a few candid photos. I'll say I want to save them for teasers on my social accounts. Marketing wanted me to start taking a few candid shots anyway."

"Perfect. Let's go."

They ascended back up to the office floor, her stomach now growling in worry and not hunger. During the short ride up, Hermes updated her on how her former team was doing, but she could feel the buzz of his anticipation.

"Wait over there." Persephone pointed towards a hot beverage bar where Hermes could watch but remain hidden. From there, he could see her take the group into the conference room, then could scurry off towards the lunch area.

Her heels tapped the concrete floor, loose pants swooshing as she approached the dev team. Eurydice waved, and Persephone forced a smile, trying to ignore the sweat gathering under her arms. She could pull this off, even with her heart pounding like a drum.

"Hey, Eurydice. Could I get a quick photo with you and the dev team in the conference room? It's booked the rest of the day, but no one's in there now and the lighting's fantastic."

Eurydice dabbed the corners of her mouth with a napkin before standing up. "We'd be happy to." Of course she would. After their first quick conversation in the Underworld office, Eurydice had made an effort to win back Persephone's favor after playing a role in Hades' trickery.

A few confused faces gawked at Persephone, but they all rose after setting down their food. When Persephone saw Sophia go to reach for her phone, she quickly instructed, "Leave your stuff! It'll be fast, I promise."

Sophia nodded and set her phone back down on the table. *I can do this.*

"Thank you. Follow me." Persephone waved them along.

Like little ducklings following their wayward mom, the team walked towards the conference room. As they filed in, Persephone said, "Sit around the table and talk about your favorite food." A few raised eyebrows were sent her way, but they obliged nonetheless.

With a glance over her shoulder, she caught the blur of Hermes headed towards the break room. This was stupid. Hermes had his share of mishaps, but this had to be the most ridiculous one yet.

The developers found seats around the long table, and Persephone guided them to gather in a way where she could get all of them into one shot. Once she finished directing them into position, she balanced her phone using its pop-out stand.

"It'll keep snapping photos so just keep talking to each other." *What a farce.* She was a phony and surely this group would rather be anywhere but in this conference room, pretending to be stock photo models. She waited as long as she could before the awkwardness grew so heavy it'd suffocate them all.

She checked her phone to look at the photos she never intended to use. "Fantastic. Thanks, everyone." They gave her polite smiles, but Eurydice lingered as her team left the conference room.

"Are you worried about the app?" Eurydice asked, voice shaky. "Everything's breaking at once."

Persephone forced a reassuring smile. "It's normal to have issues before launch. We'll figure it out."

Eurydice's eyes dropped. "It almost feels like sabotage."

Persephone felt a rise of anxiety, but she kept her expression calm. "Persistence will pay off. Trust me."

Persephone tried not to shudder. Who could be behind it? One of Hades' brothers?

My mom?

Shaking herself from her own worry, Persephone added, "Eurydice. The part where you feel like giving up or quitting is when you're the closest to having your breakthrough. Keep moving forward and trust that you'll get to the bottom of the issue before the app goes live. It sounds like there are lots of brilliant minds working alongside yours, so I have every confidence it'll be sorted before you know it."

Eurydice gave a small smile and nodded. "Thanks. I hope we figure things out fast before the team loses hope."

"You will." Persephone squeezed Eurydice's arm. "Let's get you back to your lunch."

With a soft chuckle, Eurydice opened the door, and Persephone followed her through.

"I'll catch up with you soon," Persephone called out as she headed towards the hot beverage counter where the unopened box housing her sandwich sat.

Lunch in hand, she scanned the main office space, looking for Hermes. She checked her phone and released her breath when she saw a message from him.

HERMES

All good! THX!

When she looked up from her phone, Persephone's breath caught in her throat. Hades stood barely a step away, arms crossed, his shadow looming over her like a storm cloud.

"Photoshoot in the conference room?" he asked, suspicion lacing his voice.

"Perfect lighting." She shrugged, despite her pounding heart, and forced a calm smile. In a desperate attempt to convince him, she tried to push a calming warmth from her chest using her magic. She lifted her sandwich and asked, "Lunch?"

He studied her, then nodded. "Join me in my office."

Her stomach twisted, but she managed to keep her shoulders relaxed as she walked past him.

CHAPTER TWENTY SEVEN

THE ICE IN HIS VEINS

HADES

The blue-tabbed folder on his desk held proof: Demeter had meddled with the *Flowers Near Me* app, infecting it with a virus Hecate aptly named "snake bite." Its magic spread like venom, slowly poisoning the app from the inside. Demeter had planted a beta tester to sabotage his project, a revelation confirmed after the traitor was granted immunity by Hades' legal team.

But now, a bigger problem loomed. Persephone had snuck Hermes into the building and distracted the development team. Hades clenched his mug, ice spreading over the ceramic. His power, laced with anger, threatened to burst through the walls. Yet, across from him, Persephone seemed unfazed, eating her sandwich. How did she remain so unreadable?

Hades took a breath, his fingers drumming on the folder. "I have news."

Persephone's eyes narrowed. "Yes?"

"It's about *Flowers Near Me,*" he said, his voice low and

measured. "We know what the problem is, and Eurydice should be able to fix it."

She nodded, her expression cool and collected. "That's good to hear. Will it be a quick fix or a bigger issue?"

Hades studied her. "We'll know after I speak with her." Her floral scent drifted toward him—usually pleasant but now bitter on his tongue.

"Good thing you and Eurydice have worked in the shadows together before," she added, her voice laced with sarcasm. Beneath her calm facade, there was fire.

Hades rose, shedding his suit jacket and draping it over his chair. "Speaking of old friends," he said, his tone darkening, "was it nice seeing your former assistant?"

Persephone paused mid-bite, eyes flickering. "Come again?"

"Hermes." Hades sank back into his chair, crossing his ankle over his knee. "Did you enjoy catching up?"

She swallowed, nearly choking. "Right. Yes. It was fine."

Hades' lips pressed into a thin line. "Persephone," he said, his voice dropping into a growl, and she shivered. He leaned forward, elbows resting on his knees, eyes locked on hers. "Tell me why you cleared the dev team out of the break room. The *real* reason."

She exhaled sharply. "The lighting was good. I wanted a picture."

"Try again," he said, his voice sharp enough to cut. His anger was palpable, the temperature in the room dropping further. "Why did you help Hermes access Sophia's phone?"

Persephone rolled her shoulders, meeting his gaze with defiance. "It's irrelevant."

"My brother's errand boy came into the building, then checked one of the key developer's phones." His voice rose in volume with each word. "It's very relevant given that we had a breach that threatened the existence of the app."

She made a breathy noise from the back of her throat. "It has no relevance to that or the app itself."

"You won't tell me?"

"If Charon or Hecate asked you to keep a secret, and you promised, would you keep your word or betray their trust?"

"What about *my* trust?" Pain and anger filled every syllable. The glass windows creaked as frost spread over the panes, catching Persephone's attention. Her slender neck flexed before she met his eyes again.

When no reply came from her, he scoffed. "It doesn't matter what you promised him. You gave him access to a member of our team's phone and then tried to hide it."

"He's Zeus' messenger... or *errand boy,* as you said. He's free to come and go as he pleases." She wasn't yelling, but her voice was starting to match the volume of his.

He bent forward at eye level with Persephone. "He's free to move at the behest of the gods and goddesses. Tell me, little goddess, did *you* send him off on a task? And if not, whose business was it? Because he didn't come to deliver a message. He snuck in to spy."

She stiffened. "I don't have any information that is of value to you. You can either take that at face value and trust me, or take whatever recompense you need in order to satisfy your security protocols. If you're not going to do either one of those things, then I think it's a good time for me to finish my lunch elsewhere." She packed the remaining half of her sandwich into the box then rested her interlocked her hands on top of it.

Hades' mouth twisted into a sneer. "Get out." He gestured with his chin towards the door, straightened his back, then unlocked his computer.

Without a sound, Persephone stood up and left while Hades kept his eyes on his screen. At the sound of his office door shutting, he held his head in his hands and swallowed hard.

A throbbing pulse banged his temple and disappointment

stabbed his chest. He sat up again and grabbed his phone, determined to deal with his anger later. Why wouldn't she tell him the truth?

He texted Hecate.

HADES

Bring Hermes to my office.

Both the young messenger and the Goddess of Sorcery appeared before him in a flash.

"Take a seat, Hermes," he said. Hermes promptly dropped into the seat.

Eyes locked on his computer, Hades pulled up the lobby's security feed and rewound to the moment Persephone and Hermes had started talking.

Sweating and shivering, Hermes squirmed in the chair. "Hades, I didn't mean any harm! I just wanted to check Sophia's text from an old ex of mine—"

Hades held out his palm. Wisps of his power leaked from his hand and squeezed Hermes until he released a pain-filled cry. "Don't lie to me. Why were you in my building?"

"Do you know Sophia? On Eurydice's team?"

He gave a single nod but didn't loosen the strangling grip his power kept on Hermes' torso.

Gasping for air, Hermes managed to say, "W—we've been seeing each other then, one night, I saw my ex had texted her."

Hades scowled. "Hermes, are you telling me you had Persephone help you into a secure area so you could check your lover's text messages? Because if so, then it's the dumbest thing I've heard all year. And think about that because your boss is my brother and by now you know what an idiot he can be."

Hermes released a weak groan. "I know it's dumb, but I needed to know what my ex said." Hermes sucked in a long breath as Hades loosened his power's grip.

"And that was reason enough for Persephone to let you in and compromise the app she's promoting?"

Hands shaking, Hermes waved and shook his head. "Shit! No, it's not like that. I asked her because I knew she'd help me. I just wanted to read the text."

Hades rubbed the bridge of his nose. It was a tempting story to believe because it exonerated Sephy from any major wrong-doing. Sure, she shouldn't have just let Hermes in, but if she was simply covering for a friend, insecure in his relationship, then Hades' rising fears of her possible treachery may not be true.

"What did you see on Sophia's phone?" Hades picked up his phone.

HADES

Bring Sophia's phone to my office. Tell her I'm doing random security checks.

CHARON

Got it.

"My ex told her I shouldn't be trusted and would cheat on her the second I lost interest," said Hermes.

Hades raised his brows at him. "Well, is that true?"

"What do you mean?"

"Is your ex telling the truth? Would you do that?" Now he was toying with Hermes. A little out of spite for causing the ruckus, but also curious if one of his developers was headed towards a messy break-up.

"I-er... no," Hermes replied, as his eyes danced around the room. Hecate laughed from the corner.

Charon opened his office door, and Hades greeted her with a nod.

"Here." She handed him the phone. He hovered his hand over the device, unlocking it then opening her messages.

"What's your ex's name?" he asked Hermes.

"Thaddeus."

He typed the name into the search bar, and "Thad" popped up in the results. He opened the thread and read a message very similar to Hermes' version. The only part Hermes had left out was the fact that Sophia had reached out to her friend Thad, asking if Hermes was the guy who'd cheated on him a couple of years ago.

Hades locked the phone, then handed it back to Charon. "Tell her all clear."

Charon nodded and headed out.

"Hecate, thank you for your help."

Hecate wiggled her fingers at Hermes, who shrunk back in fear. "Until we meet again," she said, then disappeared in a cloud of smoke.

"You're done seeing Sophia. Find someone outside my company, and if you involve Persephone in another stunt, my brother will be scraping you off Underworld's walls."

Hermes nodded. "Yes, sir. I'm sorry."

"Leave," Hades commanded, sending him through a portal to Zeus' office. He didn't care if Zeus was irritated by the intrusion.

Hades leaned back, exhaustion and frustration gnawing at him. He'd accused Persephone of betrayal, but perhaps she hadn't meant any real harm. Still, he'd needed to be sure.

Rushing out of his office, he approached the developer, Sophia, offering her a warning to stay clear of Hermes. Then, with a heavy heart, he made his way to the conference room, hoping he hadn't destroyed the fragile trust between him and Persephone.

But when she met his gaze with a glare, his heart sank.

Damn it.

CHAPTER TWENTY EIGHT

FLOWERS NEAR ME

PERSEPHONE

*I*f Persephone could've melted Hades with her glare, she'd have done it without a second thought.

But her anger soon drained, leaving only guilt and embarrassment behind. What had she expected—Hades to laugh it off? Hermes wasn't there on business and hadn't been invited. The more she reasoned and rationalized Hades' reaction, the sicker she felt at her petulance.

I pouted like a Fates-damned child.

Now she sat in an acrid wasteland of shame. Hades kept his eyes averted since she'd pierced them with hers, and now he scrolled on his phone. The marketing team resumed their presentation and moved on to preparations for the social events that would begin after they'd recorded their interviews. A few appearances around the city at choice vendors and public spaces, then ending with a massive gala to celebrate the launch.

As the marketing team outlined the gala's events, Persephone scribbled jagged lines in her notebook, her stomach churning with regret.

Why did I think I could get away with it? And Hermes? Did Hades find him? What did he say?

Knowing Hermes, he probably spilled out the truth the way she should have as soon as she'd sat in Hades' office.

She'd almost done it—told him everything with the hope he'd be merciful. Instead, she held fast to the story she'd conjured. She dug her heel into her foot, using the sting to steady her nerves.

There was a small part of her that felt her actions were justified. Hermes was a loyal and dear ally. He was far from perfect, but so was she. And years of working together had bonded them as work siblings and true friends. It wasn't fair to him if she blabbed about his romantic troubles—no matter how small. She'd known Hermes for fifteen years and had lived with Hades for a little over two months.

She flicked her gaze back to Hades, who was watching the presentation, but turned his head towards her as if he sensed her attention. She gave him a weak smile, which he returned with his own, along with a playful wink.

After the marketing presentation concluded a little while later, Persephone asked Hades to step into her office.

As soon as her door closed, she turned to Hades who was standing nearby. "I'm sorry I lied about Hermes. It was immature and reckless."

Hades paused, then nodded. "I appreciate that. No hard feelings, though I'm more annoyed that Hermes exploited your kindness."

"He's loyal, if nothing else," she said, managing a small laugh.

Hades' mouth quirked. "A meddlesome imp, more like."

Persephone's smile faltered, but she pressed on. "I mean it—I jeopardized everything. Underworld Unlimited deserves better."

His eyes softened, but the tick of his jaw betrayed lingering tension. "All is forgiven, Sephy," he said, though she couldn't help but wonder if he truly meant it.

Was he angry that she hadn't opened up to him? He told her afterwards that Hermes immediately spilled out the whole truth. If Hermes had no problem telling him, shouldn't she have confessed when he first asked? But if she'd asked Hermes to keep a secret for her, she knew he would've, damn the consequences.

Strangely enough, she cared about how Hades felt about her sneaking Hermes into the office. And when faced with the reality of what could have happened to the rest of the team if security was breached by someone nefarious, her palms sweated. Wasn't she better at thinking these things through?

"Thank you. I'm glad we talked about this," she said. Regret coiled around her chest, and she swore she felt the inkling of her magic stirring within her.

THE NEXT WEEK, before Hades and Persephone's first interview, flew by in a rush of meetings, presentations, and media training. Although that last bit was for Persephone only; Hades went off somewhere else during those sessions. It might've been the only real time he got to fulfill his other duties. How he had managed to keep Underworld Unlimited humming along while giving the lion's share of his attention to *Flowers Near Me*, she had no clue.

Today, they both waited in the green room for the producers to summon them for their first interview. The headache Persephone had woken up with that morning pounded in her temple, so she'd drunk enough coffee and water to kill a camel.

Hades squeezed her hand. "Something bothering you?"

"Oh, this headache. I can't get it to go away," she answered.

Two lines formed between his brows. "Let me check you."

She nodded. He grazed her temples with his fingertips, and she closed her eyes at the touch. More than the smell of his power filled her senses—she could *feel* a cool wave coat her skin. The pain in her head subsided as the chill on her brow turned to warmth.

"Any better?" Hades asked.

"Yes, thank you. What did you do?"

"I blessed you. It doesn't always work on pain, but I'm pleased to know it did this time."

A knock on their door and a producer shouted, "They're ready for you!"

Persephone and Hades got up from the couch. As Persephone reached behind her to pocket her phone, she saw tiny green buds sprouting from the cushion.

Bending down, she brushed her hand over the tiny sprigs, and they grew into full poppy blooms.

"*Titans*," she hissed and snap her attention to Hades. "Why is this happening?"

Hades tilted his head to get a look and let out a light chuckle. "You're blossoming." He smiled at her, but her glare had him clarifying, "I don't know why, but they're impressive. No minor goddess could conjure a living thing like this from nothing. By the Fates, I'm not certain my brothers or I could either."

It was quite the compliment coming from a powerful god, but that didn't mean it was true. She reached for her power, imagining it centered in her heart, and only felt a dull buzz. Did it even matter if she had magic or not if she couldn't harness it?

PERSEPHONE'S FACE hurt from laughing during the morning interview. It turned out that the first reporter they spoke with was a former classmate of hers from grade school. During media training, Persephone thought the photo of the woman looked familiar but didn't recognize her last name. As soon as she went to greet Persephone on set, she gave her maiden name and it clicked.

With more energy than she had at the start of the day, Persephone went back to the green room to gather her bag and thermos. Halfway slumped on the couch—which still had a garden of poppies blooming on it—was a passed-out crew member.

"Oh Fates!" She rushed to the crew member's side to check her face. Thankfully, she was still breathing, but despite Persephone shaking the woman's shoulders and calling to her, she didn't wake.

"Help!" she shouted, and Hades appeared next to her.

"Hades, I can't get her to wake up. Are there medics here?"

Hades narrowed his eyes on the unconscious crew member, then placed his palm on her cheek. "She's alive, but..." He sniffed the air and pursed his lips. "I think she's been poisoned."

"*Oh Fates... oh Fates...* I'll call the hospital." Fumbling with her phone, she dialed the emergency number. As she relayed the scene to the dispatcher and flagged down a producer—who knew the studio's address—Hades moved the unconscious woman to a different couch, away from the poppy-covered one.

The producer checked on his crew mate, then stared at the poppies. "Why is the furniture covered in flowers?" He stepped closer to examine them, but his legs buckled beneath him, and he crumpled to the floor.

Persephone and Hades shot a look at one another.

"It's the poppies, Sephy. Let's get both of them out of this room."

With her phone still pressed to one ear, she nodded. Hades carried out the two studio employees. They waited with the unconscious pair and a small group of staff who'd gathered to check on them before the medics arrived. Within minutes of treatment, both parties were awake and coherent.

In a low whisper, Hades said to Persephone, "Your poppies, Sephy. I think they may emit a poisonous fume."

"I was worried that was it." Her face went hot and sweat broke out against her skin. This was terrible. Not only could she not control her magic, but it was the kind that could harm others. She was dangerous. Would this mean she could no longer visit her niece, Helena? How could she trust herself around the girl if she knocked out grown adults? Somehow, both her and Hades were fine. "Why weren't we affected?"

Hades shrugged. "Well, you'd be immune to your own poison, I'd think, and I'm your soulmate so it wouldn't harm me."

"*Hades.*" She groaned. "We need to get rid of those flowers, but I don't know how."

He caressed her shoulders, then said, "Leave it to me, love."

Stepping into the green room, he released dark, billowy smoke from his hands and all the poppies turned to dust. Like sand funneling down an hourglass, the remaining powder traveled towards Hades' shoes. He conjured a glass vial and held it close to the floor. The dusty remnants near his feet gathered in a tornado and flew right into the small glass enclosure. Corking the vial, he handed it to Persephone. "Want to keep it? Poison can come in handy, you know."

Her mouth flew open. "No! Just get rid of it."

With a snap, the vial disappeared, and Hades laughed. "Poisonous flowers. That's quite a gift, little goddess."

Persephone crossed one arm over her stomach and covered her mouth. *I could've killed those two people.* Bile rose in her throat, but she closed her eyes and tried to will it back down. "They could've died."

"You think so? It looks like they passed out from a sedative. And even if they had, we could've fixed that." Sometimes Persephone forgot that life and death were trivial to the gods, like the flip of a switch. Not Persephone, though. Killing wasn't in her nature. *Or is it?*

Was she the opposite of her mother, a force of ruin instead of life?

"Sephy? Let's call off the next interview and go back home. You've been under immense pressure and anyone in your position would need a break." Hades pushed her hair back from her face, then rubbed her shoulder.

"No. Let's check on those two and then finish the afternoon interview." Stopping after the first interview wasn't an option for her. It would take more than a scare to keep her from completing the workday.

Other than some lingering lightheadedness, both the crew member and producer said they felt fine. Apologies spilled from Persephone, but neither one was upset with her. Their graciousness made her feel worse. Couldn't they be angry with her? She'd poisoned them, for Fate's sake. A little anger wouldn't hurt.

One of the crew members kept repeating that she was honored to be *blessed by Olympus' newest goddess.* Sweat beaded on Persephone's brow at the assertion. She wasn't a goddess. She was Persephone—the executive who liked gardening, spending time with her sister and niece, and spent too many hours wasting time on her phone. The poppies were a fluke, nothing more. She just needed to remain calm and move past this.

CHAPTER TWENTY NINE

PINNED, TAILORED, UNDONE

PERSEPHONE

$\mathcal{I}$n the cramped fitting room, Persephone traced the off-shoulder sleeves and sweetheart neckline of the black ballgown. The tailor worked beside her, pinning the side seam with meticulous precision. It was stunning. She couldn't wait to see Hades' reaction to it. His compliments on her everyday outfits felt lavish. This was going to blow his mind.

It had been over two weeks since her first interview, and she was grateful that no more unexpected poppies had appeared. Under Hecate's daily guidance, she'd learned to summon and banish the flowers, mastering her magic one poisonous petal at a time.

"Do you realize you're officially halfway through the term of your six-month contract?" Charon asked, holding her tablet and swiping through what Persephone assumed were an array of calendars.

As instructed by the tailor, Persephone twisted side to side, making the dress fan and sway. Fluttering black petals sewn to cover her chest waved along. She answered, "That's not possible. I thought I had at least a week or more before I was halfway."

Charon leaned against the wall, giving the tailor room to work around Persephone. "If you count the gala as the final date, then no, you're not halfway. But remember, under the original terms, you have no legal obligation to attend." Charon didn't look up from her tablet, and Persephone sensed a slight strain in her voice. Was Charon worried she wouldn't attend? Or was she suggesting that Persephone miss it? She hoped it was the former, as the assistant was becoming a welcome companion at these events.

Lifting her arms so the tailor could adjust the floral appliqués of the bodice, Persephone said, "I'm going to the gala, don't worry. I can't wait for the app to launch—I think it'll take off fast."

"You and Hades have done your part to get the word out."

"We all did, Charon. And how is Eurydice?"

"Better now. The 'snake bite' forced her to rewrite a significant portion of the code, but her team got it working again."

"I can't wait to see the newest version and how much it's changed."

"*Which fitting room?*" Both Persephone and Charon's attention snapped to the familiar deep voice outside the closed fitting room door.

Persephone gawked at Charon. She couldn't believe he'd showed up here. "Can you stall him?" *Would he portal into the fitting room?!*

Charon's hand was on the doorknob before Persephone finished her question. "On it."

"How close are you to finishing?" Persephone asked the tailor.

"Just one more minute and we'll be set. It's mostly there." She tapped the waist of Persephone's dress. "How's it feel?"

"Perfectly tailored." Persephone smiled at her. The tailor smiled back with a few pins pinched in between her teeth.

She heard Charon's muffled voice from the other side of the door. "You're supposed to be uptown for a meeting. Why are you here?"

Hades laughed. "Oh, so *that's* why I was booked across town today."

"What happened to your meeting with the director, then?" Charon asked, and the door frame creaked as something or someone pushed against it from the other side.

"We finished early. Shocking, right? Try to contain your excitement." Persephone pictured the smug look he probably wore on his face, matching his mocking tone.

Charon replied, "That *is* great. Now you can get back to the office. Hecate has urgent items for you to approve."

"Good idea. I'll just check on Sephy then head there." Hades gave three knocks before shouting, "Sephy, I'd like to see your gala dress."

One locked door was nothing to a god. Hades could've portaled in by now, so he must've wanted permission. That knowledge didn't stop Persephone from covering her chest with crossed arms despite being already clothed by the midnight flowers decorating the bodice.

"As soon as the tailor's done, you can come in."

"Finished," said the tailor who began gathering her things.

Carefully pinching the satin fabric nearest her knees, Persephone lifted her skirt and stepped off the miniature platform. Hanging on a hook, a silk robe was within reach. She grabbed it, then quickly threw it on and tied the belt with shaky hands. Was she ready for him to see the dress?

Equally excited and terrified, Persephone opened the door and the tailor left.

Hades' face lit with joy. "Sephy, it's wonderful to see you."

Hades held out his hands and gave her a chaste kiss on each cheek. "May I see the dress?"

Cross-armed behind him, Charon said, "No. She's already told you she wants it to be a surprise, so off you go."

Looking past Hades at Charon, Persephone said, "It's alright. I've changed my mind, Charon. Give us five minutes." She appreciated Charon having her back, but she was too curious to see his reaction.

Leaning in to whisper in Persephone's ear, a smirk on his face, Hades said, "We'll need more than five minutes, love. I *am* a god."

Persephone laughed. "It's fine, really. I've got a plan."

Hades cocked an eyebrow at her while Charon threw her a stiff nod and closed the door.

"Alright," Hades said, his tone light and playful. "What's this plan of yours? Does it involve me helping you out of that dress? Because, trust me, I'm exceptional with my hands."

"No," Persephone replied with a sly grin. "It's even better. I'll show you the dress today, but only if..." She trailed off, letting the anticipation build.

"Only if?" he prompted, leaning in.

"You agree to grant me a future favor. No questions asked. Deal?"

His mouth pressed into a thoughtful line. "That's quite the price."

"I know. So, what's it going to be? See the dress now and owe me, or step out and apologize to Charon? Actually, you should apologize to her regardless."

Hades studied her, a flicker of intrigue in his expression. "Fine. One favor, Sephy. Now, let me see the dress."

"And the apology to Charon?" she pressed.

He sighed, mumbling, "Yes, yes."

Persephone reached for the robe's silk tie, but Hades caught her hands. "Let me," he murmured, his voice a seductive promise.

A rush of adrenaline climbed its way from her stomach to her throat and she gave a small nod. Her breath stopped as he undid the hastily tied bow and dropped the strands to the sides. His fingers skimmed along her collarbone, pushing the silk robe over her bare shoulders and down past the delicate sleeves. His eyes wide and appreciative and his mouth parted, he laid her robe over his shoulder.

He gripped her waist, lifting her in a smooth motion. Feet off the floor and her long silk skirt billowing as he turned her. She clutched his forearms, but his suit jacket slipped over the fabric of his shirt underneath, causing her grip to falter. It didn't matter because he held her steady and placed her on the pedestal she had stood on moments ago.

Unable to make a sound, she pressed her waist where his hands had just been to feel the shadow of his touch. The simple woven satin across her hips somehow stayed in place when he lifted her, and the black skirt cascaded elegantly towards the floor. When she met his eyes, they were rapt on the dress. Focused as if he were disarming a bomb, Hades' gaze traveled over the intricate bodice and sweetheart neckline.

"I'm never letting you go, Sephy. Now that I've seen how perfectly you belong in my world, there's no escape." Hades stared with the barest hint of a smile gracing his lips.

Persephone straightened her shoulders. "Sounds like you approve, then. Well, I'm glad. Now you need to leave so I can change. And don't think for a second that I'll forget about that favor you owe me."

"With all those pins, you'll need some help getting out of that dress." He tilted his head, his gaze lingering on her hands as a playful smirk curved his lips. "At least let me have the pleasure of unfastening it before I go."

She could undo the buttons at the back of the bodice

without a fuss or have him call Charon or the tailor back in to help. But she didn't want to. Here, he'd offered assistance and even gave her an excuse to have his hands on her again.

Before he could see just how red her face was at the prospect of him undressing her, she said, "That'd be helpful. Thank you."

She cupped the underwire to lift some weight off the buttons while turning her back to him. His fingers brushed the space between her shoulders as he slowly unclasped the top, then took his time undoing each tiny button and exposing more of her back. Soft, warm touches of his fingers skimming along her spine sent her heart racing. He moved leisurely and she felt every touch of his knuckles tracing a path.

Ready to tell him to stop as he neared her hips, he kissed the back of her neck while squeezing her waist. Then he went towards the closed door.

Holding the handle, he turned over his shoulder with a mischievous smile and said, "Every god and goddess in Olympus will envy me standing beside you at the gala." His voice lowered to a gravelly whisper. "If I kissed you again, I'd be tempted to ruin that gorgeous dress just to feel you beneath it."

Without another word, he opened the door and stepped out, taking her breath with him.

CHAPTER THIRTY

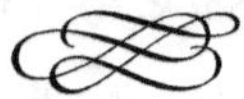

A HOPE IN FATE

HADES

"*H*ermes." The clipped greeting did little to console the fidgeting messenger in his office, but that wasn't Hades' problem.

"You summoned me?"

Hades leaned over his desk to bend closer to Hermes' sweaty face. "I have a message for your former employer."

Hermes' eyes widened, but he remained quiet. The man's timid look coaxed a smile on Hades' face.

With his elbows leaning on his desk, Hades set his clasped hands down in front of him to see if the continued silence would prompt Hermes to spill more of his worries. When Hermes' gaze started to move around the room, Hades said, "Tell Demeter the 'snake bite' virus is dead and the app's better than ever. And, oh—" A cruel thought popped into his head. Something he knew would rattle Demeter. "One more thing. Let Demeter know Sephy's magic smells incredible."

Hermes' bewildered expression confirmed his suspicion. *Most don't know she has power.*

Sephy had denied having powers on par with the rest of the gods. Initially, he'd assumed she was lying to him to protect herself while in his domain. But the past few months had proved Sephy was only now discovering her divine abilities. Her astonishment at seeing the poppies appear was his first clue, but as she tried her hand at using her power, the newness of it all was written in the bright look on her face.

Hermes asked, "What's she the goddess of?"

Shoulders stiffening, Hades stared at Hermes for a few beats. "Maybe one day you'll get to ask her." Hades flicked his hand. "We're done." The messenger disappeared, cast out from Hades' office into Underworld Unlimited's lobby.

Hades left Sephy in the dressing room of the tailor's hours ago, but the image of her in the satin dress lingered. The way she lifted her head, back straight, and kept her eyes locked with his—unfazed by the fact he'd barged in—made him want to kiss her and never stop. She was beautiful in everything she wore, but seeing her in a gown tailored to her body made his heart pound and his pants tight.

Of course, Charon tried to hide the date and time of the final fitting from him, but she couldn't remove the transaction history from his account. Ever since the dress fitting conversation at his apartment between Sephy and Charon, he periodically checked to see if there were any boutiques listed in his ledger. One day he recognized the name of a well-known clothier and scoured Sephy's calendar for it. Realizing that Charon would schedule it as something else, he set an alert on his phone if Sephy entered the shop's location. It pinged today during his meeting with the director of Helena's school, and he fled as if the place had caught fire. Fortunately, the director was a woman of few words and seemed almost relieved that the meeting ended early.

Work was not providing enough of a distraction for him to forget the way the black silk wrapped around Sephy's waist and hips. She had the body muses raved about and artists toiled to capture. Nothing compared to her.

Finished with the interviews, but not yet time for in-person events, Hades planned to take Sephy on their proper date in a few days.

Outside his office door, the sounds of Hecate's portal magic crackled like one of Helena's "fairy slimes" she'd left at his apartment after their last dinner.

Two knocks and Hecate opened the door. "Where's Sephy?"

With a flippant toss, Hades threw one hand in the air. "Hello, Hecate. Good to see you too. I'm well. Thanks for asking."

Hecate sat in the chaise near the window and looked out at the city. "I thought I was meeting Sephy."

"Since when were you on a nickname basis?" Hades clicked open his email to see if Charon had tagged any new messages for his review.

"Well, if you're allowed to say it, then we all must be able to."

Hades turned to see the wide grin on Hecate's face.

"That so?" He laughed, and Hecate shrugged.

Hades got up to stand next to the chair Hecate sat on. "How has training been going with Sephy?"

"Slowly, but not for lack of effort. It's as if her magic is hiding."

"Strange," Hades replied. His lips pressed in a line.

Hecate asked, "Do you have any idea what sparks it? Any pattern?"

"That's the problem. It's inconsistent. I've had her try a few basic things around our place, but beyond lifting objects, nothing else has worked."

"Has she tried to portal?"

Hades' chest felt tight. "I didn't want her to get hurt. I have no clue how to teach that."

"You have no clue? Or you didn't want her to get away?" Hecate scoffed.

Lowering his brow at her, Hades said, "I don't have her chained in a dungeon. And I think she's moved on from hatred of me towards curiosity."

"Maybe she has, but sounds like Demeter hasn't. Have you told Sephy her mom sent the 'snake bite' virus?"

"Not yet." Hades stared out at the streets below and cracked his knuckles. "Do you think Sephy helped her mom infect the app?" *Titans*, he hoped not. He was desperate for her to reciprocate his feelings. The thought of her sabotaging their work together sawed a hole through his chest.

After a silent minute, Hecate repositioned herself on the chaise and said, "You've tracked all of her communications. Did anything seem strange to you?"

"Nothing stood out." Why hadn't Hecate dismissed his fears? "Do you think there's any way Demeter could've spoken with Sephy without me finding out?"

"I honestly don't know," replied Hecate.

"Between Demeter and me, I'd wager that Sephy is still more loyal to Demeter."

"Demeter's her mom, Hades. And they've worked together for a long time. But I think she's grown fond of things here at Underworld. Especially Charon."

"And me," Hades replied in a firm tone.

Hecate chuckled. "Yes, you too. I think she might actually like you despite your questionable methods to get her to spend time with you. Anyway, she doesn't strike me as the breach-of-contract type. And the worst thing she's done here was let Hermes into the building and technically, he's free to go wherever he pleases now that he's working for your brother."

"When on assignment, yes, but it wasn't smart of her to let him in without a good reason," said Hades.

"Considering how she came to work for you, I think it's the

least terrible thing she could've done. Had you done the same to any other goddess, you wouldn't have much of an app left."

With a soft laugh, Hades replied, "I suppose that's true. But I wouldn't bother with anyone else. Still, she lied to me."

"Ah, yes. And you are the God of Truth, I forgot. Anyway, have you told her your true intentions?" Hecate raised one brow and crossed her arms.

"It's… in progress."

Hecate narrowed her gaze at him.

Hades gritted his teeth.

"I wouldn't assume it's a sure thing, simply because she's warming to you now. Although I don't think she's conspiring against you, there's a lot we don't know about her. And she's been going along with your plans, but agreeableness and fondness are not the same thing."

"You're wrong, Hecate. I *know* she'll eventually agree."

Staring at him, Hecate scowled, and puffs of purple smoke trailed from her fingertips. "*How* do you know?"

With a smug look, Hades answered, "I consulted the Fates."

Hecate's eyes widened. "And they answered you? Without an invitation?"

Hades nodded. "We have an understanding."

"Do either of your brothers know you asked them about her?"

"I think Zeus does. Poseidon is too busy to care."

Hecate huffed a laugh. "I can't believe the Fates answered you."

"Like I said, we have an understanding. And I don't use them like a personal magic mirror. I wanted to know if Persephone would marry me."

"You're sure you love her?" Hecate's voice dropped lower, her face impassive except for the straining tendon in her neck. The same look she gave whenever Hades informed her of a risky endeavor he planned to pursue.

"There's no question in my mind. All the uncertainty lies with her. *Would she come willingly to work for me?* No. *Would she say yes to marrying me?* Not the first few hundred times, no. But eventually? Maybe."

"So what did the Fates say? That she *could* love you?"

"That was my second question, and they wouldn't answer me," Hades answered.

"Ouch." Hecate grimaced. "What was your first question?"

One side of his mouth quirked up. "I asked them if she was my wife. They said yes."

"When did you ask them?" Hecate turned her face towards him, the glimmer of intrigue in her deep brown eyes.

Hades returned to his desk chair and sat down. "A few weeks before I brought her here."

Hecate pressed her lips together, but her cheeks lifted as she bobbed her head. "Who knows about the Fates' pronouncement?"

"Charon, you, me." He paused and leaned back in his chair. "And Demeter. I asked for her blessing, which she refused to give. Then I told her I'd asked the Fates, and she said I was lying."

"Oh my." Hecate's gaze grew distant, as if deep in thought. "When will you tell Sephy?"

"Not until she agrees to marry me."

"Otherwise, you'd always question whether or not she would have agreed if she didn't think it was inevitable."

Hades nodded. "She was never going to work for me or spend time with me unless she was coerced. Binding her to a contract was simple. Persuading her to love me is complicated."

"Yes, but having the Fates on your side puts you at quite an advantage."

With an affirmative hum, Hades said, "It's been a comfort."

"Well, I'm relieved to hear it. I was worried about the time when she'd return to her old life. It was going to be inconvenient if I had to avoid you for months or years as you recovered from her exit, sulking around and what not."

"You'd have to avoid *me?*" Scoffed Hades.

"Yes. You're clearly smitten with her. Completely obsessed. Single-mindedly focused on winning her affection." Hecate's mouth slid into a feline smile. "I have things to do, you know. I'm working on something that involves Charon, and your heartbreak would've caused a lot of problems."

"Really? What are you and Charon working on that I'm not involved in? Last I checked, she's Sephy's and my assistant, not yours."

"I'm aware," said Hecate, "but I've found a good match for her. We both know all she does is work, so she'll never pursue love on her own. But I met another psychopomp, and he asked about her."

"It sounds more like you *stumbled* upon a match than *found* one."

Hecate laughed. "If things work out, I'm taking credit for this one."

"I hope it does." The idea of Charon dating brought warmth to his heart. Perhaps Charon would treat Hades as sweetly as she treated Sephy, if she were in love.

THE MUFFLED drone of water through pipes buzzed on the other side of Hades' guest room wall. *Sephy's taking a shower,* he thought, then hurried out to the kitchen. He grabbed the kettle and filled it from the tap. With the coffee grounds and pour-over filters in place, he lit the stove, then drummed his fingers on the countertop.

"Cerberus?" He called for his dog, but didn't see him in the living room. *Must've slept with Sephy.* He rolled his eyes, feeling ridiculous that he was jealous of the hound. Cerberus split his nights between the two of them, but the little beast was lighter on his feet every morning after staying in Sephy's room.

It had been weeks since Sephy had figured out his primary bedroom was upstairs, but she made no fuss when he remained in the guest room next to hers.

Yesterday, when he'd crashed Sephy's fitting, he had a moment where he questioned if it was a good idea. She wanted to keep it a surprise from him for the event, but he wanted an excuse to be near her. When he saw her in the gown and how hard she tried to stifle the joy in her face, he almost portaled her out of there and into his bedroom. Now he regretted it, because the image of her in that dress consumed his consciousness.

Strolling around, he plucked Cerberus' toys from the floor and shot them like a basketball into the dog's basket. He didn't use his power, simply tried to see if he could make each shot or not. When he found he'd collected them all, he summoned the entire contents of the basket, then scattered them across the room. Meandering around the furniture, he scooped up toys one by one and continued to toss them back into their container.

A shriek sounded from Sephy's room and Hades' throat caught. He portaled to her and was immediately hit with an overwhelming earthy scent. With his front paws on the bed, Cerberus was eating the garden of poppies that had sprouted all over Sephy's blanket. Wrapped in a robe with soaked hair, Sephy screamed, "Stop, Cerberus!"

Hades held out his hand, and Cerberus froze. He guided the frozen dog away from the bed, then released his hold. Cerberus sat at his feet and tilted his head from side to side.

Bending down on one knee, Hades scanned his dog by placing his hands on either side of his fur covered neck. No hint of poison or malady.

"Don't worry, he's fine," he told Sephy.

"They're poisonous. We have to get him to a vet or he's going to die," she said in a hurried breath.

Hades released a chuckle and patted Cerberus' head before rising back to his full height. He turned to Sephy, and his pulse spiked. Her wet hair trailed over her silk robe, soaking her shoulders.

His eyes snapped to hers. "Sephy, he's an immortal watchdog. He's fine."

"He's a shepherd, Hades! We need to get him to the vet. Portal him!" she yelled.

He restrained his laugh. "Listen to me. He might look like a normal dog, but this isn't his true form." Hades whistled with a trill and Cerberus barked in reply. The fluffy, merle canine grew to Hades' height and two more heads shot forth from its shoulders. Cerberus' unique, splotchy pattern remained but was in all dark grey hues now. Wisps of smoke leaked from each breath.

Looking back at a gawking Sephy, Hades said, "See? He's fine. If he wasn't, then he wouldn't be able to morph into this."

Sephy turned towards him, then closed her eyes. Her fingers flew to her temples. She muttered, "Fates kill me," before asking, "Why doesn't he look like this all the time?"

Hades cocked a brow at her and smirked. "He's a bit lazy to be honest. It takes a lot out of him to transform and remain in this shape all day, so he sticks to his smaller form. Can't say I blame him." Hades whistled again and Cerberus sunk back into the size of a regular dog.

Sephy held out a hand towards Cerberus and used the other to clutch the top of her robe. Bending at the waist, she rubbed Cerberus behind his ears. "I'm so sorry, buddy, but you can't eat those."

Swiping his hands over the flowers, Hades disintegrated them into a fine dust, which he scooped up. Out of curiosity, he smelled the remnants, expecting it to be a mix of his power's cedar scent and Sephy's floral one. Instead, it smelled like vetiver—grassy and bright. He was going to offer Sephy the powder but went rigid when he saw her staring back at him, blushing and holding her robe tight.

"I'll let you get back to it." He made a weak gesture with his fist, then portaled himself and Cerberus into the kitchen.

Looking down at his dog, he asked, "Why did you eat the flowers, Cer?"

Cerberus twisted his head back and forth and kept his big, unblinking eyes on Hades' face. Hades added, "I was looking for you earlier, you know."

Back at the stove, hot coffee in his cup, he pictured Sephy in her silk bathrobe in his main suite. It was much larger than the one she was using, and he cursed himself for not putting her in the primary suite by herself to start. It would've been the *gracious host* thing to do, but would it have pushed her over the edge? Wasn't it enough to show up on her sister's doorstep and whisk her away without the added stress of putting her in the bed he'd been sleeping in for eons?

She'd sleep there soon enough. He clung to the hope.

A little while later, Sephy emerged from her room, wearing a pressed linen dress and her hair undone in waves. Fighting the urge to grab her by the arms and kiss her, he said, "You look beautiful, love. Where are you meeting Laura?"

Sephy thanked him as he handed her a cup of coffee and replied, "At her place. Helena has a day off from school and wanted to make loukoumades."

Hades' mouth watered at the mention of the mini fried donuts. They'd pair well with the coffee he was drinking. "Sounds delicious. Please tell them all I say hello."

Slipping her feet into her flats, Sephy replied, "I will. Are you sure you can't make it?"

The night before, she'd asked him if he wanted to tag along. He did, but it had been months since Sephy had seen Laura without him around. Between their demanding press tour and

Laura's tight schedule, Sephy barely saw Laura and she deserved to have some time with her sister. Besides, he needed her distracted while he sorted out a few remaining things for their upcoming getaway trip. They'd have time together soon enough.

"Next time, I'd love to. I've never tried making them before. We could bake them here." Fussing with the cuff of his jacket, he shot her a smile.

Coat and bag in hand, Sephy smiled back. "Alright. Next time."

Hades tried to temper his grin. "Are you ready?"

Persephone nodded, then took his offered hand before he portaled both of them to Laura's front door.

CHAPTER THIRTY ONE

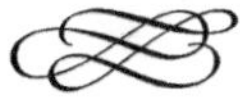

MORE THAN FLOWERY WORDS

PERSEPHONE

After rolling her thirtieth fried donut, Helena traded her apron for a tablet, leaving Persephone dusted with honeyed pistachios as she sprinkled them onto the crispy dough. Beside her, Laura fished the loukoumades from sizzling oil, setting them on paper towels.

"I'm so hungry I might risk burning my mouth," Persephone joked.

Laura laughed. "Same. I had a decent breakfast, but there's always room for sweets." She tossed more dough into the pot, the oil crackling.

Laura's eyes flicked to Helena, who sat entranced by her screen. With a careful glance back at Persephone, she asked, "So... what's going on with Hades?"

Persephone's chest tightened. "It's confusing. I'm very attracted to him, but I don't trust him. He says he cares, but the more I let my guard down, the worse it'll be when things fall apart."

Laura softened. "Are you sure it's bound to fizzle out?"

"How could it not? He's a god. This is a game to him. Even Mom, who liked your dad, discarded him. They move on faster than aphids swarming a dahlia." Persephone rolled a donut in crushed pistachios.

Laura dropped more dough into the oil. "Mom's real love is Demeter's Bounty. Hades, on the other hand, seems to prioritize you."

"As far as I know," Persephone muttered.

Laura set down the ladle. "Feelings only get stronger if you fight them. If you get bored, you walk away. Maybe it won't be so catastrophic."

"I'm not like that. If I let these feelings in, I'll create a fantasy that's not real. It's dangerous," Persephone countered.

Laura raised an eyebrow. "You? You're not the head-in-the-clouds type."

"But I *am* getting swept up," Persephone confessed. "I want to believe him. I've even been happier at Underworld Unlimited than I was at Demeter's Bounty."

"Maybe you've outgrown DB."

Persephone swallowed, a lump forming in her throat. Was she ready to leave her mother's company for good? The idea was overwhelming. "I agreed to go on a real date with him—a weekend getaway," she added.

Laura's eyes lit up. "A whole weekend?"

"Yeah, but I don't think I can handle it. If we're alone without work as a distraction, I might let my guard down."

Laura grinned. "Don't shave your legs."

"What?" Persephone laughed.

"It'll keep you from getting too cozy. Trust me," Laura said with a smirk. "Old trick."

"That's actually genius," Persephone admitted. "Why didn't you tell me before?"

Laura's smile widened. "You've never been serious about anyone before."

"Okay, fair. But I've had relationships."

"Not like this. You were never this worried about your feelings," Laura pointed out.

Persephone's shoulders slumped. "Work was my main relationship. Now that it's gone, I feel exposed."

Laura placed another batch of dough into the oil. "And yet, you've taken things slow with Hades. Have you even kissed?"

Persephone's face went hot. "We did. I thought he was going to do it for the photos during one of our fake dates, but he kissed me in private."

Laura's brows shot up. "When?"

"During a lunch date. I came out of the bathroom, and he kissed me in a quiet hallway," Persephone said, a smile sneaking onto her face. He'd kissed her in the fitting room too, but those few kisses he'd placed on her cheeks and the back of her neck felt too personal for anyone else to know about. And when she'd planted that rough kiss on him to see the lofted space… she needed to keep that one locked up tight.

Laura grinned as she set more dough into the pan. "That's actually kinda sweet."

Persephone's face lit up. "I thought so too. It was nice that it wasn't for show and he didn't wait long either. We had agreed to one kiss before we got to the restaurant and the second we had a moment alone, he did it."

"I like that. It's nice when a man's confident but respectful. It's a hard thing to find. Has anything else happened? In the apartment or out in public?" Laura paused for a second before turning to Persephone and adding, "Or at work?"

"No. Not like that," Persephone said. "He showed up to my dress fitting for the gala."

"What do you mean 'he showed up?' Did he portal into the

fitting room?" Laura's eyes sparkled through her questioning look.

Persephone stifled her snort. "No, he walked through the door after I let him in. I was surprised he showed up."

"Mad surprised? Or happy?"

"Excited, actually. I told him if he wanted to see the dress, he had to grant me a favor. A future one with no strings attached."

Laura released a low, huffed laugh. "I'm sure he hated that. Remember trying to get Mom to promise us a blessing?"

How could Persephone forget? Their mom wasn't stingy with her powers, but everything was on Mom's terms. If they asked her to make their kitten strong, then the favor would come with something they'd have to uphold on their end, like it'd be strong as long as they kept a tidy bedroom.

"Yes, she blessed my wildflowers one summer and said they'd keep their petals all season unless I touched a male. She said, even if one brushed my arm, then every bloom would fall off. I was twenty-three."

Laura flicked her eyes to the ceiling and shook her head. "Titans, she can be an ass sometimes." Tugging the dry towel from her shoulder, Laura wiped flour remnants off the counter. "So did Hades grant you this favor? And what did you ask for?"

"He agreed, but I didn't specify what it would be."

"What will it be?"

Persephone shrugged and used tongs to place the finished donuts on a porcelain platter. "I'm not sure. I did it because I figured whatever advantage I can get between us, I should take. I'm living in his world and slowly making allies, but if things go south, who there would help me? And did I tell you about what happened with Hermes?"

Laura shook her head.

"He asked me to help him distract his girlfriend so he could sneak into the building and read her texts. She's one of the app's developers."

Flinching, Laura turned towards Persephone. "I hope you said no."

With a wince, Persephone replied, "No. I got him onto the developer's floor, then distracted Eurydice's whole team by telling them they needed to take a group picture with me."

"Oh shit, Sephy. You snuck someone into Underworld Unlimited. Why?"

Persephone looked off to the side at her content niece, still engrossed in the game on her tablet. "I know. It's never wise to sneak someone into a god's domain—uninvited—but at that moment, I wanted to help Hermes. He'd do the same for me if I asked."

"Sure, and if he snuck you into some god's place of business, he wouldn't be a good friend, having you act like a fool. So what happened?"

Persephone caught up Laura on the events of that day, even telling her about Hades speaking with her afterwards in his office.

"Yikes. You've got to be more careful."

Hearing the admonishment from her older sister stirred the regret anew in her chest. "I know. I'm not saying I'm proud of it. Stupid, really—" As she fussed with the edge of a dish towel, Persephone's shoulders slumped. "But he was gracious about it and it hasn't come up again. Almost makes it more embarrassing."

"Don't be embarrassed. You apologized and admitted it was stupid, so you can move on." The slotted spoon swung between the pan and paper towels as Laura rescued more fried dough.

Persephone nodded as she finished rolling another donut.

"Go back to the dress fitting story. What did he say when he saw the dress?"

Blushing, Persephone kept her focus on covering the dough with its toppings. "He said he was going to keep me and that I was made for his world."

"How do you feel about that?" Laura asked.

Persephone met her sister's gaze. "Comforted, to be honest. He seems committed and thinks I belong there. Maybe it's dumb, but I like how attentive he is with me. He's close with Charon and Hecate, but treats them like siblings. He treats me like I'm his top priority." It was nice to get to talk with Laura like this. It'd been way too long since the two of them could spend time together cooking. Promotions for *Flowers Near Me* had monopolized every waking moment during the press tour, and now her and her sister were finally catching up.

Laura inclined her head. "Good. He should treat you well."

"This doesn't bother you at all? That he's a god and has been around Olympus bullshit for ages?"

The edges of Laura's mouth quirked the tiniest bit up. "Of course I care, but I've been thinking a lot about his reaction to finding out you were made—"

"Then born," Persephone cut in. The topic had been discussed during that first dinner together at Hades' apartment when Laura, Peter, and Helena visited.

"Right. I think he figured out you're an immortal goddess, like the rest of them. You just came later."

"You think I'm immortal?" Hades always talked like Persephone was a goddess, but he acted as if he worshipped the ground she walked on.

"You have to be, Sephy. You came from a goddess. After that conversation in Hades' penthouse, I've been thinking about it and it makes sense that you're immortal. You're tall like the rest of the gods are, you've got power, and now we know that Hecate enchanted the flowers that Mom ate to become pregnant with you. There's no way you're mortal. Think about it."

She could feel her power surging in her veins and it made her feel incredible. Although it did make sense, it was a lot to take in. "Then does this mean you're immortal as well?" Hope blossomed in Persephone's chest as she continued, "Does it work that way with a goddess and demigod?"

"I asked my dad and he said he didn't think so, but would look into it. Sounds like it's a little tricky to discern with hybrid parentage."

"Well, I hope he finds out it's true."

"Time will tell."

If the way Laura had aged was any sign, then Persephone assumed her sister was immortal. Laura could be mistaken for a young twenty-something even though she was mid-forties.

Laura continued, "Anyway, going back to that night when Hades asked about you being made. Things clicked for me. You're one of them, but it wasn't as obvious since you were a child first. But you reached thirty and haven't aged since."

"Same with you. But it hasn't been a full decade for me to really know," clarified Persephone.

Laura nodded. "Think about it for a minute. You could always open locked doors or cupboards, and your ability to maintain a garden is otherworldly. Nothing dies on you, ever. And it turns out you can create poisonous flowers."

Straightening her neck, Persephone thought back to her years of gardening and their bountiful blooms. Not to mention that miracle plants that were thriving in Hades' underground penthouse. "I always assumed the gardens did so well at Mom's estate because of Mom."

Washing the now dough-less bowl, Laura said, "Maybe I'm wrong, but there were plenty of seasons where she didn't go to the estate, but the plants stayed lush. Peter and I were just there for a weekend away, and your gardens were dead."

A stab of sadness hit her gut. She loved those gardens and to hear they weren't faring well, broke her heart. "Oh, that's so sad." Hopefully she could return and breath some life into them.

"I guess it's colder this time of year..." Trailing off, Persephone thought back to previous cold seasons. Her blooms always kept their vigor. "You're right, though. When I've been there, the gardens stayed vibrant. And now I have poppies sprouting from me."

Laura tapped her finger in the air towards Persephone. "I think you're in the newest generation of gods, so you're Hades' equal. You're worried about your heart and getting hurt, but the more I think about how you are and what it was like growing up, I really think Hades is right and that you're the goddess of... *something*. Poppies and poison, maybe?" Laura chuckled. "You're worried because you think you're at a disadvantage in this relationship, but I think you have just as much or even more power than Hades because he's so in love with you and would do anything to make you love him back."

Now Persephone's skin prickled. "He's been accommodating." *And a perfect gentleman.*

"There's no hiding for you anymore. You've got to own your power and be open to some of these more uncomfortable possibilities. Hades could be a good partner for you, despite what Mom has led us to believe."

"I appreciate your confidence, Laura. I hope I have it soon, too."

"You will. Try to be kinder to yourself for liking someone who would be a good husband."

"Oh my Fates, he jokes about us getting married. It's absurd."

Chuckling, Laura said, "Check that contract again and make sure you aren't already."

"I did, and it's not in there."

"Would you marry him? Is that a possibility?" Laura asked.

"How could I know at this point?" *Would I?* She wasn't sure.

"Well, I think the gods act quickly, despite living forever. Remember how Mom said she knew she was meant to love my dad but could never marry him?"

They each groaned in annoyance.

Persephone replied, "I do. It never made sense to me until I saw how dedicated she was to DB. You're right to say that's her true love." The memory of her mom leaving Laura's dad stirred a long-held ache. *If I found someone I loved, I could never let them go.*

Persephone loaded the dishwasher as Laura put away the clean dishes from the drying rack. In the back of her mind, Persephone marveled at how accepting Laura was of Hades.

Have I missed something?

A FEW FLOORS ABOVE HADES' apartment but still well underground, Persephone sat cross-legged on the floor in Hecate's home. Now, with relative ease, Persephone could summon and recall her poppies.

"Keep practicing with the poppies so your magic has an outlet or it'll burst when you don't want it to," Hecate explained.

"Good to know," said Persephone. The poppy meadow on Hecate's woven rug swirled into a mist that retreated into Persephone's chest.

Both goddesses held hands as Hecate recited an incantation she'd told Persephone would draw out her magic. Hair twirled around Hecate's head as if submerged under water. Poppies bloomed around them with a thick, stifling scent, more earthy than floral.

"Anything?" Persephone asked.

Eyes closed, Hecate shook her head. "It's there, but I can't make sense of it. Almost like your power is hiding and isn't ready to come out."

With a sigh, Persephone asked, "Should I try to portal instead?"

"Patience." Hecate released the word with her exhale.

Sweat formed on Persephone's brow. It must've been an

hour by now, and Persephone wondered when Charon would come and collect her.

"I think I need to stop, Hecate. All I can think about is this event tonight. We both need to get ready soon. Can we give it a go later?"

Hecate opened her eyes and her hair cascaded to her shoulders. "Of course. We may be better off waiting for it to show itself when it's ready."

"You speak of my power like it's another person." A chill ran down Persephone's back.

"Until you know what you're capable of, it sort of is. But don't worry. I think it wants more time before it'll manifest in full." Hecate stood up and offered her hand to Persephone. Using Hecate's help, Persephone rose and stretched her legs.

Gathering her bag and looking for shoes, Persephone asked, "If you had to guess, what power would you say I have?"

Hecate bit her bottom lip. "Well, we know you can poison mortals and that most of the Underworld crew is immune to them. Even Cerberus... whatever that means."

"Yes, thank the Fates. My heart stopped when I saw him eating them in my room."

"Ah, don't worry about Cerberus. He's one tough puppy." Hecate's mouth lifted at the corners. "We know Hades can command your poppies."

Persephone's body felt hot. "He's powerful. Of course he can."

Humming low with a sultry grin, Hecate said, "Magic and power between the gods isn't like that. One doesn't control another unless there's a deeper connection."

Cheeks reddening, Persephone fussed with her sleeves. "I didn't know that."

"How could you? Until a few weeks ago, you still thought you had no real power. Turns out, you're as much a goddess as your mom. Try to embrace it."

Persephone nodded. "I understand how we're connected. You created the field of poppies my mother ate to become pregnant with me. But what's my connection to Hades?" With her head high and attention directed at Hecate's face, Persephone straightened her shoulders.

Hecate bit her bottom lip. "I think you know."

A thought bubbled to the surface, and it felt right.

He's my future.

CHAPTER THIRTY TWO

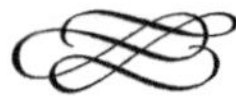

THE WITHERING BLOOM

PERSEPHONE

Inside Olympus' premiere conservatory, sunlight streamed through towering glass walls, lighting rows of crepe myrtles and blooms of hydrangeas, roses, and gardenias. Influencers posed for photos in front of *Flowers Near Me* backdrops, their laughter and carefree energy a stark contrast to Persephone's growing fatigue. Despite Hecate's lessons keeping her poppies from sprouting, the constant strain of controlling her powers left her with relentless headaches.

Wearing a sleek black kaftan, Charon directed the influencers from behind a ring light. Persephone made a mental note to ask where she'd found that dress—Charon's style exuded effortless elegance.

Persephone's mind replayed a conversation she'd had with one of the models.

"Aren't you worried people might steal flowers to sell them on the app?" the young woman had asked, her tone light but curious. Perse-

*phone had responded with the company's official stance, that users
had to agree not to misuse the application after they downloaded it,
but the woman had laughed. "No one reads the fine print," she'd said.*

Bringing her back to reality, Hades rested a warm hand on
her lower back, his touch grounding her even as her thoughts
churned. She leaned closer, her voice low. "It feels wrong,
doesn't it? Promoting an app like this in a place meant to
protect flowers, not sell them."

"That's the point." He tilted his head, a grin tugging at his
lips. "If people think it's an odd choice, it'll keep them talking."

Her stomach twisted. "If people started stealing flowers from
public places, it'd be chaos."

His smile didn't falter, and something in his eyes—satisfaction, perhaps—unnerved her. "Publicity is still publicity. As long
as they talk about the app, we win."

Anger flared inside her, heat rising to her cheeks. "That's
reckless."

He leaned in, voice smooth as silk. "It's calculated. The more
they hear about it, the more it becomes part of their lives." His
hand traced slow circles on her back, as if soothing her anger.
"Is it working? Are you giving in?"

Her lips pressed together, but a reluctant smile broke
through. "Don't use your tricks on me."

He pulled her closer, his arm sliding around her waist. "Then
tell me what works, little goddess, and I'll do it."

She arched an eyebrow, meeting his gaze. "You're clever.
Figure it out." But her teasing gave way to genuine curiosity.
"Can you tell what I'm the goddess of? Hecate has guesses, but
we're still in the dark."

Hades' grin faded, and he seemed to weigh his words. "If I
had to guess... protection, maybe preservation. The poppies
defend you, after all. But sometimes, knowing too soon isn't a
blessing."

Persephone mulled over his words, acknowledging the truth in them. Ignorance had its comforts, but it didn't quiet the yearning in her heart. She picked up a drink from a passing tray, hoping to calm the nervous flutter in her stomach. The pressure behind her eyes built, and she rubbed her temples.

Hades' hand tightened on her back. "Are you alright, Sephy?"

"A headache," she admitted. "It's getting worse."

Concern flickered in his eyes. "Want me to help?"

She remembered how he'd eased her pain before and nodded. He threaded his fingers through her hair, massaging her scalp. Slowly, the tension unraveled, and her breathing steadied.

"Better?" he asked, his voice quiet.

She opened her eyes, her shoulders relaxing. "Much."

Charon called for Hades, and he pressed a kiss to her cheek before walking away. As he left, Persephone's vision blurred, and her limbs grew heavy. Her stomach lurched, and she clutched the edge of a nearby table. Her body locked up, and her vision went dark.

COLD SEEPED INTO HER SKIN, and a damp cloth pressed against her neck. She coughed, trying to clear the tightness in her throat. Familiar fingers combed through her hair, and Hades' voice cut through the haze. "Charon is bringing tea and water."

Persephone blinked, the room coming into focus. She realized she was sprawled across Hades' lap, his suit jacket warming her shoulders. His strong hold kept her steady, and she leaned into his chest, grateful for the support.

"Sorry," she muttered, attempting to stand. His grip didn't loosen.

"Stay," he commanded, his voice firm but gentle. "You collapsed. Give yourself a minute."

Her cheeks flushed, but she let herself settle against him. "How long was I out?"

"Only a few minutes," he said. "Charon screamed as soon as you fell, and I caught you."

She shivered. "Were there poppies?"

"No." He brushed a stray strand of hair from her face. "How do you feel now?"

"Better." Persephone accepted the glass of cold water Charon handed her. "Thanks."

Charon's worry etched deep lines into her usually serene expression. "Do you have any idea what caused it?"

Persephone searched her memory. "It was sudden. My limbs went numb, and then… nothing."

Hades and Charon exchanged a tense look, and he turned back to her, his jaw clenched.

Had Hades orchestrated this?

His schemes weren't always harmless, and she couldn't ignore the unease creeping into her mind. It was a ridiculous, fleeting thought but it still gave her pause in that moment.

Hecate appeared in a burst of sandalwood-scented smoke. "You're awake. Good." She knelt beside Persephone. "Mind if I check for lingering magic?"

Persephone shook her head, and Hecate's energy washed over her, soothing and warm. When Hecate pulled back, her frown deepened. "Nothing. No trace of poison. Maybe your own magic is to blame."

Persephone's hands clenched. "You think it's me?"

Hecate sighed. "Magic can be unpredictable. But if you believe someone harmed you, trust your instincts."

Persephone glanced at Hades, his face an unreadable mask. "Did you do this?" The question slipped out, heavy with suspicion.

His eyes widened, genuine hurt flashing across his features. "Never. I'd never risk you."

The raw vulnerability in his voice cracked something inside her. But trust was fragile, and she wasn't ready to let it take root. "I want to believe you," she whispered.

Hades took her hand, his touch warm and steady. "Then let me prove it."

CHAPTER THIRTY THREE

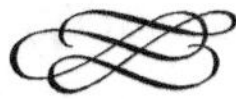

WHEN PASSION GROWS

PERSEPHONE

Several days later, headaches turned into migraines and dizziness into unexpected falls. Meanwhile, Hades continued on with the press tour, leaving the apartment empty most days, except for Cerberus and Charon. She felt sorry for him. His face twisted in worry each time he said goodbye before leaving. She reassured him that she'd be fine, but the pallor of his skin betrayed his distress. It was clear he cared about her, and she was finding it easier to trust him and his intentions with her.

The mornings were the worst, with joints screaming from disuse and a head sloshing with a congestion that wouldn't clear. Simple remedies like rest and water failed to bring relief. It was as if her body raged war against her, and she was not the victor.

After a shower, Persephone trudged to the kitchen and found a note from Hades along with a warm cup of tea, honey, and lemon slices.

My love, Sephy,

Sorry I had to run out again this morning. I'll be back with a basket of pastries and egg sandwich before you finish your tea. Can't wait to spend the rest of the day with you.

Your future husband and favorite fellow god,
Hades

Her cheeks heated, and a smile broke out on her face as she folded the note and stashed it in her pocket. She'd add it to the collection of messages he'd penned while she'd lived there. It'd be an adjustment when she'd go back to her mom's estate where there was no handsome god to leave her love letters or run his fingers through her hair.

Somehow, he'd become a staple in her life, accompanying her when she worked out, procuring food at any hour of the day or night—regardless of how busy he was. She hadn't cooked anything herself beyond the loukoumades Laura and she had made a week ago. Even before then, the most she did in the kitchen was make coffee or tea.

She took the tray her cup and tea accompaniments sat on and placed it on a low coffee table next to the strange looking reading cushion Hades had bought after the night she'd passed out.

You need to rest, even during the day, so why not take up reading? He'd suggested when he showed her the new low, ergonomic chair in the living room. It was an unusual piece of furniture with thousands of reviews claiming it helped keep the reader's posture intact during hours of reading.

Sadly, the chair had gotten a lot of use that past week. Simple tasks caused migraines or triggered uncontrolled muscle cramps. Laura's dad, Dr. Asclepius, ruled out natural health issues and Hecate couldn't discern problems with her magic. Charon pushed several events out in hopes of Persephone recovering soon. But Persephone had grown so frustrated with her inability to fulfill her work obligations, that she was ready to have Hades hold her body upright at events even if she collapsed.

The pleasant scent of cedar filled the room as Hades appeared in the kitchen holding a brown cardboard box big enough to fit a sleeping Cerberus. It was a relief to have Hades' help even if she hated feeling helpless. She trusted him to care for her and felt bad she'd thought that maybe he'd poisoned her at the influencer event. But she remembered what it was like growing up with her mom. Gods could be fickle and use you as a means to an end. It seemed like the only end that Hades truly cared about was one spent with her.

"Little goddess, I hope you're hungry because the chef said they taste best when they're fresh." He set the box on the counter, threw her a wink over his shoulder, then started pulling out pastries.

Mug in hand, Persephone watched him plate the goodies on a tray.

"It looks like you bought a bakery." Overloaded with buttery pastries and glazed masterpieces, the box was stuffed, each treat more enticing than the next.

Hades wiped crumbs from his hands, then leaned down to squeeze her to his side and plant a quick kiss on her cheek. A soothing warmth flooded her from the touch and the faint headache she'd woken up with dissolved. "I didn't buy the bakery. I opened it a long time ago. Eat what you can. I think you're not eating enough and that's why you're losing energy so quickly."

Missing meals wasn't the problem. For the past few months, Hades brought a revolving buffet of every variety of food a goddess could hope for.

"I think I've been eating just fine. This is way too much food. Can we give some away?"

Hades grabbed two plates and motioned his head towards the sitting area. "Whatever we don't eat, I'll send to the developer's break room. How are you feeling?" He set down the plates, and they sat at arm's length from each other on the couch. Persephone's knee touched his hip and from the point of contact, another cozy rush of energy thrummed in her veins.

"I'm okay, I think. I still feel weak, but that's got to be from my body's lack of use."

"Do you feel like you could take a walk or do yoga?" he asked before biting into a croissant. Crumbs fell towards his lap but disappeared into thin air. Persephone made a mental note for him to show her how to do that when she was feeling well again.

"Maybe? It's worth a try. I wouldn't mind some work. Answering emails, phone interviews, things like that." If she could ease back into things, she'd be more prepared when the live events resumed.

"I have something I could use your clever mind for. Not *Flowers Near Me* related, but a new acquisition I want to explore." Hades set his croissant down and picked up a cup of coffee she hadn't seen him bring over.

Persephone perked up. "How can I help?" She hadn't stretched her strategic business muscle in too long.

"With the app launching soon, it got me thinking about community gardens. Underworld Unlimited's buildings could house micro gardens and rent plots to schools and individuals."

Possibilities raced faster than Zeus' chariot in Persephone's mind. Underworld Unlimited owned tons of real estate throughout Olympus. "Do you own the rooftop of all of your buildings?"

He shot her a curious look. "Yes. Is that not how it works when you own a building?"

Persephone shook her head. "There are companies that buy rooftop space so they can sell them to telecommunications groups that build cell towers. The intermediary company facilitates the rental agreement and even gives a cut to the building owners."

Tapping one finger to his mouth, Hades nodded along. "Use our rooftops."

"Any outdoor space, really. I follow a few gardeners who try to bring homesteading practices into the city. They'd be good consultants for choosing the locations and then spreading the word."

Persephone pulled out her phone and brought up an account she'd been looking at the day before. "He's set up container gardens with plastic bins from the trash. He grows enough produce that he doesn't need a weekly grocery trip." She swiped to another account and held up the photo. "Here they've grown trailing nasturtium. They sell the flowers to a local restaurant and the vines hide the HVAC equipment."

"May I?" Hades gestured at her phone.

"Please." She handed it to him, then scooted closer to watch her screen over his shoulder. His piney scent smelled so inviting that she ran her fingers over his dark gray cashmere sweater. The touch was a subtle invitation for more, yet still on her terms. He couldn't reach her easily and his hands stayed on her phone, but his slight lean into her body made it clear he liked the contact.

Hades thumbed through the accounts, taking screenshots which he forwarded to his phone. "This is an entire world I knew nothing about."

"You were thinking about it, though. Community gardens are great for people who don't have a yard." A nagging, sinking feeling tugged at her chest. For all of her life, she'd lived on her mom's estate and never once thought about bringing the vibrancy and energizing force of nature into the city. A few months into owning a flower app, and Hades had the idea all on his own. Why hadn't she thought of it before?

Hades handed her phone back and smirked as he motioned for her to sit on his lap. "Tell me more of your ideas." He laid one arm across the back of the couch.

She sat across his lap with her lower back against the couch's armrest. Hades pulled her tight to his chest for a short hug, then kept his arm around her waist. A tinge of her poppy magic prickled under her skin and she imagined the sensation flooding back to her heart. Confident she had subdued the threatening burst of flowers, she smiled back at Hades and leaned into him.

"When she was a high school student, Laura worked for a food bank that partnered with a community garden. They donated fresh produce twice a week and the food bank agreed to send volunteers to tend the garden. For those who rented plots, they got a discount if they contributed."

Hades' fingers trailed up and down the side of her leg. "Do you remember which food bank it was?"

"Laura lived with her father in the city at the time and said she could bike there. Northern Olympus Food Bank, or something like that."

"Interesting. I assumed she'd volunteer at one of your mom's food banks."

Persephone shook her head. A follower, Laura was not. Her sister had never wanted to pursue her mom's interests and went to great lengths to find a place to volunteer at where Demeter had no influence. "Laura was looking for more independence from Mom. But I have no clue who owns it."

The smirk on Hades' face said everything.

"It's yours," she said in realization.

Persephone's heart swelled at the revelation. Hades, the formidable god with a reputation for ruthlessness, secretly supported a local food bank.

"Tell me more," he urged, his hands growing bolder as they caressed her legs.

She laid out her vision: community partnerships, incentives for businesses, the potential to transform Olympus with greenery. His gaze never left hers, his interest genuine and intense.

"I'll assemble a team," he said, his voice a low rumble. "We'll make this happen."

Pride surged through her, but so did desire. His touch, growing more confident, sent heat pooling in her core. Hades' hands slid up her back, and he nuzzled the side of her neck, making her shiver.

"Sounds good to me." She smiled back, fixing her eyes on him.

No dizzying nausea or limp extremities. It was the closest to full health she'd felt since the fainting episode.

Hades' shoulders filled his sweater the way a lion filled its velvet skin. The cashmere screamed to be touched. And his smokey white hair accentuated the olive tones of his face. If he kissed her now, she wouldn't stop him.

The knowledge there were no meetings, events, or responsibilities on the calendar that day, made this moment even more thrilling. Hades hugged her by the waist and ran his nose up the side of her neck. Her arms wrapped around the tops of his shoulders. He pulled back just enough for them to be face to face.

"I hope you choose to stay with me, Sephy." Hades closed his eyes and kissed her. Full lips with gentle pressure. Returning the kiss, her lips parted and tugged his lower one between them. Florals and pines mixed in the air with heady abandon. She grazed his scalp with her nails, putting weeks' worth of yearning into the slow drag. Their lips fit together as if made for each other. Perfect.

With her legs now on either side of his hips, chest to chest, the evidence of his desire pressed in into her. His grip kept her planted on his lap, allowing mere centimeters of desperate movement. When softer touches of her kiss turned needy, a gravely moan sounded in Hades' throat. That noise spurred her hands to stroke the shell of his ears and trail a path towards his strong shoulders.

Like a warm statue. She recalled the first touch of her fingers on his sides in the hibachi restaurant where they'd shared their first kiss. She ran her fingers over the length of his torso as he continued kissing her. Time stood still to unlock a new heaven.

The rock of her hips sparked a building release. Chasing the mounting pleasure, she leaned further into the kiss as his grip pushed her deeper into his lap.

CHAPTER THIRTY FOUR

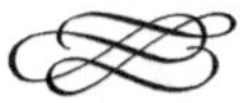

NO ROOM FOR REGRET

HADES

The Fates were smiling upon Hades. Sephy sat astride his lap, returning the kiss with equal fervor. Too scared to breathe or break the contact, he pressed his fingers deeper into her hips, willing the moment to never end. Want turned to need, coiled and wound so tight, he thought he might burst.

Sephy smelled like flowers and sugared treats and tasted better than anything he'd ever eaten. Days and nights of imagining this exact scenario paled compared to the heat of her center pressed on his lap. Tension radiated low in his stomach. Every point of pressure from her sent frissons of pleasure through him.

Without warning, Hades stood, holding Sephy against him with one arm and cradling the back of her head with the other. He turned them both and slowly laid her back down on the couch. Covering her body with his, he watched her half-lidded eyes staring at his mouth and settled himself on top of her. He leaned over her, pressing a kiss to her neck and savoring the light scratch of her nails on his back.

He parted her lips with his tongue and rocked his length against her. Reaching under the hem of her shirt, he pushed the fabric up and traced the curved line of her waist. Her smooth skin under the pad of his thumb ignited need deep in his gut.

His hand roamed higher until it met the satin fabric around her chest. Fingertips traced the skin under the band. In response, Sephy arched her back and pulled his head deeper into the kiss and his body closer with her leg. Dragging his finger back and forth under her bra, he moved higher to meet the soft underside of her breast.

A purr-like moan stirred from his chest as his palm cupped her breast and his thumb brushed her nipple. The faint whimpers from her spurred him on to keep a gentle rhythm as he ground his hips on her center.

"You're perfect, Sephy," he whispered in her ear. She shuddered as he licked up her throat, then lightly dragged her earlobe between his teeth.

She grabbed his sides and tugged him towards her, almost causing him to press his full weight on her. "Careful, little goddess, or I'm going to crush you."

Persephone gave a breathy laugh and said, "Good," as she yanked him to her again with more force.

He lowered himself, pressing fully onto her with one arm wrapped behind her head, tangled in her hair, and the other circling her breast. The press of their bodies, the way their lips fit, felt right to Hades. He'd been chasing this high and now that he'd caught it, he wouldn't let it go.

Persephone's hands slid under his sweater, roving over his back. When she ran her nails over his skin, a sigh of pleasure escaped his lips. The waves of release stirred, so he slowed the stroke of his hips and pulled away. He'd pined for this and the build-up created a wildness within him that needed to be tamed.

Opening her eyes and placing her hands on his chest, still under his shirt, she asked, "What's wrong?"

"If I keep going, I won't stop," he breathed out.

"Then don't stop." She twisted the hem of his shirt in her hands to yank him towards her, but he held himself still.

"Little goddess. I'm not taking you like this until I can have *all* of you and we're not ready for that."

Her brow furrowed. "What do you mean? Are you worried I'll get pregnant? Because Hecate already gave me a preventative elixir."

Of course Hecate had. What a meddlesome goddess.

"No, it's not only that. If we continue, I'm afraid you'll always wonder if being with me was *your* choice. Don't give regret an opportunity." His body roiled against him, screaming, *Take what's being offered.*

"Would *you* regret it if we continued?" The question cut more than expected.

"I'll give you anything, but I'm not taking something this significant in a moment of passion." He sat up and pulled her with him to set her on his lap.

"Why is it problem? We're both willing." The pleading in her eyes almost had him relenting.

He shook his head. "When we do this, I need it to be after we've committed ourselves to one another."

Her face pinched in confusion. "It can only happen *after* we're married?"

He nodded. "I'm not taking something from you until you've decided I'm right for you."

She trailed her fingers along the waist of his pants and tension built in his groin. Frustration wound itself in his chest as he sat back, but the thought of their first time happening like a tryst on the couch made his insides burn with acid. Sephy deserved to be properly bedded like a goddess and this wasn't it. But the hope of it coming sooner than expected stirred his desire.

"I understand," she finally said, "but if you turn me down again, I will take it personally." Persephone stood up, putting much needed space between the two of them. Had she pressed him to continue what they'd started, he wasn't sure he'd have had the resolve to stop. "Alright, mister. Let's eat these pastries then." She reached for a croissant, but the chill of the air left in her wake did little to temper his craving for her.

CHAPTER THIRTY FIVE

FALLING INTO DARKNESS

PERSEPHONE

"I wish I didn't have to leave again," Hades said as he trailed his fingers through Persephone's hair. It drove her mad that she kept having weird health issues. One moment she'd be perfectly fine, the next, she'd feel like she was going to pass out. She'd never felt this pathetic before.

It should've been the two of them attending the afternoon meet and greet with the flower vendors and farmers, but earlier that morning, standing and waiting for the coffee to brew had proved to be too difficult a task for Persephone. She'd fallen right after a sharp pain erupted in one temple. Thankfully, strong arms had caught her before she hit the floor. They'd cuddled for a while after that, and she'd felt so much better. It was like Hades was the drug her body craved.

"I *should* be going with you," Persephone said. "I feel better than I did earlier. I'll be fine." Her knees sank into the cushion as she gripped the back of the couch, hoping the position reminded him of how she'd straddled his lap yesterday. She really needed to get out of the penthouse too because being inside doing practically nothing was making her insane and depressed.

Buttoning his cuff links, Hades closed the distance from the kitchen to Persephone in three strides. "Your well-being isn't worth the risk. Save up that energy for our date, little goddess." He gave her a wink, then held her face in his hands and planted a slow kiss on her lips.

Gripping the sides of his jacket, she tugged him closer and rose higher on her knees to push her body against his.

Pulling back while keeping his palms on her cheeks, Hades said, "I know what you're doing, love, and it's going to work if you don't stop."

Persephone simpered and pressed harder into his chest with hers, parting her lips in a deeper kiss before releasing him with a light giggle. "Fine. Try not to miss me too much."

Hades' eyes narrowed and his mouth turned into a mischievous smirk. "I always miss you when we're not together. Try to behave while I'm not here. Save the strenuous activity for me." He winked and disappeared as he portaled away.

Emptiness settled in her gut. It was bad enough that Hades' kindness monopolized her thoughts. Now their amorous encounter from the day before consumed her. Both happy and frustrated at his conviction to stop, Persephone wasn't sure committing to marriage at this point made sense. Why did it matter to him if they were married or not? She was afraid of the answer. That he really did care for her and that what was blossoming between them was more than mutual attraction between two people in proximity. Their potential as a lasting couple was feeling more and more like an inevitable fate.

Cerberus whimpered nearby and lifted his head in a huff.

"What's bothering you, friend?" teased Persephone. His smooth ears felt like velour under her fingertips. "You've been with Hades for a long time. Why have you stayed?" she asked, stroking the fur on his neck now. It dawned on her that the dog didn't have a collar. He never had, come to think of it. The beast was formidable in his true form. He could venture out on his own. So why hadn't he?

SEVERAL DAYS LATER, hundreds packed into the covered amphitheater, and under cloaked darkness, gawked at the huge screen. Persephone watched Eurydice's presentation as she jumped from function to function, citing features unique to the app's experience.

"It makes custom recommendations for items to buy and sell based on users in your area. Connect with friends—" Taking a sip of water, Eurydice continued on as Persephone's mind wandered and she shifted on her feet.

At the edge of the curtain lining the stage, Charon bumped Persephone's shoulder. "Are you alright?"

"I'm fine." A lie, but the truth meant another hour sitting on a couch while a carousel of staff brought tea, water, and crackers. To spend one more sedentary minute in a bed or chair would destroy the little hope gained from watching the app take flight. Exercising wasn't an option, but standing on the sidelines as Eurydice dazzled the crowd was just as invigorating.

Charon bent closer. "Truly? Because you keep clenching your jaw."

"Truly. Let's listen to Eurydice." Fates, why did everyone have to treat her like she would break at any moment. On top of feeling useless, she felt pitied by those around her, too. Her thoughts turned dark as she wondered if she was ever going to be able to be on her own without fear of crippling migraines or dizzy spells.

"Persephone, please sit down." Charon set the items in her hands on the floor and urged a folding chair behind her knees.

"It's okay, Charon. It's been a while since I've been upright this long. I just look tired."

"Sit down or I'm calling Hades." Charon stared. Unblinking. Stone still.

Bending to sit, instead of meeting the chair's padding, Persephone fell into a never-ending pit of black.

CHAPTER THIRTY SIX

THE PRICE OF LETTING GO

HADES

With sluggish effort, Persephone reached for the glass of water at her bedside table, but Hades scooped it up and handed it to her before her back lifted off the pillow. The once well-fitted silk pajamas hung loosely on her bony shoulders.

"Thanks," Persephone muttered. His heart cracked at the sound of her raspy voice, stuck in the back of her throat.

At the sight of her, dull-eyed and pale, he struggled to form words. The color in her face was *wrong* and her half-lidded eyes hadn't met his when she'd offered a weak *good morning*. She'd perk up for a little if he sent his power into her, but it hadn't been enough to sustain her for more than a few minutes at a time.

"Dr. Asclepius said you need constant monitoring," said Hades. "It's not good for you to be down here with me. You need sunlight and your family."

Half-truths cut him. Asclepius never said she needed to be

moved from the apartment, but what if moving her to Laura's home made the difference in her recovery? She ought to be with her sister. If she became more sick, he couldn't bear it. And what if she thought he'd made her ill? He had no clue what was causing it, but if he was hurting her, then she needed to get away.

Better she's healing than wasting away with me.

"Okay." Defeat coated her reply.

"Obviously, anything related to the contract is void. You need proper rest without this project looming over you." Hades offered a tender smile.

She nodded. "Thank you. I appreciate that."

"Hecate's coming over to help collect some of your things and take you to Laura's."

Persephone nodded again and looked at her bedside table.

Standing up, Hades said, "I'll be back," and headed to the kitchen.

Hip cocked and leaning on the counter, Hecate pinned Hades with her stare as he grabbed a drink from the fridge.

"You're sending her away? Now?" Hecate's words burned a hole in his chest.

"Good to hear you understand the plan," he bit back, scanning the living room, looking anywhere but at Hecate's face.

"This is silly, Hades. She's getting care now, and I heard Dr. Asclepius and Laura when they said they didn't mind making regular visits here."

He gritted his teeth. "I can't keep her here when she's this ill. What if there's a part of her body that's failing because she's not with her family?"

Hecate rolled her eyes. "What a sack of shit. You know she's immortal, so that's no excuse. Look at how all these plants are flourishing down here. Her illness is unrelated to living here. I mean… think about how long she's lived with you without issue. Wouldn't it have come up sooner?"

"Maybe it took time to set in?"

"*Maybe* she's been cursed, and this is the best place for her?" Hecate spat back.

Rubbing his face, Hades rolled his shoulders.

"Hecate… what if I've gotten her all wrong? What if she's been holding it together and now her body's given up?" He paced and his stomach dropped. The scent of Hecate's magic filled the air, and he slowly drew in air.

"Don't send her away. We'll figure this out. Dr. Asclepius will help too."

The chime of the door drew their attention to Charon hurrying into the room, phone in a white-knuckled grip.

"Is she stable?" A few strands of dark hair clung to Charon's forehead.

"Hades is trying to throw her out," Hecate said.

"That's—" Hades started, but Charon cut him off.

Charon's lip curled. "Why?"

"She's getting worse—"

Hecate cut in, "No. That's not what Dr. Asclepius said. He told you to monitor her but let things run their course. Healing takes time."

Hades shook his head. "What if she needs something different *now*?"

"Help me out here, Charon. Talk some sense into him," begged Hecate.

Charon's strained expression silenced them both. "Hades might be right." Hecate went to speak, but Charon held up her hands. "Look, I hate this too, but she's been sick for over two weeks now and it isn't like her. We should give every option a try to see what works."

"Thank you." *Finally, someone sees reason.* "Staying here could be a death sentence for the young goddess, and there'd be no recovery for any of us if *that* happened." Bitterness filled his mouth.

"You call Laura, and I'll gather her things," said Charon, before she headed off towards Sephy's room.

Hecate glared back. "You're a fool."

Hades shook his head. "I *hate* this, Hecate, but we must try something different. She's getting worse."

"Her power responds to yours, you idiot. It didn't manifest until you were together. It doesn't take much to put two and two together. How do you not see it?"

His heart ached. "I want what you're saying to be true, so badly that I would risk her life to find out. But that's not fair. It's selfish, and I've already upended her life, forcing her to spend time with me."

"What about the contract?"

"Dissolved. She's done more than enough. The app is ready and we have all the content she recorded months ago. Now she can recuperate in a place that's familiar."

Hecate's voice was cold as she said, "Is that what she wanted? Did you ask her or simply tell her she's leaving?"

Hades reared back his head. "Why are you fighting me on this?"

All the lights in the main living space flickered in response to Hecate's rising fury. "Because she will not get better if she's away from you... you fuck-wit." Plumes of purple smoke obscured everything but the goddess of witchcraft. "You're backing off now that she's reciprocating feelings? What in the Fates has gotten into you?"

Her cloying scent of sandalwood burned his eyes, but he rose taller. The icy chill of his power snaked up his body and the water pipes in the wall moaned against the strain of ice threatening to burst them to pieces.

Stabbing a pointed finger, he replied, "How are you so sure she won't get better as soon as she leaves?"

The swirls of Hecate's magic faded to the floor, spinning near her feet. "*Titans fuck me.* You're impossible sometimes, you realize that? Aren't you the one who tricked her into a contract so you could try to date her all under the pretense of promoting an app? *With* the intention of trying to marry her. Yet with all your wisdom, can't see how she blushes when you compliment her? The woman can't do anything but smile when your name is mentioned. Her power responds to you and we're both old enough to recognize what that means. Fuck, Hades. Didn't the Fates tell you she's going to be your wife? You absolute—"

Charon coughed loudly as she approached them, returning to the kitchen after visiting Sephy's room. His power retreated back into his body and Hecate's scent no longer battered his lungs. "Persephone's things are ready. Did you call Laura?"

"Not yet." He shot Hecate a scowl before dialing Laura's number.

After a couple of rings, Laura answered, "Hi, Hades. What's up?"

"Sephy's gotten worse, and we need to move her in with you until she recovers. Can I bring her over today?" Fortunately, the words came out strong.

"Oh Fates, what's happened?"

"She's gotten weaker. I think we need to get her somewhere more familiar and see if that helps," said Hades. Nearby, Hecate mumbled something derisive which Hades caught parts of. *He's forcing her away* was muttered the loudest.

"That's concerning. Yes, of course she can come here. Bring her as soon as you can."

"Thank you, Laura. I'll portal her there after lunch."

When Hades ended the call, Hecate said, "Coward."

Hades sneered, "Harpy."

Hecate narrowed her eyes into slits. "I wonder if Poseidon wants to bring Sephy a get-well-soon gift? I should ask him."

"Enough." Charon stared both Hades and Hecate down. "One week. If Persephone doesn't improve in one week, then we bring her back. And Hades needs to visit her twice a day."

He didn't know if he'd have the strength to visit her after she left. If he saw how happy and healthy she was without him, it'd crush his heart.

Hecate crossed her arms. "Fine by me, but if she asks to come back, I'm bringing her immediately." She disappeared in a cloud of purple smoke.

Hades gestured at Hecate's vacated spot. "Why is she so opposed to this?"

Charon's face sagged in sadness, tears filling her eyes. "None of us want to let Persephone go." She clutched her necklace as she turned and headed towards Sephy's room.

It killed him to send Sephy away, but if he hesitated any longer, he might never do it and she may hate him for it.

What if she perished? He struggled to breathe.

CHAPTER THIRTY SEVEN

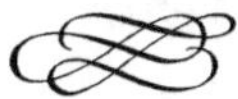

ROOTS AND THORNS

PERSEPHONE

The familiar scent of a field of wildflowers woke Persephone from her fitful sleep. It took a breath to remember she was in Laura's guest room and not Hades' apartment. She'd half expected Cerberus to nudge her leg.

"Mom?" Persephone's voice cracked.

Warm arms embraced her and pulled her into a hug. "*Sephy, my heart. How are you feeling?*"

Tears streamed from Persephone's eyes. "It's so good to see you." After weeks of feeling ill, unable to work or do anything productive, it was good to see her mom. She needed someone familiar or else she was truly going to lose her mind.

Demeter held Persephone's arms in her hands and looked over her face. "Tell me what he did to you. We'll fix this, I promise. Did he make you eat something? Inject you? Did he touch you?" Demeter swallowed, choking back her cry.

Shaking her head, Persephone answered, "No. I was never in danger."

Demeter ran her fingers through Persephone's hair. "You've been in danger this whole time, and it's my fault."

Persephone's eyes felt heavy. She was too tired to say everything she wanted to. "*Mom.*" She groaned. She needed answers. After months of waiting to hear *something* from her mom—beyond their short interaction in Zeus' office—she finally had the chance. Using as much vigor as she could, she asked, "Why wouldn't you answer my texts or calls?"

"I knew he was targeting you, Sephy. He asked me about you as soon as I introduced you as my daughter. After photos and videos of you began circulating, he tried to negotiate a marriage agreement between you two."

The bed felt like a shoddy raft on rapids. "What?" She must've gone insane because whatever her mom had said made no sense.

Demeter nodded at Persephone with a long face. "But that's not why I'm here. I don't want to talk about him. I needed to see you."

Persephone had wondered what this reunion would be like, what she would say to her, but now she was at a loss for words, fighting through the fog of sickness.

Demeter said, "I've heard you're showing signs of power."

Persephone struggled to not break down and sob. What good were these powers anyway? "Why didn't you tell me I'm immortal?" Magic prickled over her skin.

Her mom's eyes softened, and she inhaled a deep breath. "Because I wanted you to grow up to be kind and with an understanding of mortals that the rest of us lack. I wanted you to be better than me. I wanted you to *live and feel* and for those to be natural things for you."

Demeter looked up at the ceiling and her throat bobbed in a teary swallow. "You're different from the others because you work hard for your power. It's hard not to raise an entitled child. When you're a goddess and can give them everything they want… it's even more difficult. And I didn't want you to be hard like me. I wanted you to be better, Sephy. And you are."

Persephone rubbed her face. She needed her mom in this moment, and she needed a strength she didn't have. "Well, I've been a mess, actually. I almost killed two people." She kept the fact that Hades was immune to herself. How would her mom respond to her change of heart regarding him? *Not well,* if she had to guess. A problem for another time when she didn't feel like she was spiraling into the depths of depression.

There was a tenderness in Demeter's smile that Persephone recognized. Part pride and part sympathy.

"I've heard about your magic, Sephy. Have you tried to conjure the poppies?" Demeter asked. Persephone felt the rush of her mom's power wash over her body, giving her energy.

"Yes. Hecate's been a huge help with controlling my power. The poppies aren't a problem anymore. Now it's whatever's causing me to be so weak."

Demeter's nostrils flared, and her mouth pressed into a flat line. The scent of earth and grains hit Persephone. "He had no business using you like that. Trying to run you into the ground so you'd be too weak to leave."

"It wasn't like that. He was the one that sent me here to Laura's. Said it'd be better for me to be above ground with family and sunlight."

Demeter's brow shot up. "That's the only thing he's done right."

She doubted she could win Demeter over to Hades' side—especially not when she was in such poor health—but she felt the need to still defend him. "Things have been busy, but I've not been overworked. Their office culture is like ours and you'd love his assistant, Charon."

Leveling her gaze at Persephone, Demeter replied, "I have no qualms with Charon, but I'd imagine you'd be a dream to work with after working for him for as long as she has."

"No, not just—" A stabbing pain erupted on Persephone's side, and she clutched at the spot. She held her breath, willing the pain to fade. A powdery floral scent preceded an eruption of sprouting poppies. The spasm in her side relented, and she took in a full breath.

"Oh, my…" Demeter trailed off, staring wide eyed at the blooms now covering the bed. "This is what you were telling me about." With a featherlight touch, Demeter stroked a silken petal. Golden pollen sparkled. "It's beautiful, Sephy. A sign of potent magic. Soon you'll conjure objects and will portal all on your own."

A mother's confidence could dispel any fear of inadequacy. If Demeter thought Persephone had potent magic, then it had to be true. "I hope so. I haven't gone longer than a day without shooting pains. Why is this happening?"

Plucking a flower and breathing in its scent, Demeter replied, "It's residual decay from Hades' power. You've been stuck in Underworld Unlimited for so long and needed to get out. You're not meant to be hidden away like that and brought out like a doll when someone wants to flaunt you around."

You had no problem keeping me a secret. It pained her to admit it even to herself, when she knew her mom only wanted to protect her. And right now, she needed her mom to know that she had been fine these past few months.

"Listen, it wasn't like that. I've been well taken care of."

"Of course. Why would he break his favorite toy once he got it?" Demeter waved her hand over the poppies and they turned a light pink. She gathered them in her hand, then conjured a vase to set them in.

"Mom. There's a lot we need to catch up on. It was not bad there at all. I enjoyed my time with him." Fates, did she sound like a wayward teenager pleading with her mom that her new boyfriend 'wasn't that bad?'

Demeter's eyes snapped to Persephone's and the thick scent

of wheat fields and summer sun enveloped her. Her mom set the flower-filled vase on the dresser and sidled next to Persephone on the bed. Those familiar dark green eyes softened. "Do you love him?" Not harsh, accusatory, or biting. Just sadly inquisitive.

"I don't know, but I'd like to find out."

Her mom gave a tight nod and looked down at her inter-locked hands sitting on her lap. She returned Persephone's gaze. "And you're certain you're under no compulsion or spell?"

"Does it seem like I am?" Rubbing the center of her chest, Persephone sucked in a deep breath.

Her mom sighed. "I don't sense any enchantments."

Grasping her mom's hand, Persephone gave it a tender squeeze. "I've missed you. Why didn't you respond to any of my messages? Were you disappointed?"

Shaking her head, Demeter closed her eyes, then focused on Persephone. "I didn't handle things well, Sephy. I'm very sorry about that. I tried to get you out of that contract. When Zeus affirmed it, I finally gave up and by then, felt terrible I'd aban-doned you. I didn't want to make things harder, but I can see how I did. I even tried to give you a helpful warning when we last spoke."

Don't make a fuss and don't involve my team. Her mom knew bigger things were at play and did her best to protect her.

"You didn't fail me, Mom. I made a mistake, and you had to scramble."

"You've done nothing wrong. With the Fates, meddling only makes things worse. I was worried if you bucked against the contract, it'd give him more reason to force you to marry him sooner."

"Hold on." Heart pounding, Persephone asked, "What do you mean by *sooner*?"

Demeter's throat bobbed. "He asked me for my blessing for your marriage."

Persephone's head spun. Air left the room. Tiny stars danced a jig across her vision.

"What are you talking about? When did he contact you?" Hand on her stomach, she waited for her blurry sight to sharpen and slowed her breathing. Hades had asked her to marry him, but it was playful banter, not a proposal.

"Before all of this happened. He reached out saying he consulted with the Fates and that you two would be married and he wanted my blessing. I, of course, said no, and he said he'd marry you, regardless. I thought I'd protected you from him. I even had Hermes block all Underworld Unlimited numbers in our phones' contact lists. I should've known he'd find some other way." Demeter shook her head and peered out the window.

"Fates... Mom. What does this mean? That I'm destined to marry him? Is this how it works among gods? Fates decree then we obey?"

With a grimace that did nothing to diminish her beauty, Demeter replied, "Afraid so. There's usually a high cost to fight it and you'll lose."

Persephone's mind reeled. On top of feeling awful—both physically and mentally—this was quite the earth-shattering revelation.

Do I like him because it's destined to be so?

Why am I not more mad about this?

"I-I'm not sure what to think. I'll admit I'm fond of him." A thought struck her. *Does he only like me because he thought he had no choice?* The blood in her face retreated and her stomach lurched.

"Sephy, I know this is a lot to take in. I was hoping there was more time."

Tears pooled in her eyes. Wiping at soaked eyelids, Persephone stifled a cry.

"Oh, honey. We can fight this. You don't have to marry him soon. There are ways we can delay this."

Persephone swallowed, then sucked a breath through her mouth. She grabbed a tissue. "He only likes me because he knows he has to." She blew her nose, then dropped her head in her hands. The motion caused the mounting pressure in her face to throb painfully.

Her mom rubbed soothing circles on her back. "Oh, my sweet Sephy. No. You're a goddess of immense value. Any god or goddess would be thrilled to wed you. If he wasn't interested in the first place, he never would've consulted the Fates. Us gods only do that when we desire something so desperately that we're afraid it's an instrument of our demise."

Of course she'd think that. "You're terribly biased. You don't know what he feels." She leaned more of her weight onto her mom, feeling tiredness pressing down on her. She was going to need to sleep again soon, and it made her so angry. This conversation had been months in the making—she was desperate for it and had to fight through the pull of whatever this illness was.

Her mom released a long exhale. "Sephy, dear, I know how gods think. I've been a goddess for far too long to claim ignorance. He's locked onto to you and will never let go." Demeter continued brushing her fingertips up and down Persephone's back. "You're a goddess. I'm sure by now you've figured out that we don't do anything we don't want to."

Persephone managed a soft laugh. She'd seen as much with the gods and—to be honest—realized that few could force her to do anything unless they convinced her first. She leaned towards her mom, Demeter's warm chest and arms wrapped around her. As she melted into the embrace, the tears stopped.

Demeter kissed the top of Persephone's head, and both goddesses released each other. "Let me get Laura in here to check on you before I go. I've come here and riled you up."

"I'm glad you came. Thanks, Mom." Demeter portaled away, leaving Sephy to contend with her conflicted feelings.

Her mom's support—albeit closer to sympathy—chipped her spirit. Hades had sent her away without hesitation and now her mom pitied her. Worse, her mom thought Hades had damaged her. What would her mom say if she knew how easily Hades had let her go? A raw, unrelenting ache saturated her chest.

I'm weak and alone. What can I do?

Months ago, she was poised to become Olympus' next mogul. Now she'd be lucky if she could stand long enough to brush her own teeth.

BEFORE SHE'D FALLEN ASLEEP, Persephone had told Laura a quick, stilted version of her conversation with their mom. After Persephone's long nap, Laura returned with a pot of tea and an eagerness to hear more.

"She said *what* now?" Laura stared slack-jawed at Persephone as she sat next to her in bed.

"He's my Fates-ordained husband, apparently. Asked Mom for her blessing before I signed the contract with Eurydice. Mom knew and tried to save me from it, but was too worried if she meddled, it'd cause more problems."

Laura laughed, then slapped a hand over her mouth. "I'm sorry, but that's archaic. Right? I believe in the Fates or whatever, but didn't that type of divination die out a long time ago? Do the Fates bill gods when they're consulted? Does Mom have them on payroll?"

Persephone released a small, airy laugh despite feeling like a shell of what she once was. "Perhaps they make them sign a statement of work before fortune telling?"

"How are you feeling about this? Are you okay?"

Persephone took a slow sip of her tea. "Relieved. Knowing we're fated to be together makes it feel more like a sure thing, but I'm worried it influenced his initial interest. Mom claims he must've been interested if he went to the Fates in the first place, but she's biased."

"No, I'm with Mom on this one, but it's not our place to convince you he's committed. Leave that to him."

"Shouldn't you be cautioning me to guard my heart?" Persephone set down her tea.

"Sephy, you're not some lust-crazed simpleton. You've barely dated. And we knew Hades was good-looking and successful and it turns out, he's kind and is obsessed with you. I think it makes sense that you've developed feelings for him. Plus, Peter, Helena, and I like him and he owns all the best restaurants."

"So, is it because he's kind, or because he owns the best restaurants?" Persephone cracked the joke, but her insides felt hollow.

"Why can't both things be true? Expand your mind, goddess." Laura winked at Persephone and then brushed her hand lightly down Persephone's arm. "Want me to help you get ready for bed?"

Persephone nodded with tears filling her eyes because she knew she wouldn't make it more than two steps before she'd be needing Laura's help again.

THE DAY after her mom's visit, Persephone woke with the worst migraine she'd ever experienced. Back in Laura's guest room, groaning into the pillow, Persephone pushed up to a sitting position on the bed. The movement caused the room to wobble, and a sharp spasm tore through her stomach. One hand clutching her waist and the other extended to steady herself, she shuffled towards the bathroom. Exhausted, she sat on the closed toilet seat, resting her head on the nearby sink and needing the chill from the porcelain to cool her.

The bedroom door creaked open, followed by Hecate's voice. "Sephy, it's Hecate. Can I come in?"

Clearing a hoarse throat, she called, "Yes."

The door clicked shut, then Hecate laid a hand on Persephone's shoulder.

"Laura said you're feeling worse. May I check you?"

Five days ago, Persephone could stand without trouble and now she struggled to make it the short distance to the bathroom.

Nodding, Persephone tried to sit tall as Hecate placed her hands on Persephone's neck. She felt pathetic. She couldn't live like this, needing the constant help of others to do simple things. She wanted to cry but felt too weak to even do that.

"A little pressure." Hecate pressed lightly under Persephone's chin for three seconds. With a gentle touch, Hecate traced her thumbs down the column of Persephone's throat to her heart. "Your magic is starving, so it's taking energy from you." Hecate crouched down, resting her forearms on her thighs. "Power functions a lot like our metabolism does. The more you feed it, the hungrier it becomes. I have a few guesses what was feeding it before, but I may need to relocate you to be certain. Are you well enough to portal?"

"Let's try it." Anything was worth a shot at clearing the constant pain.

Hecate stood up and pulled out her phone. "Is it okay with you if I take you straight to Hades' bedroom?"

"Alright." Hecate could've laid Persephone in the middle of the streets of Olympus, and she wouldn't care. Every atom of her being waged war against her.

"Fates, you poor thing. I never should've let you leave his place." Hecate wrapped her arms around her, and the familiar whoosh of a portal swept over them both. Engulfed in the purple smoke and sweet sandalwood scent of Hecate's magic, a large bed appeared in a suite decorated with velvet furniture and an open door to a spacious walk-in closet filled with suits.

Cerberus perked his head up from the intricate wool rug he laid curled up on. He then hopped up to nudge Persephone's leg.

The dark oak bedside tables shone in the low light of the room, and flanked the pressed pillows lined so precisely, they looked like tiles in a palace wall. The fresh, masculine scent was unmistakably Hades.

"Hecate, it's too clean to have me stay in here. Put me in my old guest room." The thought of sweating on the silk sheets made bile rise in her throat. *Poor Laura. Her guest room must smell like an open grave now.*

Scoffing, Hecate pulled back the covers just as Hades appeared beside Persephone.

"Come here." Hades scooped her up and cradled her to his chest. Her muscles relaxed and her eyes drifted shut as she laid her head on his shoulder.

Hades lowered her to the bed, between the sheets. Shedding his jacket, Hades scooted next to her and pulled her partway onto his lap. The dizziness and nausea from seconds before faded, leaving a pleasant calmness in her bones.

On the other side of the bed, Hecate stroked Persephone's hair. "When you're feeling up to it, try conjuring the poppies."

Persephone nodded.

Before leaving, Hecate glared at Hades, narrowing her eyes in a challenge, then portaled away. Odd given the fact that Hecate had brought her here.

A welcome coolness washed over her, bringing with it a light evergreen scent. "Little goddess, I am so sorry I let you leave."

The reminder stirred an emptiness in her gut. Was he relieved she was back? Or burdened again by his future Fates-ordained wife? *Why did you send me away?* Even thinking about the question churned humiliation to the surface.

"It's okay." The words tasted sour. Turning her head away from Hades, she reached out her hand and imagined poppies blooming around the bed. Bright orange and red blooms sprouted across the floor and parted around a sitting Cerberus.

A low rumble in Hades' chest preceded his reply. "I thought I was being selfish, keeping you here as you struggled. I didn't believe Hecate when she said you were better off staying. I was wrong, Sephy. Will you forgive me?"

Relieved to hear his regret, she smiled. "Of course. I mean, we still don't really know what's going on. And I'm sorry I've missed so many events. I feel terrible."

Hades ran his fingertips over the back of her neck. "I kept you from going to events. Besides, you should save your strength for our weekend getaway."

In the struggles of her illness, she'd completely forgotten about their trip. Would it even still happen?

Do I tell him what my mom admitted? Maybe if she could go a day without searing pain, she'd bring it up.

CHAPTER THIRTY EIGHT

A GODDESS AWAKENS

PERSEPHONE

Back in Hades' apartment, Persephone's no longer suffered from headaches or dizziness. Instead, she felt better than ever. When Hades touched her, her powers came alive. Those few days of full health made her recent illness a distant memory. Had she known being back with Hades would cure her, she would've never left.

Cerberus slept at the end of the bed like a furry donut. Eyes closed, the gentle lift and dip of his breathing made him too irresistible not to squeeze. His fluffy fur scrunched like fleece.

With a loud knock, Hecate entered the room with Hades close behind. "We figured it out," Hecate cheered.

Sitting straighter on the end of the bed, Persephone knew he could only be talking about one thing: what had made her sick in the first place.

Hecate said, "You've got to purge your magic more regularly. If you don't start using it for daily activities, it'll get stored up and make you sick again. Hades' power seems to draw it out, which is why you feel better when he touches you, but you've got to push it out as well."

"So, I need to release and recall the poppies more often?"

Hades shook his head. "No, you need to portal when you want to get somewhere. Conjure your morning coffee, summon your clothes to get dressed, enchant your laptop to record notes in a meeting. Once you're exercising your powers regularly, you won't have those terrible headaches."

A wave of relief washed over her. *Thank the Fates.* There was life after migraines and fainting spells. "How did you two figure it out?"

Hecate said, "After I portaled you back here from Laura's place and saw how you immediately perked up at his touch, I knew it had something to do with the flow of your magic. Hades must've awakened it but you had so much pent-up power it drained you trying to escape."

Hades cut in, "You should try to use your powers this morning so you feel your best. We've got a meeting with the launch team, and I want you there."

Persephone sprung up from the bed, Cerberus hopped off and Persephone fixed the sheets with a wave of her hand, just as Hecate had shown her. "How soon until we leave?"

"We have a couple of hours." Hades smiled at her.

Hovering her hands over her face, Persephone imagined her makeup from one photo of Hades and her on their first fake date. Olive tinted foundation, dark mascara, and light pink blush. A warm breeze radiated from her palms and brushed her skin. A thrill spiraled from the soles of her feet to the top of her head. Power flowed with abandon through her, and a beaming grin spread across her face.

Opening her eyes, she asked Hades and Hecate, "How do I look?"

"Stunning," said Hecate.

Hades replied, "Perfect."

"Good. I'll meet you two in the living room. I want to change my outfit with magic."

"Great idea," Hecate said and portaled with a purple cloud in her wake.

Hades stepped closer. "Sephy, before you finish getting ready, I have something I should confess." He sat down on the bed, patting the open spot next to him. He leaned onto his side getting comfortable, but the strained expression on his face looked anything but relaxed. "Before we ever met in person, I asked the Fates about you."

So this was it. Her Mom had said as much—that he'd asked them if they'd marry.

"It only took one look at you and I felt it deep in my being that our paths would intertwine." His gaze bore into her with such sincerity that she held her breath. "I bargained with them for an answer to the question: *would you marry me.* I was drowning in my infatuation with you, even before I knew how incredible you truly are. There was no rationalizing or explaining why I was so captivated by you from the start. I'd never experienced a longing as strong as this and I needed to know if I had an iota of a chance to be in your life, because if I didn't, then I needed to leave Olympus." He paused, sucking in a deep breath. "But here's the tricky thing about the Fates: they expect payment for their answers. Even still, I knew the answer was worth the cost."

"What did it cost?" she barely whispered the words. It felt like her body had left her. To know that someone as strong as him was desperate for answers about her was surreal.

He sat up and moved closer to push some of her hair behind her ear. "Nothing that wasn't worth losing."

She swallowed. "So what did you bargain?"

With a lopsided smile, he said, "Underworld Unlimited."

Her hand covered her mouth. There was no way. He owned

and ran the empire, so why was he saying he'd bargained with it? "Did you end up not having to pay?"

"Oh, I paid. Legally-speaking, I'm the president but no longer CEO."

Her throat went dry. "Who's CEO then?"

He traced his finger down her cheek, trailing along the side of her neck. "You are, Sephy. The papers are awaiting your signature for it to be official, but in all practical terms, Underworld Unlimited is yours."

Coherent thoughts evaded her. She shook her head. "Why would you bargain that?" She examined his face for any sign of jest but found none. Just his handsome face watching her with the shadow of a grin.

"Ask Charon, she'll verify everything I'm saying. You're Underworld Unlimited's CEO, Sephy. We're just waiting for when you're ready to take over."

"I..." Her voice trailed off. She twisted her hands together, unsure what to say.

"It's not something you have to do *anything* about today. Especially since you've barely recovered from weeks of your power weakening your body."

His palms held the sides of her arms. She wanted to kiss him, even if it was to keep from continuing the conversation. It was simply too much to process.

"Sephy," he prompted, and she looked up at him. "You haven't asked what their answer was."

Right. Hadn't she been wanting to talk about what she knew? "What was it?"

"Do you want to know?"

No fear, only excitement. "They said we'd marry."

He nodded. "Are you disappointed?"

Not even a little. She frowned, worried that he'd assume she would be. "No. Are you?"

"Not at all. If anything, I'm surprised the Fates were this kind to me."

She fussed with the hem of her shorts. Gods rarely gave compliments without a clear motive, but she believed he adored her and *that* made her melt. Still, she wasn't sure what to say.

A mischievous grin crept over his face. "You said you wanted to change outfits. Should I stay and help? In case things go awry? One can never be too careful."

The welcome change of conversation kept her from gushing her insecurities that had bloomed along with her growing affection for him.

With a snap of her fingers, two pillows flew from the bed and smacked his chest. "You can help me dress another day." Whether it was the impressed look on his face or the lightness in her chest, she felt unstoppable now that she had control.

Hades flicked his hand, sending the pillows from the floor back to their original spots by the headboard. "I'd rather *undress* you, Sephy." He winked, then whistled at Cerberus. "If I'm not getting to watch, then neither are you. Come on." Cerberus bounded towards Hades as he exited the door and blew her a kiss.

Once the door clicked shut, she pictured the dark gray, monochromatic shirt and skirt combination Charon had set out for her weeks ago before her first in-office visit and imagined it appearing in her hands. Silk landed softly in her palms.

Setting the clothes on an upholstered chair, she stripped off her loungewear set, not wanting to ruin two outfits if it didn't work. Her mom could change clothing, makeup, and even hair at will. Baby steps for now. She pictured the blouse and skirt wrapped around her and smiled when the clothes disappeared from the chair and reappeared on her body.

She examined how the shirt tucked into the waist, then swiped her hands down the length of the skirt. Holding her head higher, she swept fingers through her hair, creating soft, wavy curls and checked the end results in a floor-length mirror. Pleased with the ensemble, she portaled to the kitchen.

CHAPTER THIRTY NINE

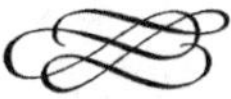

POPPIES AND POISON

Time flew once Persephone was feeling well again. Hades and her had completed their promotional tour and all that was left was the gala celebrating the *Flowers Near Me* launch. Technically, Hades had released her from the contract, but she was too invested in the app to step away now. She owed it to the Underworld Unlimited team and herself. And she wasn't ready to leave Hades' side.

Sunlight streamed through the glass ceiling overlooking the botanical garden's conservatory. What a sight it'd be once all the decorations for the gala adorned the space.

Persephone and Hermes stood off to the side as Hades, Zeus, and Poseidon argued over the seating arrangement chart. A quiet Charon stared at her tablet while another psychopomp nearby intently watched her. Poseidon had introduced his assistant, Vanth, when they'd arrived. Dressed in dark suit that matched his dark features, Vanth had mastered the same untouchable, signature look that Charon wore, but he'd failed to hide the glances he shot Charon's way.

"So..." Persephone bumped Hermes' shoulder with hers. "How do you like working for Zeus?" Although they'd spoken over the phone, she hadn't seen him in person since she'd snuck him into the Underworld offices.

Hermes gave her a grin. "Good. He's not as nice as you, but things are going well. I was worried we might never cross paths again after… you know."

Keeping her voice low, she leaned in. "Me too, but I think Hades has moved on. I heard he interrogated you afterwards."

Hermes glanced at Hades, who was now pinching the bridge of his nose as Poseidon moved names around on the board. "He wasn't happy. I told him everything. That I had begged for your help."

"Oh, I heard. You didn't have to do that. I was ready to keep your secret for eternity." She gave him a half smile.

"It's fine. I think he was more concerned that you had double crossed him by tampering with the app."

"Right. I'd almost forgotten. How did you hear about that? Did he accuse you of being involved?"

Across the garden patio, Zeus picked the seating chart off of its stand and held it away from Poseidon. The God of the Sea swatted at his brother's shoulders.

Hermes spun his head and gaped at Persephone. His curls bounced. "You know it was your mom that messed with the app, right? She sent some kind of virus called a 'snake bite' and Hades found out. She was livid when I delivered his message to her."

It was Mom? "How long ago was this?"

Hermes shrugged. "A few months."

Fates. Mom tried to take down the app. Why didn't Hades tell me? And Hermes' nonchalant delivery of the news made it seem like it wasn't a big deal whatsoever. Demeter had tried to sabotage *Flowers Near Me* and Persephone was the last one to find out?

"So…" Hermes pulled her from her spiraling thoughts. "Hades said you have powers. What are you the goddess of?"

She looked up to see Hades staring back at her. She clamped

her mouth, and Hades cocked his head to the side. Beside him, Vanth restrained Poseidon who was still trying to swing at Zeus.

Keeping her eyes locked with Hades from across the solarium, she replied to Hermes, "I don't know. My only unique power is creating poisonous poppies. I'll tell you if I figure out more."

"I want to know." Hermes gaze moved towards Charon and Vanth standing near the three brothers and he made a low groan. "Poor Vanth. Can you imagine working for Poseidon?"

Now Poseidon pouted, arms crossed, scowling at Zeus. Vanth dusted his suit jacket, smirking and shaking his head.

"No, but I'd bet Charon could whip him into shape in a week," said Persephone.

"I don't know. Managing his liaisons would take up so much time."

Persephone huffed a laugh. "Fates. Think of all the rides you'd have to call after his one-night stands."

Hermes rolled his eyes. "You mean all the calls to the clinic for STD testing?"

Persephone turned and pretended to gag. It felt great to joke with Hermes and not be worried about fainting or trying to fight through the painful fog of a headache.

Off to the side, Vanth moved closer to Charon as Zeus placed the seating chart back on its stand. Hades and Poseidon circled around the chart. "What do you know about Vanth?"

Hermes shrugged. "Not much. He's a psychopomp like Charon, so naturally everyone is saying they should hook up. He seems nice."

"I haven't heard anything about him."

Charon scrolled through her tablet as Vanth regarded Charon's ensemble. It should've been creepy but only admiration shone in his eyes.

"Think he has a chance with her?" asked Hermes.

Persephone wondered, did Charon focus on anything other than her work? Charon's eyes remained on the screen in her grip, while Vanth now stared longingly at her face. "I don't know, but it would be sweet to watch Charon fall in love. See if you can find out more about Vanth. I want to know if he's good enough for her."

Hermes said, "I'll try."

CHAPTER FORTY

LOVE IN BLOOM AND STONE

HADES

*H*e'd postponed their trip until he knew Persephone had fully recovered. After seeing her thrive in *Flower Near Me*'s final promotions, he felt confident she was hale and whole.

The gala was only a few days away, but there were still a few things left to do before he and Sephy would leave for their getaway. Inside the gala's event space, Hades marveled at the vines cascaded over the balcony, nearly touching the floor of the three-story domed conservatory. Dozens of staff navigated carts around marble pillars, like ants building a marvel for their queen, all in preparation for the massive gala.

Tomorrow, Sephy would join Hades for their first genuine date—a weekend getaway to one of his favorite secluded properties. The thought consumed him, but his little goddess was shooting daggers his way from across the bustling room. He hadn't gotten a moment with her since they'd arrived at the gala's location to finish preparations for the event. Even when they moved from the conservatory to the greenhouse to finalize seating arrangements, Sephy had stuck close to Hermes.

After a painful hour, Poseidon relented to Zeus and Hades' plans and stormed off, citing another meeting that Hades was certain didn't exist. If the timing wasn't suspicious enough, his brooding assistant's surprised reaction confirmed his theory. He'd met Vanth—the man Hecate said would be a good match for Charon—earlier that morning. The poor psychopomp had a long road ahead of him, given that Sephy and his assistant barely looked Vanth's direction.

With a few parting words to Zeus, Hades made his way towards Sephy. Hermes gave him one look, then flitted off.

"Good time catching up?" he asked Sephy.

"Very enlightening. Sounds like you had him pay my mom a visit to correct bad behavior." She held his gaze, and his heart dropped.

In the chaos of her magic-induced illness and the subsequent months, he'd forgotten to tell Sephy about her mom's involvement with the app's virus. "He told you about the 'snake bite.'"

She slowly crossed her arms. "Strange hearing it from him and not you, though."

He looked away, unable to hold her stare. "I should've told you when I found out, but at the time I needed to know you didn't have a hand in it as well."

She sighed. "I would've preferred to hear about it from you and not Hermes."

"That's fair." Guilt gnawed at him but dissipated when the lines between her brows faded.

Smirking, Sephy asked, "Are your brothers happy now that they get to sit with all their friends?"

Purring a light laugh, Hades stood next to his little goddess and placed his hand on her back. The warm silk of her shirt brought images of the sleep sets he'd requested Charon pack for Sephy for their trip. *Better if she wears nothing at all.*

"Yes, every child's got their assigned seat. Though we might need Charon to write Poseidon's name in giant, glittering letters —just to keep him from causing a tidal wave. Maybe his new assistant can help."

Sephy's head swiveled to him faster than Cerberus to spilled ambrosia. "What do you know about Vanth? He seemed very curious about Charon."

He met her gaze, a grin blooming on his face. "You noticed his interest too. Hecate speaks well of him. Maybe I should ask Charon to look into him?"

"Sounds like I need to reach out to my private investigator." Sephy pulled her phone from her skirt. He imagined sliding his fingers into her pocket and pulling her against him.

"Who's your PI, Sephy?"

"Laura. No one can find skeletons in the closet faster than a motivated sibling."

He laughed, knowing he could *never* trust Poseidon to help him research anyone. Zeus... maybe? "I'll take your word for it. Let me know what she finds. I'm not too bad of a detective when I need to be."

Sephy typed a message, then pocketed her phone. Smiling at Hades, she asked, "So, our trip starts tomorrow. Will you tell me where we're going?"

"Want to bargain for the information?" He wrapped his arm around her and pulled her to his side.

"Hm. Depends. What do you want?"

He leaned down an inch from her ear and whispered, "Don't tempt me, love. I've got a trove of fantasies to choose from." Goosebumps covered her soft neck.

Still tucked in his arm, she scrutinized his face. She dragged her knuckle down the center of his shirt. "Don't start something you won't finish, Hades. It wasn't me who asked to stop back at the apartment."

His insides went molten. "Patience, Sephy. We'll have all weekend to pick back up where we started."

Eyes unblinking and lips parted, Sephy's face blushed in a delightful pink hue.

Using his power to deepen his voice, Hades added, "You know, that first time we *really* kissed and I heard your little moans, it seemed like the right time to get you to agree to marry me. Didn't want to waste the opportunity when I had you pliant and needy." He trailed his fingers down the back of her arm. "Besides… there's no world where our first time *together* happens on a couch. You should expect more from your lover."

He pressed a gentle kiss to her flushed cheek, then strode away towards nothing, going nowhere. He'd been careful ever since she'd returned to the apartment after her magic sickness, to not push anything too far physically—at least not until their getaway. The want inside him had nearly killed him. But this was not the moment to stir the longing, yet he'd managed to fuel the flames higher. After months of careful planning, trying to win her heart, now he was close to convincing her to marry him. It'd been agony to wait.

Hades portaled to the guest bedroom he'd been staying in since Sephy had started staying in his private suite. Ripping a pillow from the bed, he slammed it to his face and screamed. Cerberus bounded through the door and nudged at his feet. Laughing to himself, he tossed the pillow on the bed and bent down to pet Cerberus. Whenever he removed his hand, Cerberus huffed and poked him with his nose. After a few minutes of trying to satisfy the fluffy beast, Hades stood up and adjusted his jacket.

Cracking his neck, he took a deep breath, then portaled back to Sephy, still standing in the large hall of the botanical garden's central building.

"Sorry, little goddess. Did I miss anything?"

Her eyes traced up and down his body. "Where did you go in such a hurry?"

He smirked. "Just headed off to scream into a pillow as one does." He hoped his wink was convincing. She cut right through his defenses unlike any other—immortal or otherwise—had.

"You're funny." She turned back to watch the flurry of staff moving carts and boxes.

The familiar clack of sandals on the tiled floor caught his attention. Hecate approached, giving Sephy a squeeze on her delicate arm.

"Hades, are you ready to go through the decor?" Hecate gestured towards a wire archway covered in flowers.

"What else is needed? The building already looks fit for a gala." Sephy looked between him and Hecate.

He turned to Sephy. "Just some final touches I need Hecate to make. Please excuse us."

"No worries," Sephy said with a polite smile and gave him a quick kiss.

Scanning the room for Charon, he sent a pulse of power her way. With a stack of garment boxes in her arms, Charon met his eyes. He casually dipped his head, gesturing at Sephy.

"Persephone," Charon called out. "Could you join the marketing team as they get some photos of the setup?"

Once Sephy was out of earshot, Hecate asked, "So these enchanted vines... you want me to charm them so that whenever Sephy is near, they'll bloom?"

"Precisely."

"Show me which ones to enchant."

They toured through the building, Hades pointing to green vines being hung with tiny solar-powered lights attached to them. Buds dotted the twisting stems. He doubted Sephy understood the depth of her influence on plants, but he knew.

With the Underworld Unlimited event planning machine in full force, Hades snuck off to a shop back in the ironworks district of Olympus. Hephaestus' workshop had a large 'closed' sign across the door, but Hades portaled through anyway.

"Hades, I'm almost finished," Hephaestus greeted him. The god bent over a workbench, working his hands around a small piece of jewelry.

"Good." Hades leaned on a glass counter and unbuttoned the top of his dress shirt.

"Yours is finished if you want to see it. Over there." Hephaestus motioned a fist behind him to a black metal box sitting on the desk.

Pushing through the gate between the displays, Hades picked up the box. Inside, a wide wedding band of obsidian sat tied to a velvet pillow. Removing the satin string, he pinched the ring between his fingers and squinted at the stamped design adorning it. "Well done, Hephaestus. They look just like her poppies."

Hephaestus grunted and stood up. Cradling three small rings, he held them out to Hades. "Check out hers."

Each one had a white gold band with melanite in the center. The largest band boasted the widest polished gemstone.

Untying a thick, charcoal stained apron, Hephaestus asked, "Why does she want three rings for her ring finger?"

Hades released a low sigh. "She doesn't. I wanted a ring to be seen on each part so everyone knows she's taken." He gave Hephaestus a smirk.

Hephaestus' jaw ticked. "I can understand that."

CHAPTER FORTY ONE

A DIVINE PROPOSAL

PERSEPHONE

The primitive image *hot springs cave* brought to mind was nothing like Hades' palatial residence built into the caverns. Although they had portaled there, it was clear from the forested mountains surrounding the property that they were far from the metropolis. Even on the coldest night, the city of Olympus could never be this quiet.

Equipped with ambient lighting and modern bathrooms, most of the rooms sat along an exterior wall with natural light flooding through large windows. The same style of lush furniture Hades had in his apartment decorated the space.

"Take a bath while I gather a few things," he said then pointed to a rose-colored silk robe and fluffy towels placed on a sprawling, god-sized bed. He opened a pine wardrobe built within the wall—its edges framed by an overlapping lip of stone—and pulled out a basket filled with oils and soaps.

"This place is gorgeous," said Persephone. "Why don't you live here instead of the apartment?"

"Remember how much Cerberus sheds?"

Picturing the dog shaking off, water droplets scattering over a pile of towels, brought a grimace. "Good point."

"Make yourself at home." With a hand gesturing to a carved archway between a velvet loveseat and a desk cut from a large, dark stone deposit in the wall, he added, "That hall leads to a spring-fed bath."

"Thank you." She scooped up the items from the bed.

Hades left and Persephone walked down the hallway into the bathing chamber. She marveled at the carved ceiling twice Hades' height with snaking veins of lapis running throughout the light gray stone.

Persephone sunk into the effervescent springs and stretched her arms overhead, relaxing against the submerged curved bench. Faint trickles echoed in the cavern. Would too much bliss melt an immortal body into a puddle? It seemed possible as she closed her eyes.

When her body felt warm and loose, she got out and wrapped herself in a fluffy towel. Using her poppy-scented power, she finished drying her hair and body before heading back to the bedroom.

Inside the wardrobe were sleepwear sets, reverse seam sweaters, and tailored joggers, each in a variety of soft fabrics of silk or silk-like cotton. She pulled out a long-sleeved top and matching pants. Dressing quickly, she kept one eye on the arched doorway.

Using the mirror on the inside of the wardrobe door, she ran one finger over her lids, imagining her eyelashes lengthening and sending magic through her veins. Picturing a dark pink rose, she pressed her lips together, and they turned a deeper shade. Would her mom be proud to see how far she'd come in her power? She hoped so.

An evergreen scent announced Hades' presence in the hall-way. "Sephy, love. Are you done with your bath?"

She called back, "All done," and he joined her in the bedroom. Despite her advances and protests, Hades refrained from becoming *too* intimate. He claimed it was so they could be extra certain that her powers wouldn't reignite the sickness. But it had been two months since she'd healed. She sensed he was holding out for her to agree to marry him.

"You charmed your face." Hades ran his hands up and down the sides of her arms.

"How can you tell?"

Tapping the side of his nose, he said, "You get a sense of these things." With a bright smile, Hades asked, "Ready to eat? Or want to play a game of Sevens?"

She'd lost the last time they'd played and now they were on the date she'd agreed to because of that gamble. It reminded her to ask if he'd swayed the outcome in his favor. Even if he did, she wasn't upset but she was curious.

"Hades, did you cheat when we played before?" Arms crossed, she let a smirk peek through.

He stiffened and took a breath. "I may have tipped things in my favor."

"Damn it. When you won after all those losing rounds..." Persephone shook her head.

"Are you upset with me?"

Pressing into him, her face on his chest, she replied, "No. If you hadn't won, I may have never gotten to see this place."

He met her eyes when she looked up at him. "The contract's complete. And I always planned to bring you here as soon as you would let me."

Pulling away, Hades kept her in his hold with his hands on her back.

"Well, thank you for bringing me. The bath alone has made the visit worth it."

Hades' eyes roamed her face, his lips parted and eyes narrowed slightly. "Persephone." Hearing her name from him sent a shiver up her spine. "There's something I want you to agree to, but only if you're ready."

Another contract? Was he worried she wouldn't attend the gala?

"What is it?"

He held her hands and knelt on one knee. No mistaking which kind of contract he meant now.

"Persephone, I'd be honored to be at your side. You're the only partner for me."

Heart speeding, she nodded. "We make a good team." Hades owned the key to her heart, and he knew it.

With a kiss on her hand and a glimmer in his eye, he said, "Come with me. I want to give you something."

He stood up, a surprising move given how certain she was that he was going to propose. Instead, he led her down the corridor connecting the rooms on the cave's outer wall, into a sitting area. Plump cushions atop a huge, curved couch jutted against steel framed windows looking out the mountainside.

A present wrapped in floral fabric sat on a polished wood tray on the sofa. Written on its tag in flowing script was 'Sephy.'

Hades picked up the tray. "Sit here."

Settled on the sprawling couch, Persephone took the present off of the tray as Hades sat next to her.

Small like a jewelry box. Her heart danced as she untied the satin bow. The fine wrapping fabric slid from the black box.

Three rings of varying sizes lay in a jewelry cushion. Each silvery white band had a smooth, dark stone in their center. Her brows pinched in confusion, looking at the different sizes. Was Hades unsure of her ring size? Unlikely. What detail did Hades —or Charon—ever miss?

A chill cut through the air as Hades' power enveloped her like a wintery cloud. Her own power rose to meet it, a tangle of cedar and florals filling the room.

His deep voice warmed her chest. "Persephone..." His throat

bobbed. "I'm not sorry that I tricked you into working for me—or living with me. But I am sorry that I made you think you were a pawn that day I moved you—"

"Forced," she interjected with a smirk and bright eyes.

He laughed with a wink. "Yes. Well, let's call it the first day you came to our apartment."

Her smile grew wide and he continued, "You thought you were a pawn, but you've never been one to me." The sincerity of the sentiment shone through his softened gaze. He scooped her hands in his. "You're the most exquisite immortal to exist. You've unlocked a yearning I didn't know I could feel. I love you, little goddess. You're everything I want but don't deserve. And I wish I had something as valuable as you to offer in return, but all my love, commitment, and loyalty is yours. Marry me, Sephy."

Peacefulness washed over her. A future with him made her feel like she could conquer more than just Olympus.

She met his silver eyes. "I'll marry you, Hades."

He leaned in for a kiss which she returned. He pulled away to pick up the ring box.

"May I?" Hades held up his palm to her.

Placing her hand in his, she whispered, "Please." Magic crackled in the air—tiny sparks surrounded them, leaving wisps of smoke in their place. The scent of their commingling power was thick yet pleasant.

He plucked each ring from its bed then slid the largest one onto her finger. A blanket of contentment wrapped around her.

Mesmerized by his gentle movements, she watched him slide a second one, stopping right before going over her knuckle. Now the varying sizes made sense. Each ring was built to fit a different section of her finger. The largest worn normally, the middle one in between her knuckles, and the smallest right behind her nail bed.

"They're beautiful." Time stood still as she admired the jewelry.

With a tender smile, he said, "These symbolize my intention to love and care for you. As long as you wear yours, they represent your commitment to me. Once you place my ring, it'll secure our marriage bond."

"We'll need a ceremony, right? And to get a marriage certificate?"

Hades shook his head. "It's different between the gods. Our word is law. Once we exchange these rings then the oath is complete. There's nothing else to it unless we want a ceremony or a certificate to commemorate our promise. No need for witnesses or officiants."

No wonder the gods expected the world. Everything was simpler for them, yet more powerful. And now Persephone knew she was one of them too.

He hooked a finger under his collar to fish out a black chain holding one obsidian ring.

"Here's mine." He unclasped the necklace, allowing the ring to slide down the chain into his palm.

Carefully, she plucked it from his hand. Adorning the dark band were carved images of poppies—*her* poppies. Each intricate flower was a sibling of the ones next to it. As she traced the pad of her finger over the design, a warm sensation ran up her arm.

"Is it enchanted?"

"No. It responds to you, though. Similar to most things and people in your environment." He paused and grinned at her with a glint in his eye. "I think I've finally figured out what you're the goddess of."

"Tell me after I put this on you." She wanted Hades to be hers as much as he wanted her to be his.

Between pinched fingers, Hades' ring vibrated a low tone.

His hand remained still as the ring slid over his knuckle. Was he breathing? She wasn't sure she was.

With gentle and slow pressure, she placed the ring on his finger. A fullness entered her chest as their agreement settled into place.

His hands cupped her cheeks in their tender kiss, then wrapped behind her back, tugging her to his broad chest.

CHAPTER FORTY TWO

THE GODDESS AND HER KING

PERSEPHONE

Cuddled against Hades' firm chest, Persephone sipped the ambrosia, then guided it through the air to the low coffee table by one of the sets of bookshelves.

"Do you want a ceremony?" she asked him. She did, but couldn't deny the relief flooding her veins knowing the marriage bond was in place before they held a public wedding.

The app's promotional events had helped acquaint her with mass attention, but this was too personal a thing to do in front of hundreds of guests—most of whom would be strangers. She'd heard that Zeus and Hera's wedding had lasted days with droves of mortals and immortals alike. She doubted even almighty Zeus had known more than half of his guests.

Hades ran his fingers through her hair and teased, "I see its appeal." She recalled the first time they'd met when she'd said the same thing about living in the city of Olympus, and she gave him a playful swat on his leg.

"Is that a yes? Or are you trying to hide how much you want a ceremony?" she asked.

"I want whatever makes you happiest, Sephy." He kissed her temple, then nuzzled her hair. With a low, throaty sound, Hades pushed his nose and mouth against the side of her neck, sending a tickle down her spine. "You know, there is *one* more thing we need to do to seal this bond."

Understanding dawned, and her body wound tight. She pressed harder into his muscular torso. "Oh?"

Holding her in his arms, he asked, "Is this your first time?"

She nodded. "Don't let that be an excuse to hold back."

He cradled the back of her head with one hand and used the other to draw her closer to him. "Hold on," he whispered. The quiet tone was at odds with the sudden jolt of his portal-ing power.

The soft couch disappeared from under them, replaced by a bubbling hot spring. She released a small gasp as she registered her new surroundings—and *lack of clothes.*

Warm candlelight glowed in carved alcoves. The cedar decking surrounding the pool led to a large bed on the other side of the cavernous room. It was difficult to see into the water, but she felt his strong, naked form under her. He was sat on the polished stone bench carved into the pool's perimeter, she on top of him. Water lapped at his chiseled torso and a thin sheen of sweat coated his tanned skin.

Envisioning the body under his clothes was one thing, but to see it up close—to be sitting half-pressed against it—was unreal. His half-lidded eyes roamed her exposed waist and chest.

She released a small laugh as he cocked his thigh higher, lifting her out of the water and into his view. The trickling water and fresh air invigorated her skin. He stroked his fingertips down the column of her neck, slowly moving towards the center of her chest while his other arm held her waist.

The yearning in his gaze pinned her in place. A heady feeling rushed through her when he met her eyes. Her cheeks flushed hotter than before and she placed her hands on his wide shoulders to lean in to kiss him.

"Not yet. I'm not done admiring you." Hades backed away enough to grant his gaze the freedom to roam her face, throat, chest, and stomach.

His admiring smirk sent a pulsing need to her core. Delighted by his appreciative perusal, she raked her eyes over the definition sculpting his torso. Even with their famed likeness, the masterpiece renderings of Hades in marble and paint paled in comparison to the god in front of her.

He traced his fingers across her chest, down her stomach, and back up over the sides of her breasts. "Come here," he said, before placing her between his legs so that her back pressed against his chest.

With a firm grip, he held her against his groin. The result of his desire pressed into her lower back as he slowly ground into her. He lifted her higher and used his knees to ease her legs apart, spreading her wide. The position forced her to lean back against him, and her nipples pebbled in the cool air. He kissed behind her ear and down her neck.

"You are everything, Persephone," he whispered as he traced his fingers up the inside of her thighs. Touching so close to her center, he drew tiny circles, stirring a feverish craving in her gut. "I've thought a lot about how I've wanted to touch you. How I've wanted to taste you. How I'd try to take my time exploring every inch until you burst."

His words drove her heart to beat against her chest. If he didn't touch her where she needed it most soon, she would flip around and take her pleasure. The want to do just that—slowly slide his length inside her—grew until he ran one finger along her seam. He dipped into her, hooking his long finger into a place that ignited her longing. Alternating the pressure of his palm and fingers dipping inside, he struck a dizzying rhythm, building sparks from his touch. She felt him grind against her lower back.

Nipping her ear with his teeth, Hades said in a low voice, "I want to feel you come on my hand." She pushed and pulled as his steady ministrations responded to each whimper.

An orgasm stirred inside her and built so suddenly that she gripped his bicep. Now his cedar-scented power filled her lungs, sending a flood of arousal through her body. The keen sensation spread and she held her breath, frightened by the intensity of what was about to explode within her. Hades didn't break his pace and whispered a gravelly encouragement. "You feel amazing, Sephy."

Her muscles seized from the bliss, eyes rolling back in ecstasy. Warmth spread up from his fingers inside her up through her chest, dissipating into a boneless euphoria. He lessened the pressure as she bucked against the intense sensitivity. With a slow roll of his hand, he massaged her entrance as the high faded.

"I can't wait to see how good it feels when you're gripping my cock."

He turned her so her side rested against his chest. She cuddled against him, laying her head over his thumping heart. She planted kisses along his neck. He swept an arm under her knees and stepped up and out of the water. Persephone held tight to his shoulders in anticipation of the strain it'd take to lift them both cleanly out, but Hades' heart kept its even beat. He offered her a devious smile. Drops splashed to the ground, but by the time his foot stepped onto the cedar decking surrounding the bed, their skin and the soaked ends of her hair were dry.

Cushions like clouds billowed around her as he laid her down. Persephone reached out an expectant hand, but Hades stood up to stalk around to the end of the bed. As she took in the whole of him, her chest fluttered. Imposing yet refined in a suit, Hades naked with his eyes piercing halted all rational thought. Aware of her body bared to him, she sat up, bringing her pressed legs to the side.

"Lie back down. I need to see all of you," he said in the deep timbre of his voice. Eyes serious and nostrils flared, he waited. Pressing her lips together, Persephone sunk back onto the pillow and kept her knees bent but touching. The soles of her feet pushed into the downy comforter.

"I said all of you, Sephy." His voice was a command.

She raised up on her elbows and stared back. "Or what?" Maybe it was the afterglow of their time in the pool, but the question in all its boldness spilled out.

He cocked a brow, and one edge of his mouth lifted. "You're challenging the God of the Underworld?" The bed dipped with the weight of each knee and hand as he crept towards her feet.

She smirked. "Maybe."

Hades wrapped his fingers around one of her ankles and tugged her leg straight. "Well, you are the Goddess of Spring, Sephy. Empress of the Underworld. I guess that's why I'm the one at your feet." He trailed kisses up the inside of her leg, rubbing the scruff of his jaw along the sensitive skin of her inner thigh. Her other leg fell to the side as she lay back.

Goddess of Spring. It made little sense given the dangerous blooms her powers produced, but Fates, did she like how it sounded as he moved up her body.

Still caressing her skin with his lips and stubbled cheek, Hades added, "Everything and everyone comes to life around you. And your poisonous poppies..." He dragged his tongue up her leg and over her hipbone. "It's more than a clever defense. They're a symbol of your protective nature. Something earthy, alluring, yet dangerous."

His sweet words wash over her, building the anticipation of what he'd touch or kiss next. "I wonder how the Goddess of Spring and protection tastes."

He moved down her body, his hands firm on her hips, and settled between her legs. His tongue flicked against her clit, causing her to squirm. One finger pushed inside her, and he established a toe-curling pace before adding a second. Persephone's hips struck their own rhythm until whimpers escaped her lips.

Frenzied and charged, she tugged his hair and the crisp scent of his power filled the air. He'd already wound her up so tight but another wave of desire pulsed through her when she smelled his magic.

Once his eyes met hers, she said, "Come here," and pulled him up. Instead of meeting her in a kiss like she thought he would, he turned to lick her ear which had her shuddering.

She helped position him at her entrance and the realization of how big he was, striding at the end of the bed minutes before, came crashing down.

"Sephy, are you still with me?"

This would be uncomfortable before it felt good again, and with all of her experience—or lack thereof—she'd jumped into murky water without the faintest idea of where the bottom was. But she wasn't about to stop. "Yes, keep going," she replied, her voice full of need.

"You have my heart, Sephy." He slowly pushed into her and the sharp pinch disappeared before she could register the pain.

Releasing a soft moan, she met the drive of his hips with the roll of her own. The angle of each thrust hit that sweet spot she wanted pressed over and over again. The fullness of him inside her and his unchanging, pleasure-building tempo drove her higher.

In a gravelly whisper, he said, "I could stay inside you forever and it'd never be enough. I knew you'd feel *perfect*."

She pulled him towards her in a kiss, swept away by the sensations. Let him do all the talking—it was her first time, and she was going to savor the ecstasy wracking her body. His mouth left her lips to press frenzied kisses into her neck. Her head sunk further into the pillow as she arched her neck and back. She wrapped one leg around him to pull him tighter towards her and his satisfied grunt spurred her to wrap her other leg around him as well.

The slow increase of pleasure rose like the crest of a hill. She braced for impact before her body snapped. "You're made for me, Sephy," he whispered but she could hardly speak as an orgasm rolled through her, sending wave after wave of rapture through her core. She pressed her nails into his back and Hades released a strained grunt, slowing his movement at the same time. He murmured something incoherent that sounded like muffled expletives.

With a desperate breath in, the scent of his power filled her lungs. She hadn't thought to use her power during sex, but he had, and she'd *loved* it. He gave her a long, slow kiss before pulling out and resting on his side. Stretching his arm around her waist, he pulled her against him and rubbed his chin on the top of her head.

"From the moment I saw you, little goddess, this is all I've wanted. To have you in my arms forever."

She hugged him tighter. By the way she'd lost herself, she wondered if he was bleeding from when she'd clawed at his back. "Did I hurt you, Hades?"

With a throaty reply, "Fates no. You could've driven a knife through my heart, and I wouldn't have stopped. Nothing has ever felt as sublime as being inside you."

SHE WOKE from a short nap on Hades' chest to find him gazing at her, running his fingertips up and down her spine.

"Sleep well?" he asked.

"Very." Stretching her neck and back, she sat up to lean against the plush pillows. With the excitement of their joining, she'd barely noticed the silky sheets and impressively large bed. "Did you fall asleep?"

He shook his head. "I couldn't. The most beautiful goddess the Fates ever made was asleep in my arms."

A blush crept onto her cheeks. "Such a sweet talker." She ran her hand over his stomach, enjoying how every muscle tensed under her touch. "We'll have to do this again soon." She shot him a wink to which he chuckled.

"That a promise?"

"Listen. If you'd like to bargain for a prom—"

He cut off her retort as he grabbed her by the waist, bringing her into his lap. She yelped in delight, squirming as he playfully bit where her neck met her shoulder, causing goosebumps to erupt over her skin. His fingers tickled her sides as he squeezed her and continued to kiss her collarbone. "Try again, little goddess. I'm not letting you get away. You're mine now."

Giggling and struggling to catch her breath, she replied, "No, you have to bargain to get all this again." The boldness she felt fled when his eyes narrowed and felt the chill of his power swept through the room.

He pulled her into his chest. A low hum rumbled from him before he whispered into her ear. "Is that right?" He ran his nose along her neck, his hands roaming over her ass then under her thighs. He lifted her to settle her astride him. "So if I tried to slide you onto my cock right now, you'd try to slip away?"

Fates. Hoping he'd make good on that threat she arched her brow. "You wouldn't dare."

A sly grin was all she got from him before he slowly lowered her all the way down his hardened length. His eyes stayed locked with hers, and her heart sped. Hands still gripping her hips, he lifted her until only the head of his cock was still inside her.

"Should I stop?" he said with feigned coldness. After months of living together, she now knew that harsh look on his face was one of desire and not anger and it thrilled her to no end.

His Fates-given strength held her in place as she leaned back to push her chest out and run her fingers down her chest and towards her navel. "If you need to stop, that's fine. I'll take care of—"

She released a heady whimper as he slammed her back down on his cock. Her hands flew to his shoulders to brace herself. "You win, little goddess." He moved her up and down until she started to roll her hips.

His palms covered her breasts. "Take what you need, Sephy. I can do this all day and night."

So can I.

CHAPTER FORTY THREE

SETTLE THE SCORE

PERSEPHONE

"I need to call Laura," Persephone said as she reached for her phone. After a long shower which Hades had prolonged with his flirty interruption, she'd relaxed with her *husband* in a cozy sitting room with tall windows and short bookshelves.

After telling her sister that she was *married*, Hades and she reclined on the large sofa. The unhurried manner of Hades as they'd cuddled calmed her heart.

Laura and Peter were thrilled to hear the news, and she, Laura, and Helena, had set a date to dress shop. Picturing Helena in a flowing gown as she spread petals down the aisle coaxed a permanent grin on Persephone's face.

"When are you telling Mom?" Laura had asked her.

"In a few days, at the gala."

"She'll demand the wedding be at the estate," Laura said.

Persephone looked at Hades, who smiled back and ran his

fingers back and forth across her collarbone. "Good. It should be there."

Hades had texted Charon and Hecate, who both gushed their congratulations. Dozens of notifications popped up from Charon on Persephone's calendar for wedding planning details. Tastings, meetings with potential vendors, photographers. Meanwhile, Hecate sent her links to her favorite lingerie and sex toy sites.

THE EVENING OF THE GALA, inside Hades' SUV, Persephone went to wipe the sweat off her hands onto her legs. Hades intercepted her with a handkerchief before she marked her satin dress.

"*Fates,* I'm nervous," she said, drying her palms.

Hades held out his hand to take the handkerchief and folded it back into his front pocket. "Trust me, you were made for this." He leaned over and gave her a kiss on her temple.

"You're still feeling good about making the announcement tonight? Even with every god and goddess there?" Persephone watched Hades' face for any hint of hesitation.

Smiling back, Hades skimmed his fingers over her shoulders. "Of course, my love. I don't want to wait a second longer to let them all know we're married."

Persephone nodded. "And you'll wait until I talk to my mom first, right?"

He dipped his head. "I won't say a thing until you give me permission."

Sucking in a slow breath, Persephone straightened in her seat. "Thank you. I'm not sure how she'll take it." She turned to Hades. "Do you think your brothers will be angry or not care?"

Hades gave a light laugh. "I think Zeus already knows, and

Poseidon will care for all of two seconds before he's chasing down his next victim."

"Speaking of Poseidon, has he mentioned anything about us not following up with a get together?"

"Charon followed up with him, but he went quiet after she asked him who his date would be. I don't think he's stayed with anyone long enough to schedule more than three days in advance."

Huffing a laugh, Persephone looked out of the car window and saw the botanical gardens.

"I can't wait to see it fully decorated." Persephone loved the lighted flower displays Charon had shown her.

The car stopped in front of a purple carpet strewn across the marble staircase. Lines of reporters edged the velvet ropes and Persephone took another steadying breath. She looked at the three rings on her finger and prayed they weren't a beacon.

Hades exited first then helped her out of the car. He placed his left hand in his pocket, hiding the obsidian band. His large hand covered hers when they entered, ensuring no onlookers or photographers would notice her new jewelry.

"You look like a princess." Persephone hugged Helena but mouthed the word *sorry* over her niece's tiny shoulder.

Back when Helena was barely a week old, Laura had cautioned Persephone not to compliment the girl's appearance as a way of greeting.

She'll associate her worth with how she looks, and we don't need to perpetuate that, Laura had said to Persephone as she'd held baby Helena to her chest.

But Persephone couldn't help it. Helena, in all her adorable glory, looked regal in the lavender ball gown.

"She *does* look like a princess," Peter agreed and shook Hades' hand.

"Have you seen Mom?" Laura asked Persephone as they exchanged a quick air kiss.

"Not yet, but I need to find her." With a reach of her power, she felt around for the familiar hum of Demeter's magic.

"She doesn't know yet, right?" Laura nodded at Persephone's not-so-hidden wedding bands.

"Not yet. And she doesn't know that I know she was behind the 'snake bite' virus."

Laura's lips pressed into a thin line. "I'll keep an eye out for you. Want me to be there when you talk to her?"

Persephone tilted her head. "Why?"

"Morbid curiosity."

Appreciative as she was for her sister's support, she needed to do this on her own. "I'll come find you afterwards."

With a few parting words, Hades and Persephone made their way further into the main hall, where guests gathered in small groups, chatting around the dance floor. As she stepped past a hanging vine, tiny buds blossomed to reveal bright pink and orange petals that looked to be following her movement. Curious about the strange flower behavior, she tested her theory by stopping, then doubling back over her steps. Sure enough, the blooms moved with her.

Her face snapped to Hades. "What flowers are these? They look like a tropical morning glory. Maybe a hibiscus? But they move?"

Eyes bright, Hades replied, "Hecate enchanted them to respond to your power."

"Awe, thank you." She squeezed his hand and kissed his cheek. "That's so thoughtful. I love them." His gesture warmed her heart. They continued, greeting guests.

Finally, the feel of the warm sun and smell of flowing fields wafted over one side of her face. Turning towards the sensation, she spotted her mom sauntering in, wearing a dress of iridescent green that matched her intense eyes.

"Would you bring Laura over in a few minutes?" she asked Hades who nodded, then kissed her before heading off.

Her jaw tightened with each step. Her mom's smile faded as she met eyes with Persephone.

"Sephy, sweetheart. You look stunning." Demeter held out her hands, and the women exchanged a stilted hug.

"As do you. Beautiful as always, but we need to talk… in private." Without allowing a reply from her mom, Persephone picked up her mom's hand and portaled them to a secluded garden path in one of the connected greenhouses.

Demeter's mouth hung open for a moment. "A smooth portal, Sephy. Your power is so fragrant and strong." She cupped Persephone's chin. "Everything alright?" The stern yet focused mask returned to her mom's face.

"Yes, and no." Persephone took a deep breath. "No, because I heard you had a hand in the 'snake bite' that almost killed Eurydice's app." Steeling her eyes on her mom, Persephone waited for the reply.

Demeter sighed and looked away. "I wanted you back, Sephy. I won't apologize for trying, but I am sorry it hurt the people you care about." Demeter waved her hands at their surroundings. "Although it seems like my efforts did nothing to diminish *Flowers Near Me*'s success."

Persephone bit the inside of her lip. "Thank the Fates for that." As far as Demeter and apologies went, that would have to suffice. And if Persephone showed mercy, then maybe her mom would as well once she dropped the news of her marriage to Hades. Her gaze remained steady. "There is something I wanted to tell you in person."

She looked up to see a strange smile on her mom's face. Something akin to bitterness with equal parts happiness and disappointment. "You married him."

Persephone held back a gasp. "How did you know?"

With a hand lifted in the air, Demeter answered, "You're my daughter and I notice everything about you. Your magic smells different. It has this evergreen scent that wasn't there before. That's Hades' doing. Not to mention you've kept your left hand hidden since you spotted me from across the room. And lastly, I received a dowry payment from Hades."

"What?" Persephone practically sneered. *Why would he do that?*

Demeter chuckled. "Don't be cross with him. DB received a sizable donation in the form of a new app. He gifted *Flowers Near Me* to us and I knew there could only be one reason why."

"Because I asked him to?"

"Because this is how it is among the gods. He gets you, so I get something in return. Hardly an equal transaction." There was a glint of coquettish satisfaction in her mom's stifled grin. "Besides, you're glowing, and if this agrees with you, then I'm happy for as long as you're happy with him."

"Thanks, Mom." It was more than acceptable given the long-standing battle between Hades and Demeter. Two top-tier gods united by Olympus' newest Goddess of Spring. It all sounded workable enough.

"I love you very much, my clever girl. I always will. And I'll honor the things you honor." Demeter glanced over her shoulder, looking statuesque with soft lines tracing her long neck. "You should get back to your launch party and dance with your new husband. I'm certain he's counting down the seconds to flaunt you in front of all of Olympus."

Persephone's cheeks turned to lava, but she straightened and clasped her mom's hand. "I'll take us both back."

HADES' arms wrapped firmly around Persephone's waist, pulling her close after a graceful spin. Since announcing their marriage and the upcoming celebration, he hadn't let her go. His hand pressed gently against her back, fingers tracing delicate patterns between her shoulder blades when they weren't intertwined with hers.

Persephone stretched her sore jaw, her endless smiles leaving indents even godhood couldn't erase.

"Remember that first night at the restaurant?" she whispered as they swayed together. "I thought I'd outsmarted you, marked my territory in Olympus by getting the app you wanted before you could sink your teeth into it."

Hades' deep laugh rumbled through his chest. "Sitting with you in that booth only confirmed what I already knew: you were dangerous. Irresistibly so. And now, it's clearer than ever."

"Dangerous?" she teased, but a thrill danced up her spine.

He leaned in, his lips brushing the shell of her ear. "I knew then I had no hope of resisting you. You're as kind as you are breathtaking, and even though I don't deserve you, the Fates gave you to me anyway. I just had to trick you into spending time with me, hoping you'd take pity on me and fall in love." He smirked, pulling her impossibly closer as he inhaled softly, the warmth of his breath sending tingles down her neck.

Persephone smiled, her heart swelling. "We do make the perfect team, you know. Partners in every way."

Hades' lips brushed her ear. "Yes, partners for eternity, my love."

EPILOGUE

CHARON'S DILEMMA

A YEAR LATER...

Flowers cascaded from the modern chandeliers, creating a lush, floral canopy over the bustling crowd at Narcisi. The restaurant was the perfect choice for Laura's baby 'sprinkle,' and Persephone had enjoyed collaborating with Charon to create this magical, garden oasis. After all, with Laura and Peter's surprise second baby on the way—years after they thought they were done with midnight feedings—the occasion called for a celebration.

Hades, ever the doting husband, waved a hand to light the candles, brushed a kiss against Persephone's cheek then went to place their gift with the others. As Charon nestled bottles of sparkling mineral water into an ice bath, she cast a glance at Persephone. "Have you heard from Laura?"

"She'll be here in ten minutes," Persephone replied, stacking a tower of colorfully wrapped presents on a cloth-draped table. She propped up a large poster board decorated with glittering flowers. "She's going to crack up when she sees this baby voting board."

Charon grinned. "I've got my vote on 'coffee.' Laura swears the baby already reacts to the smell."

Persephone laughed. "I'll bet Peter will suggest 'no,' and Laura will choose 'mama.'"

Before they could share more, a swirl of fragrant, violet smoke heralded Hecate's arrival. She stepped out, glamorous in a fitted black dress, her lips curled into a knowing smile. "A contest over the baby's first word? How wicked."

Charon's face went pale as Hecate sauntered over, her heels clicking in time with the background music. "Wait—is this too much?" Charon asked, her voice uncertain.

Hecate looped an arm around Charon's shoulders, her eyes sparkling with mischief. "Relax. It's perfect. And much tamer than a game I'd suggest."

Persephone waved off Charon's concern. "Laura loves stuff like this. She'd be disappointed if we *didn't* make it competitive."

"How's Helena feeling about becoming a big sister?" Hecate asked, grabbing a glass of wine from a nearby table.

Persephone's face softened. "Oh, wait until you see her. She's taking her responsibilities very seriously and has a list of 'big sister duties' only she's allowed to handle."

"That's adorable," Charon said, but her smile seemed forced.

Hecate's eyes narrowed on Charon with curiosity. "Speaking of taking things seriously… how was your date with Vanth?"

Charon's cheeks flushed, and she fidgeted with the torch pendant hanging from her neck. "I canceled."

"What?" Persephone and Hecate gasped.

Charon managed a nervous laugh. "Well, us psychopomps aren't as impulsive as you gods," she joked, but she didn't quite meet their eyes.

Hecate cocked an eyebrow. "Canceling dates? When have you ever canceled something in your own schedule?" She exchanged a knowing glance with Persephone. "Come on. Do you even *want* to give him a chance?"

Persephone leaned in, her eyes bright with curiosity. "Or should we tell him to back off? The poor guy is head over heels for you."

Charon's gaze darted between the two goddesses, her fingers twisting her pendant. "It's complicated."

Hecate's voice softened, but a hint of intrigue remained. "How complicated?"

Charon swallowed, her cheeks paling further. "We work together. If it doesn't work out, it could ruin everything."

Persephone rolled her eyes. "That's all?"

Charon sighed, but her voice dropped to a whisper. "No. There's more."

Hecate leaned in, her expression intrigued but less intense. "Go on."

Charon took a shaky breath. "I stole something important from him. And I think he wants it back."

Persephone shot Charon a worried look. Hecate asked, "What did you steal?"

Charon winced, clutching her necklace. "Let's just say giving it back isn't an option, but keeping it has made things… messy."

Hecate sipped her drink, murmuring, "Well, this baby sprinkle just became a lot more interesting."

ACKNOWLEDGEMENTS

Did I write this book?

It's a silly question meant to contextualize how much outside input, edits, critiques, and support went into this story. I shouldn't say I wrote this book, because I had loads of help from a group of magnanimous folks. I'm just the last one who touched it before it went live.

I tried to capture the sisterly bond—in a small way—with Persephone and Laura's relationship, because my sister, Lindsay, is precious to me. Just like Laura, she's smart, funny, and reliable. Without her constant support and her willingness to read every version of what I wrote, I can't say that I would've kept going.

To the world's best editor (that by providence I somehow found on the internet!), Candida, you're brilliant, talented, and an all-around, top-notch human. How you willingly kept reading my work, knowing how *awful* other projects and versions were, I don't understand. You have a massive heart for newbie authors, and I hope it takes you to great heights in your career.

To my fellow debut authors, Aster, Delani, and Sienna, thank you for the hours you poured into helping me refine this craft. And thank you for sharing your delightful stories with me and even your own experiences as new authors. Your encouragement validated the struggle, and I am better for it. I hope every great thing that can happen to a best-selling author comes your way a hundredfold.

How great is it to find high quality alpha readers / critique partners? Pretty fucking great! Elizabeth and Audrey, you lovely souls, thank you for giving me a chance as a complete stranger with no social media following or any relative clout. You're both unexpected friends that will forever be my close book buddies. Your critiques kept me from completely embarrassing myself. Thank you for not giving up on the story!

And to my best friend and husband, Matt, I love you so much. No matter how expensive one piece became or how many hours I needed to get away to finish this, you didn't flinch. You spurred me on in a way only a loving spouse can. Thank you for never wavering.

ABOUT THE AUTHOR

When not writing or recording a romance author skit, Alexis spends time with her husband, two kids, two dogs, and two cats. Originally from Pittsburgh, PA, she now lives on a barrier island along the southeast coast of the US where she enjoys the warmer weather that lets her garden all year long. As an avid romance reader (aka insatiable smut goblin), she's always chasing a good HEA. She's embraced her inner old soul through knitting, crocheting, and baking but still can't resist a good video game.

Flowers Near Me is her debut novel, but she plans on revisiting Olympus in her next book, Carry My Torch, starring Charon and Vanth.

For book updates and general frivolity, sign up for her newsletter at alexisrex.com.